SPRING MAGIC

Dorothy Emily Stevenson was born in Edinburgh. Her Father was a first cousin of Robert Louis Stevenson and grandson of the Robert Stevenson who built the Bell Rock Lighthouse. He himself carried on the tradition by being Civil Engineer to the Commissioners of Northern Lights. She was educated privately, travelled in France and Italy, and is deeply interested in history and art. She is married to Major James Reid Peploe, Highland Light Infantry. Many of her novels are published in *Fontana*.

D. E. STEVENSON

Spring Magic

Collins
FONTANA BOOKS

First published in Fontana Books April 1960
Second Impression May 1962
Third Impression March 1966
Fourth Impression October 1968
Fifth Impression March 1969

*Printed in Great Britain
Collins Clear-Type Press
London and Glasgow*

CONTENTS

PART I

FRANCES ASLEEP

Chapter One

A GOOD INN run by a good-tempered landlord is always an important social centre in village life, and the Bordale Arms at Cairn is no exception to the rule. It is the place where men congregate when they want to talk to other men when their homes are disorganised by washing-days or noisy children. The bar counter is broad and polished; men lean upon it and discuss the prospects of the fishing season or argue about the war. Cairn is a small fishing village, a mere handful of fishermen's cottages built of grey stone from the quarry on the hill. The main street slopes up from the harbour; it is steep and paved with cobbles and is lined with small dark shops. Painters sometimes come to Cairn; they set up their easels and mix their colours and paint strange pictures of the place—pictures which, as far as the villagers can see, bear little or no resemblance to the scene. It was Mr. MacNair, the innkeeper, who put the matter in a nutshell when he said: "If they are making a picture of this place why is it not like this place at all? And if they are not making a picture of this place why do they trouble to come? Could they not stay at home and paint a picture out of their heads?" "But it is as well for you that they have not thought of that," replied Alec MacNair, his nephew. Alec usually had an answer ready, and on this occasion it was very much to the point, for the painters were a fruitful source of income to Mr. MacNair—or had been before the war.

The inn had belonged to Mr. MacNair's father, and to several generations of MacNairs before him; it was an ancient rambling place, dark and gloomy and none too clean, but the present owner is a thrifty man and has the good fortune to possess a capable and far-seeing wife. They saved enough money to rebuild part of the house and to put in a couple of bathrooms, and now the gaily-painted sign, which hangs over the front door and is apt to squeak somewhat dolefully when the wind is in the north-west, bears the inscription BORDALE ARMS HOTEL. It is a grand name—every one agrees to that—and it confers distinction upon the whole village, but the Cairn people continue to speak

7

of it as "The Inn," and even the MacNairs rarely use the new title.

The war affected Cairn in various ways. The young men departed to serve their country and the old men joined the Home Guard. They turned up at the first parade with a curious assortment of weapons, and Mr. MacDonald, the Laird, who was a keen historian, was so much interested in the weapons that it was some time before he was able to settle down to the enrolment of his recruits. He was aware that the shot-guns had been used for poaching upon his land and that some of the rifles might be described as loot from the last war, but there was one ancient weapon which looked as if it might have lain under the thatch since Culloden. . . .

"It will shoot a German if he lands upon the shore," explained old Donald Fraser, the bootmaker. "Aye, it will do that—and a fine noise it makes too."

Mr. MacDonald believed him.

The odd thing was that there was scarcely a man in the place who could not produce some sort of firearm. They had no right to possess firearms without a permit, but Mr. MacDonald shut his eyes to this well-known fact and welcomed the motley collection with enthusiasm.

Cairn had its A.R.P., and a few of the more timid inhabitants covered their windows with strips of sticky paper, but after a week or two the sticky paper peeled off and the village settled down to its usual routine. The boats went out to the fishing, and the women cleaned and cooked and minded their children or sat upon the steps of their houses mending their husbands' nets and conversing with each other from doorstep to doorstep in strident tones.

The war was there, of course; it was at the back of their minds (they followed its course in the papers and listened to the wireless bulletins), but the war was a long way from Cairn and somehow or other it was not very real to them. An epidemic of whooping-cough which was racking the children and disturbing their parents' nights seemed much more real than the war.

The winter passed—it was the second winter of the war—and one day in early spring a fleet of enormous lorries suddenly appeared and rumbled down the cobbled High Street with a noise like thunder. It was a friendly invasion, this, and the people who crowded into the street were greeted with cheers and amicable waves by the khaki-clad figures of the invaders.

"'Ere we are again!"

"'Ere we are—but where are we?"

8

"Is this the end o' the world?"

"Hi! where's the nearest pub?"

Cairn was too bewildered to respond. It watched the lorries draw up at the inn and saw the men climb down and disappear into the bar.

"It is the Tower of Babel come back," declared Mr. MacNair as he strove to understand and to satisfy the demands of his un-expected customers.

It certainly seemed like it, for there were men from London and Yorkshire, from Devon and Lancashire and Wales, and although they all spoke the same language it sounded like a dozen foreign tongues. They were not fighting men, they were Pioneers, and were recruited from all over the British Isles. In twenty minutes they had drunk the place dry, and, returning to their lorries, they moved on to a field about a mile from the village, where they proceeded to erect enormous huts. A few days was sufficient to turn the field into a camp, and Cairn was just beginning to get used to its visitors when they vanished as suddenly as they had appeared.

"So they have gone," said old Donald Fraser in his slow Highland voice as he leaned upon the bar counter and sipped his drink.

"M-hm, they have gone," Mr. MacNair agreed. He was not quite sure whether to be glad or sorry at their departure. They had brought business to the house, but on the other hand it was pleasant to feel that the bar was once more his own peace-ful preserve. It had not been the same place at all in the last few days.

"Mr. MacDonald will have let them have the field," said Fergus MacNair. He was the innkeeper's cousin.

"There is some law now by which they could take it," replied Mr. MacNair vaguely.

"But they would pay him, surely?"

"Och, they would pay him."

"There will be little need of the Home Guard," declared Fergus with a hoarse chuckle. Fergus was one of the few men in Cairn who had not joined the body, and he lost no opportunity of poking fun at it in his pawky way.

"I would not be so sure," said old Donald gravely. "The Home Guard is to defend Cairn. . . . M-hm, and what will the soldiers know of the paths over the hills?"

"Donald is right," agreed Mr. MacNair, nodding.

"Aye, I'm right," said Donald in his squeaky voice. "I'm the auldest man in the Home Guard, but there's nobody can beat me ower the hills!"

"There will be men coming to the camp," said Alec, drawing upon his pipe in a ruminative manner.

"Men!" exclaimed Fergus. "You would not expect women to come to a camp!"

"That is what I said. There will be soldiers . . . and soldiers drink beer."

Mr. MacNair took the point. "Alec's right," he said. He hesitated for a moment and then added: "Maybe it would be a good thing to order six barrels. . . ."

"Six barrels would be a little better than none at all," remarked Alec dryly.

He had scarcely finished speaking, and his uncle was still standing with his mouth agape, trying to envisage the enormous quantity of beer which might have to be procured, when the door was pushed open and a woman looked in. She was a stranger, of course, for no Cairn woman would be likely to come into the bar, and the six men turned their heads and looked at her. The heads turned quite slowly, and the looks were neither friendly nor hostile. It was the way in which a herd of cows turn their heads and look at a stranger when he opens the gate of the field in which they are grazing.

"Oh!" exclaimed the newcomer, somewhat nervously. "Oh, is this . . . I mean I thought this was the hotel."

"It is the Bordale Arms Hotel," said Mr. MacNair, nodding.

"Yes. That's what I thought. I tried the other door but I couldn't find anyone."

"Annie will have gone out with Shiela," said Mr. MacNair after a moment's thought.

"Shiela is better, then?" inquired Alec with interest.

"Och, there is not much the matter with her," Mr. MacNair replied.

"I should like a room, please," said the stranger.

There was a short silence. Mr. MacNair stroked his chin—he had shaved that very morning so it felt nice and smooth. "You will be painting pictures," he said at last.

"No."

"M-hm!" said Mr. MacNair. The exclamation was one of slight surprise, and his voice rose on the second syllable.

Alec looked at the newcomer with more interest. He wondered why she had come to Cairn if she did not intend to paint pictures. She was nice to look at, Alec thought. She was slight, and rather tall, with short fair hair which curled softly about her ears. Her eyes were very large, they were a strange deep blue, shadowed with violet, and they had a wondering expression which is more often seen in the eyes of a child than of a grown-up person. In some ways (thought Alec) she was like the artist lady who had come to Cairn last year, but in other ways she was quite different . . . she had not painted her face at all, Alec noticed. The suitcase, which she had put down on the floor when she came in, bore a green label, and by twisting his head to one side and using his extremely long-sighted eyes Alec was able to make out the name on the label—it was " Miss F. Field."

" The lady will have come off the bus," Alec said.

The lady agreed that she had done so. There was no other way in which she could have arrived unless she had walked.

" It will be the soldiers," said Fergus thoughtfully.

Every one in the room understood what Fergus meant by this somewhat enigmatic statement—every one except Miss Field. She turned her eyes upon Fergus and inquired: " What soldiers?"

" The soldiers at the camp," said Fergus.

" Are there soldiers here?" asked Miss Field in surprise.

" No, there are none at all," replied Fergus, shaking his head. Miss Field looked thoroughly bewildered.

" Not yet," explained Alec kindly.

" But they will be coming soon, no doubt," added Mr. Mac-Nair,

" I don't understand," said Miss Field.

" You will be here on account of the soldiers," suggested Fergus.

" No," said Miss Field firmly. " No, I didn't even know there were any soldiers here. . . ."

" There are no soldiers here—not yet," Fergus reminded her.

There was another silence—quite a peaceful sort of silence—the clock on the wall ticked away busily and Donald finished his drink.

" Perhaps you haven't got a room for me," said Miss Field at last.

" We have five rooms," replied Mr. MacNair with some pride. " Five good bedrooms, we have. Two of them are a wee bit small, but they are not bad——"

" They're grand rooms, so they are," declared Donald in his squeaky voice.

" I spent good money on them," Mr. MacNair admitted.

Miss Field looked relieved. One room was all she required,

11

but it was pleasant to know that she had such a wide choice of accommodation.

"You could not have the east room," said Mr. MacNair doubtfully. "It would not be nice for you at all. The paper has come off the wall in the corner, so it has. Alec has been too busy to paste it."

"I have been busy with the boat," explained Alec. "I did not think there would be anybody coming so soon—but I will get on to it to-morrow. It will not take long once I can get started to it."

"There is the south room——" began Mr. MacNair.

"Och, you would not put her in there!" exclaimed Fergus. "A dark room, it is, with a wee window in the corner and no view at all."

"The west room has a view of the sea," Alec pointed out.

"That would be lovely," declared Miss Field.

"The north room is nice too," said Mr. MacNair.

"It is the biggest one," agreed Fergus, nodding his head.

"But you would need to move Shiela!" said Alec.

"Och, Shiela would not mind," declared Mr. MacNair.

The other men had been listening to the discussion with interest. One of them now leaned forward and said: "There is the room over the kitchen where the old lady was—the old lady that had the operation——"

"Och, that wee hole!" exclaimed Fergus in disparaging tones.

Mr. MacNair said nothing. He drew another glass of beer for Donald, wiped it carefully and set it on the counter. Miss Field felt—and looked—exactly like Alice in Wonderland. She waited for a few moments and then she said: "I think the room with the view of the sea would suit me best."

"But you have not seen it," Mr. MacNair pointed out.

"It is a nice room," Alec declared.

"It is not bad at all," agreed its owner.

"I should like to see it," said Miss Field in desperation.

"And why not?" inquired Mr. MacNair, taking a chamois duster out of a drawer and polishing the shining counter.

Miss Field was so exasperated by this time that she felt inclined to pick up her suitcase and depart—she would have done so, but she was aware that there was no other hotel in the place and the bus had gone—and then suddenly, just as she had reached the limit of her patience and had opened her mouth to inquire whether or not she could be given a room in the Bordale Arms Hotel, Alec straightened himself and came across the room. He lifted her case as if it were packed with feathers and led her through a side door which communicated with the residential part of the house. Miss Field found herself following Alec across a stone-flagged hall and up a flight of steep, narrow stairs.

The house was old, the walls were very thick and were panelled in oak, darkened with the smoke of bygone fires, but Miss Field was glad to see that the place was clean and well kept. At the top of the stairs there was a square landing lighted by a skylight. The floor was covered with flowered linoleum and with several deerskin rugs.

" This is the west room," said Alec, opening a door and standing aside to allow Miss Field to precede him. " It is the nicest room too. It is the one I would choose for myself."

The room was a good size and well proportioned, it was full of late afternoon sunshine.

" Oh, how lovely!" cried Miss Field, running to the window and gazing out at the wide expanse of sea. " Oh, how magnificent! I've never seen such a heavenly view before."

The view was certainly very beautiful, it was wide and varied and colourful. There was the harbour with its little boats bobbing up and down in the gentle swell, there were rocks and cliffs and stretches of green grass. Southward was the lovely sweep of Cairn Bay glistening in the late afternoon sunshine. The sea was a deep blue and, far away, floating in a haze of mist, Miss Field saw the faint outline of an island with jagged mountains. " Oh, how lovely!" she cried again.

" The room is comfortable," said Alec. " The carpet is new and the bed is not bad at all. It has a real hair mattress."

She realised that he wanted her to admire the room, so she turned away from the window. She felt that she owed Alec a good deal for the way in which he had rescued her from her plight. It was a little difficult to " place " Alec, she found. He was dressed in a fisherman's jersey and an old pair of blue trousers, but he seemed different from the other men she had seen. He was tall and dark and very good-looking in a weather-beaten sort of way, and his voice was pleasant and musical.

" It is a nice room," said Miss Field, smiling in a friendly manner. " It's so nice to have a comfortable chair. I shall be able to sit here and read and enjoy the view. Why didn't the other man want me to have this room?"

" The other man!" echoed Alec in surprise. " Is it my uncle you mean?"

" The hotel-keeper . . . is he your uncle? He didn't want me to have this room, did he? It was so nice of you to—to persuade him." She hesitated, wondering whether she could possibly tip him . . . but, no, it was out of the question.

" Och, that is just his way," Alec declared.

" Just his way?"

" This is the only room that is ready for visitors," he added.

" Then why—then I suppose he didn't want me to stay?"

" What would be the use of a hotel if people did not stay in it?" asked Alec in surprise.

" I mean," began Miss Field, struggling to find her way through the fog of misunderstanding. " I mean . . . well . . . why didn't he give me a room when I asked for it?"

" There was no hurry," replied Alec comfortably.

" No, but still——"

" Och, it is not every day that a visitor comes to Cairn."

He went away after that, and Miss Field sat down on the edge of her bed and laughed to herself. She laughed because it had been so funny, but also because she felt happy. She was going to enjoy her holiday; it was quiet and peaceful, the air was clear and sparkling, and for the first time in her life she was free. She could do exactly as she liked all the time. She could do silly things if she wanted to do them—there was nobody to worry her with questions as to where she had been and what she had done and why she had done it—she could go out when she liked and stay out as long as she liked; she could go to bed early or stay up late.

Miss Field began to unpack and to hang up her clothes in the big old-fashioned wardrobe. Her fingers were busy loosening the band of her skirt when the sound of a gong, beaten in a peremptory manner, boomed throughout the house. Miss Field hesitated and looked at her watch; it was half-past six (which seemed a strange hour for a meal), but as she had had no tea the idea of something to eat was distinctly pleasant. She washed her hands and tidied her hair and went downstairs.

The dining-room was a long-shaped room with a low ceiling and panelled walls. There were two large tables in the middle of the room and two small ones in the window, and they were all empty. Miss Field was the only visitor at the Bordale Arms. She had guessed as much from the conversation in the bar . . . five bedrooms and all empty except one which was occupied by Shiela. Perhaps Shiela was the daughter of the innkeeper, thought Miss Field. She was hesitating at the door when a plump, rosy-cheeked maid came forward and conducted her to her place.

" I thought you'd like the table in the window," said the maid

14

in a friendly manner. "Most of the people like it best. You can see the wee boats going in and out of the harbour while you're taking your meals. Mistress MacNair said would you sign the papers. They're awful particular about it since the war started."

Miss Field took the pen and began to fill in the forms, and the rosy-cheeked maid watched the process with unconcealed interest. "Frances Field!" she exclaimed. "It's a nice name, so it is. My name's Annie Fraser . . . and you're British, so there's no need for you to fill in the other questions. . . . Och, your home's in London, is it?"

Frances Field laughed. She could not take exception to Annie's curiosity, for it was so friendly and natural. It was like the curiosity of a child.

"Fancy your home being in London!" said Annie, looking at her with wide eyes. "My, weren't you frightened of the raids?"

Miss Field admitted that she was very frightened indeed, but added that one soon got used to it.

"I wouldn't, then," declared Annie. "I'd be scared all the time. It's a wonder to me that people can stand it. Are you an evacuee?"

"I suppose I am in a way," replied Miss Field doubtfully.

"Was your house bombed?"

"No, it wasn't. A bomb fell in the square and some of our windows were broken, but——"

"Och, I wouldn't like it at all!" cried Annie in horror-stricken tones.

Miss Field settled down to her meal. She had wondered what sort of meal would be provided for her at this hour—whether it would be tea or supper—and now she decided that it was a mixture of both. There was a dish of herrings fried in oatmeal and a couple of large potatoes roasted in their jackets. There were scones and oatcakes and butter and jam and a square of heather honey. The beverage was tea.

"Would that be enough?" asked Annie, hovering round and rearranging the plates. "Would you take an egg, Miss Field?"

"I shan't want anything else, thank you," Miss Field replied.

If she had hoped to get rid of Annie and to have her meal in peace she was disappointed. Annie was far too interested in the newcomer to leave her in peace. There were all sorts of things that Annie wanted to know—things that everyone in Cairn would want to know—and the longer she talked to Miss Field the more she would find out. You couldn't ask people too much all at once, but you could talk to them and tell them things and then most likely they would tell you what you wanted to know. She was a nice lady, Annie thought. She wasn't stuck-up like some of the people that came. . . .

"It's quiet here," said Annie. "There's a picture house at Rithie—that's the place you got the bus. Rithie's a nice place, and the picture house isn't bad at all. Do you like the pictures?"

Miss Field nodded. She was eating a mouthful of herring, so she could not speak.

"I do," said Annie with a sigh. "I like Clark Gable. Do you like him?"

"I don't know," said Miss Field. "I don't think I've ever seen him."

"Not in London?" inquired Annie in surprise.

"I didn't go to many films," explained Miss Field. "I lived with my aunt and she—she wasn't very strong. She didn't like me to leave her."

"Is she dead?" asked Annie sympathetically.

"No," replied Miss Field.

Annie waited for more information, but none came. She said: "Weston is a nice place. It's much bigger than Rithie and the shops are fine. I go there when I get a whole day off. It's a nice place to go. Maybe you'll go over one day."

Miss Field nodded.

"Are you staying here long?" asked Annie.

"It depends how I like it."

"There's not much to do here."

"Isn't there?"

"Not unless you paint pictures."

"But I can't paint," said Miss Field, laughing. "My governess did her best to teach me, but I never got beyond the tulip stage."

"That's a pity," said Annie regretfully. "Maybe you've come for the fishing——"

"I don't know how to fish either," declared Miss Field.

"There's a lot of people come here in the summer. It's the bathing they like. There was one man swam out to the Black Rock. But it's too cold for the bathing yet—I'm thinking you'll maybe find it a wee bit dull."

Miss Field shook her head.

"After London!" said Annie with a surprised inflection. "My, I should think Cairn would seem awful dull to a person who was used to London!"

"It depends on the person," Miss Field replied.

Annie considered the matter. "There was a lady came here

16

last year. She'd had an operation, and the doctor sent her here. It's a grand place for people when they've been ill."

"I haven't been ill," said Miss Field, smiling. "I came here because I wanted to think."

Annie looked at her in amazement.

"I saw a picture of Cairn," continued Miss Field, helping herself to another herring and dismembering it carefully. "I saw a picture of it in the Academy—it's a place in London where pictures are hung and people can go and look at them—and I made up my mind that some day I would go to Cairn and see it with my own eyes—and here I am."

"In the name of fortune!" exclaimed Annie in heartfelt tones.

Chapter Two

MISS FIELD was very much amused at Annie's interest in her affairs; she realised that it was friendly interest and not mere idle curiosity. She would have been quite willing to tell Annie the whole story of her life, but it was not the sort of thing one could do. Annie would have to make the most of the small tit-bits which she had succeeded in obtaining from Miss Field—though no doubt she would elaborate them.

Frances Field had lost her parents before she was four years old. Her father had been killed in the last war, and her mother, losing all interest in life, had followed him shortly after. Frances went to live with her uncle and his wife in London. They were old-fashioned people with no children of their own, and their house was like a little bit of Queen Victoria's time set down in the bustle and hum of modern London. They did not want a child in the house, but there was nobody else to take her and, although she was not actually penniless, it was out of the question to send her to strangers.

"After all, she's your own flesh and blood," said Mrs. Wheeler with a sigh. "She's your own sister's child——"

Mr. Wheeler agreed that she was—he always agreed with his wife, for it was the easiest thing to do. "But I hope she won't disturb you, Zoë," he said anxiously.

Frances did not disturb her aunt. She was a quiet, gentle child and soon developed a taste for reading, which was a good thing for every one concerned. At ten years old she discovered Dickens, and, as there was a whole set of Dickens in the book-case in the dining-room, the discovery kept her quieter than before . . . after that came Thackeray and Jane Austen, but Dickens was her first love.

Frances was not sent to school—she might have learnt to be rough and noisy—she was educated at home by a governess, and when she had learnt all that the governess could teach her it was decided that her education was complete. Mrs. Wheeler had always talked of " sending Frances abroad to finish," but when the time came she discovered that Frances was useful and could not be spared. Mrs. Wheeler had always been extremely lazy, and now she decided that she was " not very strong." Dr. Digby—the old Scottish doctor who had attended the Wheelers for years and had seen Frances through the usual childish ailments—could find nothing the matter with Mrs. Wheeler, or at least nothing that a little exercise and dieting would not cure, but Mrs. Wheeler disliked exercise in any form and was incapable of self-discipline. She relapsed into a state of semi-invalidism, and Frances took over the housekeeping. She did the shopping, ran messages, exercised the dog in Wintringham Square Gardens, did the flowers, filled hot-water bottles, and made Bengers Food. " I don't know what I should do without her," Mrs. Wheeler would say, as she lay on the drawing-room sofa and devoured chocolate creams and novels from the library, and Mrs. Wheeler's friends would nod and reply: " But it's so nice for Frances to have such a comfortable home."

It never occurred to Frances that any other life was possible for her. Wintringham Square was her home—the only home she knew. It never occurred to her that she was working very hard and receiving nothing in return except her board and lodging. She had a little money of her own which had been left to her by her father. It was not very much, but it was more than sufficient to buy her clothes. She was neither happy nor unhappy, for she had a contented nature and no standard by which to measure her life. Uncle Henry was kind to her in an unimaginative fashion, and Aunt Zoë was quite pleasant as long as she had everything she wanted. Unfortunately, however, Aunt Zoë's wants were not always easy to satisfy, and when Frances failed her in any way she was not a pleasant person to deal with. The library books were a constant source of trouble. Aunt Zoë liked romance—it went so beautifully with chocolate creams—and above all she liked the romances of Janetta Walters; but as Miss Walters wrote three romances a year and Aunt Zoë read three a week—and sometimes more—there were forty-nine weeks in the year when Aunt Zoë had to make do with other

18

authors. Every time a new book written by Janetta Walters appeared amongst the publishers' advertisements Frances was informed of the fact and was sent off to the library to procure it, but Miss Walters's books were popular and many other people rushed to the library upon the same errand—people with a good deal more push and drive than Frances. " They've put it on your list," Frances would say as she presented her aunt with a couple of romances by some other (less absorbing) writer, and Aunt Zoë would storm and rave and declare that if only she were able to go to the library herself she would be able to obtain the books she wanted. " I want *Her Prince at Last*," declared Aunt Zoë, " and I want it *now*. I don't want it in three weeks' time when everyone else has read it." Frances would never forget her struggle to obtain *Her Prince at Last*. She did not care for the book herself. It seemed to her that it was a trifle insipid. She knew very little about life, so she was not a very good judge as to whether or not the books of Janetta Walters portrayed life as it really was or people as they really were, but she had her doubts on the subject. Frances did not care for any of the books on Aunt Zoë's list, but she was obliged to read them, for she had nothing else to read—you cannot go on reading Dickens indefinitely, however much you may enjoy him.

When the war came Frances was anxious to attend Red Cross lectures, but Aunt Zoë received the suggestion coldly. " You have plenty to do at home," she said. It was quite true, of course ; the days were not long enough for all she had to do, and the servant problem was becoming increasingly difficult. Wintringham Square houses were designed in the days when no servant problem existed, and to run the house comfortably half a dozen servants would not have been excessive. Frances struggled to run it with four, and did a good deal of the work with her own hands.

" I think you should go to the country," said Mr. Wheeler to his wife when the bombs began to fall. " You and Frances can go to Devonshire—Clara has offered to have you."

" I couldn't leave home," declared Mrs. Wheeler in alarm.

The fact was she was so deeply sunk in her rut and so wedded to her comfortable routine that the thought of moving made her quite ill. She would rather risk the bombs—so she thought —than go and live with her energetic and somewhat unsympathetic sister. As she never went out—except to totter round the square with Frances in attendance—Mrs. Wheeler did not see

19

any of the damage which had been caused in other parts of London, and, being of an unimaginative nature, she was unable to believe that a bomb might fall upon Wintringham Square.

One morning in February when Dr. Digby came to see the "invalid" Frances accompanied him to the door. He hesitated a moment and, looking at her from beneath his bushy eyebrows, said in his brusque way: "Why aren't you doing something?"

"I haven't time, really——" began Frances, raising her eyes to his face.

"Time!" said the doctor. "No, I suppose she keeps you busy. It's a pity."

"I *wanted* to do something," said Frances, who was very fond of Dr. Digby and was anxious that he should understand. "I wanted to go to a bandaging class, but Aunt Zoë doesn't like me to leave her."

"It would do her good," said Dr. Digby. "You do too much for her—there's nothing the matter with your aunt except laziness——"

"Nothing the matter . . ." echoed Frances in surprise.

"Nothing," replied Dr. Digby. "It would do her good if she had to hustle round a bit. Why don't you take a holiday?"

"A holiday!" cried Frances in amazement.

He laughed and said: "Everybody needs a holiday now and then," and hastened away.

Dr. Digby's words lingered in Frances's mind and started a train of thought . . . it was really two trains of thought, but they arrived at the same place. "There's nothing the matter with her except laziness. . . . Everybody needs a holiday."

Frances had slaved for Aunt Zoë for years, had borne patiently with all Aunt Zoë's vagaries, because she had been so sorry for her (it was dreadful to be ill, to lie on the sofa all day and never go out), and all the time there had been nothing the matter with her, "nothing except laziness." Now that the idea had been put into her head Frances found a hundred proofs of its truth without the slightest difficulty and wondered how she could have been so blind. Why hadn't she realised that Aunt Zoë was always well enough to do anything she wanted to do?

The other train of thought led Frances into strange places. "Everybody needs a holiday," that's what Dr. Digby had said, but Frances had never had a holiday in her life. She began to look at her life and to compare it with other people's lives, and she began to realise that it wasn't a life at all. Even Mary, the seventeen-year-old between-maid, had her afternoon off and went to the pictures and, sometimes, to a dance. She received regular wages and was given three weeks' holiday every year and an occasional week-end into the bargain. In all these respects—and in others as well—Mary's life was infinitely better than hers.

Frances thought of this as she went about her daily routine, and the daily routine became more and more irksome. The big gloomy house seemed to grow bigger and gloomier every day. It was more and more of a battle to keep it clean. Smuts drifted in and settled upon the newly washed curtains in greater numbers than ever before. The house pressed upon her spirit, it was like a huge vampire sapping her strength. Aunt Zoë was more exacting than ever—or perhaps it was Frances who was less patient. It was so much more difficult to be patient when you knew that Aunt Zoë was not really ill. . . .

Until now her life had been bearable because she had never thought about it; when she began to think about it and saw her life going on just the same for ever and ever until she was old and her hair turned grey and her teeth dropped out . . . then it became unbearable. She had thought of marriage, of course (what girl has not?), but she had only thought vaguely: Some day I shall be married and have children.

Now she began to think seriously, reasonably and frankly, and she saw that unless a miracle happened there was not the slightest chance of her getting married and having children, for she had no opportunity of meeting people of her own age. The Wheelers had friends, of course (elderly ladies and frumpy old gentlemen who dropped in to tea on Sunday afternoons), but Frances had no friends at all. She had never been to school, she had never been allowed to romp in the square with other children, she had never been to a dance in her life. Day after day Frances moved about the streets of London, doing the shopping and exchanging books at the library, and she saw hundreds of young people—men and women of her own age—dashing hither and thither, leaping in and out of cars and buses, or sailing past her on the tube escalators, but she had no means of getting to know them (she lived in a sort of glass ball cut off from all communication with her kind). These people were always seen by Frances in groups or in couples chattering to each other or waving to each other as they parted; calling out that they would see each other on Monday, or meet at lunch on Tuesday, or would ring up and make a date. What fun they had, thought Frances, as she went her solitary way.

She was beginning to feel quite desperate when a bomb fell in the middle of Wintringham Gardens and broke most of the windows in the square. It happened in the middle of the night and made the most ghastly noise. Frances, who had seen a good deal of the damage done by bombs in other parts of London, had a sudden and most unpleasant conviction that her last hour had come and that the house was about to fall like a pack of cards, as so many other houses had done . . . but nothing disastrous occurred, and the only thing that was destroyed irrevocably was Mrs. Wheeler's morale. Mrs. Wheeler had been certain that no bombs would fall upon Wintringham Square, and now that this comfortable assurance was dissipated she went to the other extreme and was convinced that every bomber in the Luftwaffe was making a bee-line for Wintringham Square with the intention of wiping it off the face of the earth.

"I can't bear it," she wailed. "It's too *awful*. It's far worse for me than for strong, active people who can go about and *do* things. I just lie and think about it all the *time*—I can't *bear* it."

"We'll shut up the house and go to Devonshire," said Mr. Wheeler in soothing tones. "It will be a nice change for us all."

"Do you mean you're coming too?" inquired his wife in surprise. "Can you leave the business?"

"The business has left me," replied Mr. Wheeler dryly.

Frances realised that this was her chance. The spell which had bound them all together in the big gloomy house had been broken by a German bomb.

It was exceedingly difficult for Frances to take her chance, for she had never asserted herself before, but she knew that it was now or never. It was her last hope of escape from Aunt Zoë, and if she didn't seize her opportunity she would be a prisoner for life.

"I'm not coming to Devonshire," said Frances bluntly.

"Of course you're coming," said Mrs. Wheeler. "Clara knows that you're coming and she's quite pleased. You will be very useful in the house."

"I'm not coming," said Frances.

"Don't be silly, Frances," said Mrs. Wheeler firmly.

"I want a holiday."

"We're all going to have a lovely holiday in Devonshire."

"I want a holiday by myself."

"I shall need you," said Mrs. Wheeler. "It's a busy house and Clara has several evacuees. There will be plenty for you to do——"

"I'm not coming," said Frances.

She said the same words over and over again. She clung to them as a drowning man might cling to a raft, but more than once she was tempted to let go of the raft and drown.

"Why not let Frances have a holiday?" inquired Mr. Wheeler, who was sick to death of the eternal argument. "It will do her good to be on her own for a bit."

"On her own!" screamed Mrs. Wheeler. "Henry, what nonsense you talk! How can she go and live in a hotel by herself?"

"I'm twenty-five," said Frances desperately. "I can look after myself perfectly well. I want a holiday . . . I've never had a holiday in my life."

"Where would you go? What would you do with yourself?"

"I'm going to Cairn."

"*Cairn*—where is it?"

"I don't know, but I'll find out."

"Who told you about it?"

"Nobody told me."

"Who lives there?"

"I don't know."

"You're mad," declared Mrs. Wheeler. "You're stark staring mad. Why do you want to go to a place you've never heard of?"

"I saw a picture of it," said Frances, driven to desperation by the catechism. "I saw a picture of Cairn in the Academy. Oh, I know it sounds mad, but I can't help it. I must get away . . . I want to think. . . ."

"Think!" exclaimed her aunt, gazing at her in amazement. "Can't you think here? Who prevents you thinking as much as you want?"

"You do," replied Frances firmly. "I can't be myself at all. I can't even choose a hat without your approval."

"You must be ill——" began Mrs. Wheeler, but Frances interrupted her.

"No," said Frances firmly. "No, I'm perfectly well, but I must go away by myself. I'm twenty-five and I've never done anything that I wanted to do."

Mrs. Wheeler had been very angry, but now she was alarmed. She was so much alarmed that she summoned Dr. Digby and explained the matter to him (Frances had taken the dog for a walk, so she was able to explain her own view of the case without fear of interruption). "It's so strange," said Mrs. Wheeler. "We've been so *good* to Frances. We couldn't have done more for her if she'd been our own daughter—and now her one idea is to go away by herself. I can't think where she got the extraordinary idea, it's absolutely beyond me. She's so worked up about it that she's quite unlike herself. I thought you might prescribe a sedative for her, and perhaps a tonic would do her good."

Dr. Digby laughed. "I'm the culprit," he said. "I told Frances to take a holiday, and I'm glad to hear the suggestion has borne fruit."

"But, Dr. Digby——"

"It's not often a patient requires a sedative and a tonic at the same time," he continued with a twinkle in his eyes, "and in any case Frances needs neither the one nor the other. She needs a holiday, and I'll not answer for the consequences if she doesn't get it."

"But what about me?" cried Mrs. Wheeler, who had pinned her hopes on Dr. Digby.

"You don't need her," replied the doctor.

Mrs. Wheeler felt the ground sliding from beneath her feet. "Whatever can you mean?" she quavered. "Who's going to look after *me*? I can't do without Frances."

"Of course you can," said Dr. Digby.

Frances was free. She had enough money for her holiday, and when it was over she would find useful work. Her plans were vague, but she would have plenty of time to think things out when she got to Cairn. One thing only was certain—she was never going back to prison again.

Chapter Three

FRANCES FIELD went out to explore Cairn.

The sun was bright this morning and there was a westerly breeze blowing in from the sea. A few white clouds came sailing by. The sky was the bluest blue that you could imagine. When Frances had seen the picture of Cairn she had decided that the colours were exaggerated—no sea and sky could be as blue as that, no rocks so red, no grass so green—but now she decided that far from exaggerating the colouring the painter had failed to reproduce it with sufficient brilliance—she did not blame him, of course, for she felt sure there could be no paints on earth to do justice to the sparkling atmosphere of Cairn.

She walked across the street and looked at the fishing boats which were tied up along the harbour wall. There was a man in one of the boats ; he was sitting on the thwarts mending a net, but he raised his head as Frances passed and she saw that it was Alec.

"It is a fine morning for you, Miss Field," said Alec in a friendly fashion.

Frances agreed that it was. She talked to Alec for a few minutes and learned that the boat was called the *Kittiwake* and that it was the best boat in the harbour. It belonged to Mr. MacDonald, but Alec had charge of it and could use it when he liked. It had brown sails and a petrol engine—but petrol was scarce.

"Maybe you would like to come out some day," suggested Alec in his soft Highland voice.

"Would Mr. MacDonald mind?" asked Frances doubtfully.

"Why would he mind?" inquired Alec.

Frances wondered who Mr. MacDonald was. There were all sorts of questions she wanted to ask but she did not like to appear inquisitive. She wanted to know about Alec himself—last night she had decided that he was attached to the hotel in some sort of capacity, but this morning he seemed to be a fisherman. She had begun to realise that these people used the English language in a way of their own. They did not ask a question in a straightforward manner but merely made an observation with a questioning inflection in their voices; they never answered a question with a plain yes or no but preferred to answer it with another question. Frances liked to hear them talking. It made her holiday so much more adventurous, for she felt as if she were in a foreign land. She had had no idea that Cairn would be so "different" and the people of Cairn so unlike any people she had ever seen before.

"Do you ever wear a kilt?" she asked.

Alec laughed. "Och, you are like the other visitors," he said. "Would you want me to wear the kilt when I'm in the boat? A kilt is a fine thing to wear on the hills but trousers are better for fishing."

Frances looked round. She said impulsively: "What a lovely place this is! It's so peaceful. The war seems far away—as if it were being fought in another world."

"It was not always peaceful here," he replied. "There were wars here—and bloodshed and murder—there were battles fought on this very spot, so there were."

Frances found it difficult to believe.

"It was long ago," Alec continued. "The Vikings landed here and ravaged the country. Some of them settled in these parts and gave their own names to places—Bordale is a Viking name—then when the Vikings went away there were wars amongst the clans. The Campbells and the MacDonalds were not often at

25

peace with each other . . . maybe there will be battles here again," added Alec hopefully.

"Battles *here*?"

"Och, we are ready for them," he declared. "There is no need for you to be afraid. The Home Guard is in fine form . . ."

"But I don't think——" began Frances.

"It would be a grand place for them to land with their flat-bottomed boats," explained Alec, pointing to the lovely sweep of bay which stretched southwards from the harbour. "But maybe they would not get so far before the Navy would be after them . . . they would need to come round the north of Scotland, Mr. MacDonald says."

"Who is Mr. MacDonald?" asked Frances, who could contain her curiosity no longer.

Alec looked at her in surprise. "Who would he be but the Laird?"

"Oh, I see."

"He is of a younger branch of the clan. He is a very proud gentleman is the Laird."

"Does he live here?" asked Frances.

"Where else would he live?" replied Alec. "He will be asking you up to the Castle in a day or two."

Frances thought this most unlikely. "But he doesn't know me," she said. "He doesn't even know that I exist!"

"There is nothing goes on at Cairn without the Laird knowing about it," replied Alec firmly.

She would have liked to ask more, for the information she had been given had roused her interest, but Alec had finished mending his net and he began to prepare to put out to sea. "They are wanting fish at the inn," he explained, "but it is too rough for you to-day——"

She agreed that a calm day would be much more pleasant.

"You will need oilskins," he added thoughtfully. "It is no fun going out fishing without proper gear."

"Where could I buy oilskins?" asked Frances.

"Och, you could get them in Weston. You take the bus to Rithie and get the train from there. There are fine shops at Weston, so there are, and it's a nice day's outing."

Frances watched the little boat put out to sea—it was rather pleasant to think that it was going out to catch fish for her supper—and then she turned northwards and took a path which wound its way amongst tumbled boulders and climbed steeply to the top of the overhanging cliffs. The cliffs stretched for

26

several miles—sometimes they were high and straight, sometimes they were broken and jagged, here and there they had crumbled on to the shore in masses of tumbled rock. Frances wandered along and her thoughts strayed in and out amongst a whole heap of material. How odd it is to think I am here at last, thought Frances, *here in Cairn*! How odd it is to think that if I hadn't happened to see the picture I shouldn't be here at all! Alec is nice; I wonder who he is, and why he is so different from the other men . . . it would be fun to go out in the boat, but not unless it is calm. I might be sick and that would be perfectly frightful. . . . I must go to Weston and buy the oilskins. I could buy a torch there, and some notepaper. . . . I want a warm scarf. I shan't go for a day or two because I want to explore first . . . it would be silly to rush away the moment I got here . . . but it doesn't matter (thought Frances, with a surge of pure delight), it doesn't matter whether I'm silly or not. I can do exactly as I like. I can do silly things if I want to do them.

Frances strode along, she leapt from rock to rock. She felt a different person from the timid, nervous girl who had moved about London, solitary amongst the crowd; who had battled with the dirt and smuts in Wintringham Square . . . and I *am* a different person, she thought. I *want* to be different. The only thing is I don't know what sort of person I want to be.

It was odd that she had reached the age of twenty-five without having decided what sort of a person she was—or wanted to be. It was because she had never had a chance to follow her own inclinations nor to develop her personality. Her nature was gentle and yielding and she had a horror of " scenes," so her one idea had been to keep the peace, to propitiate her uncle and aunt, and to keep things smooth and pleasant. All her energies had been directed to this end, and she had scarcely been aware of her own existence until the old doctor's words had set her thinking.

Frances rambled along, stopping here to gather a little bunch of primroses which were growing in a sheltered hollow, and pausing there to watch the white seagulls hovering and diving in the brilliant blue sea. She was so happy that she was almost frightened. Is it horrid of me? she wondered. Am I selfish and ungrateful to want to live my own life and to try to find out what I really am? But I must have a life of my own. I must be able to think my own thoughts. I'm twenty-five years old and I'm nothing at all.

She saw quite clearly that this was partly her own fault. If she had had a strong character she could have lived with Aunt Zoë and kept her own soul. It was because she was too yielding, too frightened of unpleasant scenes, that she had allowed herself to be dominated and repressed.

The path which Frances was following dipped down into a narrow ravine full of rowan trees. There were no leaves on them yet, but the sap had risen and the buds had begun to swell. A burn leaped merrily over a ledge of rock and flung itself into the sea. The path forked here, one branch continuing along the cliff and the other mounting steeply by the side of the burn. Frances hesitated. She was unused to choosing for herself—even in unimportant matters—and it was difficult for her to make up her mind which path to take, and as she stood there, hesitating, she began to feel a quickening of her imagination. She began to have the feeling that something had happened here. Vikings had landed here. Perhaps they had landed at this very spot, and kneeling down had drunk their fill of the pure sparkling water of the burn. They must have been glad to drink, for, after their long voyage, the water in their barrels would be musty and tainted . . . perhaps a Viking had stood where Frances stood now with his sandalled foot upon this very stone. She visualised the man from pictures which she had seen—a tall, proud figure with flashing blue eyes and yellow hair, with a circlet of gold upon his brow and golden armlets. He would be carrying a shield emblazoned with his arms and there would be a sword—a long pointed sword—in his hand. He would stand very still, looking about to see if there was danger—he would listen for a rustling in the bushes. The scene could not have altered much in a thousand or more years, for the sea, the rocks and the burn were all immutable in their different ways. . . .

Frances had frightened herself pretty thoroughly by this time but she had sense enough to laugh and throw up her chin. She began to climb the path which led inland by the side of the burn, and in a few minutes she found herself in a wood of pine and fir trees. The trees were straight and tall, with rough bark and gnarled branches which spread fanlike above her head and creaked a little in the wind. Their roots were shallow in the rocky ground, creeping across the path and amongst the stones, seeking for soil. Beneath these trees the ground was bare of vegetation ; it was covered with withered needles, but here and there she found a clearing in which stood an oak, ancient and lichened, or a noble beech. These trees were bare, of course, and the sunshine rained down between the branches so that each little clearing was like a bowl of gold. It was very quiet in the woods, the sound of the sea—of the waves falling rhythmically upon the

28

far-off shore—filled the air with a gentle murmur. There were no birds: that was why the woods were so quiet. It seemed to Frances that no living thing moved in the woods except herself. Her town-bred eyes were not trained to country sights, so she was not aware that a little red squirrel had streaked across her path and was watching her somewhat anxiously from a fork in the branches of a pine tree.

Suddenly the path turned round the edge of a rock and Frances found herself standing in a blaze of sunshine. It was dazzling after the green gloom of the woods. She hesitated until her eyes had recovered from the sudden light and then went forward again. She came to a ruined wall and then to a large slab of stone half-buried in grass and brambles. It was a strange-looking stone and she bent down to examine it, pushing back the grass so that she might see it better. It was a large slab, about six feet long and three feet wide, deeply carved with a pattern of interlaced stems and leaves. The pattern went round the edge of the stone and up the middle, dividing it into two panels; in the left panel there was a sword with a carved hilt and a long tapering blade, and in the right panel a stag's head with branching antlers. The carving was roughly done but it was boldly conceived and the design was simple but effective . . . there was something very satisfying about it.

Chapter Four

FRANCES WAS still looking at the curiously carved stone and wondering what it was and how it had come here, when something made her raise her head and she saw a man come out from amongst the trees at the other side of the clearing. He stood for a moment dazzled—as she had been—by the sudden blaze of sun and Frances caught her breath . . . just for a moment she thought it was a Viking come back from the past.

The man was very tall. He was carrying a scythe over his shoulder. He wore no hat and at first she thought that his thick wavy hair was golden, but as he approached she saw that it was silver. . . . He's old, thought Frances, with a slight feeling of disappointment. Then, as he came still nearer, she changed her mind again for, although his hair was silver, his eyes were young eyes, blue and piercing and very active.

She stood up, waiting for him to approach and wondering who

29

he was and whether he would be annoyed with her for trespassing. She had seen no notices to say that these woods were private property, but of course they must belong to someone. . . .

"Are you interested in burial slabs?" asked the man in a pleasant cultured voice which had a lilt in it that reminded her of Alec.

"Burial slabs?" said Frances, a trifle breathlessly. "Oh, that's what it is! I might have known——"

"I'm afraid I startled you," he said.

"It was because—because the woods feel so empty," she explained. "I didn't expect to see anyone . . . and so when you . . . but I hope I'm not trespassing."

He smiled and replied: "There's no need to worry about that."

Frances was still nervous. She didn't know what to say, so she said the first thing that came into her head. "Are you going to cut the grass?" she inquired.

He nodded. "It seems rather a waste of time but I like to keep this place tidy. So many men have gone that it isn't easy to manage . . . but I like working here."

He began to hone the scythe with a long white stone and Frances watched him and wondered who he was. She had thought at first that he might be Mr. MacDonald, but Alec had said that the Laird was "a very proud gentleman," and there was no pride in this man—or none that she could see.

"I suppose this is a burial ground," she said at last.

The man nodded. "Yes, it's one of the earliest Christian burial places in Scotland. There's a little ruined chapel behind those rocks. I'll show it to you, shall I?"

"Tell me about it first," said Frances.

He smiled at her. "You're quite right," he said. "It's much more interesting to know about places before you see them. The chapel dates from about A.D. 504. It was built by St. Kiaran. He was a friend of St. Columba. The old name of this place is Kilkiaran, which means the cell—or living-place—of Kiaran, but gradually it has been shortened to Cairn."

"Did he live here?" asked Frances, looking round the little clearing with interest.

"I have no absolute proof that he lived here, but I believe he did. These monks came over from Ireland. Sometimes they came alone, sometimes several of them came together. They were missionaries and they spent their lives amongst the pagan people of this wild land. They lived in caves or tiny huts, moving from place to place, spreading the teaching of the early

Columban Church and caring for the sick. This was one of the places which St. Kiaran visited. I feel sure of it . . . though, of course, ancient history is a debatable subject. We can only build it up by deduction and by the examination of the data at our disposal."

" I don't know anything about Scottish history," Frances said.

" Very few people do, and yet it was those saintly monks who first brought Christianity to Britain. St. Ninian was probably the first Christian to set foot on our shores and St. Kiaran was not long after him. One might think that fact was at least as important as the Battle of Hastings, 1066."

Frances saw that he was smiling, so she smiled too. " I thought St. Augustine was the first——" she began.

" Good heavens, no! St. Kiaran died in A.D. 548, and that was more than forty years before the Augustine mission came to England."

" So you were Christians before we were," said Frances in surprise.

He nodded. " Of course we were, but the Norsemen started ravaging our coasts about A.D. 700. . . . We had no chance to develop the arts of peace."

" Are there books about it?" Frances asked.

" These are our history books," replied her companion, pointing to the stone slab which lay between them on the ground. " The whole history of the district is contained in these burial slabs—that's what makes them so interesting. First we have the crosses and burial slabs of the early Columban era—the carved basket-work is the earliest pattern, for it was a familiar pattern to primitive people who were in the habit of weaving osiers and rushes into baskets for domestic use. The sword is often depicted. It means that the slab commemorates a brave and gallant fighter. The stag's head means that he was a hunter as well."

Frances saw the idea. She said: " It was a splendid idea to carve people's characteristics on their tombstones, wasn't it? It seems so much more individual than just writing: ' In loving memory of Thomas Smith, a good husband and a loving father.' "

Her companion laughed heartily. " How would you depict a loving father?" he inquired.

Frances did not reply to this. She was feeling the carving of the stone with her fingers. " How deep it is! " she exclaimed. " And they can't have had very good tools to work with, can they? It must have taken *ages* to do."

" Time was no object in those far-off days."

"No . . . besides, it was a labour of love. If you were very fond of someone it must have been nice to be able to do something for them. It would be comforting, wouldn't it? You could spend days—or even weeks—making a really distinctive tombstone."

There was a little silence and Frances glanced up to see why he had not replied. He looked down at her gravely. "That's a new idea to me," he said, "and a very delightful one. Thank you, Miss Field."

"Then you *are* Mr. MacDonald!" exclaimed Frances.

He nodded. "Yes, but may I ask how you have suddenly arrived at the conclusion?"

"Because Alec said you knew everything."

"Cairn is a small place and the arrival of Miss Field has created a good deal of interest amongst the inhabitants." He smiled as he spoke and Frances smiled back. She had decided that Mr. MacDonald was very nice indeed. At first she had felt shy, for she was unused to talking to strangers, but her nervousness had vanished now and she felt quite comfortable with him.

They walked through the long grass towards the little heap of ruins which was all that remained of St. Kiaran's chapel. The ruins were overgrown with brambles and a rowan tree had rooted itself amongst the stones, but there was still an atmosphere of holiness about the place—a strange peaceful feeling of goodness and kindness—and Frances suddenly understood what Mr. MacDonald had meant when he said that he liked working here. Beyond the chapel was a rocky hill, and a spring of water bubbled out of the ground and ran past the ruined entrance. It was the source of the burn which Frances had followed from the sea.

"These early chapels are always situated near springs," said Mr. MacDonald in a quiet voice. "It was essential for the monk to have his cell near running water. The people believed the water to have miraculous properties—usually the power of healing—but St. Kiaran's spring is supposed to have stranger powers than those of healing. Legend has it that any one who drinks the water will be married within a year."

Frances was hot and thirsty. She had knelt down beside the trickle of water and cupped her hands, but now she started back. "They don't believe in it nowadays, do they?" she inquired.

"No, of course not," replied Mr. MacDonald, looking down at

32

her with a twinkle in his eyes. " Nobody believes in fairies nowadays—or in magic wells—but all the same I'm told that quite a number of village maidens come to Kilkiaran to drink at this spring. . . . It's perfectly safe to drink," he added. " It's as pure as any water could possibly be."

Frances shook her head.

" Why not?" inquired her companion. " Are you afraid that the spell will work? I believe you're every bit as bad as the village maidens."

The bubbling water looked delightful but it was quite impossible to drink it after what Mr. MacDonald had said. Frances had not the necessary *savoir-faire* to carry off the situation—she was shy and embarrassed again.

" I don't want to be married," she said awkwardly. " I like being free——" and then, before he could ask any inconvenient questions, she changed the subject by asking if there were any more burial slabs to be seen. She had a feeling that her companion would not be able to resist this question, and she was right.

" Not here," he said, " but there are many scattered about the district. Many of them are very fine indeed with deep carving and beautiful designs. Some of the slabs are carved with the ancient emblem of the Trinity—three legs in the form of a wheel —others depict a pair of shears which represents the cutting of the thread of life. Swords are very common, of course, and so are emblems of the chase. After the Columban era we find stones which show the influence of the Norsemen—or Vikings—the galley with its pointed prow and stern, mermaids, whales and dolphins, and sometimes a hunt with dogs in full cry. Then comes the Norwegian era—the district was actually a part of Norway until 1225 when it was ceded to Alexander III for a yearly tribute. The Norwegians professed Christianity but were pagans at heart, full of strange superstitions, and during their occupation we find burial slabs depicting winged beasts and strange birds and animals which were never seen on earth, all of which are intended to convey some meaning."

" And after the Norwegians?" asked Frances.

" Soon after the Norwegians we begin to find effigies," he replied. " These are intended to be actual likenesses of the departed. The best examples are of blue schist, which is very hard and can be cut into delicate fretwork. They date from about 1335. The warriors are depicted wearing the peaked helmet and the solleret with curved and pointed toes——" He stopped suddenly and then added in a different tone: " But I'm so interested in these things that I'm apt to bore people. My cousin says I scare all our visitors away."

" I think it's very, very interesting," said Frances, looking up at him with large serious blue eyes. " I had no idea that history was written on tombstones."

" It does seem curious," agreed Mr. MacDonald. " The people who carved them had no idea that they were writing history books . . . but stone is the most enduring material we possess, and much of the history of the human race has been handed down to us in stone. To take a few random examples: there are the flint weapons and implements of prehistoric man, there are the Pyramids, the Druidical altars, the ruins of ancient Rome . . ."

" Shakespeare should have said: ' history in stones,' instead of sermons," said Frances thoughtfully.

Frances had a great deal to think about as she walked back to Cairn. She looked at everything with new eyes. The woods did not seem so empty now, for she could imagine the people who had lived here all those hundreds of years ago . . . quiet, in-offensive people, living peaceful lives, catching fish and culti-vating their little plots of ground, welcoming the holy man when he visited them and taking small presents of milk and meal and fish to his lonely cell. They might have continued like this, and become a little nucleus of Christianity and civilisation (they might have developed the arts of peace under the guidance of the monks), had not the Norsemen invaded them and laid waste their land. Even in those days there was aggression, thought Frances rather sadly, even in those days people could not live peaceably upon their own soil and allow their neighbours to do the same.

She had reached the cliffs now and she stood there for a few moments gazing out across the blue sea to the distant islands, and, as she looked, she seemed to see a great galley rounding the point, the sun flashing upon its dripping oars and on the torcs and armlets of the yellow-haired crew. . . .

Could it happen again? she wondered, and, although the sun was still warm and brilliant, she shivered suddenly, and hurried back to the hotel for her belated lunch.

Chapter Five

EVERYONE at the Bordale Arms seemed to be aware that Frances intended to go to Weston for the day, and everyone was anxious to advise her as to how she should go and what she should do when she got there ; indeed she received so much advice that she began to feel quite dazed. She was tired of saying : " Yes, thank you, I'll remember that . . . a large shop called MacTaggart at the corner of the square," or " Oh, thank you, I mustn't forget that . . . the first turning on the left after I leave the station." The advice was somewhat conflicting—as advice so often is—and the only point upon which everyone was unanimous was that she must catch the half-past seven bus from Cairn.

" I'll wake you, never fear," declared Annie. " I'll be up at six and you'll get your breakfast at a quarter to seven sharp. Maybe you would get me a wee red belt if you have the time. It's to wear with my new spring outfit."

Frances could not help smiling. She reflected that " a wee red belt " sounded a very modest request, so much more modest than a large red belt, and the joke was that the belt would have to be a fairly long one to encircle Annie's ample waist. Frances took the pattern and put it in her bag and promised to do what she could.

The journey was completed without a hitch. Frances caught her bus to Rithie, and from there she was conveyed to Weston by a small but fussy train which bustled its way through some of the most gorgeous scenery she had ever beheld. There were mountains and forests and lochs, there were dashing rivers and deep ravines. She rushed from one window to the other, gazing out at the magnificent country . . . it seemed strange that she was getting all this beauty for the price of a third-class ticket.

Arrived at her destination Frances lunched and shopped ; she enjoyed her shopping, for it was a new experience to be able to buy exactly what she liked (there was no need to ask for the goods on approval so that they could be changed if Aunt Zoë did not like them), and, because it was so new, the experience went to her head and she spent a good deal more than she had intended. She bought the oilskins and a torch and several pads of notepaper and envelopes ; she bought a lovely warm scarf and knitted gloves to match ; she bought two woollen jerseys and a pair of stout walking-shoes, and—most daring and exciting of all—she bought a pair of navy-blue trousers and a polo jersey. By this time she had so many parcels hanging on to her fingers by loops of string that she was obliged to buy a cheap suitcase to hold them. The belt caused Frances more trouble than all the rest of her shopping put together, for Annie's spring outfit was an unusual shade of red. In pursuit of a belt which would tone with the pattern—or at least would not clash with it so violently as to set one's teeth on edge—Frances very nearly missed her train to Rithie. She tore down the platform as the whistle blew; the guard wrenched open the door of a third-class compartment and shoved her in, and the train moved off with a jerk that sent her backwards into a corner seat.

It was an old-fashioned compartment designed to seat eight people, and when Frances had recovered herself a little she looked round and saw that there were other three women in the compartment sitting together at the other end. As she had not had time to buy a paper she amused herself by trying to determine their relationship to each other and to guess their business —it was a game in which she had often indulged as she went about London by herself. People's faces were so interesting; there was a story in every face, and Frances adored stories. These three women were difficult to place. They were all much the same age—about her own age or a trifle older—but they were not sisters, that much was certain. After a second glance Frances decided that they were not related to each other at all. She took her fellow-travellers one by one, scrutinising them with growing interest. They were talking to each other earnestly and never glanced in her direction; in fact they seemed oblivious of the fact that there was anyone in the compartment besides themselves. Perhaps I'm invisible, Frances thought, and a faint smile touched the corners of her mouth. It would be fun to be invisible, to move about unseen amongst one's fellow human beings. " A chiel's amang you takin' notes." Frances had discovered a whole set of Waverley Novels at the Bordale Arms and had been reading *The Heart of Midlothian*. She had found the quotation from Burns on the title page and had been very much struck with it. She was not quite sure what a " chiel " was, but she felt certain that an invisible chiel would be able to gather volumes of notes without any difficulty.

Having decided that she was an invisible chiel, Frances set to work to observe her fellow-travellers. They were well worth the trouble, not only individually but collectively. They were all quite different, as different as three women of much the same age could possibly be, and yet there was something common to all three, something which Frances could not define. Perhaps they all belong to some sort of club or society, thought Frances, but what sort of club could include such different types?

The woman in the corner seat was wearing a dark-green tweedy coat with a squirrel collar. Her shoes were neat brown brogues, beautifully polished. They had attained that dull gleam which only comes after long and meticulous care . . . neat feet she had, and slim ankles clad in heavy silk stockings. Glancing at her face Frances saw that it was a " heart-shaped face," fair and slightly freckled. Her hair was the colour of old mahogany, her green eyes sparkled with life. Her lips were slightly reddened, but apart from that she was not made-up at all . . . she couldn't be an actress with those freckles. Beside her sat an older woman —she might have been thirty—with a keen thin face and dark eyes. She was in black, with a white frilled shirt and long jade earrings. Everything about her was in exquisite taste—fine silk stockings, patent-leather shoes and a patent-leather bag to match. The third woman was not so easy to see, for she was sitting in the corner seat on the same side as Frances, but Frances could see her feet—and what strange feet they were— shabby and slightly bulgy in their black strapped shoes. What on earth were those black strapped shoes doing in company with the gleaming brogues and the shining patent leathers?

The conversation which was taking place was baffling in the extreme. Frances could not help overhearing it, for it was con-ducted in voices raised to carry above the rattle of the train.

" I know," the owner of the brogues declared. " I didn't want to, of course, but she asked me straight out. I couldn't say no, could I?"

" I'm glad she didn't come herself," declared the owner of the black-strapped shoes.

" Why?"

" Because she would bag the best for herself."

" She always does, doesn't she?" nodded the owner of the brogues.

The woman in black laughed somewhat cynically and re-marked: " Yes, and she always will. You don't imagine that she will be content with less, do you? She asked Tommy to find her a house, so Tommy will have to offer her the nicest."

" I shan't," declared the owner of the brogues in savage tones.

" Of course you will."

" But, Elise, why should I?"

" Because she'll be impossible if you don't."

"Elise is right, Tommy," said the shabby woman regretfully.

There was a few moments' silence. The woman with the brogues—who had been addressed as "Tommy"—took out a packet of cigarettes and handed them round and they all lighted up, even the bulgy-footed woman in the corner. She leant forward to light her cigarette with Tommy's match and Frances saw her face. It was a round face with an indeterminate sort of nose, and was framed in fair hair which straggled a trifle shaggily from beneath an old-fashioned helmet-shaped felt hat.

Who are they? wondered Frances. Where can they be going, and why? What is it that has brought them together and made them so intimate?

"Let's decide what we want," said Tommy suddenly. "It's easier if we make up our minds beforehand. Tillie must have the biggest, because of the children. I want to be as near as I can—that's all I mind about . . . but it must be cheap, of course. . . ."

"We're absolutely on the rocks," announced Tillie. "It's school fees—they're simply terrific—and Winkie's operation cost fifty pounds."

"Fifty! Good Lord!" exclaimed Tommy. She had taken a small writing-pad out of her handbag and was making notes upon it in a businesslike way, but now she paused and looked at Tillie in dismay.

"It can't be helped," said Tillie in a resigned voice, "and, anyhow, Winkie is all right . . . nothing else matters."

Tommy returned to her notes. "What do you want, Elise?" she inquired.

The woman in black laughed and uncrossed her elegant feet. "I'll tell you what I want," she said. "I want a small house with all modern conveniences, electric light, company's water, and two bathrooms. I want it facing south, of course, with a nice garden and a garage——"

"Elise!" exclaimed Tommy, pausing, pencil in air.

"And now I'll tell you what I shall get," said Elise blandly. "I shall get a pigsty with no water laid on but plenty coming through the roof, or else a mansion standing in an enormous park."

Tommy smiled. "Our little optimist," she said indulgently.

The compartment was beginning to get hazy with smoke, and Frances decided to smoke too. She had started smoking as a gesture—it was a practice that Aunt Zoë abhorred. She opened her bag, took out a cigarette, and began to search for her matches, and then she saw that Tommy had a box of matches in her hand and was offering it to her with a shy but wholly delightful smile. So I'm not invisible, thought Frances, as she accepted a match and smiled back.

The ice was broken now and Tommy addressed her in a sweet high voice—it sounded quite different from the voice in which she had addressed her companions. "Could you tell us——" asked Tommy. "Could you possibly tell us whether we have to change at Rithie for Cairn?"

"Cairn!" exclaimed Frances. "You can't be going to Cairn; that's where I'm staying."

Elise laughed. "Do you require the whole of Cairn for your own use?" she inquired.

"No, of course not," said Frances, somewhat taken aback. "But there isn't anything *there*—I mean, nothing for you to do—nothing that you would want to do——" She stumbled over the words, for it was difficult to express her meaning without seeming rude.

"I told you it was a one-horse hole," said Elise with a sigh.

Frances had not intended to convey this impression of Cairn. "Oh, I *love* it!" she exclaimed. "It's perfectly beautiful. I just meant that you—that there isn't much to do——"

Three pairs of eyes were fixed upon her with interest, and Frances was so embarrassed by their gaze that she wished she was invisible again.

"If you like it, why shouldn't we?" asked Elise.

Frances could find nothing to say.

"Shut up, Elise," said Tommy quickly. "It's a shame to tease her. It's because you look like Bond Street—that's why."

"Bond Street!"

"Exactly like Bond Street," said Tommy firmly. "You create an impression of elegance and affluence, of jewellers' shops and cocktail bars."

"How frightful!" exclaimed Elise with a light laugh.

"Of course, we know Cairn is bound to be a one-horse hole," Tommy continued, "but even in one-horse holes one can find amusing things to do. Is there a cinema?"

"I don't think so," replied Frances.

"What about houses?" asked the shabby woman, leaning forward and looking at Frances anxiously.

"Houses?" echoed Frances.

"Buildings with four walls and a roof," explained Tommy with a grave expression. "Places where people live—do you happen to know of any at Cairn?"

"You don't mean you're going to—to *settle down* in Cairn!"

" Of course we are," said Tillie.

" If we can," added Tommy.

" For as long as we are allowed," declared Elise.

Frances gazed at them in amazement. Why were they going to Cairn when they knew nothing about the place?

" It's a shame to tease her," said Tommy, laughing. " She thinks we're mad. She thinks we're escaped lunatics or something."

" We're the people who are supposed to live on puddings and pies," said Elise with a quiet smile.

" On two and ninepence a day," added Tillie grimly.

" Officers' wives, you know," explained Tommy, taking pity upon the bewilderment of their new acquaintance. " It's quite simple, really, and not nearly so crazy as it sounds. The battalion is going into camp at Cairn, so we must have houses—furnished houses—you see that, don't you?"

" Oh!" exclaimed Frances.

" Did you say ' No '?"

" No, I said ' Oh,' " replied Frances hastily. " I was just trying to think . . . I don't believe there *are* any houses at Cairn."

" None at all?"

" None that would suit you."

Tommy laughed with relief. " Oh, anything will suit us. I thought you meant there were no houses at all."

" There are fishermen's cottages," said Frances in desperation.

" Fishermen's cottages," said Elise. " That will be a new experience. I've never lived in a fisherman's cottage before."

" We had a cowman's cottage at Barnhurst," said Tillie in a reminiscent voice, " and then we moved to Stapleton and took Stapleton Place. It had twenty bedrooms. I preferred the cottage every time, it was so much easier——"

" We'll find *something*," said Tommy comfortably.

" I suppose there's some sort of pub where we can stay while we have a look round?" asked Elise.

Frances assured her that the Bordale Arms was quite a comfortable place to stay. " It's rather primitive in some ways, of course," added Frances, glancing at Elise, who looked as if she usually put up at the Ritz.

" No bathroom, I suppose?" said Elise with a sigh.

" Oh, quite a nice bathroom," replied Frances hastily.

" Splendid!" exclaimed Tommy. " How lucky we met you!"

Frances could not see that she had been of much service, and she looked at Tommy in case the remark was intended to be sarcastic, but Tommy's heart-shaped face wore a perfectly innocent expression. Tillie was smiling, and even Elise (whom Frances had credited with a somewhat cynical disposition) was looking at her in a friendly way.

"You can tell us all about Cairn," explained Tommy. "It *is* lucky, isn't it?"

"I've only been there three days——"

"Three days is ample," replied Tommy. "You can turn a place inside out in three days if you set your mind to it."

Frances could not help laughing. "I'm afraid I didn't," she said. "I just walked about and explored and talked to one or two people." She could not make up her mind whether she was glad or sorry that these people were coming to Cairn. It had been very quiet and peaceful and she had enjoyed it immensely, but on the other hand these people seemed interesting and unusual. . . . After all, thought Frances, I can always go up to my room and read. . . . I needn't see much of them unless I want to. . . .

"I'm Mrs. Widgery," said Tommy, who had suddenly decided to introduce herself and her companions. "That's Mrs. Crabbe, and that's Mrs. Liston."

"I'm Frances Field," said Frances.

They all smiled at each other—the acquaintanceship had gone a step further. Frances thought it would be difficult to remember that they were Mrs. Widgery, Mrs. Crabbe and Mrs. Liston after having fixed them in her mind as Tommy, Elise and Tillie.

Now that they had introduced themselves, they began to ply Frances with all sorts of questions about Cairn, and Frances answered to the best of her ability. She was somewhat surprised when Elise (now to be known as Mrs. Crabbe) admitted to a baby and inquired whether it was possible to procure certified milk.

"Alec would know," said Frances confidently. She found herself making the same reply to a good many questions.

They arrived at Rithie and Frances explained that the remainder of the journey must be performed by bus.

"Why on earth didn't one of you bring a car?" asked Tillie a trifle fretfully.

"Because I had no petrol," replied her companions with one voice.

Three suitcases and a hatbox were retrieved from the van and placed in the bus which was waiting in the station yard. The bus was already full of people, but they managed to squeeze in —Frances found herself sandwiched between Tommy and a fat woman with a fish basket.

41

"I'm glad it isn't onions," whispered Tommy in her ear. "I hate onions—I know it's extraordinary of me—the only bright spot for me in this foul war is no onions."

They rattled over the cobbled market-place and swung round the corner, and a fisherman in a jersey bumped against Tommy's shoulder.

"Sorry, miss," he said.

"Quite all right," declared Tommy, smiling at him. "You couldn't help it, could you? Do you live at Cairn, by any chance?"

The man replied that he had lived at Cairn all his life.

Tommy's eyes glistened and she proceeded to pump him about the place, asking all sorts of questions about houses and shops and whether one could buy fresh fish from the boats that went out from the harbour. At first the man was inclined to be suspicious and a trifle grumpy, but Tommy did not appear to notice this. She had a gay friendliness of manner which was difficult to resist, and before the bus had covered half the distance to Cairn he was eating out of her hand.

Frances now began to worry about their reception at the Bordale Arms—her own reception had been so strange. She explained this to Tommy as best she could, but Tommy refused to be cast down.

"It will be all right," said Tommy. "Hotels are bound to take you if they have room—unless you're drunk or something— there's a law about it, isn't there? Besides, that's how they make their money. I don't mind doubling up with Elise—it wouldn't be the first time—Tillie snores."

There was a good deal to be read between the lines in Tommy's simple statements, and Frances was silent for a few moments while she assimilated the information contained therein.

"Don't worry," added Tommy kindly. "You needn't have anything to do with it. You can pretend you don't know us, if you like."

This offer was so remarkable that Frances was struck dumb, and before she had recovered her power of speech the bus drew up outside the post office at Cairn. She was now the interested spectator of the manner in which an experienced traveller can get things done. When Frances arrived at Cairn she had been obliged to carry her own suitcase from the bus to the hotel, but Tommy, Elise, and Tillie had scarcely set foot upon the cobbled street before they had provided themselves with porters in the shape of three hefty-looking boys who had been lounging against the wall with their hands in their pockets. The boys looked a trifle surprised to discover themselves laden with suitcases, but they made no objection. The small suitcase which Frances had bought in Weston, and which contained all her parcels, was seized out of her hand and bestowed upon Tommy's boy.

"I can't give him less than sixpence, so he may as well carry them both," said Tommy frankly.

After this display of competence Frances was not really surprised when her new friends asked for, and received without demur, three bedrooms at the Bordale Arms Hotel.

Chapter Six

"Do you play bridge?" inquired Tommy as Frances came into the lounge.

"Or poker?" asked Tillie hopefully.

Frances did not. She had played backgammon with Uncle Henry, but she did not mention this.

"There are some books here," murmured Elise, who had been wandering round the room.

"Drivel, I expect," remarked Tommy.

Frances sat down with *The Heart of Midlothian*. She had decided that she must not force her company upon her new acquaintances. They were obliged to share the lounge because it was the only place to sit, but there was no need to listen to the conversation.

"Janetta Walters," said Elise.

Frances uttered a muffled exclamation.

"What did you say?" inquired Tommy.

"Nothing," replied Frances. "It was only—I mean, my aunt reads all her books. I used to pursue them at the library."

"There's a whole row of them here," said Elise in a disgusted tone.

"I like them," Tommy declared. "They're frightfully funny."

Frances was surprised to hear this; she had never found any humour in them.

Tilly was surprised too. "Funny?" she asked incredulously. "Screamingly funny," Tommy repeated, nodding her head. "I've read them all, so I know what I'm talking about. You see, we were in a furnished house at Hythe and there was a complete set of Janetta Walters bound in tooled leather. The first thing I did when I got there was to fall down the stairs and

43

sprain my ankle, so I read the whole lot straight off. They're much funnier than Wodehouse."

" But why——"

" Oh, I don't know," said Tommy. " It's because they're so crude or something. You can hardly believe that the woman isn't writing with her tongue in her cheek. There was one that outdid all the others for sheer unadulterated sloppiness—the man was so strong and silent that he was almost dumb, and the girl was as frail and delicate as a hothouse flower—they met and fell in love at first sight, and spent the rest of the book misunderstanding each other. Then, quite near the end, when everything seemed absolutely hopeless, they got marooned by the rising tide and everything came right with a bang."

" It sounds the most awful drivel," said Elise.

" Oh, it is," agreed Tommy. " Everything in Janetta's books happens quite differently from the way things happen in real life. Did you ever hear of any real person—anyone you know— getting cut off by the rising tide?"

" Never," said Elise.

" That's why they're so funny," declared Tommy triumphantly.

" They aren't meant to be funny," Tillie pointed out.

Frances noticed that Tillie was often left behind in arguments of this nature. She was apt to lose the point and stray from the beaten path. She had done so again, and Tommy did not bother to answer her. Tommy had lighted a cigarette and was turning over the leaves of an illustrated paper in a desultory manner. The subject of Janetta Walters seemed to be closed, and Frances was sorry, for she had been very much interested in Tommy's reactions. She was aware that the book to which Tommy had referred, and of which she had given such a spirited *résumé*, was *Her Prince at Last*, for, although all Janetta Walters's books were full of strong men and flower-like maidens who fell in love with each other at first sight, it was in *Her Prince at Last* that Edward and Rose had been marooned upon the island by the rising tide. (Frances remembered the incident well—she had had so much trouble over the book that it had been imprinted for all time upon her memory.) Edward and Rose had been obliged to spend the night on the island, but Edward was too chivalrous—or perhaps too dumb—to speak to his beloved and clear up the frightful tangle of misunderstandings which enveloped them. Edward had taken off his coat and wrapped it round the feet of his companion—it had seemed to Frances a foolish thing to do—and then he had gone to the other side of the island and left her by herself. As Rose was an exceedingly highly strung individual and was terrified of the waves, this seemed foolish too ... it was all the more idiotic because the other side of the island was swept by a strong east wind, and Edward, sitting there in his shirt-sleeves and musing upon the innocent beauty of his love, was unfortunate enough to contract a severe chill, which developed into pneumonia. The pneumonia solved everything. Rose, believing him to be dead, flung herself upon his breast and confessed that she had adored him for years. Edward did not die, of course—Frances had not been the least anxious about him, for she was aware that he must recover so as to be able to marry Rose. All Janetta Walters's books ended in marriage bells; her large and admiring public would have been disappointed if they had ended in any other manner.

Elise said suddenly: "I don't know how you can have read them *all*, Tommy. They sound such tripe."

"But I like tripe," replied Tommy gravely. "I like tripe, but not onions."

"I didn't know you could have it without onions," Tillie said.

"Brown sauce," explained Tommy. "It's terribly good. Midge loves it. I'll give you the recipe, if you like."

Once again they had strayed from the subject—it was most tantalising. Frances was wondering how she could reopen it, when Tillie reopened it for her. "I suppose it must be hard work writing books," she said regretfully.

"Are you thinking of writing one?" Tommy inquired.

"I wish I could," declared Tillie. "She must make thousands —Janetta Walters, I mean."

"I believe I could write fairy tales," said Tommy thoughtfully. "Let me see. . . . Once upon a time there was a fairy princess and she had four husbands and——"

"She was a film-star," interrupted Elise.

"No," said Tommy. "You don't understand. She had four husbands all at once—on her permanent staff, I mean."

"Keep it clean, Tommy."

"Oh, of course," agreed Tommy. "I mean, only people with minds like sewers will be able to read anything between the lines."

"I suppose that's why you liked Janetta Walters?"

"I believe it was," said Tommy with a surprised inflection. She hesitated for a moment and then went on with her story. "The princess was called Princess Carginamel, and——"

"Why?" inquired Elise.

"I hoped you'd ask that," said Tommy. "It was because she was sweet with a little bit of ginger inside."

"She was full of gin, you mean?"

"No, ginger is much more subtle," replied Tommy firmly.

"I love ginger," said Tillie in a dreamy voice. "You can't get real ginger here—except at Fortnum's—it was when we were at Hong Kong that I developed a taste for it."

"You get it at Sierra Leone," put in Elise. "It grows almost like a weed and has a pretty flower. The boys used to bring in the roots and scald them. It was black ginger, of course—Ned loved the stuff, but it was rather strong for me."

Frances had given up all pretence of reading, and was listening to the conversation with all her ears. She was being given a peep into lives so different from her own that they might have been lived by a different species of being, and because they were so different they fascinated her. The indubitable fact that Aunt Zoë would have disapproved of her new friends made their society all the more adventurous and desirable. Frances had never before met people who talked nonsense with the grave demeanour of judges, nor people who spoke of Hong Kong and Sierra Leone as if these places were just round the corner, and as if it was all in the day's work to travel half-way round the world and back again. Frances remembered the case of Mrs. Bagnet, who, left in another quarter of the globe with nothing but a grey cloak and an umbrella, made her own way home to London and turned up fresh and smiling at the end of her journey. Now, as then, following the drum seemed to entail travel on a wide scale.

"What are you thinking about, Miss Field?" asked Tommy suddenly.

Frances blushed. She said: "I was thinking what different sort of lives you have had—different from mine. I've never been anywhere or seen anything. It must be so interesting to go all over the world and meet all sorts of people."

"We don't, really," replied Tommy. "I mean, we go about but we don't meet other people very much. We go about together—it's silly, really."

"You don't seem quite *real*, somehow," said Frances.

"Perhaps we aren't real," put in Elise with a thoughtful look.

"What *do* you mean?" inquired Tillie in surprise.

Frances came down to breakfast in good time. She had put on her trousers and polo jersey and was feeling a trifle self-conscious. The trousers were not as comfortable as she had expected—there was a strange flappy feeling about the legs—but whether they were comfortable or not she was determined to wear them, for

46

they were symbolic of her new life. She was half-way through her breakfast when Mrs. Crabbe and Mrs. Liston appeared. They said " Good-morning " and sat down and began to talk about food.

" We ought to get plenty of fish, at any rate," said Elise, pointing to the sea.

" Have you found out about milk for Jennifer?" asked Tillie Liston.

They discussed milk earnestly, and were still discussing milk when Tommy Widgery came in. She waved to Frances in a cheerful manner and sat down with the others.

" How did you sleep, Tommy?" asked Tillie.

" With my eyes shut—how did you?" replied Tommy, smiling.

" With her mouth open, of course," said Elise quickly.

Tilly laughed—she did not seem to mind being teased. " The beds are really *quite* decent," she said.

Frances saw very little of her new friends that day. They were busy with their own affairs, and she did not want to bother them. It was a damp, misty sort of day, so Frances decided to spend the morning writing letters (she ought to have written before, but letter writing seemed such a waste of time when the sun was shining and Cairn was waiting to be explored). She wrote to her uncle and aunt saying that she was very comfortable and was enjoying her holiday, and then she proceeded to write to Dr. Digby. There was no real need to write to Dr. Digby, of course, but Frances felt that he would be interested to hear how she was getting on. She intended to write him a short note, thanking him for his help and telling him that her holiday was a tremendous success, but once she had started to tell him about her holiday her pen raced on . . . the truth was she needed a friendly ear, and Dr. Digby was the only real friend she had. When Frances had finished her letter and read it over she was quite surprised at herself. Shall I send it? she wondered. Will he think it odd of me to write such a screed? She hesitated for a moment or two, but finally decided that it would be foolish not to send it after having spent most of the morning writing it. At the end of the letter she wrote a postscript saying that she had decided not to go back to the Wheelers when her holiday was over, and asking Dr. Digby what sort of work she should do. " You know my limitations," wrote Frances modestly. " I cannot do typewriting nor drive a car, and I should be no use in an office. Have you any idea what I could do?" She signed the letter and folded it up and put it in its envelope.

After lunch it was still gloomy and misty, but Frances put on her oilskin coat and went downstairs. Mrs. MacNair was in the hall—she was a short, plump woman with dark hair and brown eyes.

"Are you going to the post, Miss Field?" she asked, smiling at Frances in a friendly way.

Frances replied in the affirmative. As she had her letters in her hand it was fairly obvious that she intended to post them, but the little exchange of words was not altogether superfluous; if it did not convey any information it betokened a friendly feeling.

The hall of the Bordale Arms was an odd place—so Frances had found—for there was nearly always someone there, either passing through or lingering in it in a purposeless sort of way. In fact, the only time Frances had ever entered the hall without finding someone there was the occasion of her arrival at the place. She had found, too, that the moment any sort of conversation began the doors round the hall would immediately open and heads would appear. Mr. MacNair would appear from the bar, or Annie from the pantry, or sometimes the cook—a large comfortable-looking woman with snow-white hair—would open the kitchen door and beam placidly upon the conversationalists. Alec, also, had a habit of appearing suddenly and unexpectedly at the window which opened into the yard, or from the dining-room with a handful of cutlery, or from the lounge with a coal-scuttle . . . it was all very friendly. To-day was no exception to the rule. No sooner had Frances replied that she did intend to sally forth to the post office than Annie emerged from the pantry and Alec from the lounge.

"Is Miss Field going out?" inquired Alec.

Miss Field repeated that such was her intention.

"Shiela should get out," said Annie. "Will I put on my things and take Shiela for a wee turn, Mrs. MacNair?"

"You'll get on with your work, Annie," replied Mrs. MacNair firmly.

"I would take her," said Alec, "but I've a lot to do."

"Perhaps she would like to come with me," suggested Frances.

"She would not go with you," said Mrs. MacNair.

"No, indeed," agreed Alec and Annie with one voice.

Frances opened the door and went out. She had made the offer on the spur of the moment, because she was feeling friendly towards the MacNairs, and she was a trifle hurt at the manner in which it had been rejected . . . she had been well snubbed. As she walked up the street to the post office she wondered again who Shiela was. It seemed odd that she had been living in the same house for nearly a week and had never set eyes upon her.

The bright colours of Cairn had vanished to-day. The mist was thickening, and it was scarcely possible to see across the street. Frances did not walk far, and perhaps it was just as well, for the mist played strange tricks with her and she had some difficulty in finding her way back to the hotel for tea. Later in the evening her three new friends initiated her into the mysteries of vingt-et-un, and Frances, who had never played a game for money in her life, was amazed and thrilled beyond measure to discover that she had won tenpence from her more experienced adversaries.

Chapter Seven

FRANCES DID not sleep well that night. She awoke several times and heard a sound which reminded her of distant traffic. It could not be traffic, of course, because this was Cairn—not Wintringham Square—it must be some sort of engine, a pump or an electric-light plant.

There was nobody in the dining-room when she went down to breakfast, so she rang the bell and sat down and looked out of the window. It was nice to see Cairn again ; the mist had vanished and the sun was struggling through the pale-grey clouds. She saw the boats leaving the harbour—there were five of them—and she recognised the *Kittiwake* by its big brown sails. She was still watching the boats when Annie came in with her porridge and inquired whether she would rather have a kipper or a boiled egg.

" A boiled egg, please," replied Frances promptly—she was not very fond of kippers.

" The new ladies are not in yet," said Annie.

" Perhaps they would like their breakfast in bed," suggested Frances. " They were very tired last night——"

Annie laughed. " But they're not in their beds," she declared. " They've been out most of the night. Did you not hear the soldiers, Miss Field?"

" The soldiers?" Frances exclaimed.

" The Green Buzzards," said Annie, nodding. " That's what the regiment's called. They've got a wee green toorie in their caps. Och, they're fine-looking fellows and no mistake."

"Were there many of them?" asked Frances, who had no idea of the size of a battalion of infantry.

"Thousands of them," replied Annie, who was given to wild exaggeration in moments of excitement. "Thousands and thousands. They had a band, too, but it wasn't playing. You should have been out like the rest of us, Miss Field, and then you'd have seen them yourself. There was scarcely a person in their beds—the whole of Cairn was in the street, and that's a fact. It might have been four in the afternoon, let alone four in the morning. They marched right through the street and away out to their camp, and their lorries with them—thousands of them there were. You'll take a kipper, then?"

"No, a boiled egg," replied Frances. "I wish I had known they were coming."

"Nobody knew," said Annie. "The Germans might have bombed the road. . . . I'll get your kipper in a moment."

"A boiled egg," repeated Frances firmly.

"Will they get time off?" asked Annie, hesitating and looking down at Frances anxiously. "Will they be allowed into Cairn?"

"I should think they would be," replied Frances, smiling with amusement.

"They must get off sometimes . . ." nodded Annie as she hastened away.

Frances was still eating her porridge when the door opened and Tommy Widgery came in. She looked pale and tired, but her eyes were more sparkling than ever. "They've come!" she exclaimed. "Did you hear them? We were over at the camp. It was fun. . . . Elise and Tillie are coming. I didn't wait, because Midge was so busy. He's the Adjutant, you see. May I come and have breakfast with you, or would you hate it?"

"I'd like it," Frances declared.

Tommy sat down and sighed and ran her fingers through her thick hair—it was a gesture which Frances was beginning to know. "Don't marry a soldier," she said a little sadly, "or, if you have to marry a soldier, don't let yourself get too fond of him. . . . Of course, sailors are worse . . . and, of course, in war every one is in the same boat. As a matter of fact, I've seen more of Midge since the war started . . . he was training recruits for a bit. I *must* get a house. . . ."

As usual Tommy had packed a deal of meaning into a very small space. Frances thought: She packs her sentences in the same way as she packs her suitcase when she is starting off, like Mrs. Bagnet, to meet her husband at the other side of the world.

She fills her shoes with bottles and rolls up her stockings into tight balls and pushes them into the corners. . . .

" I *must* get a house," repeated Tommy in desperate tones.

" I thought you had heard of one," said Frances.

" We've heard of two," replied Tommy. " There are two bungalows on the hill. They belong to the grocer and the butcher. They let them to people who come to Cairn in the summer."

" What are they like?"

" I'm going to see them this morning. Tillie must have one, of course, because of the children, and we've got to offer the other to the Colonel's wife. If she doesn't want it, Elise and I will toss."

It seemed a curious way of taking a house, and Frances said so a trifle diffidently. " Perhaps neither of them will be suitable," she added.

" Oh, suitable!" exclaimed Tommy. " Anything would be suitable as far as that goes . . . I'd put up a tent . . ."

" Couldn't you stay on here?" asked Frances in surprise.

" Yes," said Tommy. " Yes, it may come to that. . . ."

When they had finished breakfast Frances followed Tommy to the door and watched her walking up the street. Her small, slight figure was full of courage and determination, her step was light, her head was high, her short skirt swung like a kilt from the hips. We owe a good deal to people like that, thought Frances, with a surge of admiration and affection for her new friend. We think of the men who spend themselves in the service of the Empire, but who thinks of their women?

Frances was so stirred by all that was happening that she decided to go for a long walk, and soon she was wending her way along the shore in a southerly direction, the opposite direction from that which she had taken before. She left the harbour and the fishermen's cottages behind her, and was suddenly out of sight of all signs of human life. There were no straggling cottages at Cairn ; they were all built closely together, and around them was wild and rocky land. Before her was the wide sweep of Cairn Bay ; it was full of water this morning, grey tumbled water, and all that was left to walk on was a strip of white sand and shingle between the sea and the woods. At first Frances tried to walk along by the edge of the sea, leaping back when a wave broke and rushed up to her feet, but after a few minutes she decided that it was too soft—her legs were already aching from the effort of ploughing through the sand—so she went up over

51

the seaweed and the shingle and found a little path which twisted along between the trees at the edge of the wood. They were all fir trees here, she noticed, dwarfed and distorted by storms, and their roots were like fingers clutching the sandy soil. It was easier walking here, and she strode along swinging her arms and humming cheerfully to herself. Her trousers felt much more comfortable to-day; they gave her a feeling of absolute freedom. Presently she came to the other side of the bay and found herself upon a little headland which jutted out into the sea; and here, to her surprise, Frances found a house. She had been thinking about houses all the morning; thinking of Tommy and wondering how to help her, so the moment she saw the house she decided that this was the very house for Tommy.

Frances went up to the little house, noticing as she went that the place looked deserted and somewhat unkempt. There had been a little garden, but it was overgrown with weeds. The fence was down, and heather had crept in and invaded it. Frances went up the path and peered in through the dirty windows and saw that the house was empty. It was very small, but it was " a house " in the sense that it had walls and a roof. Whether or not Tommy would like the place Frances did not know . . . but she had spoken of a tent, and this was certainly a good deal better. She was still poking round the place and flattening her nose against the windows when a woman with a basket on her arm came swinging up the path. She was a tall, big-boned woman with dark hair and dark eyes. She did not take any notice of Frances, but produced a key from her pocket, opened the door, and went in. Frances looked in and saw her on her knees before the little fireplace, kindling a fire.

" Is this house to let?" asked Frances.

" To let!" repeated the woman in surprise. " Who would want it?"

" I know someone who might take it," replied Frances, looking round the room. It was a good-sized room and of a pleasant shape, square, with one wall slightly rounded. It was dirty, of course, but the wallpaper was in fairly good order. The windows faced seawards. Cairn harbour and the grey stone cottages of the fishermen looked for all the world like a toy village set down at the other side of the bay. The house was built on a low cliff, and was so near the sea that when you stood in the middle of the room and looked out of the window there was no ground visible. It was like being in a ship, Frances thought. She had never been in a ship, but still——

"It's my house," the woman said. "It belonged to my grannie. She died at the New Year and left it to me. I'm thinking to sell it."

"Why not let it?"

"I'd need to do it up."

"You couldn't sell it now," continued Frances. "Nobody wants to buy a house just now."

"Maybe not," said the woman in a disinterested fashion.

She said no more, but busied herself lighting the fire, and Frances found herself up against the stone wall of her indifference. The woman did not seem to care whether she let the house or not; it was an attitude which was exceedingly difficult to tackle. When she had lighted the fire she proceeded to open the windows, and the breeze, blowing in from the sea, dissipated the slightly musty smell. Frances looked into the other rooms which led off the main room. There were two—one fairly good-sized room and one small room. The kitchen was a pleasant place with an old-fashioned range and a large cupboard. There was a sink in the window. Frances was examining the sink when she heard the woman come into the kitchen.

"It's called Sea View," said the woman in a grudging tone of voice. "It was my grannie called it that. It was called another name before. It's an old house."

She flung the information at Frances ungraciously, but in spite of her awkward manner Frances thought that she was coming round and was willing to consider letting the place.

"There's no bathroom, I suppose," Frances said.

"There's nothing but the sink," replied the woman. "I could have sold it if there was a bathroom. There's no light either. It's lamps you have to have—you wouldn't care for that."

"I don't know," said Frances doubtfully. "It's for a friend of mine."

"How long would you want it for?"

"Several months," said Frances.

There was a short silence. "Och, well," said the woman at last. "I'm not caring much one way or the other, but maybe it would be better than standing empty. You can take the key and let me know in a day or two."

Frances was rather amused at this sudden change of heart. She realised that the woman was quite anxious now to obtain a tenant for the house. She accepted the key and asked the woman's name and where she lived, and was informed that it was Mrs. MacNair and that she lived in Cairn.

"But where?" asked Frances. "I mean, what's your address? I want to know because of returning the key."

"You can give it to Alec," she replied. "He's my husband's brother. . . . I'll clean the house, but I'll not do anything else. It wouldn't be worth my while."

The sea had retreated a little by this time and had left a narrow path of golden sand. Frances walked back along the golden pathway with the key of the house in her pocket. (It was a large, heavy key, an old-fashioned door-key, with curiously shaped wards.) She had no idea whether the little house would be any use—whether Tommy would be disgusted or delighted with it—but she was determined that if Tommy wanted the house she should have it.

The three ladies were having lunch when Frances went in. They looked up and smiled and went on talking. They were discussing the bungalows on the hill.

"I dare say it isn't so nice, but it's bigger," Tommy was saying. "And Tillie had much better take it, because there won't be room for the children in the other one. Freda can have the small one, and Elise and I must just stay on here."

"I don't mind," said Elise Crabbe. "It's quite nice, really. I was talking to Mrs. MacNair, and she doesn't mind having baby and nurse. I shall have some trouble getting them away from mother, I'm afraid."

"She's your own child," Tommy pointed out.

"I know," replied Elise, "but mother likes having her—that's the trouble. Mother has had her there off and on ever since she was born, and every time I say I want her, mother says she'll keep her a bit longer. Nurse isn't particularly keen to move either. I don't blame her, really."

"It's nonsense," Tommy said. "If you want Jennifer you've only got to say you want her——"

"It isn't as easy as that," replied Elise. "Tillie knows what I mean, don't you, Tillie?"

Tillie nodded. "Oh, yes," she said. "You daren't offend your relations, because you never know when you may have to ask them to have your children back again. Jack and I have had vast experience, " she added a trifle bitterly.

"So you walk like Agag," Elise continued, "and when you aren't walking like Agag you're grovelling on the floor. . . ."

Frances had found a folded note on her table ; she opened it and was surprised to discover that it was an invitation couched in formal language and containing the information that Mrs.

Crabbe, Mrs. Liston, and Mrs. Widgery requested the pleasure of her company at dinner that night at eight o'clock.

"Oh, how nice!" exclaimed Frances, looking across at the authors of the note.

"It's a party," said Tommy, somewhat unnecessarily. "We had to make it eight o'clock because the husbands are coming. It's going to be a proper dinner—we've squared Mrs. MacNair. I do hope you can come."

"I don't see how she can get out of it," said Elise.

Frances did not want to get out of it. She was quite excited at the prospect of a dinner-party.

When she had finished her lunch Frances pursued Tommy Widgery to her room and found her resting on her bed. She took the key out of her pocket and handed it to Tommy.

"What's this?" asked Tommy, laying down her book and looking up at Frances in surprise.

"It's a house," replied Frances. "I mean, it's the key of a house. I found it this morning—the house, I mean."

"You found a house!"

"A very tiny one," said Frances hastily. "It hasn't any bathroom or electric light. It's a small cottage on the cliff at the other end of the bay. You can have it if you like—at least, I'm almost sure you can."

"Is it furnished?" asked Tommy eagerly.

"No, it's completely empty except for a few spiders."

Tommy shook her head. She explained that it would cost thirty pounds at least to bring their furniture from the south. "And I don't *want* to bring it," added Tommy gravely, "because if I send for the furniture Midge is certain to be moved."

"But surely——"

"No," said Tommy. "No, it *isn't* superstition or coincidence or anything like that. It's just plain fact. It's happened over and over again. The moment I begin to think of getting the furniture out of store Midge is wafted away to the other side of nowhere."

"You wouldn't want much furniture," said Frances thoughtfully—somehow or other she was very anxious for Tommy to have the little house.

"No," agreed Tommy. "No, that's true, we shouldn't want much. Perhaps we could hire furniture—just beds and chairs and things. It's frightfully good of you to bother——"

"It wasn't a bother——"

"It was frightfully kind," repeated Tommy. "I hate hotels."

Frances was rather surprised. She thought hotels—and especi-

55

ally the Bordale Arms Hotel—were pleasant places to stay in. It was pure bliss to have everything done for you; to have your food cooked and brought to you without having to order it from the shops; to live in a place which was cleaned and swept by people for whom you had no responsibility whatsoever.

"You see," said Tommy, sitting up in bed and hugging her knees. "You see, I do like to have Midge all to myself, and you can't be by yourselves in a hotel. You can't do as you like ... there are too many people about. Elise and Ned will be here, and that makes it worse. Midge wouldn't mind so much, of course, and so—so I should mind more."

"What——" began Frances in bewilderment.

"You'll see Midge to-night," said Tommy with a dazzling smile.

Chapter Eight

TWO CARS drove up to the door, and in a moment the quiet hotel was full of laughter and the sound of men's voices. Frances was dressing for dinner when the cars arrived, and all at once she was overtaken by shyness. Her face looked back at her out of the mirror, rather white beneath its recently acquired tan, and her eyes seemed larger than ever. They all knew each other, and she knew none of them—she was an outsider, a mere chance acquaintance. She saw suddenly that they had had to ask her—it would have been impossible not to have asked her to join the party—but they didn't really want her. "You can't get out of it now," said Frances to the white-faced nincompoop who stared at her from the mirror. "You'll just have to go through with it. If you were worth your salt you could make friends with them and enjoy yourself." She slipped into her frock—it was an afternoon frock of heavy navy-blue silk with white frills at the neck and elbows. She smoothed her hair and pinched her cheeks to bring the colour back, then, summoning all her courage, she ran downstairs.

The lounge seemed full of men. There were only four of them, but they seemed to fill the room. They were all big men, and their uniforms made them look massive.

"Here she is!" cried Tommy's voice above the din of conversation. "Here's Miss Field. For goodness' sake be quiet till I get you all introduced."

Everyone immediately stopped talking and turned and looked at Frances, and Tommy made the introductions. "Major Crabbe, Major Liston, Captain Tarlatan, Captain Widgery," said Tommy, waving her hand.

". . . And here's some sherry to revive you after the ordeal," added one of the officers, offering her a glass on a tray.

Frances accepted it gratefully. She felt she required it.

"It's quite decent sherry," declared another officer with a surprised inflection in his voice.

"Yes," agreed Tommy. "Elise tried it. She said it was all right."

"Elise has a palate," said someone else, and they all laughed.

"Mr. MacNair has a cellar," said Elise. She was perched on the end of the sofa with a cigarette in one hand and a glass of sherry in the other. Her cheeks were slightly flushed with colour and her eyes were very bright. Frances, looking at Elise, thought that she was one of the most attractive creatures she had ever seen—she was so beautifully *soignée*, she was so elegant.

"He's got an enormous cellar under the hotel," continued Elise in her soft, slightly husky voice. "He took me down to see it this afternoon. You're going to have some real old cognac later."

"Heavens!" exclaimed one of the officers in amazement. "Heavens! d'you know what the stuff costs?"

"I know what he's going to charge," replied Elise, smiling. "He was so thrilled when he found that I appreciated the beauty of his cellar and its contents that I believe he would have given me a bottle for nothing. He says nobody appreciates wine nowadays; everyone drinks whisky if they can afford it, and beer if they can't."

The men began to discuss the wine, and to conjecture whether Mr. MacNair's grandfather had smuggled it into his cellar in the good old days when such things were more easily accomplished. Frances was glad that they had found a subject which interested them, for she was so nervous and miserable that she could not open her mouth. It was not until they were seated at table and Annie was handing the soup that she managed to collect her scattered wits and to look at her new acquaintances. They had been introduced to her *en masse*, and it was impossible to determine which was which. The two majors belonged to Elise and Tillie, one of them was fair and the other mouse-coloured, they both had close-cut moustaches. Frances then turned her attention to the captains, and tried to decide which of them belonged to Tommy.

"Interesting, isn't it?" asked a voice in her ear.

She blushed and turned her head and found her next-door neighbour looking at her with twinkling eyes.

"I don't know any of them," stammered Frances.

"But you will know them soon. They aren't at all difficult to know. I'm the unattached member. Guy Tarlatan is my name."

"Oh!" said Frances. "I didn't know. Of course, I ought to have listened when Mrs. Widgery . . . but I didn't . . . I mean, I didn't know which was which."

"How could you?" asked Captain Tarlatan. "We all look alike. We're all squeezed into the same mould. We're all dressed in the same hideous garments—all have red faces and short hair."

Frances did not know how to reply to this. She was not sure whether Captain Tarlatan was in earnest or whether he was pulling her leg. His face was grave, but there was a fleeting twinkle in his grey eyes. She was still frightened and nervous, for she had scarcely ever spoken to a man in her life.

"The garments make it more difficult," he continued, after waiting vainly for some reaction to his words. "If you had seen us attired for golf you would have had less difficulty in disentangling our personalities, for they would have been expressed in our choice of clothes. Harris for me, of course, with a plain Shetland pullover. Grey flannel bags of indeterminate shape for the much-married Liston. The Lobster is always neat, and Midgey is invariably gaudy."

He paused again, but Frances was still inarticulate.

"Difficult for you," he said in a thoughtful voice. "Extremely trying for you to be plunged into a sort of family party without any preparation. Elise should have given you a short *résumé* of our careers, an *exposé* of our characters. She didn't do that, I suppose?"

"No," said Frances.

"Tommy might have done you some thumbnail sketches of us—she's rather good at it. Have you seen any of her things?"

"No," said Frances.

"Get her to show them to you. They will be a great help in introducing the regiment. She has us all taped. The only person who is safe from Tommy's somewhat malicious pencil is Midgey Widgey himself. She can't draw him—or says she can't—yet to a casual beholder his features seem to offer scope to a caricaturist. Don't you think so, Miss Field? Add a trifle more hook to his nose and give his lips a slight twist, put rings in his ears and a bloody scarf round his brow, and you have a pirate chief."

58

Tommy's husband was dark—so dark that he had a slighty foreign appearance. He was very good-looking in his own way, but Frances saw quite well what her companion meant; there was something lawless and ruthless about him ... it was something in the curl of his nostrils, in his flashing dark eyes.

"Yes," said Frances a trifle breathlessly. "Yes, it's true."

"The mousy-haired major is Liston," continued Captain Tarlatan. "I suppose that's why he's usually known as Mouse. And the fourth member of the party—he should have come first, because he's the senior major—is Ned Crabbe, one of the best fellows you could meet in a day's march."

Frances was feeling better now. She smiled at her companion and said: 'Thank you. It makes a difference knowing who they are."

The conversation had now become general, and Tommy was holding the floor. She was elaborating her fairy story about the Princess Carginamel and everyone was listening.

"She was a very clever princess," declared Tommy. "She ran her kingdom awfully well. It was a benevolent autocracy."

"That's a good one, Tommy!"

"Yes, isn't it?" Tommy agreed. "She made all the laws and tried all the criminals herself. That kept her pretty busy, of course, but she was never late for anything. She——"

There was a storm of protest at this point in the narrative—it was led by the three husbands.

"She wasn't human," Major Liston declared.

"Of course not," cried Tommy, raising her voice above the din. "Haven't I just told you she was a fairy princess? It was quite easy for her to be ready for things at the right moment, because she had an arrangement with the Time Fairy. She could borrow time whenever she needed it. If she wanted to catch a train she could borrow ten minutes or even half an hour ... and that's why she was never late for dinner or for—for opening Parliament."

"Could she borrow it whenever she liked?" Major Crabbe inquired.

"Whenever she liked," said Tommy firmly. "If she found she was going to be late for anything she just put back the clock. It was most awfully useful. The only nuisance was that she had to pay it back to the Time Fairy, otherwise something funny would have happened to the calendar."

"How did she pay it back?" Elise inquired.

"The Time Fairy just took it," replied Tommy, screwing up her eyes in an effort to explain. "I mean, Carginamel just lost an hour—or whatever it happened to be—and she couldn't choose *when*, so sometimes it was very inconvenient. She would be dressing for dinner and the clock would be pointing to one minute to eight, and then, quite suddenly, it was nine."

"So she missed her dinner altogether!" exclaimed Major Crabbe in dismay.

"I can't make up my mind about that," replied Tommy gravely. "I haven't quite decided what became of her during the lost hour——"

"Everyone lost an hour," said Captain Tarlatan, nodding his head. "That was what happened, of course. Everyone in the palace was frozen stiff in the same position until the debt was paid. The cook, who was basting the joint, stood with his ladle poised in the air; the Foreign Minister was just getting into his car, and there he was for a whole hour, half in and half out, with his chauffeur standing beside him with a rug over his arm. The ladies-in-waiting were frozen stiff with combs and brushes and powder-pots in their hands; the porters' children who had been playing hop-scotch in the yard remained balanced precariously upon one leg; the scullery-maid——"

"Is this my story or yours?" demanded Tommy.

"Yours, darling," replied Captain Tarlatan unblushingly. "Your story, of course, decorated and embellished by a master hand."

"What was the scullery-maid doing, Foxey?" Major Crabbe inquired.

"Oh, the scullery-maid!" said Captain Tarlatan. "Perhaps we'd better leave the scullery-maid alone for the present. . . ."

"Talking of sculleries," said Tillie Liston suddenly. "I noticed there was a funny sort of smell in one of those bungalows—it seemed to come from the sink. I wonder if it is quite healthy."

"Take the other one," suggested Captain Tarlatan. "Mrs. Thynne won't notice the smell, because she always uses scent—a most reprehensible habit, in my opinion. I mean, any woman who drenches herself with scent deserves a house with a nasty smell in it."

The subject of the bungalows having been raised, the company proceeded to discuss them thoroughly. No detail of their situation, construction, or sanitation escaped criticism; the plumbing was commented upon by one and all without reserve. The subject of plumbing led quite naturally to sappers. Major Liston propounded the ancient axiom that they were all mad, married, or methody, but Major Crabbe disagreed, declaring that he knew quite a lot of sappers and they were most awfully decent fellows.

"Quite a lot of decent fellows are married, aren't they?" inquired Captain Tarlatan innocently.

"Yes, of course, but I mean——" began Major Crabbe, but everyone was laughing, so his meaning was never made clear.

After dinner, when they returned to the lounge, Frances suddenly discovered that nobody had mentioned the war, and she realised, looking back at her previous conversations with Tommy and Tillie and Elise, that they never talked about the war either. She wondered why it was. They had all sat down by this time, and it was obvious from the manner in which they had arranged themselves that husbands and wives were partial to each other's company.

"Disgusting, isn't it?" said Captain Tarlatan as he sat down beside Frances on the sofa. "If I ever marry I shall take care not to parade my felicity before the eyes of the world."

"I think it's rather nice," replied Frances. "They like each other, and they don't see as much of each other as ordinary married people, so——"

"The wrong conjunction," declared her companion. "Otherwise sound. You really meant to say that they like each other *because*——"

"No," said Frances quickly. "I didn't mean that at all. It isn't fair to twist what I say until it means something quite different."

Captain Tarlatan looked at her in surprise. "Dear me!" he said. "Dear me, I seem to have struck a spark. I was beginning to think the tinder was too damp."

Frances laughed at that. She couldn't help it. "I was frightened," she said frankly, "but I'm feeling better now. I think my dinner has done me good. It was a good dinner, wasn't it?"

"Excellent," agreed Captain Tarlatan. "It was an excellent dinner, and the brandy is superlatively fine. I feel sure that a little brandy would complete your cure."

Frances shook her head. She had been offered brandy with her coffee but had refused it, for she was not used to strong drink and had no idea what effect it would have upon her.

"Midgey Widgey can sing," said Captain Tarlatan suddenly.

"Can he?" asked Frances.

"Yes, he makes rather a pleasant noise. Shall I wind him up?" and, before Frances could reply, Captain Tarlatan leaned forward and said in a loud voice: "Midgey, I've been telling Miss Field you can sing, but she won't believe me."

Nobody seemed surprised at this perversion of the truth, and Captain Widgery required no pressing. He rose at once and crossed the room and struck a few chords upon the piano.

"It isn't bad," he said. "Are you going to play for me, Tommy?"

"I'll fetch your music," said Tommy, rising from her chair.

"Couldn't he fetch it for himself?" asked Captain Tarlatan.

"He doesn't know where it is," declared Tommy as she sped away.

"Bad training," explained Captain Tarlatan in an undertone. "Terribly bad training. When you're married you should make a point of teaching your husband to fetch and carry for you."

"I'm never going to be married. I like being free," replied Frances seriously.

Her companion looked at her in some surprise, but by this time Tommy had returned with a large pile of music and the subject was closed.

"I brought it all," said Tommy a trifle breathlessly. "There are some new songs here. I thought someone else might like to sing too."

"Perhaps Miss Field sings," suggested Major Liston.

Miss Field declared that she could not sing, that she had not sung for years.

"You can join in the chorus," said Tommy firmly.

Frances did not know much about music, but, like most people, she knew when she heard something good. Captain Widgery's voice was beautiful—it was deep and velvety. He sang Tosti's *Parted* with such expression that there was a little silence when the last notes had died away . . . and then a chorus of thanks.

"It was lovely," Elise said, "but couldn't we have something a little more cheerful now?"

"What would you like?" asked Captain Widgery.

Elise thought for a moment, and then said she would like *Where E'er You Walk*. So Captain Widgery sang it. Major Crabbe asked for *Drake's Drum*.

"You sing it," suggested Captain Widgery. "It doesn't suit my voice."

"What about *Pale Hands I Love*?" asked Tillie Liston. "I know it's supposed to be hackneyed, but I like it awfully."

Captain Widgery seemed quite pleased at the suggestion. He sang it extremely well.

Tommy wanted *Speak to me of Love,* and after some argument he sang that too. Then he sat down and said that someone else had better sing now.

"Nobody wants to sing after you," declared Major Liston, shaking his head.

"Just one more," said Tommy. "You haven't sung *You Alone Have My Heart.*"

"Sing *Shenandoah*," said Major Crabbe.

He shook his head.

"I'll say *The Wreck of the Hesperus,* if you like," said Captain Tarlatan.

"You can't," replied Tommy firmly.

"Why not?"

"Because Miss Field wouldn't like it."

"But I know it," said Frances. "I used to say it when I was a child."

"Oh, that must have been another wreck," declared Tommy. "Guy's wreck is quite different. It isn't the sort of wreck that you could teach a child."

"Couldn't we have *Mad Dogs and Englishmen*?" asked Major Liston.

Every one—or nearly every one—immediately clamoured for the song and urged Major Liston to sing it, and after some persuasion he agreed to "have a dab at it" if everyone joined in the chorus. Frances had heard the song before, but not until now had she realised its real meaning. She understood it now because these people made the song real to her. It was real to them—in a way it was their creed—and as Frances listened she seemed to see white-clad figures striding along sun-baked streets while, behind closed shutters, the native population rested and slumbered.

"Mad dogs and Englishmen go out in the midday sun."

Everyone knew the words, everyone was singing them . . . except Elise. Elise looked tired, Frances thought. The glow had faded from her cheeks and the shadows round her eyes had deepened. All at once she looked years older.

"Let's go out," said Captain Widgery when the song was over. He strolled to the side door, which opened on to a little terrace overlooking the sea. Tommy seized a scarf and followed him. The others hesitated and then decided to go too, and in a few moments Frances discovered that she was alone with Captain Tarlatan.

He sat down at the piano and began to pick out a tune by ear. "That's *A Pocketful of Dreams,*" he said. "I dare say you wouldn't know it. . . . I wish I could play. . . . I never wanted to learn when I was young, but now I'd give a good deal to be able to do it. . . , They're awful, aren't they?"

" Who?" asked Frances.

" All of them," he replied. " They want to talk to each other, so off they go and leave us."

" I don't mind," said Frances, quite innocently.

He laughed and replied: " Oh, neither do I for that matter. I mean, I don't mind for myself. It's a bit rude, don't you think —or perhaps crude describes it better."

" You mean fading away like that?" inquired Frances.

He nodded. " I'm here to amuse you, that's why I was asked. Tommy is always throwing me at people's heads, and usually they hate it."

Frances laughed. She said: " Perhaps I was asked so that I could amuse you. I'm afraid I haven't been very amusing."

" No," he said thoughtfully. " You haven't exactly sparkled, but I'm not sure that I like sparkling people."

" I like sparkling people," replied Frances—she thought of Tommy as she spoke.

" They're fun sometimes," he agreed. " There's Angela, for instance, Angela Thynne—you haven't seen her yet."

" Shall I see her?"

" Definitely. The regiment always moves *en masse*. Already a house of sorts has been allocated to the Colonel and his lady. Angela is the Colonel's ewe lamb."

" I see," said Frances.

" You see, but only through a dark glass," replied Captain Tarlatan. " There's wheels within wheels. Tommy thinks it would be nice if I were to marry Angela, but neither Angela nor I see much point in the idea. Tommy is a confirmed match-maker, she can't leave things alone."

" She's so happy herself," Frances said.

" She's devoted to Widgery."

" That's what I meant."

" I don't think it is—quite. It's possible to be devoted to a person without being happy, you know." He hesitated, as if he were going to say more on the subject and then changed his mind. " Shall I play *Too Romantic*?" he asked. " It seems suitable at this point in the conversation. . . ."

He was still playing the catchy tune with one finger when the Widgerys passed the door leading on to the terrace. It was slightly ajar and Frances heard Tommy's sweet high voice.

" . . . but I'll do it *all*," she was saying. " The house is frightfully cheap and we shan't need much. . . . I'll do it *all*."

Chapter Nine

THE LOUNGE was full of sunshine when Frances came in from her walk, but the windows were all tightly closed and it smelt fusty and stale. She went across to the windows and opened them widely and the sea breeze swept in, scattering the papers on the table.

"I see you like fresh air," said a voice from the corner, and Frances saw that Captain Tarlatan was sitting there reading a paper.

"I see you like fug," said Frances, laughing.

"I don't," he replied. "I just accept things as they are. Neither fug nor a gale from the Atlantic has the power to upset my equilibrium."

The gale from the Atlantic to which he referred was so strong and boisterous that Frances was obliged to moderate her passion for sea air. She shut one of the windows and left the other slightly open and sat down.

"Where is Tommy?" inquired Captain Tarlatan.

"I think she has gone over to the little house," replied Frances. "I think so, but I'm not sure. Did you want to see her?"

"She asked me to tea but she's probably forgotten," replied Captain Tarlatan quite cheerfully.

Frances asked him to have tea with her, so they had tea together and chatted about various matters in a friendly manner. He was a little alarming to talk to, Frances found. He said the most incredible things with a perfectly serious face; but Frances had her trousers on to-day, she crossed her legs and felt rather dashing; she lit a cigarette.

"What's the joke?" inquired her companion.

"The joke?" asked Frances in surprise.

"You were smiling in an enigmatic manner," he explained. "It seemed to me that you must be enjoying a particularly good joke and I wanted to share the fun."

"You wouldn't see anything funny in it."

"I'm sorry you consider me lacking in a sense of humour."

"It isn't that," she replied quickly. "It was just that I was thinking of someone I know. . . ." She had thought suddenly of Aunt Zoë and had wondered what Aunt Zoë would have said if she could have been a spectator of the scene . . . it was no wonder that Frances had smiled to herself in an enigmatic manner.

He handed his cup for more tea and said in a resigned voice: " In that case I shall have to remain in ignorance, I suppose. It seems a pity, doesn't it?"

Frances was unused to this sort of conversation, and although she was aware that he was teasing her she was unable to reply in kind. She was still searching for something to say when Captain Tarlatan changed the subject.

" Are you a painter?" he asked.

" No ; everyone asks me that. Do I look like one?"

He looked at her critically. " No," he said. " No, you don't. As a matter of fact it was what is usually known as a leading question. I wondered what you were doing here."

" Having a holiday."

" A holiday from what?"

" From work," said Frances, laughing.

He laughed too. " All right," he said. " All right, I shall find out for myself."

" How will you find out?"

" By using my powers of observation. By deduction and elimination. To begin with, I'm quite sure you aren't an actress."

" How do you know?"

" You haven't the poise," he replied frankly. " For the same reason you aren't a mannequin. You aren't a nurse, and you aren't in any of the women's service organisations."

" Perhaps I'm nothing at all," suggested Frances.

" In less than a week I shall find out," he said gravely.

Frances scarcely knew why she was disinclined to clear up the mystery. Perhaps it was because she was ashamed of having so little to tell. Her life—compared with the lives of these people—had been dull and unadventurous. . . .

" Hallo, here's Midgey!" exclaimed Captain Tarlatan.

" Why do you call him that?" asked Frances as the tall broad-shouldered figure came up the path and hesitated for a moment at the door of the lounge.

" I don't know," replied Captain Tarlatan. " Everyone calls him that. . . . Midgey, Miss Field wants to know who gave you that name."

He was passing through the lounge and he stopped and put his hand on the back of a chair. " Middleton is my name," he said evenly. " Perhaps Miss Field would be interested to know that my mother was a member of a well-known South American family. Her surname was Middleton."

66

He hates me, thought Frances in surprise and some alarm as she met the strange veiled glance of his dark eyes.

"So that's the reason," Captain Tarlatan said lightly.

"Yes. I suppose you have told Miss Field why your nickname is Foxey?"

"I told her my name was Guy and left her to draw her own conclusions."

"Are you sure it's that kind of fox?"

Frances looked at the long-fingered hand which was gripping the back of the chair and noticed that the knuckles were white. There was a strange tenseness in the air. The air had suddenly become difficult to breathe.

"I am quite sure it's that kind of fox," said Captain Tarlatan in level tones, "but if you have any doubts about it I am willing to convince you."

Captain Widgery hesitated, and then he said: "The house—Tommy's crazy about it. There's no bath and the lavatory is in a hut outside the back door. . . ." He turned and went up the stairs.

It was funny—Frances saw that quite clearly—but somehow or other she did not feel inclined to laugh, and although Captain Tarlatan was smiling it was a grim sort of smile.

"Some day I shall have to strangle Widgery," he said, and the mere fact that he had avoided using the absurd nickname gave the idle words a strange significance.

A good many things happened in the next few days. Tillie Liston moved into her bungalow on the hill; the Thynnes arrived in a large but somewhat shabby Austin and moved into theirs, and Tommy busied herself with preparations to move into Sea View. Cairn village, and in particular the Bordale Arms Hotel, became alive to the presence of soldiers in the vicinity. There was nowhere for the officers and men to go and nothing for them to do when they were off duty except to stroll into Cairn and make friends with the inhabitants. The officers discovered that the Bordale Arms was quite a decent place and kept good wine, and scarcely a day passed but some of them dropped in for a meal. Mrs. MacNair was a capable woman; she realised her opportunity and took fortune at the flood. The meal at six-thirty vanished and, instead of it, Mrs. MacNair provided tea at four-thirty and an excellent dinner at eight o'clock. Frances was sorry to see the change, for she had enjoyed the odd mixture of tea and supper, but it was quite amusing to see the officers dining —there were different ones nearly every night. Meanwhile the men had discovered the bar, and by eight o'clock it was always full of soldiers, laughing and talking and singing at the tops of their voices. Mr. MacNair had never served so much beer in his life. Sometimes the bar was so full that the men could not get in and benches and tables were put out in the street. It was a strange sight to see the khaki-clad figures sitting there, drinking their beer and smoking and swopping stories. They sat there long after darkness had fallen and, owing to lighting restrictions, they were forced to sit in the dark, but this did not seem to worry them. Sometimes at night, as Frances lay in bed, she could hear them talking beneath her side window, and, unlike their officers, they were always discussing the war. They would talk of Dunkirk and of various other places in France and Belgium, and would discuss with absolute freedom the vicissitudes of that ill-starred campaign and the conduct of their allies. . . . She heard some strange language winging its way through the darkness, but somehow or other it did not shock her as much as one might expect. She realised that it was just " soldiers' talk "; it was an unfortunate habit but it meant little or nothing—even to the men themselves. They would talk and talk . . . and then someone would start to play a few bars of a song on a mouth organ and in a moment they would all be singing at the tops of their voices. They sang *Over the Border, Down Mexico Way,* and all the songs made popular by Gracie Fields, and sometimes they sang songs from the last war, and sometimes ballads. Then Alec and Mr. MacNair would come out and Frances would hear the chink of glasses being collected, and there would be a good deal of joking and teasing and horseplay before the men strolled off down the road back to the camp. Frances lay and listened to the sound of their voices and the tramp of their feet dying away in the distance until she could hear nothing more and all was silence and darkness.

Oddly enough, the noise did not worry Frances in the least. She liked to hear the men enjoying themselves—they deserved a little enjoyment after all they had been through. Whenever she saw them, strolling in the street or sitting at the wooden tables, her heart went out to them in a flood of warm friendship and gratitude. They were *her* soldiers—so she felt—they were ready to defend her country with their lives. There was nothing she would not have done for them in return. She would have liked to speak to them, but she had no idea what to say and she was far too shy to attempt it. One evening when she was coming back from a walk she passed near a table at which four men were sitting, and suddenly she felt that she must do something for them, so she took a packet of cigarettes out of her pocket and put it on the table as she passed, and then fled for her life before the men had recovered from their astonishment sufficiently to thank her for it. Afterwards her cheeks burnt with shame at the gauche way in which she had presented her gift—how differently Tommy would have done it!

Chapter Ten

TOMMY HAD been so busy preparing her new home and ordering the necessary furniture that, in the last few days, Frances had only seen her once—dashing into the hotel for a belated meal—but now the arrangements were almost complete and Frances received an invitation to come over and see the results of Tommy's labours. Frances had seen possibilities in the house but, even so, she was surprised at the transformation. She stood in the doorway for a moment and looked round in amazement. The last time she had been here the room had been empty and dirty, the windows streaked with salt from the sea spray, the corners festooned with cobwebs, but Mrs. MacNair had been as good as her word and the place was now as clean and shining as soap and water and elbow-grease could make it, and the hired furniture which had arrived that morning had been put in place.

" It's perfectly lovely," Frances declared.

" It's the darlingest little house in the world," agreed Tommy with satisfaction and some pride.

" . . . and you've been most awfully clever about it," added Frances. She was surprised to find that Tommy had a practical side to her nature; the carpets fitted exactly, the curtains were the right length and breadth, and the furniture was neither too large nor too small.

When asked how this had been achieved Tommy replied: " I measured everything, of course— what else could I have done?"

It was the only thing to have done, but Frances could not see Tommy doing it . . . she had thought Tommy a trifle scatterbrained.

The kitchen was nice too. It was clean and shining, and shelves were well stocked with pots and pans and china dishes of all sorts. Frances remarked on the numbers of cups and saucers and plates. " It looks as if you were prepared to entertain the regiment," she said with a smile.

" It's because I hate washing up," explained Tommy gravely.

"Mrs. MacNair is coming every morning for a few hours and I shall leave all the dishes for her to wash. She said she didn't mind."

They were working about as they talked, putting the finishing touches to the little house—the little touches that are so important.

"Is Mrs. MacNair going to do the cooking?" Frances inquired.

"No, I'm going to do it myself," replied Tommy. "I'm rather good at cooking—you wouldn't think it, would you?"

"Why shouldn't you be good at it?"

"I don't know, but nobody believes that I can cook. I suppose I must have an un-cooklike appearance or something."

Frances looked up at her (she was standing on the steps arranging the sitting-room curtains). It was true that her appearance was unlike the general idea of a cook. She looked young and fairy-like and there were blue shadows round her eyes.

"You're tired," said Frances in concern. "You've been doing far too much. Why didn't you let me help?"

"There was nothing much that you could do," said Tommy. "I mean, I had to think it all out myself—it's thinking that tires me, not doing things." She finished the job and came down. "There," she said, looking at the curtains critically and giving them a tweak to arrange their folds. "There, it's finished and I hope to goodness they're really light-proof. The blackout was the worst part."

"It always is," said Frances.

Tommy was looking round the room now. "It's the nicest house I've ever had," she declared. "The very nicest. I've chosen the furniture myself and I've never been able to do that before. It's a home—a real home, isn't it?"

Frances remembered the big gloomy house in Wintringham Square and decided that this little house—with all its drawbacks—was infinitely preferable. Tommy had chosen comfortable modern furniture for her sitting-room: there were three easy-chairs and several smaller ones; there was a round gatelegged table and a small bookcase; the carpet was green with little sprigs of flowers; there were a few good prints on the walls; Tommy had filled a brown jar with pussy willows and had stood it in the corner.

"Nice," said Tommy with a little sigh.

Frances nodded. "Awfully nice," she agreed.

"And all your doing," added Tommy, looking at her affectionately.

" My doing?"

" Yes, of course. If it hadn't been for you we should have had to live in the hotel. Thank you, Frances."

" I hope you will be very happy here, Tommy," replied Frances. They looked at each other and smiled.

" I shall be happy," declared Tommy after a little pause. " It's what I've always wanted—I've always thought it would be lovely to have a tiny cottage and nobody in it at all except Midge and me. I've thought how lovely it would be to cook and wash for Midge, to be alone at night, miles from everyone. I've often envied ploughmen's wives. Life would be so simple—and love would be simple too."

Frances had been laying the fire in the sitting-room fireplace. It was an old-fashioned cottage grate and there was a little platform at the side for a kettle. She sat back on her heels and looked up at Tommy. " Love would be simple?" she asked, wrinkling her brows in bewilderment.

" Yes," said Tommy. " Love's a most awfully difficult thing to manage—but don't listen to me, Frances, I talk too much. Shall we have tea?"

" Tea here?"

" Why not? I think it would be fun. I've got all the doings—and biscuits and things. Light the fire."

" You ought to light your own fire."

" Light it for me," Tommy said.

Half an hour later they were sitting by the fire having tea. It was the first meal in the new house and it was a friendly, cheerful meal. Frances was pouring out the tea and Tommy was sitting on the hearthrug.

" That's one of the *things* about your own house," Tommy declared. " I mean, you can sit on the floor. I always do."

" It seems rather a waste to have hired three perfectly good chairs."

" One is for Midge and one is for you," replied Tommy gravely. " and the other is for any chance visitor who happens to drop in. You'll come often, won't you?"

" If you want me," Frances said.

" I do want you—I always say what I mean."

They cleared away the tea-things, locked up the little house, and strolled back to the hotel. " It's lovely to think that it's all ready," said Tommy suddenly. " We could sleep there to-night, couldn't we? He's sure to like it when he sees it—nobody could *not* like it, could they?"

" Nobody," said Frances with conviction.

71

The hotel was very quiet for dinner, but after dinner the Listons appeared and a car came in from the camp with Captain Widgery and Guy Tarlatan; a few moments later the door opened and a girl looked in and said: "Hallo, everybody!" and was greeted with shouts of "Hallo, Angela!" from the assembled company.

Frances had taken up her position in a corner of the lounge, and from this strategic point she was able to see everything that was going on without having to talk to anyone herself—this was what she liked, for she found these people interesting to watch. The thought crossed her mind that it must be rather fun to belong to a regiment. They all knew each other so well, they were so friendly and cheerful, laughing and talking and teasing each other. She was interested in the arrival of Angela Thynne— this was the Colonel's ewe lamb, the girl who sparkled in an amusing manner! Frances, looking at her with critical eyes, decided that she was too brilliant to be real. She was wearing navy-blue trousers and an emerald-green shirt, open at the neck; there were long gold ear-rings in her ears, and her lips and nails were scarlet. Her hair was fair and she wore it in loose curls round her neck; her eyelashes were long and dark and curling. She was pretty and vivacious; even Frances—who for some reason had taken a dislike to her on first sight—was forced to admit that she was very pretty indeed.

Mrs. Liston came over and sat down beside Frances. She said: "I've been on my feet all day. There was so much to do. The children are coming to-morrow." She was very pale and her hair was more wispy than usual.

"You're tired," Frances said sympathetically.

"Yes. Yes, I am. I didn't know I was tired until suddenly— suddenly I felt as if I were going to cry . . . but it's quite a nice bungalow." She hesitated and then added in a vague sort of voice: "This place reminds me of India."

"This place—do you mean Cairn?" asked Frances in amazement.

"Oh, I don't mean it's really like India . . . and, of course, if this were India you wouldn't have to do anything yourself. You couldn't. Nobody thinks of doing a hand's turn. It was this room that reminded me of India—all the meeting and talking and the noise—like the club, you know."

Frances did not know.

"The club," explained Mrs. Liston. "There's always a club where everyone in the station meets and talks. Sometimes they have dances. Jack and I didn't go over to the club every night, but most people do. It was too expensive—we've always had to scrape. I didn't mind for myself, but I minded for Jack. Men like standing drinks and that sort of thing—you know what I mean. It's harder for men not to have as much money as other people. It was because of the children, of course. We've got four."

"How lovely!" Frances said.

"Yes," agreed Mrs. Liston, still in the same vague tone. "Yes, of course. We wouldn't be without them for anything, but—but it *has* made things a little difficult sometimes. Of course they're worth it. They're worth everything that we have had to give up—all the struggles. John and Helen are at boarding-schools now, but Winkie and little Dolly are coming to-morrow. You'll come and see them, won't you, Miss Field?"

"Yes, I should like to see them."

"They're darlings," said their mother with a little smile that lighted her wan face like a lamp. "They're terribly sweet and precious—and it is so lovely to be able to have them with us. We were in India when John and Helen were little, so we missed years of them—all the funny little things that children say and do. Then, when we came home, they didn't know us—they couldn't remember us at all—it was like trying to make friends with strangers. They were shy, you see. They liked Jack's brother and sister so much that they didn't want to come and live with us. Jack was a little hurt—you see, we had given up so much for them, to pay for their education and everything—but you couldn't expect children to understand, could you? We were strangers to them . . . nothing but names. . . . It all came right in the end. Things usually come right in the end if you just go on doing your best . . . if you keep on loving people. . . . I'm afraid I'm talking nonsense, but it's because I'm so tired," added Mrs. Liston apologetically.

Frances did not think it nonsense. In fact Mrs. Liston, who had always been a shadowy and insubstantial figure, had quite suddenly become a real person. She was still as shabby as ever, and her hair was a mess, but these details had ceased to matter. "It was dreadful for you!" Frances exclaimed.

"It wasn't their fault——"

"No, perhaps not, but surely your husband's brother and sister could have talked to the children about you."

"That was what Jack said," admitted Mrs. Liston. "Jack said that they had deliberately stolen the children's hearts, but I

73

don't think they had. It just happened. They were very kind to John and Helen, so I couldn't feel angry with them."

Frances was casting about in her mind to find something friendly to say—something to show that she understood—when Major Liston detached himself from the group at the other end of the room and came over to them.

"Tillie, you're worn out," he said, looking down at his wife with solicitude. "You're almost asleep—come along home to bed." He held out his hand as he spoke and pulled her up. "Sorry, Miss Field," he added. "Sorry to drag Tillie away in this unceremonious fashion, but she's been working like a navvy all day."

"Have you spoken to Fox?" asked Tillie in a low voice.

"No, but it doesn't matter. I can ask him to-morrow," replied her husband. He seized her cloak, which was lying on a chair, and put it round her shoulders.

Tillie smiled at Frances. "Come to tea to-morrow—do come," she said, and was dragged away before Frances could reply.

Now that Frances was alone she had time to observe the rest of the party. Miss Thynne was standing in front of the fire smoking a cigarette in a long, green holder. Frances decided that Miss Thynne's figure was not shown to its best advantage in trousers. She bulged in the wrong places. She would have looked better in more feminine apparel. Captain Widgery was leaning against the mantelpiece talking to Miss Thynne, smiling down at her from his immensely superior height . . . somehow or other he looked more like a pirate than ever. The Crabbes and Tommy and Guy Tarlatan were sitting near the window talking and laughing in an animated way. Tommy seemed to be doing most of the talking; there was a bright colour in her cheeks and her voice was a trifle shrill.

Miss Thynne knocked her cigarette into the fire. "Hallo!" she exclaimed. "The Listons seem to have gone. Daddy said I was to walk home with them."

"I'll walk home with you," said Captain Widgery.

They had turned to go when Guy Tarlatan jumped up and seized his cap. "I'll walk home with you, Angela," he said.

For a moment all three of them stood there indecisively—then Angela laughed. "Well, which of you is coming?" she inquired. "Or are you both coming?"

"I'm coming," declared Guy. "You know you'd rather have me."

"I don't know anything of the kind," retorted Angela.

74

"Come on," said Guy. "I've something to tell you—something frightfully important." He put his arm through hers and dragged her towards the door.

"Farewell!" cried Angela, waving her other hand. "Farewell, farewell, the maiden cried——"

Captain Widgery did not look too pleased at having his companion snatched from under his nose in this unceremonious manner. He hesitated for a moment and then straightened his back. Frances had a feeling that he was going after the other two, but instead of that he walked across the room to his wife.

"Well, Tommy," he said, "it's getting late. What about this house of yours?"

Tommy rose at once. She was quite pale now, but her eyes were shining like stars. They said good-night and went away.

"So that's that," said Major Crabbe.

Frances had seen all that had happened, and somehow she was aware that she should have been able to understand what it all meant, but it was an enigma to her. She went up to bed, leaving the Crabbes sitting by the fire, but it was a long time before she could sleep.

Chapter Eleven

SEA VIEW was bathed in golden sunshine, and as Frances approached she heard the sound of Tommy's voice—Tommy was singing *Never in a Million Years* in a high, sweet treble—it was like a boy's voice, Frances thought. She smiled and quickened her steps, for it was obvious that Tommy was happy . . . everything was all right, after all. . . .

Tommy came to the door to shake a duster. She saw Frances and waved cheerfully. "We're going to have coffee," she cried. "You're just in time. Mrs. MacNair is making it."

Frances followed her into the sitting-room. She had wanted to ask if everything was all right, and whether Captain Widgery had liked the house, but she was too shy—besides, there was no need to ask, for Tommy was on top of the world this morning.

"Mrs. MacNair is splendid," declared Tommy, flinging herself on to the hearthrug and hugging her knees. "She was here at eight o'clock. We were just sitting down to breakfast. She's washed up everything and tidied the kitchen cupboard—— Hurrah! here's the coffee!"

Mrs. MacNair brought in a tray with coffee and biscuits and two cups, and put it on a chair beside Tommy.

" It smells lovely," said Tommy appreciatively.

" I make it in a saucepan," said Mrs. MacNair. " It was a French cook showed me the way. Most people seem to like it."

" I'm sure we shall like it," declared Tommy. " Have you kept some for yourself, Mrs. MacNair?"

" Yes, thank you. It isn't rationed, so I thought you wouldn't mind." She hesitated, and then added: " I was in service before I was married. It was in Glasgow. My name's Ellen."

" Ellen," repeated Tommy. " I wish my name was Ellen. Tamara is such a silly name."

" It's better than Ellen," said Mrs. MacNair firmly.

" What a pity we can't exchange," said Tommy. " I'd like to be called Ellen—only, if I were, everyone would call me Nelly. I'm that sort of person, you know."

" I was called for my grannie," said Mrs. MacNair. " The only good I got out of it was this house. She left it to me on that account—because I was Ellen."

" I never got any good at all out of being called Tamara," said Tommy regretfully.

When the woman had gone Tommy smiled at Frances and said: " She's rather sweet. She's got a wonderful face. I think she must have a history."

Frances was surprised at the way in which Mrs. MacNair had come out of her shell. She thought: I might have known the woman for years and have got no nearer to her.

Tommy was pouring out the coffee. She went on talking. " It will be much easier to call her Ellen," said Tommy. " That was what she meant, wasn't it?"

" Yes," said Frances.

" Of course everyone has a history—even you—but I mean she must have been through a good deal. She looks as if she had."

" Why do you say ' even you '?" asked Frances.

The green eyes regarded her thoughtfully. " You haven't begun to live, that's why."

" I don't know what you mean."

" That's just it. If you had begun to live you *would* know. We're probably just about the same age, but I've knocked about the world since I was six years old. I've been utterly miserable and wildly happy. You've never been either. I don't know what you've been doing with yourself, but you haven't lived."

" I'm different from you," said Frances.

"Yes," agreed Tommy. "Yes, you're a looker-on at life—but some day you'll find yourself in the thick of it. People can't look on for ever. I hope you won't get hurt——"

"Tommy, you're frightening me!"

"I didn't mean to," said Tommy gravely. "I just wanted to warn you, because you're such an infant, but it isn't any use, really. Everyone has to find their own way through the jungle. Some people come through all right and others don't. . . . The coffee is lovely, isn't it?"

It was four o'clock precisely when Frances rang the bell of the Liston's bungalow—it was the kind of bell which buzzes just inside the door—and almost immediately the door was opened by a nice-looking girl in a blue overall. "Oh, are you Miss Field?" she said. "I'm Mrs. Liston's nursery governess. We've just arrived. Mrs. Liston is expecting you."

Mrs. Liston was sitting in an arm-chair with a baby girl on her knee and a small boy leaning against her shoulder. She looked much happier and less lost, and her hair was a good deal neater than usual. She held out her hand to Frances and said: "I'm so glad you've come, Miss Field. I can't get up, because Dolly weighs about a ton. I don't know what Miss Cole has been feeding her on."

"Coal," said the little boy.

Miss Cole laughed. "Yes, we've been feeding her on coal—or rather she has been feeding herself on coal—hasn't she, Winkie?"

"She takes it out of the coal-scuttle and *eats* it when nobody's looking," Winkie said, nodding gravely. "I think perhaps she thinks it's chocolate, don't you?"

"Chocklit!" cried Dolly, bouncing up and down.

"There—you shouldn't have said it," declared Miss Cole. "She thinks she's going to have some. I wish you'd *think* before you say things like that."

"She's looking very well," said Mrs. Liston in a pacifying tone.

"Yes, isn't she?" agreed Miss Cole. "I've been feeding her up. She's put on nearly two pounds in a fortnight. I was sure you'd be pleased when you saw her."

Frances knew nothing about children, but she could not help feeling that it was Winkie—not Dolly—who required feeding up. Dolly was a solid child with fat pink cheeks and beady brown eyes. Winkie was thin and pale, so pale that the veins in his temples showed blue through his transparent skin. She remembered that something had been said about Winkie having an operation, so perhaps he had not recovered from it yet.

Miss Cole had been putting the finishing touches to the tea table, and now it was ready. She removed Dolly from her mother's lap and strapped her firmly in her high chair.

"Mick!" cried Dolly, seizing a spoon and hammering on the wooden tray. "Mick—ben butter—mick."

"Dolly is always hungry," explained Miss Cole, cutting a large slab of bread and plastering it with butter.

It was obvious that Winkie did not share his sister's enthusiasm for food. He climbed on to his chair with reluctance and eyed his slice of bread and butter with distaste. "I don't think I want it, really," he said. "It's rather a waste to eat it when I don't want it."

"It's much more of a waste not to eat it," replied Miss Cole. "There are thousands of little boys who would be glad of a nice piece of bread and butter."

"I wish I could give it to them," Winkie declared.

"That's very naughty," said Miss Cole. "You're to eat it up at once. Look how good Dolly is!"

Dolly was ploughing through her meal in a determined manner—every now and then she would pause and gaze at Frances, fixing her with an unblinking stare, and then she would seize another piece of bread and butter and cram it into her mouth.

"Have you been out in a boat?" asked Winkie suddenly.

"No," replied Frances, "but I know a fisherman, and he's promised to take me some day when the sea is nice and calm."

"I wish I knew a fisherman," Winkie said.

Frances hesitated. It would be foolish to raise the child's hopes by offering to take him until she had found out whether he would be allowed to come . . . besides, the prospect of making herself responsible for Winkie, of having him on her hands for a whole morning, was somewhat alarming.

"Perhaps Miss Field would take you," said Mrs. Liston, smiling.

"Yes, of course," agreed Frances, trying to make her words sound cordial, but not succeeding very well.

"Will you?" cried Winkie, fixing her with his enormous eyes. "Will you really? It is a true promise?"

Frances was obliged to reply that it was a true promise. She suggested that Miss Cole might like to join the party, but Miss Cole showed no enthusiasm for the idea.

"I am not fond of the sea," said Miss Cole. "Dolly and I will
78

come down to the pier and see you off. Go on with your tea, Winkie. Miss Field won't take you if you don't eat your bread and butter."

"She didn't say that," Winkie pointed out. "She didn't say that she wouldn't take me unless I was good, did you, Miss Field?"

"No," said Frances, rather uncomfortably.

"You said it was a true promise," Winkie reminded her.

"Yes, of course," she agreed.

"When will it be?" asked Winkie. "Will it be to-morrow or the next day or the next day? Will it be this week?"

Frances was about to reply that they must wait for a calm day when Dolly interrupted the conversation by shouting "Maw tate!" in a shrill, penetrating voice. "Maw tate!" shouted Dolly, thumping on the tray with her spoon. "Maw tate!—maw tate!—maw tate!"

"She can't say cake," explained Miss Cole, cutting a large chunk of cake and putting it on Dolly's plate.

"Isn't she sweet?" said Mrs. Liston fondly.

Frances could not make up her mind whether she liked Dolly or not; there was something rather attractive about her, and her greediness was so naked and unashamed that it disarmed criticism. There was a vital force in Dolly's small body, a savage instinct which demanded the necessaries of life. One felt that if Dolly had been cast away upon a desert island she would have managed to find food somehow, she would have managed to look after herself and struggle through. There was humour in Dolly too, for when Frances was offered a piece of cake, and accepted it, Dolly made a little grimace which was first cousin to a wink and said "Dood" in a voice which was somewhat muffled by crumbs.

"*Did* you see that?" cried Miss Cole, laughing. "Isn't she a one? She *has* taken to Miss Field, hasn't she?"

Frances had already begun to suspect that Miss Cole was a foolish young woman, and now her suspicion was confirmed. She knew nothing about children, of course, but she had a feeling that Dolly, though somewhat inarticulate, was capable of understanding a good deal. The grimace had been spontaneous and extremely funny, but it would have been wiser to take no notice of it. They'll spoil her, thought Frances, rather sadly. It seemed a pity that anything so natural should be made self-conscious.

Mrs. Liston was so taken up with her children, smiling fondly at Dolly's antics and trying to coax Winkie to eat, that it was

79

quite impossible to converse with her, and Frances could not help wondering why she had been asked to come. She took her leave soon after tea, saying that she must write a letter before post time, and Mrs. Liston did not press her to stay. Winkie walked down to the gate and opened it with an old-fashioned gravity which Frances found rather pathetic. He looked up at her as she went out and said: " I won't be any trouble *at all* if you take me in the boat. I'll do what I'm told *at once.*"

" We'll arrange it," Frances promised. " The very first calm day I'll get hold of Alec and ask him to take us."

Chapter Twelve

THE WEATHER broke suddenly, and when Frances opened her eyes the next morning she saw leaden skies outside her window, and a strong westerly wind, accompanied by driving rain, was rushing in from the sea. Francis had seen Cairn in sunshine and wrapped in mist, and now she was seeing it in a storm ; she felt as if the storm had been summoned by Providence for her especial benefit. She swallowed her breakfast hastily, and, putting on her oilskins, she battled her way down to the harbour. The wind was like a living force, plucking at her coat ; the waves were breaking over the wall, leaping up in sheaves and falling in fountains. There was nobody about—the fishermen's houses had little wooden shutters fastened across their windows—Frances had the magnificent spectacle all to herself. She turned north, but instead of climbing the cliff she walked along the shore and then scrambled along a ridge of rocks, a sort of promontory which ran out into the sea. The wind came in strong gusts, so that sometimes she was forced to cling to the rocks with both hands ; the spray from the bursting waves was salty on her lips. Frances was breathless, and her hair was blown in all directions by the time she reached the end of the promontory. She found a sheltered nook between two rocks, and sat down to watch the waves.

Far out, as far as eye could see, the waves swelled into green hills and rolled slowly towards the shore. They hung for a moment and then curled over and hurled themselves against the reef. The white surf surged over the rocks and poured away, draining down amongst the crevices and falling into the trough of the next wave. Sometimes a wave burst against an upstanding pillar of rock, shooting up white as snow against the dull grey sky and falling in showers upon the rocks beneath. It had stopped raining now; away to the south-west there was a rift in the grey blanket of cloud and a patch of blue sky was showing.

Frances was watching it and enjoying the turmoil when she heard a rattle of stones behind her and Guy Tarlatan came round the corner of the rock. He was wearing his service burberry, but his head was bare and his fair hair was plastered to his head by the falling spray.

"I know what you are now. You're a mermaid," he said.

"How clever of you to guess!" said Frances.

"Do you mind if I share your cave?"

"No, I don't mind at all," she replied, moving up to make room for him.

He sat down and leaned his back against the rock. "I've got a day's leave," he said. "Twenty-four hours all to myself. It's a new idea and rather a pleasant one. The only thing is, I don't know what to do with my day; I'm so unused to having a whole day on my hands."

"You might fish," suggested Frances after a moment's thought.

"I might if I knew how—and if I possessed the necessary equipment," he agreed.

"Couldn't you borrow a fishing-rod?"

"I expect I could, but I couldn't borrow the skill. As a matter of fact, I wondered whether you'd like to come over to Rithie and go to the pictures. D'you like that sort of thing?"

"I like it if it's a good picture," Frances said, and then, feeling that this sounded somewhat ungracious, she added: "It was very nice of you to think of it."

"Purely selfish," he replied.

"How did you know I was here?" asked Frances after a moment's silence.

"They told me at the hotel, and I saw you climbing along the reef with my glasses. It looked pretty risky, to tell you the truth. Every now and then a wave broke and you disappeared from view."

"It wasn't difficult, really," said Frances. "The waves didn't actually break over me. I was enjoying every moment of it."

"Perhaps I should have left you to enjoy it in solitude."

"I don't mind *you*," she replied.

Her companion laughed.

"I mean," said Frances hastily, "I mean, lots of people would be such a nuisance that they would spoil all the fun; they would be worrying about their clothes; they would say I was getting rheumatism from sitting on a damp rock——"

"Are you sure you aren't getting rheumatism?"

"Quite sure. Salt water doesn't give you rheumatism."

"What a comforting belief!" said Guy Tarlatan with a sigh. They were silent for a few moments, watching the waves. "Aren't they magnificent?" he said at last in quite a different tone of voice. "There's something terrifying about them . . . they're like lions on a chain. They spring forward and then something draws them back. . . . Do you know what I mean?"

He was looking at her now, and, as there was not much room for two people in the mermaid's nook, his tanned, weather-beaten face was so near that Frances could see every hair of his close-clipped moustache—they were like thin golden wires. His eye-lashes were fair too, but they were of a silky texture. It was an odd feeling to be so close to a man, and Frances was a trifle breathless as she replied: "Yes, of course I do. What would happen if the chain broke?"

"The lions would spring upon us and tear us limb from limb," replied her companion cheerfully.

"Yes, why aren't we frightened?" asked Frances.

He nodded thoughtfully. "It's funny, isn't it?" he said. "We know we're perfectly safe. We trust the chain implicitly. Here we sit, just out of reach of those tremendous waves. . . ."

There was another silence—if silence it could be called in the midst of the waves' thunder. "What about the picture house?" inquired Frances at last.

"What about it?" he replied. "We'll go if you'd like it, but I'm just as happy to stay here—or we could walk along the shore. Look at that seagull!"

The seagull had dived suddenly into the bosom of a wave and now it was poised just beyond the breakers, floating up and down on the swell. Guy Tarlatan took out his glasses and focused them before handing them to Frances. For a few moments she could see nothing but green water, and then she found the bird— she could see its feathers, its bright eyes, and the down upon its breast.

"Isn't it wonderful?" she exclaimed. "It looks so near . . . as if I could touch it. . . . Now it has gone behind that rock. . . ."

"We'll have to go back," said Guy suddenly. "The tide's coming in. That rock is almost covered now." He stood up as he spoke and held out his hand to Frances and pulled her to her feet. They went back along the reef, scrambling over the rocks. Here and there the sea had invaded the pools and filled them with creamy foam. The wind was as strong as ever, but the clouds were breaking and scattering like torn grey rags.

"It's going to be a lovely afternoon," said Frances, pausing a moment to look at the sky.

Her companion agreed. "We'll have lunch at the Bordale Arms and go for a walk, shall we?" he said. "There must be lovely walks round here. We don't want to be cooped up indoors on a day like this."

They had reached the cliffs by this time, and they turned to walk back to Cairn. It was difficult going, for the firm sand was covered, and along the base of the cliffs there were heaps of tumbled boulders. Here and there the tide had come up so far that it was difficult to get past. They had to wait until a wave receded and then run across to the next heap of rocks. Frances thought it was rather fun; she was quite breathless, and the wind had whipped a wild-rose colour into her cheeks.

"Let's sit down for a few minutes," she said at last.

"No, we'd better hurry," he replied. "Give me your hand in case you slip on the seaweed . . . come on . . . put your foot on that rock . . . that's right, up you go."

"Let's have a rest," said Frances. "It doesn't matter if we're a bit late for lunch——"

"No," he said firmly. "No, we had better hurry. What a fool I am!"

"Why?" asked Frances.

At that moment they came round a bend in the cliff and stopped by one accord . . . the little bay in front of them was full of waves—green waves flecked with patches of foam—they were splashing up against the face of the cliff.

"What a damned fool I am!" exclaimed Guy Tarlatan in savage tones.

There was no need for Frances to repeat her question; she stood beside him and looked down; the bay was like a cauldron of bubbling water—a giant's cauldron.

"We'll have to go back," Frances said.

"That's just the trouble—we can't go back," replied her companion. "We should never get back past that other bay . . . and we can't get up the cliff either. I've been looking for a possible place all the way along——"

Suddenly Frances began to laugh. She laughed so much that

she had to sit down on a rock. She laughed and laughed, and the more she tried to stop the more impossible it seemed to control her laughter.

"I say——" began her companion in anxious tones.

"I'm not—hysterical," declared Frances breathlessly. "It's just—just so awfully funny. We're cut off—by the tide."

"It's damned silly," said Guy, but he began to laugh too—he could not help it. "I wish you'd tell me the joke," he said at last, taking a large white handkerchief out of his pocket and wiping his eyes.

Frances was wiping her eyes with a smaller handkerchief. She said weakly: "What would you think if you read about it in a book? Would you think it was awful drivel?"

He looked at her in surprise. "Was that what you were laughing at?"

"You were laughing at it too," said Frances.

"I was laughing at you," he replied. "As a matter of fact, I'm certain there's something more in it than meets the eye, but this is no time for explanations." He walked back and gazed up at the cliff with knitted brows. Then he went close to it and, taking out his penknife, scraped a piece of the rock. Frances remained where she was; she did not worry him with questions.

Presently he came back and said: "It looks as if we shall have to remain where we are until the tide goes down. I'm most awfully sorry about it."

"It isn't your fault," she replied.

"I should have noticed," he said. "It was idiotic, really. I'll have a try at the cliff, if you like."

"You'll do nothing of the sort," said Frances. "The rock is crumbling away. You'd just fall down and break your neck—what good would that do?"

"Not very much."

"We'll stay where we are," continued Frances cheerfully. "We're all right here. The tide won't come up much farther, will it?"

"It may come up a bit farther. It's a spring tide, you see. I'm pretty certain that these rocks are never covered, but it might be as well to find a place where we should be sheltered from the spray. You don't seem to be worrying much," he added, with a surprised inflection in his voice.

Frances wasn't worrying at all. Somehow or other she felt perfectly safe. She smiled at him and replied: "I'm leaving all the worrying to you."

"You're taking it very well, I must say."

" I don't mind—but it seems rather hard that you should be forced to spend your holiday on a barren rock."

All this time the waves were thundering against the cliff, and Frances noticed that a small rock which had been sticking up out of the sea was covered completely.

Her companion had noticed it too. He said rather anxiously: " The tide is rising. I think we had better climb higher up." He pointed to a ledge of rock which jutted out of the cliff just above their heads.

" We couldn't reach it," objected Frances.

" Of course we can reach it," he replied firmly. " I'll stand underneath and you can climb on to my shoulders—what a good thing you're sensibly dressed!"

Frances had been thinking the same thing. It would have been much more difficult if she had been wearing a skirt. The ledge was at least nine feet high and she was extremely doubtful of her capacity to carry out the acrobatic feat, but it was no use being silly about it . . . he would think she was a perfect nuisance. . . .

" Come on," he said. " It will be quite easy. Put your feet on my shoulders."

He stooped down, facing the rock, and Frances climbed on to his shoulders. There was a tuft of grass on the rock and she grasped it firmly while he straightened himself. She felt herself being raised into the air—how tremendously strong he was! The ledge was now on a level with her chest, and she stretched out her arms and tried to pull herself on to it . . . there was nothing to take hold of. For a moment she struggled vainly and then she found herself being pushed upward by her feet . . . she wriggled up and turned over.

" Are you all right?" asked Guy anxiously.

" Yes," she replied. " Yes, perfectly all right. It's quite a good place. It goes back into a sort of cave. How are you going to get up?"

" I don't think I can make it, but it doesn't matter. I shall be all right here."

Frances lay down and looked over the edge. " You *must* come up," she said anxiously. " Couldn't you scrape holes in the rock to put your feet?"

" There are several places for my feet but nothing to hold on to with my hands."

It was a bit of a problem but, after some discussion, it was solved in the following manner. Frances took off the belt of her oilskin coat and dangled it over the edge and Guy fixed his belt to the other end of it—the two belts joined together made a reasonably long rope. Frances then wedged herself firmly between two rocks and wound her end of the improvised rope round her wrist.

"Are you ready?" he asked. "Remember, if I'm too heavy you're to let go. Do you understand?"

"Yes," replied Frances. She understood perfectly.

The two belts took the strain—it was a far greater strain than Frances had expected. The belt cut into her wrist and her arm was almost pulled out of its socket. She hung on for dear life, and in another moment his head appeared over the edge and he scrambled up beside her.

"Good work!" he said. "It's a grand place—we shall be perfectly all right here. What's the matter with your hand?"

"Nothing."

He took her hand and looked at the weal on her wrist. "That was a silly thing to do," he said sternly. "I told you that if I was too heavy you were to let go. You couldn't have let go, could you? I might have pulled you over the edge. You said you understood."

"I did understand," said Frances, smiling, "but I didn't intend to let go."

He took a clean handkerchief out of an inside pocket and soaked it in a pool and tied it round her wrist. "I'm very angry," he said. "Another time you're to obey orders without quibbling."

"You mean, the next time we get cut off by the tide," asked Frances innocently.

He laughed and replied: "Yes, of course."

They sat down beneath the overhanging rock and stretched out their legs. Guy took out his cigarette case and offered it to his companion. They smoked peacefully. Below them the sea thundered against the cliff and the spray flew up in clouds.

"The lions are angry," said Frances suddenly.

"I know," he said. "I was just thinking the same thing."

"How long will it be?" she asked.

"Probably about three hours—long enough for us to get to know each other quite well."

"There certainly isn't much distraction," said Frances in a thoughtful voice.

He agreed that there was not. "We might play a game if we had a pack of cards," he added.

"We might play consequences," said Frances, smiling. "Captain Tarlatan and Miss Field met on a rock; he said to her——"

"Doesn't it sound silly!"

" Is that what he said?"

" No—yes," replied Guy Tarlatan, laughing. " As a matter of fact, he said to her: ' Doesn't it sound silly for two people sitting on a barren rock in the middle of a storm to go on calling each other Captain Tarlatan and Miss Field?' "

Frances was rather alarmed. She said: " Oh, but I don't think I could!"

" She gave him the frozen mitt," said Guy somewhat sadly.

" Oh, no," cried Frances. " I didn't mean to be horrid—it was only—I mean, I don't know you very well."

For some reason this seemed to amuse Guy immensely. He laughed and said: " What a funny girl you are! I never know whether you mean what you say or something quite different."

Frances had found the same difficulty in understanding him. " I think it's because we've led such different lives," she said thoughtfully. " You've travelled about all over the world and mixed with all sorts of different people——"

" And what have you done?"

" Lived in a cave," replied Frances mischievously.

He sighed. " The mysterious Miss Field . . . and how difficult it is to carry on a conversation with you! Every now and then —just when I think we're getting along quite pleasantly—we run slap up against a stone wall."

" I wish I had brought my knitting," said Frances.

" Yes, *it* is a pity," agreed Guy. " If you had brought your knitting and I had brought a copy of K.R., we might have spent our time in a profitable manner."

" What's K.R.?" asked Frances.

" King's Regulations," replied her companion. " It contains detailed information upon the manner in which an officer should conduct himself in every conceivable situation."

" It sounds a most useful sort of book."

" Oh, it *is*! The British Army would crumble to bits if it were not for K.R."

" You must bring it next time."

" Yes ; I shall also bring a large packet of chocolate."

Frances smiled. " I shall bring a Thermos flask and a packet of sandwiches."

" You win," said Guy promptly.

They were silent for a while but it was a companionable silence. Presently Guy said: " Are you frightened of mice?"

" Mice!" exclaimed Frances in surprise.

" I just wondered," he said. " It would interest me very much to know whether or not you are frightened of them."

"You don't mean there are mice *here*!" exclaimed Frances, looking round in an anxious way.

He shook his head. "No, the question was purely academic. It was good of you to answer it so promptly. Psychology has always interested me."

"I suppose you think it's silly to be frightened of mice," said Frances indignantly.

"Not silly, merely rather odd. The prospect of being swept off a rock and drowned had no power to daunt you, but the moment I mentioned mice you showed considerable alarm."

"It was horrid of you to frighten me," she declared.

"It was a scientific experiment," he replied.

They smoked and talked. Sometimes they talked quite seriously and sometimes Guy resorted to his teasing manner which Frances found so baffling. She had no experience in repartee, but she discovered that it puzzled him considerably if she replied to his nonsense with a serious air, and the discovery gave her confidence and poise.

The tide began to ebb, and once it had started it receded quite rapidly (they watched the rocks come poking up through the water and saw the seaweed drying in the sun), but it was three o'clock in the afternoon before it had gone out far enough to release the prisoners, and by that time they were hungry and thirsty and somewhat stiff.

"Don't tell anyone, will you, Guy?" said Frances as they went up to the hotel.

"Not on your life," he replied. "I should never hear the end of it if any of the others got hold of the story . . . mum's the word, Frances."

They looked at each other and smiled.

Chapter Thirteen

It was raining gently but persistently when Frances woke, and she decided that it was just the sort of day to go over to Rithie and see a picture. She could get a bus at ten o'clock, which would give her plenty of time to do some shopping and have lunch before the picture started.

The bus was almost empty, but several people hurried up at the last minute and amongst them was Miss Cole and Winkie. Miss Cole was very flustered. She thrust Winkie into the seat next to Frances and sat down beside him.

" It was all your fault," she declared. " You seem to have no idea of time——"

" Hallo, Miss Field!" said Winkie.

Frances returned the greeting.

" Oh, Miss Field—I didn't see you!" exclaimed Miss Cole. " I'm taking Winkie to the dentist. He's been complaining of toothache."

" Was it bad toothache?" asked Frances sympathetically.

" Oh, no," replied Miss Cole, " but he makes such a fuss when there's anything the matter with him."

" Sometimes it's bad and sometimes it goes away," said Winkie gravely.

" I've had toothache like that," said Frances.

" He makes such a fuss," repeated Miss Cole.

" Toothache can be horrid," said Frances.

They were bumping over the cobbles now and Frances felt a small hand steal into hers. She gave it a little squeeze.

" Will the dentist pull it out?" asked Winkie in anxious tones.

" You keep on asking the same thing," complained Miss Cole. " I've told you that I don't know. He may pull it out or he may drill a hole in it and fill it with stopping."

Winkie shuddered.

" It won't hurt much," declared Frances, squeezing his hand again.

" It's stopped aching now," said Winkie suddenly. " Isn't that funny? It doesn't hurt any more. Perhaps we needn't go to the dentist after all."

Frances knew exactly what he was feeling, for she had been through the same thing herself, but apparently Miss Cole was above such childish nonsense. " Don't be silly," she said. " Miss Field will think you're a coward. You know perfectly well that you've got to have your tooth attended to, so what's the use of making a fuss about it?"

" I wasn't making a fuss," he replied meekly. " I was just thinking it was rather a waste going to the dentist when my tooth was quite better, that was all."

After having made his point Winkie was silent for a few minutes, and his elders discussed various matters over his head. They discussed the war news and the calling-up of women for essential services. Frances explained that she was having a holiday at the moment but that she intended to take up some sort of work very shortly.

" What sort of work?" inquired Miss Cole.

" I don't know," replied Frances. " I've written to a friend of mine to ask his advice. I'm afraid I'm not very good at anything."

Miss Cole laughed. " It doesn't affect me," she said. " I mean, I'm doing work of national importance already. What could be more important than looking after children and bringing them up to be useful members of society?"

" Yes," agreed Frances. " Yes, it's very important."

" The future of the world, the future of civilisation, is in their hands."

" Yes," said Frances, nodding.

" We must teach them to build a better world," declared Miss Cole. " We must train them to be good citizens."

" Yes," agreed Frances.

" There is no work of more importance to the nation than the training of the next generation," declared Miss Cole.

Frances agreed that there was not.

Miss Cole laughed. She said: " I'm afraid I get quite heated on the subject. I have a friend and she's gone into munitions. She and I have the most tremendous arguments about it, but nothing she says can alter my opinion. I just tell her that everyone has to decide for themselves. I just say: ' Well, perhaps making aeroplanes is right for you, but I'm making the men and women of the future.' That always shuts her up. She can find nothing to say to that."

" No," said Frances.

" No," repeated Miss Cole, shaking her head. " No, there's nothing she *can* say, really. Mrs. Liston couldn't possibly look after the children herself—she hasn't the knack, if you know what I mean—it's so important to understand their little minds. . . . I don't know what Mrs. Liston would do if I were called up."

"No," said Frances.

"Poor little Dolly," continued Miss Cole, smiling. "Poor little Dolly is so devoted to me. She has such a sweet, loving little nature. This morning she cried when I came away. I told her over and over again that I was coming back this afternoon and that I would bring her a parcel, but she was quite inconsolable."

"Dolly cried because she bumped her head on the table," said Winkie in a detached sort of manner.

Miss Cole did not reply. Her lips were set in a straight line and her face was very red. Frances could not help smiling, but she turned her head and looked out of the window so that Miss Cole should not see her amusement.

"I had an operation," said Winkie suddenly. "Have you ever had an operation, Miss Field?"

Frances replied that she had had her tonsils out.

"Oh, mine was much worse," said Winkie with some pride. "I was very ill. The doctor had to cut me open and take out my pain—then he sewed me up again with a needle and thread."

"You talk about it far too much," said Miss Cole.

"Well, you needn't listen," replied Winkie in reasonable tones. "Miss Field doesn't know about it, so I thought she'd be interested. I haven't talked about it too much to *her*."

After these preliminaries Winkie settled down and chattered all the way, and as Miss Cole was sulky he addressed himself exclusively to his new friend. Frances knew that Miss Cole was becoming more and more furious every moment, and made several attempts to drag her into the conversation, but her efforts were in vain, and by the time they reached Rithie she was uncomfortably aware that she had made an enemy—it was an exceedingly unpleasant feeling.

"Where does the dentist live?" asked Frances as they got out of the bus.

"In Forth Street," replied Miss Cole shortly. "Come along, Winkie, we shall be late for our appointment if we hang about here."

"I want Miss Field to come too," declared Winkie, clinging to his new friend's hand. "I shall be quite good and brave if Miss Field comes too. I promise faithfully I will."

"Miss Field doesn't want to be bothered with little boys," declared Miss Cole, trying to drag him away.

"She *likes* little boys," declared Winkie, clinging on harder than ever. "I *know* she does."

" She doesn't like silly little boys who make a fuss about going to the dentist," said Miss Cole firmly.

" She likes *me*," he replied with the utmost assurance.

It was true, of course. Frances had discovered that she liked him immensely, and she would have been quite willing to go to the dentist with him, but the thing was impossible. It was Miss Cole's business to take him to the dentist, not hers. Frances disengaged herself from Winkie, declaring that she had a great deal of shopping to do and reminding him that they were going out in a boat one day—the very first day that the sea was calm. She said good-bye and fled for her life before Winkie could say anything more ... but although she had managed to escape from Winkie's clinging hand she could not escape from his large, reproachful eyes; they haunted her all the morning, and even followed her into the picture house and spoilt her enjoyment of the film. She wondered whether the dentist had been obliged to pull out Winkie's tooth ... and whether Miss Cole had been kind.

The next day Frances met Winkie on the shore. He was dabbling in a pool, and beside him was a red pail full of seaweed. She was glad when she saw him, for she felt that she had let him down, and although she could not have done anything else in the circumstances she was anxious to make amends.

" Hallo, how is your tooth?" she inquired.

" It's out," he replied, opening his mouth and showing her a small red gap. " The dentist pulled it out. I had gas, so I didn't feel it at all. I had a most awfully funny dream."

" Did you?"

" Yes, it was a horrid dream, really. I don't think I had better tell you about it."

Frances thought that this was a wise decision. She sat down on a rock and pointed to the pail. " Have you caught any fish?" she asked.

" Not fish," he said gravely. " It's very difficult to catch fish—they're so slippery, you know—but I've caught a whole lot of funny little animals. They're like snails, but they've got legs underneath them."

" They're hermit crabs," said Frances.

The hermit crabs reminded Frances of an occasion when she had been sent to the seaside for a few days to recover from the effects of whooping-cough. She had gone with her nurse and they had spent their whole time searching for hermit crabs and playing " house-agents." It was rather a curious game, and

92

she was pretty certain that it would appeal to Winkie, so she proceeded to show it to him. . . . " You see," said Frances, " you put a few hermits in a pool and you collect some empty shells and put them in beside the hermits, and then you watch for a bit and sometimes the hermits change their shells . . . they move into a new house."

" Why do they?" asked Winkie in surprise.

" I think it's because their own houses are too small," replied Frances.

They chose the hermit crabs which were to be provided with houses, and Winkie named them. " That's you, and that's me," said Winkie seriously, " and that's Jennifer's uncle. We must find a very big new house for him, because he's so big already."

" Who is Jennifer's uncle?" Frances inquired.

" Just Jennifer's uncle," replied Winkie in surprise. " I thought you knew him. You know Jennifer, don't you?"

" No," said Frances.

" She's a baby," Winkie explained. " She's only a little older than Dolly, but she's *quite* different. Jennifer is beautiful," declared Winkie in a dreamy voice.

" Is she?"

" Yes, perfectly beautiful. I'm going to marry her, you know."

" But who is Jennifer?" asked Frances.

" Jennifer!" he said, wrinkling his brows. " Oh, I see what you mean. She's Mrs. Crabbe's baby, that's who she is." He laughed and added: " She's a little crab—isn't that funny?"

Frances agreed that it was.

" Now look," continued Winkie. " Look, that teeny weeny hermit crab is Jennifer and we must find a nice house for her. Here's a yellow shell—it's pretty, isn't it?—I think Jennifer would like that, don't you?" He put the two shells close together and they waited with breathless interest to see what would happen. For a long time nothing happened at all, and then, just when they had begun to lose patience with Jennifer, she put out her little pink claws and felt the yellow shell all over . . . she hesitated for a moment, then out came her long, whitish body, it did a little somersault, and fitted itself snugly into its new home.

" Oh!" cried Winkie, raising his head and looking at Frances with shining eyes. " Oh, isn't it fun? Oh, this is the very nicest game——"

" We've let a house," said Frances, who was almost as pleased as Winkie with the success of their experiment.

" Yes, we've let a house," agreed Winkie. " I'm the house-
93

agent man and you're the house-agent lady—let's find a house for Jennifer's uncle now."

"Are you all by yourself?" asked Frances, when Jennifer's uncle had been offered a large mansion with all modern conveniences and had refused it with scorn.

"Not really," Winkie replied. "Miss Cole and Dolly are sitting behind that rock out of the wind. I'm not supposed to go very far away—and I haven't, have I?"

He was not far away from the rock, but he was completely out of sight, and Frances could not help feeling that Miss Cole was neglecting her duties. He might fall into a pool or get cut off by the tide . . . she was aware that the latter fate was not altogether impossible.

They played at house-agents for some time and then Winkie demanded a story. "You can make it up," he said. "Just make it up as you go along—that's much the nicest sort of story."

Frances was extremely doubtful of her capacity to do anything of the kind, but by this time she had fallen so completely under Winkie's spell that she could deny him nothing. She started in a tentative manner. "Once upon a time," said Frances, leaning back against a rock and clasping her hands round her knees, "once upon a time there was a princess who lived in a palace in the middle of a big city."

"Was it London?" Winkie asked.

"Yes, it was London."

"Was it Buckingham Palace?"

"No," said Frances. "No, it was—it was called Wintringham Square."

"Wintringham Square—what a funny name for a palace!" said Winkie in surprise.

Frances agreed that it was. If she had had more time to think she might have invented a more imposing name for the palace, but she was not used to improvising fairy stories for small boys. "The princess lived in the palace," continued Frances, searching somewhat desperately for inspiration, "and sometimes she went out for a walk in the city, and she saw all the people enjoying themselves and having fun, but she couldn't join in their games because she was invisible. She couldn't speak to them, and they didn't know she was there because they couldn't see her, so she was very lonely. She was very comfortable in the palace, of course ; she had lovely clothes to wear and lots of good things to eat——"

"Ice-cream?" inquired Winkie with gleaming eyes. "Ice-cream and strawberries and peaches and chocolate creams?"

"Yes," agreed Frances. " She had everything like that, but she wasn't happy because she was lonely. She had nobody to play with. Then one day, when she was feeling very sad, a kind old magician came to the palace and he——"

" Was it Merlin?" asked Winkie eagerly.

" No," replied Frances, smiling. " No, it wasn't Merlin. It was a magician called Digby. Some people thought he was just an ordinary doctor, but really and truly he was a very powerful magician indeed. He was sorry for the princess, so he broke the spell and the princess was able to escape. She left the palace and came to Cairn, and——"

" She came *here*?" cried Winkie with his eyes like saucers. " She came here, to Cairn—a real princess?"

Frances nodded. " Yes, but she wasn't a princess any more. The magician had broken the spell, so she was an ordinary person again. She was ever so much happier because she could do what she liked, and she wasn't lonely because she could talk to people and make friends with them. It was difficult at first, of course—she wasn't used to talking—but after a bit she found her tongue. She was ever so much happier," said Frances thoughtfully.

She stopped there, and Winkie looked at her in surprise. " That's not the end, is it?" he inquired.

" Yes, that's all," replied Frances. It was a poor sort of ending, but she could not think of anything more to say.

" But it *can't* be the end," he declared, looking up at her with his big, solemn eyes. " You haven't said that she lived happily ever after."

" I know, but, you see, she was just an ordinary person ; she wasn't a princess any more. It's only fairy princesses who live happily ever after—not real people like you and me—and that's why the story isn't finished," added Frances, clutching at this heaven-born inspiration, " because real stories about real people go on and on."

" Until the people are dead and buried, I suppose," agreed Winkie, nodding.

" They don't finish even then," said Frances in a thoughtful tone, " because things we do and say live on long after we are dead . . . but you aren't old enough to understand that yet."

" Couldn't I if you explained?" inquired Winkie anxiously.

Frances tried to explain it simply. She said: " You and I are friends, and we're teaching each other a lot of things that neither of us will ever forget, so when I get very old and die there will still be little bits of me alive in you."

Winkie was silent for a moment, and then he said: "That's an awfully funny idea, isn't it? I suppose there are bits of me in every one I know—bits of me in Mummy and Daddy and Dolly —and every one. Perhaps there are bits of me in Jennifer's uncle too , , , but I don't think there are any bits of me in Miss Cole."

Chapter Fourteen

NOTHING HAD been seen or heard of Tommy for two days, and Frances decided to walk over and pay her a visit. She expected to find Tommy alone, but, on approaching the house, she heard the sound of a saw and perceived a tall young man engaged in sawing up an enormous tree. He had a snub nose and a freckled face and was attired in khaki trousers, a khaki shirt, and a pair of blue braces. He stopped sawing as Frances approached, and straightened his back and wiped his brow with a large blue handkerchief.

"Are you looking for anyone?" he asked, staring at Frances in surprise.

"Mrs. Widgery," said Frances.

"Oh, she's there," he said, nodding towards the house, and with that he seized the saw and applied himself once more to his task.

Frances knocked on the door and then, as nobody came, she opened it and went in. One of the many inconveniences of Sea View was that the front door opened straight into the sitting-room, and Frances, as she walked in, nearly collided with another tall young man who was dressed in almost exactly the same garments as the first one. In fact, the two young men were so alike to the casual glance that if Frances had not heard the sound of industrious sawing going on she might have concluded that this was her second encounter with the first young man instead of her first encounter with the second.

The second young man was carrying a tray of tea-things and had a tea-cloth over his arm. "Hallo, look out!" he exclaimed. "By jove, that was a near thing!" He paused in the middle of the room and added: "I say, would you mind taking this white cloth and spreading it on the table? There's nowhere for me to put down this blinking tray."

Frances took the cloth and spread it, and the young man planted the tray in the middle of the table. "Thanks awfully," he said. " It was Mrs. Widgey's fault. She must have thought I had four hands or something."

" You could have put it on a chair," said Tommy, appearing from the kitchen attired in a bright-green pinafore. " You never thought of *that*, I suppose. No initiative—that's what's the matter with young officers to-day. . . . Hallo, Frances, have you come to tea?"

Frances said she had. She said it quite boldly, for she was beginning to get used to the free-and-easy manners of her new friends.

" Well, there isn't much to eat," said Tommy, sitting down in one of the easy-chairs. " There's nothing to eat except bread and marge. . . . Barry, go and make another piece of toast for Frances."

The tall young man seized the toasting fork and started for the kitchen. " Does Frances like her toast brown or golden?" he inquired, pausing at the door.

" Miss Field to you," declared Tommy, aiming a cushion at his head.

He ducked and said in a hurt tone: " Well, how was I to know? You never introduced us."

" Nice children, but wearing," said Tommy as the door closed behind him with a bang. " Nice children, but *distinctly* wearing. Sit down, Frances, and tell me what you've been doing with yourself."

Frances sat down. She had just opened her mouth to comply with Tommy's request when the outside door opened and the other young man appeared. His arms were full of sawn logs. " I say, will this do?" he inquired. " I mean, isn't it nearly tea-time? D'you want this stuff or shall I pile it in the shed?"

" Put it there," said Tommy, " and then say ' how d'you do ' to Miss Field and go and wash your hands."

" She's like this sometimes," explained the young man, grinning at Frances . . . " but at other times she's really quite civilised. One has to make allowances for her, because she hasn't been properly brought up. What I really need is a bath," he added hopefully.

" There isn't a bathroom," replied Tommy. " You know quite well there isn't a bathroom, Mark."

" I'd forgotten," he admitted. " Though how I managed to forget I can't imagine. Everyone in the mess has been informed of the fact, not once but several times . . . as a matter of fact, I wouldn't mind a bathe in the sea."

" In the sea!" exclaimed Tommy, shuddering.

He nodded. "We bathe every morning, Barry and I. It's pretty grim, to tell you the truth."

"Why on earth do you do it?"

He blushed and replied: "Oh, well . . . it's just an idea we had. Hardening ourselves and all that sort of rot, you know."

He piled the logs neatly beside the fireplace and stood up. "Will that do?" he asked.

"Yes, it will do beautifully," said Tommy, nodding. "Now you can go and help Barry to make the tea."

"Thank you so much," he replied. "Thank you, dear Mrs. Widgey, but I think I've earned my tea already. Please tell Barry to bring it to me on a silver tray." He sat down as he spoke and leant back and crossed his long legs—he looked the picture of indolence.

Frances was amused at the back-chat, but she could not take part in it; in fact, the only remark she had made since her arrival was the simple statement that she had come to tea. She felt that it was about time she made another remark, so she inquired whether she should go and help in the kitchen.

"Good heavens, no!" exclaimed Tommy. "Why should you bother? Barry will manage it all right."

At this moment the door opened and Barry appeared with a pot of tea in one hand, a rack of toast in the other, and a jar of honey under his arm. He placed them on the table with a triumphant air.

"Where did you get that?" asked Tommy, coming over to the table and pointing to the honey.

"In the cupboard, darling," he replied. "I opened the cupboard and there it was, sitting on the shelf. I know you like honey, so——"

"It's for Midge," said Tommy.

"Yes, of course," agreed Barry, snatching it from under her outstretched hand, "of *course* it is, but he wouldn't grudge it to us. We'll only eat the tiniest, littlest spoonful. Two spoonfuls, that's all—one for you and one for me. The others can have marge. How would that do?"

"I want honey, too," declared Mark. "As a matter of fact, I've *earned* it. You should see the lovely pile of wood I've cut up, Mrs. Widgey."

Tommy laughed. "We'll each have one spoonful," she said. "We mustn't have more, because, *honestly*, it's difficult to get . . . and I can't get marmalade, so I *must* keep the honey for Midge's breakfast."

"I'll get you some honey," declared Barry. "There must be honey somewhere, and if there is I'll find it."

They sat down to tea, and Frances noticed that in spite of all their nonsense the boys were extremely sparing of the honey— each of them taking only the slightest smear of the precious stuff on their toast. The tea was good and the toast beautifully made— neither too hard nor too soft but crisp and golden.

"I never tasted such lovely toast before," said Frances after the first mouthful.

Barry smiled complacently. "Very few people know how to make toast," he replied. "There's an art in making good toast. I learnt it at Eton. It was one of the few really useful things I learnt."

"I know," agreed Mark. "You got licked if you didn't make it properly."

"What were the other useful things you learnt?" asked Tommy with an innocent air.

"Rowing," said both the boys with one voice.

They did not explain why rowing was useful to them, so after a moment Tommy lifted her eyes and said: "Well, is it a secret or what?"

"I don't think so," replied Mark doubtfully. "It's Major Crabbe's idea. We've got two boats down at the camp and we take the chaps out and teach them to row. It's rather fun, isn't it, Barry?"

"What's the idea?" inquired Tommy with interest.

"Oh, just training," said Barry.

"Hardening 'em up and making 'em fit," said Mark.

"Makes a change from foot-slogging," said Barry.

"Frightfully good exercise," said Mark.

Tommy waited till the chorus was over and then she said: "Oh, I see. I thought perhaps you intended to row across the North Sea and beard Adolf in his den."

"That *would* be fun," said Barry in a languid tone.

"I like this house," declared Mark, looking round as if he were seeing it for the first time. "I like it awfully. There's something very cosy and comfy about it. I think I shall get married after the war and buy this house and live here for the rest of my life."

"You had better make certain that your wife can cook," said Tommy dryly.

"Oh, of course," he agreed. "I shall say: 'Dear Miss Smith, I love you to distraction. Can you cook?—if so, be mine.'"

99

"Sea View," said Barry suddenly, waving his hand towards the window. "Who on earth thought of calling this house Sea View?"

"Why shouldn't it be called Sea View?" Tommy inquired.

"It's so obvious," complained Barry. "A bit too obvious. It's as if you were to launch an ocean-going liner and christen it Sea View. . . . I wonder why they don't."

"A bit too obvious," suggested Mark in a thoughtful tone.

"Idiot!" cried Barry, aiming a punch at him across the table. "Idiot—that's what you are! Can't you see that I was expressing an extremely subtle and penetrating idea? Sea View is the sort of name they give a boarding-house at Eastbourne. Doesn't anyone understand?"

"Yes," said Frances, smiling at him. "As a matter of fact, I stayed at a boarding-house once and it was called Sea View. If you leaned out of the bathroom window you could catch a glimpse of the sea between the chimney-pots."

"There," said Barry. "That's exactly what I meant. Miss Field is the only person who understands and appreciates me."

He was so earnest about it that they all laughed uproariously, and they were still laughing when the door opened and Captain Widgery appeared; with his appearance the laughter ceased abruptly and the two boys sprang to their feet.

"A tea-party!" said Captain Widgery. "You didn't tell me you were having a tea-party this afternoon, Tommy." He came in and drew off his glove and shook hands with Frances. He nodded to the boys.

"I didn't know," Tommy was saying. "It wasn't an arranged tea-party. It just happened. If it had been a proper tea-party there would have been cakes and scones and things . . . but it just happened, and, of course, that's much the nicest kind of tea-party, isn't it?"

It was so unlike Tommy to babble like this that Frances was quite alarmed. She said: "I'm afraid I invited myself."

"I'm sure Tommy was delighted to see you," replied Captain Widgery in deliberate tones.

The two boys had put on their tunics and were busy fastening on their belts. Captain Widgery looked at them. "You aren't going away, are you?" he inquired. "I seem to have burst up the tea-party—and it was going with such a swing. I heard you laughing as I came up the path."

"Afraid we must be getting along, sir," replied Mark.

"It's been tremendous fun," declared Barry.

They were fully accoutred by this time—neatly belted and
100

hung about with tin helmets and revolvers and gas-masks. Somehow or other their faces looked different too ; their faces looked older and more responsible ; there was a tightening of the muscles about their mouths. It was as if they had armed their minds as well as their bodies. They were men and soldiers—no longer carefree boys.

"Good-bye, Mrs. Widgery," said Mark gravely. "Thank you very much indeed. Good-bye, Miss Field. Good-bye, sir."

Barry echoed his companion's words, and they retreated somewhat hastily but in good order, shutting the door after them quietly but firmly.

Frances realised that she had missed her chance . . . she ought to have gone with the others. She rose from her chair.

"You needn't go yet," said Captain Widgery, sitting down at the table and looking at Frances with a grim smile.

"I was just going, really," replied Frances somewhat feebly.

"You must change your mind. It wouldn't be polite to go away the moment your host appeared on the scene, would it?"

"No," said Frances uncomfortably. "No, I don't suppose it would."

"Besides, you have no excuse, have you?" he continued. "You aren't engaged in any work of national importance ; you aren't defending your country from the rapacious Hun. You're a lady at large."

"Yes," agreed Frances. She was somewhat annoyed, for this was beyond a joke, but she was determined not to show her annoyance. "Yes," she repeated, smiling. "I'm a useless mouth —that's all."

He looked a trifle taken aback, and there was a short silence.

"Shall I make you some fresh tea?" asked Tommy.

"I don't want tea," he replied. "Tea is a beverage which doesn't appeal to me at all. Sit down, Miss Field. Tell me what you were laughing at when I came in. It must have been a good joke."

Frances sat down. She did not want to, but what else could she do? She tried to think what it was that had amused them so much—that nonsense about Sea View—it had seemed funny at the time, but she realised that it would sound extremely puerile if it were to be repeated in this cold-blooded atmosphere. She was wondering what to say, when Tommy came to the rescue again.

"It was quite silly, really," Tommy said. "Jokes are always flat if they have to be explained. I'll go and get you a drink." She disappeared into the kitchen, and Frances was alone

with Captain Widgery. She thought—as she had thought before:
He hates me; I wonder why. She was surprised and annoyed to
discover that she was frightened of him.

"How do you like this house?" he asked, leaning forward and
fixing her with his dark, pirate's eyes.

"I like it very much indeed," she replied firmly. "Tommy has
made it so comfortable and cosy . . . and there's such a lovely
view."

"The view is monotonous," he retorted. "In fact, it isn't a
view at all; it's merely an expanse of water. I like a view of
fields and trees; I like a house with electric light and proper
sanitary arrangements. No view on earth is as important as a
good bathroom with a heated rail for towels. Perhaps if you had
knocked about as long as I have you wouldn't be so keen on a
picnic."

"The summer is coming," Frances pointed out. She was
aware, the moment she had spoken, that it was a feeble thing to
say.

"Summer!" he repeated with a mirthless laugh. "There isn't
any summer here. In this part of the world they have eight
months of bad weather and four months of worse. If you expect
to be warm here in the summer you will be very disappointed."

"They said at the hotel that people came here for sea-
bathing," objected Frances.

"I dare say they did," he replied. "These people will say anything. They just say what they think you want to hear without
the slightest regard for the truth. Some people will bathe in
Arctic water, of course—and as a matter of fact the whole regiment will probably be invited to use my house as a bathing-
machine—but I prefer warm water for my ablutions."

Tommy had now returned with a bottle of whisky and a siphon
of soda. She put her hand on his shoulder and said: "We won't
ask anyone if you don't want them."

"Ask anyone you like," he replied. "I'm sure I don't care. It
might be quite amusing if you asked amusing people. I
don't know how you can be bothered with those young jacka-
napes."

"Oh, Midge, it's good for them to come here and play," said
Tommy earnestly. "It's good for them to get away from—from
the war and all that sort of thing. They're so young . . . and
there's nowhere else for them to go."

He laughed unpleasantly and replied: "And when we were at
York—I suppose there was nowhere else for them to go there
either?"

102

Somehow or other Frances managed to escape. She was not very clear, herself, how she had accomplished it. Her host and hostess accompanied her to the door, and when she looked back to wave to them she saw them standing together in the doorway of the little house—the tall pirate chief and his fragile fairy wife —his arm was round her shoulders and she was gazing up into his face. Frances walked home very slowly. She didn't understand in the very least . . . somehow or other she didn't want to understand.

PART II

FRANCES AWAKE

Chapter Fifteen

FRANCES WAS getting ready for bed when there was a knock on her door. She hesitated for a moment and then put on her dressing-gown and opened the door. It was Major Crabbe.

"I'm frightfully sorry to disturb you," he said, "but the fact is I'm rather worried about Elise; she's—she's just had a heart attack. She has them sometimes. It frightened me . . . it always frightens me horribly," he added with rather a wan smile. He certainly looked as if he had been badly frightened; there was a strange pallor beneath the tan of his weather-beaten skin.

"I'm awfully sorry," Frances said in concern.

"She's better," continued Major Crabbe. "She's all right, really, but I've got to go. I've been sent for from the camp. I wondered if you would sit with her for a bit."

"Of course I will. I'll come at once——"

"I hate leaving her," he said unhappily.

"Couldn't you get special leave?" asked Frances, who had begun to understand the workings of the military machine.

"Not to-night," he replied. He hesitated for a moment and then added: "I shouldn't tell you, really, but the fact is we've had orders to stand to. I don't suppose anything will come of it."

"Do you mean—they're expecting—an invasion to-night?" inquired Frances in amazement.

"It means there's something up," admitted Major Crabbe. "It might be a big air-raid, or—something like that; but we've had scares like this before several times and nothing has happened. You aren't windy, are you?"

"No, of course not."

"That's right," he said, smiling at her. "There's nothing to worry about. We'll deal with the blighters—that's what we're for. In any case, I don't suppose there's a dog's chance of them coming here. It's the east coast that's the danger spot."

His voice sounded a trifle regretful, and Frances looked at him in surprise. "You wouldn't like them to make an attempt here, would you?" she added.

"No," he said, but he said it doubtfully.

"You would!" she exclaimed.

"No," he repeated. "I mean—— Oh, I don't know what I mean. We've been hanging about waiting for it for such ages . . . if it were not for Elise . . . it might be rather a good show. In fact, I'm pretty certain it would be a dashed good show. . . . You'll go along to Elise, won't you?"

"Yes, of course," repeated Frances.

He waved to her and ran downstairs, his thick boots clattering on the stone staircase.

For the first time Frances realised what an immense gulf lay between her outlook and the outlook of a man like Major Crabbe. War, invasion, the attempt of an enemy to land upon the beach at Cairn were viewed by him in a matter-of-fact way. He saw the possibilities and accepted them and placed them in his mind. He was prepared, morally and physically prepared, for these incredible things to happen—"that's what we're for," he had said. Frances stood quite still for a few moments trying to prepare herself in the same way. She tried to imagine the thing happening—tried to imagine what she herself would do if the thing really happened—but she found it impossible. I hope I should be brave, she thought. I hope I shouldn't do anything silly. I ought to have asked him what I was to do . . . in any case, I shall stay with Elise.

Frances put on some more clothes and went across the landing to the Crabbes' room. She knocked on the door and went in. Elise was lying in bed propped up with pillows. She looked even more fragile than usual, and there were dark-blue circles round her eyes, but she smiled at Frances in a friendly way.

"So nice of you," she said. "Ned was worried about leaving me alone—quite nonsense, of course, because I'm perfectly all right. I suppose Ned told you they were standing to," she added.

"Yes," replied Frances.

Elise sighed. "Poor darlings," she said. "It's so tiresome for them."

"Tiresome!" exclaimed Frances.

"Yes, they've got all the bother without any of the excitement. Ned would like to be in Libya—or even Greece. I don't mean he's a fire-eater, but soldiering is his profession, so, naturally, he would like to take an active part in the war. I shouldn't like it at all, but I wouldn't stand in his way. It wouldn't be right. If you marry a soldier you've got to marry his profession."

"You don't talk about the war much," Frances said.

"Don't we?" asked Elise. "No, I suppose we don't really.

They discuss it in mess, and sometimes Ned tells me things. I don't talk about it to other people very much, because there's always a chance that I might say something that I ought not to say. . . . It's better to get into the habit of saying nothing."

"So that's why——" Frances began.

"Only partly," said Elise, smiling. "There are all sorts of reasons, I think. The war isn't a new idea to us. Civilians have been saying for years that another war was impossible, but soldiers and sailors didn't share their views. Now that the war has come with all its horrors it's no use talking about it, is it?"

"No," agreed Frances.

They were silent for a few moments, and Frances heard the sound of an approaching plane. Its engine was making that queer, intermittent, booming noise which Frances had heard so often when she lived in Wintringham Square: "*Ba-room, ba-room, ba-room.*"

"That's a Jerry," said Elise. "I wonder where it is going."

It was odd hearing the noise of the enemy plane in the stillness of Cairn—odd and a trifle alarming. In London the guns had roared and barked and spluttered whenever the enemy planes had approached, but there were no guns here . . . no anti-aircraft defences whatever. If the pilot took it into his head to obliterate Cairn from the face of the earth there was nothing to prevent him from doing so. Of course Cairn was not a military objective—it was not worth obliterating—but still——

"I hope the blackout is complete," said Elise with a light laugh. She had hardly spoken when there was a roar like thunder and the whole house shook to its foundations. The windows rattled in their frames but did not break.

"Heavens, that was a near thing!" exclaimed Frances in some alarm.

"Not very near," replied Elise, "but perhaps you should go downstairs. Mr. MacNair's cellar would be a good place, I should think."

"Would you like to go down?" asked Frances, looking at her anxiously.

She shook her head. "I'm better where I am—my heart is still a bit funny—but there's no reason why you shouldn't go."

"I'll stay with you——"

"No, I'd much rather——"

"Honestly, I hate cellars——"

They were arguing somewhat heatedly when Mrs. MacNair knocked on the door and peeped in.

"It was a bomb," she said.

" We thought it might be," replied Elise with gentle sarcasm.

" It fell on the shore," continued Mrs. MacNair. " The dining-room windows are covered with sand. Alec says it was a Jerry and he's on his way to Ireland."

" Poor Ireland!" said Elise with a sigh.

" There's another——" Frances said.

They listened and heard the same queer booming in the distance . . . " *Ba-room, ba-room, ba-room.*"

" In the name of fortune!" exclaimed Mrs. MacNair in some alarm.

" There's nothing to worry about," said Elise. " You had better tell Alec to go round and make sure that there aren't any lights showing. They won't drop bombs unless they see a light——"

" I'll tell him," nodded Mrs. MacNair, and with that she disappeared.

The plane approached, roared over their heads, and sped away.

" Are you sure you wouldn't like to go downstairs, Frances?" asked Elise.

" Quite sure," replied Frances. " I'll sit here and read. I've brought my book with me . . . you can go to sleep."

" I'd rather talk," said Elise. Her eyes were very bright and she did not look like sleep.

" I'm sure you ought to rest," declared Frances.

Elise smiled. " I can talk and rest," she said. " It doesn't tire me to talk."

They were silent for a few moments and then Elise said: " Isn't it funny that if you decide you're going to talk it's almost impossible to find anything to talk about?"

" Yes," said Frances, " but you must have lots to talk about. You've travelled so much and met so many interesting people, haven't you?"

" You want me to tell you the story of my life!" said Elise, laughing.

" It would be very interesting."

" It would take too long. It would fill a book. As a matter of fact, I've sometimes thought it would be fun to write a book. I know it's the sort of thing people often say—silly people, I mean —but I believe I could do it."

" Why don't you?" asked Frances.

" Too many distractions," replied Elise. " Too much talking and moving about, too much worrying about Ned. It makes me so unsettled, you see. I'm either parting from Ned or planning to meet him, or meeting him and being with him for a little and wondering how long it will be before he's dragged away and sent somewhere else and whether I shall be able to go with him . . . all so unsettled," said Elise, waving her hands vaguely. " All such a strain—an emotional strain—and that's why we're all keyed up to concert pitch. It would take an Ibsen to write about us."

Frances was beginning to understand what Elise meant. She had always admired Elise but had liked her least of all her new friends; to-night Elise was quite different, for she had laid aside her slightly cynical manner and was talking with absolute frankness.

" I knew what Army life was before I married Ned," continued Elise in a dreamy sort of voice. " My parents were Army people, so we were dragged all over the world or else dumped on relations who didn't want us. I had always said I wouldn't marry anyone in the Service, but—well, I couldn't refuse Ned. We met in India and we were married there. Ned had had exactly the same sort of upbringing as I, and he was just as bitter about it. We decided that we wouldn't have children until we could settle down and give them a home. It wasn't because we didn't want children—we both wanted them—but we knew what it entailed. We should either have to be parted, and I should have to stay at home and look after the children, or else we should have to leave them to be looked after by other people, to be spoilt or neglected. I told Ned I wanted to go with him wherever he went and I stuck to it through thick and thin. I was the only wife in Jullundur one hot weather. Ned did all he could to persuade me to go to the hills, and he got the doctor to back him up, but I refused to go. I pretended that I liked the heat. The heat was terrific—you couldn't imagine what it was like—I used to lie on my charpoy all day with nothing on but a kimono. It was too hot to read. I just lay there and watched the clock and waited for the hours to pass. Sometimes I lay for half an hour trying to make up my mind to turn over on my other side . . . but men have to stick it . . . why should women be pampered and privileged? It was cooler when the sun went down. I used to get up and have a bath and put on a pretty frock. Then in the evening everyone used to come and see us. They just dropped in and lay about on long chairs and drank iced pegs. There wasn't much talk—it was too hot—but I used to sing and play the banjo and they seemed to like it. I can't sing at all," declared Elise with a smile. " I've got a miserable husky little voice, but that didn't seem to matter. They always asked me to sing. I suppose it was a change for them." She hesitated and then added: " I was the only woman in the station, you see."

108

"Where else have you been?" asked Frances.

"Where haven't I been?" replied Elise with her light laugh. "I was in Jerusalem for a bit—that was interesting. It was the time when there was rioting and most of the wives were packed home, but Ned had left off trying to get rid of me. . . . It was when we were in Jerusalem that Ned's uncle died and left him some money, and Ned said he would retire as soon as he got his majority. We were very happy about it. We planned it all—we talked about it for hours, Ned and I. There was to be no following the drums for our children ; they were not going to be carted about the country and dumped into lodgings and squeezed into furnished houses. Our children were not to be planted upon relations who didn't want them. Our children were to have a settled home. We had done our bit—so we felt—we had earned our happiness. We would find a house ; it need not be large but it must have a decent garden. There must be a proper nursery, furnished as nurseries should be, with a tall fire-guard and a basket-chair. (The basket-chair was Ned's idea. It was to be the sort of chair that creaked when you sat in it.) There was to be a window with bars and a window-seat. There was to be lino-leum on the floor. There would be a dog, of course, a spaniel with long ears and a silky coat . . . but the main thing was that it was to be a proper home with a father and a mother settled permanently in it. There was to be none of that strained atmos-phere, that grasping at brief periods of happiness, that uncer-tainty about the future which had been our lot when we were children. . . . Ned and I would settle down and have our children in peace . . . that was what we said. Wasn't it funny?"

Frances could not speak. She shook her head.

"Funny," said Elise again in a thoughtful voice. "Awfully funny, really. We came home and Ned got his majority and Jennifer was born. She was born on the eve of the most fright-ful war the world has ever seen. It just shows how futile it is to plan things out, doesn't it?"

They were silent for a few moments and in the silence they heard the sound of another plane. It was farther away than the others had been but its engine was distinctly audible.

"That's three," said Elise.

"I think it's four," replied Frances. "I heard another a few minutes ago. Go on, Mrs. Crabbe."

"Go on?" echoed Elise in surprise. "Haven't you heard enough? I've never told anyone so much about myself before—not even Tommy—and, by the way, don't you think you might call me Elise? I've been calling you Frances for several days, but perhaps you haven't noticed."

"I'd like to call you Elise," Frances said.

"You must think I'm mad to tell you all this," said Elise. She hesitated for a moment and then continued: "I wanted to tell you some of it because I saw your face the other night when they were all singing that song, but I didn't mean to tell you quite so much. It's very easy to tell you things."

"But why?" asked Frances in bewilderment. "I mean, why did you want to tell me——"

"Because I hate that song."

"*Mad Dogs and Englishmen?*" asked Frances.

Elise nodded. "The midday sun isn't funny," she said. "It's a great, glaring, blaring, brassy enemy. Nobody but a fool would go out in the midday sun if they could avoid it. The midday sun shrivels you up and sucks the marrow out of your very bones. It saps your energy so that after a little you find yourself talking in a whisper . . . there's nothing funny about it." She hesitated again and added: "Army life is fun sometimes. It's fun going about and seeing the world, especially when you're young; but it isn't all fun. . . . I don't want to brown you off completely, but it would be unfair to let you think it was all beer and skittles."

Frances was more bewildered than ever. The verb "to brown off" was not in her vocabulary. . . . She didn't know what Elise meant by saying that it would be unfair to let her think that Army life was all beer and skittles . . . why would it be unfair? She gave up the problem with a sigh, and in the silence that followed she considered the problems of her friends. The Crabbes had tried to plan for the future and their plans had all gone wrong; the Listons had not planned anything but had just battled along, taking things as they came and wearing themselves out in their struggle to make ends meet. Tommy's troubles were of a different nature but even more confusing.

She said suddenly and impulsively: "Can't anyone do anything to help Tommy?"

"No," replied Elise. "Nobody can do anything for anyone. They only burn their fingers if they try." She looked at her own long thin fingers as she spoke. "But I had to try," she added softly.

110

Chapter Sixteen

THE CLOCK on the mantelpiece was pointing to twelve when Frances opened her eyes. She looked at it in amazement and then suddenly she remembered the events of the previous night. It had been nearly five before she had left Elise and gone to bed, so she had slept solidly for seven hours. She was still lying there, and trying to make up her mind to get up and have a bath, when the door opened very quietly and Annie's face appeared round the corner. " Oh, you're awake!" said Annie. " Mrs. Crabbe said I wasn't to wake you, but I thought I'd just peep in and see if there was anything you were wanting. . . . You should see the hole in the sand. Every soul in the place has been down to the shore looking at it. I was saying to Mrs. MacNair it's a pity we couldn't charge them thrippence and send it to the Spitfire Fund."

" Was there any damage done?" asked Frances, clasping her hands behind her head.

" None at all," replied Annie. " And nobody was hurt, either . . . it's lucky, isn't it? Alec says they dropped the bomb because of Fergus MacNair's skylight—he didn't black it out properly, the wee wretch. Alec's been at him more than once about it but he wouldn't heed. He just said the Germans would never come here."

" I hope he'll do it now," said Frances a trifle anxiously.

Annie smiled. " It's been done," she said. " Old Mr. Fraser—he's Donald Fraser's brother—took a pot of paint and a pair of steps and down he went to the house when Fergus was out and painted the skylight all over . . . and when Fergus went home the house was as dark as the grave. It was Ellen MacNair told me, and she said Fergus was furious but he daren't say much, for every soul in the village is against him. It's a grand joke," declared Annie, laughing heartily.

Frances smiled. It certainly was funny but she could not help feeling that there might be trouble over it. " He hadn't any right to do it," she pointed out.

" Right!" echoed Annie indignantly. " It wasn't right for Fergus to let his skylight show. Alec says he was a danger to the community—that's what Alec says—and the whole of Cairn is saying the same thing. What's the use of other folk spending good money on great ugly curtains if Fergus lets his skylight

111

blaze like a beacon every night? He'll not do it any more, that's one good thing. We'll be able to sleep in our beds without the fear of getting blown to pieces by a German bomb."

" How is Mrs. Crabbe?" asked Frances.

" She says she's better," replied Annie, " but she's not looking very grand and that's the truth. She's had her breakfast and she's staying in bed. The Major rang up from the camp and I spoke to him myself."

" I hope you didn't frighten him, Annie."

" Not me," she replied. " I said we'd see to her. He's coming over in the afternoon. Here's two letters for you, Miss Field," she added, taking them out of her apron pocket and handing them over.

Frances looked at the letters with interest. One of them was from Dr. Digby and she opened that first. She had been hoping for a letter from the old doctor.

My dear Frances (wrote Dr. Digby),

I am very pleased to hear you are enjoying yourself and meeting some interesting people. I am also pleased to hear that you have decided to take up useful work. You are too modest about your capabilities, for although you cannot drive a car nor use a typewriter, you have had experience in running a large house. I suggest that canteen-work might be suitable. A friend of mine who is the manager of a large munition plant is opening a canteen for his work-people, and is anxious to find a capable woman to take charge of it, to look after the staff and do the catering. I feel sure that you are the right person for the job and have written to tell him so. This does not bind you in any way, of course, but I hope you will consider it. The Jerries were over here last night and were inconsiderate enough to drop an H.E. bomb upon my small establishment. Nobody was hurt, but the house is in a bad way and what is left of it will have to come down. Fortunately I was able to get in touch with your uncle and he has agreed to rent me his house in Wintringham Square. (You will be amused to think of me living in No. 9.) It is too big for an old bachelor, but I am glad to have a roof over my head. I can shut up the top stories, of course. I inquired for Mrs. Wheeler and was glad to hear that she seems a good deal better.

With kindest regards and best wishes.

I remain,

Yours sincerely,

John Digby

There was a great deal to think about in this letter. First, his suggestion that Frances should take charge of a canteen, and second, the information that he was moving into No. 9 Wintringham Square. It was queer to think of Dr. Digby in the old house —queer to think of him moving about familiar rooms and sitting in the easy-chairs. . . . It was a good idea, of course (Frances saw that). The house was better to be let to Dr. Digby than to stand empty or to be taken over for housing purposes, and it would suit Dr. Digby, for it was not far from his own house and would be convenient for his patients. The canteen idea was rather alarming when Frances came to think of it. How could she possibly take over the management of a canteen and do all the catering? She had had no experience of running a canteen. She wouldn't be able to do it properly. She would make a mess of it. Frances took up the letter and read it again. . . . " I feel sure that you are the right person for the job," that was what Dr. Digby had written, and Dr. Digby had always said what he meant. . . . Perhaps, thought Frances doubtfully, perhaps I could do it . . . perhaps I ought to try. . . .

Frances decided to think it over and meanwhile she opened her other letter. It was a short note from Mr. MacDonald asking her to go to tea at the Castle on Tuesday. Frances had been so engrossed in the affairs of her new friends that she had not thought of Mr. MacDonald, but she thought of him now and decided that it would be pleasant to see him again.

It was high time that Frances got up and had her bath, so she bounded out of bed and seized her towel . . . but as she opened the door she heard a man's voice, so she drew back and waited for him to pass. It's Major Crabbe, thought Frances, as she waited with the door slightly ajar. He's come to see Elise. . . .

The voice grew louder, and it was obvious that its owner had paused in the doorway of Elise's room for a few last words. " Good-bye," said the voice. " Take care of yourself. You aren't going to get up to-day, are you? I'll look in to-night and see you again . . . good-bye, darling. . . ."

Frances closed her door as the heavy boots passed and clattered down the stairs. She felt a trifle sick—there was a strange empty feeling within her—for Elise's visitor was not Major Crabbe, it was Guy Tarlatan.

Sitting on her bed with her towel still over her arm and her sponge tightly clasped in her other hand, Frances tried to reason with herself to explain away the facts: they're *friends*, said Frances to herself, they're tremendous friends. They've travelled about all over the world together and shared all sorts of strange

113

experiences . . . so it's quite natural that Guy should be worried about her. They're just friends—that's all—Elise is devoted to her husband. This was perfectly true and was very good reasoning, but it did not convince Frances that there was nothing serious in what she had heard, for although she might explain away the words themselves—these new friends of hers often called each other " darling "—she could not explain away the tender solicitude of the voice. . . .

It was a black day—one of the blackest Frances had known. It was a day of jumbled thoughts and strange discoveries. She had been living on the surface, talking and laughing with her new friends and trying to understand them, and so she had not had time to think of herself or to notice where she was going. Now she looked inward. She mooned about on the foreshore all the afternoon. She sat on the rocks and gazed at the sea. She rose and wandered along the cliff. Cairn looked different to-day: it looked unfriendly and forbidding, the sunshine was not so golden, the colours were less brilliant than before. Her thoughts went round and round and came back to the same place. However hard she tried to get out of the circle, her thoughts brought her back to the same place again.

It was most important that she should give her mind to the consideration of Dr. Digby's letter. She must decide whether or not she should accept the post at the canteen, but no sooner had she begun to think about it seriously, to envisage herself in charge of the canteen, ordering the food and arranging the menus, than her thoughts suddenly whizzed off at a tangent and she found herself thinking of Guy and Elise. Why was she so upset, so knocked off her balance by the discovery she had made? If they were too fond of each other—too fond for ordinary friends—it was their affair and Major Crabbe's, not hers at all. Why was she worrying herself silly over it? . . . Somehow or other Frances had not thought that Guy . . . Frances had thought that Guy . . .

At this point Frances discovered that her eyes were full of tears. She brushed them away angrily. It was absurd to behave like this—quite absurd—Guy was nothing to her, nothing at all . . . he was just a chance acquaintance. There were no distractions at Cairn and so . . . so he had been quite pleased to talk to her . . . and of course she had been quite pleased to talk to him . . . *quite* pleased. She wasn't a romantic young girl who imagined that every man she saw was in love with her. She was a sensible woman of twenty-five.

Frances walked on quickly without the slightest idea where

114

she was going. She had now begun to think of Elise, and of all that Elise had said. . . . She had not understood what Elise meant, but now she was beginning to understand. . . . Elise had been trying to warn her off . . . quite kindly, of course, but still . . .

Frances sat down and stared out to sea . . . the canteen . . . could she do it? She had arranged all the meals at Wintringham Square. She had done the catering, she had chosen meat and vegetables and paid the books. Uncle Henry had often complimented her upon her housekeeping and had told her she had a business head. This being so, perhaps she could run the canteen without getting into a mess. (This was where she and Guy had passed on their way back to the hotel after they had been cut off by the tide. This was the very rock—Frances remembered it— he had held out his hand and helped her down . . . and as they went up the beach they had made a pact together. Guy had smiled at her. " Mum's the word, Frances," he had said.) The canteen . . . could she do it? Should she try? Perhaps she had better sleep on it and write to Dr. Digby to-morrow . . . by that time she might be able to think more clearly. . . .

It was late when Frances got back to the hotel. She pushed open the front door and found herself face to face with Guy. The encounter was so sudden and unexpected that she started back with a gasp.

" Hallo, Frances, did I give you a fright?" he inquired.

" No," said Frances.

" What have you been doing?"

She tried to edge past him. " I've been on the shore," she said.

" I hope you kept an eye on the tide," said Guy in a joky voice.

Frances could not respond. It was difficult to speak at all, and quite impossible to joke with him. " I must go or I shall be late for dinner," she said, making a dash for the stairs.

Afterwards she was annoyed with herself. How much more dignified it would have been if she had carried off the situation with a high hand instead of running away from him like that.

Chapter Seventeen

" DEAR DR. DIGBY," wrote Frances. " It is most awfully good of
you to have found me a job. The only thing is I am not sure that
I could do it properly, for, although I have had considerable
experience in housekeeping, a canteen would be different. I
should not like to accept the post and then find out that I could
not manage it. Do you think your friend could give me some
idea of——"

The door opened and Tommy walked in. " Hallo, Frances!"
she said. " I thought you were dead and buried."

Frances threw down her pen and smiled at Tommy affectionately. She was not sorry to be interrupted in her task, for her
mind was still in considerable confusion. She did not want to
accept the post, and she did not want to refuse it—Tommy's
appearance upon the scene was providential.

" What have you been doing?" continued Tommy somewhat
fretfully. " Why haven't you been to see me? I thought you'd be
sure to come yesterday. . . ."

" Yesterday," said Frances, looking back on her black day.
" Yesterday I was thinking——"

" Come to lunch," said Tommy in more cheerful tones.

" To-day?"

" Yes, of course. I've got a whole bag of herring roes at the
fishmonger's and I'm going to fry them. Do you know, the fish-
woman was actually *throwing them away*."

" Was she?"

" Throwing them away," repeated Tommy in horror-stricken
tones. " She was gouging them out and chucking them into a
pail, so I asked her for some and she gave them to me for
nothing."

" Are they good?" asked Frances.

" They're marvellous—simply marvellous. Come on, Frances,
we'll have coffee and herring roes. It will be a scrumptious
feast."

Frances ought to have refused the invitation and finished her
letter to Dr. Digby, but she was beguiled by Tommy's charm.
She seized her cardigan and slipped it on, and in a few minutes
the two girls were walking along the sands towards Sea View.

" What d'you think of Miss Cole?" asked Tommy suddenly.

" Not much," admitted Frances.

"A minx, my dear," declared Tommy, nodding her head. "A minx—that's what she is. I've told Tillie to get rid of the woman but Tillie won't—or can't."

"How do you mean 'can't'?" asked Frances.

"I suppose I mean she hasn't the guts. She's a 'shall I, shan't I' sort of person, isn't she? Just the sort of person to allow herself to be trampled on by a minx. Miss Cole runs the whole family. I liked her at first."

"She doesn't understand Winkie," Frances said.

Tommy opened the door of the little house and shouted "Ellen!" and Mrs. MacNair appeared from the kitchen with floury hands.

"Ellen, we're having a party," said Tommy. "A luncheon. You know what that means, don't you? A luncheon is much grander than a lunch."

"Yes, Mrs. Widgery," said Ellen, smiling.

Frances had a feeling that Ellen MacNair would have smiled and agreed no matter what Tommy had said. She would have said, "Yes, Mrs. Widgery," to the most extravagant nonsense which Tommy's brain could devise.

"You're making scones," said Tommy, taking off her hat and throwing it on to a chair.

"Just a few," agreed Ellen. "The ones I made yesterday have all gone."

"It's because you make them far too well," explained Tommy seriously. "I mean, they're too good. If only you would make them heavy and doughy—like those I made—they would last far longer and it would be much more economical. My scones lasted nearly a week."

Ellen gave a hoot of laughter and disappeared.

"Now," said Tommy, running her fingers through her hair. "Now then, Frances, I'm going to fry the roes. . . . No, you can't come and help. I don't need help and there isn't room for three women in the kitchen. Are you hungry? I must know definitely because if you're hungry I shall cook all the roes. I'm simply starving."

Frances had not felt inclined for breakfast, but the walk, combined with Tommy's company, had done her good. "Fairly hungry," she replied after a moment's thought.

"Good," said Tommy. "I'll cook the lot. . . . Here's my book of horrors. You can have a look at it while you're waiting."

The book of horrors, to which Tommy referred, and which she now produced from the bottom shelf of the bookcase, was a large sketch-book held together by an elastic band. It was full of

117

hastily sketched portraits of Tommy's friends and acquaintances. Frances had heard of Tommy's malicious pencil and now she was to see the fruits of it. She turned over the pages of the book with interest and amusement. The portraits were small, sometimes there were three or four on the same page, and a great many of them were sketches of people that Frances had never seen—people that Tommy had encountered during her travels—but each little portrait had so much character and personality that Frances was sure the likeness must be good. Here and there she found a face that she knew, and these she looked at with especial interest—Tillie and Jack Liston, Angela Thynne, Tommy's own heart-shaped face with its small pugnacious nose, the two young subalterns, Mark and Barry, whom Frances had met the last time she was here. She decided that the sketches were neither true portraits nor caricatures, but were somewhere between the two—just where depended upon the artist's feelings. For instance, Mark's portrait was practically true, and Angela's was to all intents and purposes a caricature. Frances turned over the page and her heart gave a leap . . . this was Guy Tarlatan, of course. His thin face was just a trifle leaner here than it was in real life and his firm chin a trifle more pronounced. Tommy had caught the tilt of his head, the half-serious, half-mocking look in his eye . . . it was one of the best portraits in the book. Just opposite Guy was Elise—which was strangely significant—and her portrait was good too.

Frances looked from one to the other and suddenly it struck her that the faces were alike: they were much the same shape and their expressions were almost identical. She was so surprised to find this likeness that she pointed it out to Tommy, who had just appeared with a tray of cutlery and was scattering knives and forks about the table.

" Yes, of course, brothers and sisters are often alike," said Tommy, and vanished before Frances had found words to express her astonishment.

Brother and sister, thought Frances—brother and sister! She was so overwhelmed by this sudden revelation that for a moment she felt quite faint. The room spun round uncomfortably and the book slid on to the floor. What a fool she had been! What an idiot to worry herself silly! Why hadn't she thought of this explanation? She saw at once that it explained everything—that it was a full and perfect solution to the problem of Guy and Elise. Frances felt better now; she picked up the book and looked at the portraits again. They were very much alike, they were so alike that their relationship was obvious to the most casual glance. Why hadn't she noticed it before? The answer was that the likeness between Guy and Elise was much more apparent in the sketches than it was in real life, for the likeness lay in the bony structure of their faces and the unlikeness lay in their colouring and in the texture of their skins. Guy was fair and Elise was dark; Guy's face was ruddy and tanned and weather-beaten, and Elise had a smooth, pale, delicate complexion . . . these differences had acted as a disguise.

Frances had got thus far in her reflections when Tommy emerged from the kitchen with a rack of toast. " National bread," she said as she put it on the table. " It makes lovely toast. I hope we'll go on having it after the war."

" I didn't know they were brother and sister," Frances said.

" Guy and Elise? I thought everyone knew—but I keep on forgetting you're such a recent acquisition. Colonel Tarlatan commanded the regiment. There have always been Tarlatans in the Green Buzzards."

" So she was the Colonel's daughter! "

" Yes, of course. She came out to India when she was seventeen and all the subalterns fell in love with her. She was perfectly lovely, of course."

" She still is," said Frances thoughtfully. " Don't you think so?" but Tommy had vanished again so the question remained unanswered.

" What's happened?" said Tommy when they had settled down to their meal and the herring roes were disappearing like melting snow.

" What's happened?" repeated Frances in some bewilderment.

Tommy nodded. " That's what I said—*what's happened*? I thought you were a bit under the weather this morning, but now you're on top of the world. You needn't tell me unless you want to."

" I don't think I can," replied Frances, smiling. " I mean— I think—I think I'd rather not. . . . You know, Tommy, your drawings are simply marvellous. You ought to take it up seriously and make something out of it. Why don't you?"

" Because I'm me," said Tommy promptly. " I can do things in a hurry when I feel in the mood; I can make a rough sketch and it's like the person, but if I try to tidy it up it loses all its sting. It's the same with hats——"

" The same with *hats*!" echoed Frances.

" Yes, I can make a frightfully *chic* hat with some bits of ribbon and a few pins, but, when I take the pins out and start sewing it, the whole thing becomes a mess."

119

" But, Tommy——"

" I know," nodded Tommy gravely. " I know it's a dreadful confession, but unfortunately that's how I'm made. I'm awfully good at starting things but I'm a bad finisher. Perhaps if I had learnt to draw—or to make hats—it would have been different. I've never had any discipline, you see. I've always galloped along through life and done what I wanted when I wanted to do it. I've had some nasty falls, but they haven't taught me much. I just picked myself up and galloped on."

" You're brave," said Frances impulsively.

" Not brave, just headstrong," declared Tommy with a grin. " My mother would tell you that . . . it's a pity you can't meet my mother ; she would like you."

" Where does she live?" asked Frances.

" She lives near Aberdeen—it's our old home, you see. She hasn't been very well lately," added Tommy with a frown. " She wants me to go and see her, but the fact is I hate leaving Midge . . . and I couldn't take him, even if he could get leave, because he and Mother don't understand each other."

Frances made sympathetic sounds—it was difficult to know what to say.

" Yes," agreed Tommy. " Yes, it's very unfortunate. Mother is quite horrid to poor Midge sometimes, and of course he feels it because he is so sensitive."

" Have you done your mother's portrait?" asked Frances, who was anxious to change the subject.

" No," replied Tommy. " She's difficult—have you seen your own? . . . Oh, yes, you're in the book of horrors. I don't need to have people in front of me to draw them ; in fact I can do it better from memory."

Frances took the book off the chair and turned over the pages hastily ; she was anxious to see what Tommy thought of her . . . here she was, here at the end, on the same page as Ellen MacNair —an excellent likeness this.

" Well, how do you like it?" asked Tommy after a moment's silence.

Frances liked it immensely. " I didn't know I was so nice-looking," she declared.

" I thought it good," said the artist, leaning over the table and glancing at the sketch. " I've managed to get that wondering sort of look—that slightly blank expression you sometimes wear . . . it's as if you didn't quite know what you were going to meet round the next corner."

120

Frances laughed. "How can anyone know that?" she inquired.

"Some people know—or think they know," replied Tommy quite gravely. "I don't mean people who have second sight. Take Tillie, for instance, she knows quite well that there are going to be misfortunes round the next corner—and of course there are. Tillie is one of the most unfortunate people on earth. . . . Angela knows there will be men," added Tommy vindictively.

"I thought you liked her," Frances said.

"I used to like her, but she's got terribly spoilt. I hope Guy won't marry her."

"Guy?"

"He's taken a good deal of interest in Angela lately," said Tommy in a thoughtful voice.

Frances smiled to herself. She was not afraid of Angela. A natural sequence of thought led her back to Elise. "What about Elise?" she asked. "Does Elise know what's waiting for her round the next corner?"

Tommy hesitated and then said: "Elise knows a lot. I think Elise is prepared for anything she may meet—good or bad. I wish I were more like Elise."

They had finished their meal; Frances had moved into a comfortable chair and Tommy had taken up her favourite position on the hearthrug. Frances looked round the room and thought again how nice Tommy had made it.

"That's new," said Tommy, pointing to a large square footstool covered with green plush to match the carpet. "I saw it in Rithie the other day and I just had to buy it. Midge said it was awfully extravagant of me—he said it was quite useless—but I liked it so much that I couldn't resist it. . . ."

Frances liked it too. She liked it all the more because Captain Widgery disliked it. "Clever of you to remember the exact shade," she said.

"It *does* match nicely, doesn't it?" agreed Tommy. "Midge says it matches *too* well. He says someone will take a header over it some day—that's why I put it under the table."

Having exhausted the subject of the footstool, Frances and Tommy went on to chat of other matters. Tommy spoke of her home at Aberdeen and of her brother who was somewhere in the Middle East.

"He may be anywhere," Tommy declared. "We haven't had a letter from him for months. Mother got a cable from him the other day, but it didn't comfort her very much. She sent it to me to read."

"Didn't the cable say where he was?"

"No, of course not," replied Tommy, shaking her head and smiling. "The cable said ' WELL UP WITH HOUNDS ' and nothing else. He may be in Abyssinia, chasing the Italians, or he may be at Tobruk. . . . I hope he isn't in Greece, poor darling."

They were silent for a few moments, and then Tommy sat up and listened with her head on one side. "It's Midge," she said in a low voice. "It's Midge—I wonder—this isn't his usual time——"

Frances had heard nothing, but now, by straining her ears, she heard footsteps approaching the house. . . . It was odd that Tommy had heard those footsteps so long before she had; it was even more odd that Tommy had known for certain whose footsteps they were. Tommy was sitting erect upon the hearthrug now; she reminded Frances of a terrier with its ears cocked, a terrier listening for the approach of its master—or its god. Suddenly Frances felt that she could not face Captain Widgery, and she rose and said she must go.

"But you can't!" said Tommy quickly. "I mean——"

It was quite obvious what she meant. There was only one door to the house, so unless Frances intended to climb out of the window there was no way of avoiding her host. She could easily climb out of the window, but convention forbade this mode of exit—convention and something more. It would be a confession that she did not want to meet him, that she was afraid of him—she *was* afraid of him, of course.

The door opened and Captain Widgery appeared. He burst in, and the wind, bursting in with him, filled the room with air. The curtains flew out through the open windows and fluttered wildly as if they—like Frances—were anxious to escape.

"Hallo, Miss Field!" exclaimed Captain Widgery in quite a cheerful tone. "Hallo, Tommy—some day this house will be blown out to sea."

"Oh, Midge, have you got leave?" asked Tommy eagerly.

"Instead of Saturday," he replied. "Saturday is going to be a great day—a field day. We're supposed to manœuvre on the hills with the Home Guard." He laughed, and added: "The Home Guard! I ask you! A collection of bootmakers and bakers, most of them in their dotage!"

In spite of his derogatory words Frances received a distinct impression that he was pleased at the prospect . . . she was to remember this impression later.

" Oh, Midge—*Saturday*!" exclaimed Tommy in consternation.

" Yes, it's a blue-pencil nuisance," said Captain Widgery. " No chance of running over to Rithie and seeing a film. We shall be out all night, I'm afraid."

" All night!" repeated Tommy.

He nodded. " It's a nice prospect, isn't it? Perhaps you'd like to spend the night at the hotel. You might be a bit lonely here all by yourself."

After some discussion it was arranged that Tommy should walk over to the Bordale Arms and have dinner with Frances. " We'll ask Guy," said Tommy, brightening a little at the prospect of a party.

Her husband laughed shortly. " You'll ask Guy, will you?" he said. " Perhaps you've forgotten that Guy happens to be a member of the battalion, and the battalion happens to be manœuvring on the hills with the rag-tag and bobtail of Cairn."

" Oh, how silly of me!" Tommy said.

Frances hated to see the hurt look on Tommy's face. She burnt with rage . . . he was cruel . . . he enjoyed being cruel to Tommy.

Chapter Eighteen

THIS WAS the day upon which Frances had been invited to take tea at the Castle, and, as always, there were half a dozen people ready and willing to advise her how to attain her objective. Mrs. MacNair told her that she must go up the road towards Rithie for about half a mile and she would see the Castle gates on her left just before she got to the foot of the brae, but Mr. MacNair, appearing from the bar in his shirt-sleeves, declared that she would be better to take the path along the top of the cliff and go up past St. Kiaran's Spring. Annie, coming downstairs while the argument was in progress, joined in it with gusto ; and Alec, who had been washing a car in the yard, leaned his elbows on the window-sill and gave his opinion in his usual forceful way.

" Miss Field could go up through the fields and past the home farm," declared Alec. " That is the shortest way of all——"

" But she would never find it," put in Annie firmly.

" She would find it easily——"

" She would not."

" The road would be the best," said Mrs. MacNair. " She is

123

wearing her good shoes, she will not want to go ploughing through fields in them."

"There is quite a good path," Alec pointed out.

"But she'll not find it," Annie declared.

"You will put on your coat, Alec," said Mr. MacNair at last, "and you will go with Miss Field, yourself, and put her on the right road. It would be a nice thing if Miss Field was late for tea at the Castle!"

". . . and you will take Shiela with you," added Mrs. MacNair. "It will be a nice walk for Shiela over the fields."

The oracle having spoken, everyone disappeared and for once the hall was empty. Frances, who was neatly dressed for her tea-party in a tweed coat and skirt and a blue felt hat, went out and sat down on the seat outside the front door. It was half-past three by now, so there was not much time—she wondered how long Alec and Shiela would take to titivate. Although Mr. MacNair had registered horror at the idea of Miss Field being late for tea at the Castle, Frances was aware that none of the MacNair family was a slave to time. Meals were often late and sometimes early, and every clock in the Bordale Arms jogged along at its own sweet will . . . but Alec did not keep her waiting long; he came round the corner of the house struggling into his jacket, and with him came an enormous bobtailed sheep-dog which leaped upon him from all directions and bounded between his legs, nearly tripping him up. The dog was so large and shaggy that it reminded Frances of the overgrown puppy which had tried to play with Alice in Wonderland.

"Down, Shiela," cried Alec, pushing it away with his hand. "Quiet, Shiela . . . down, Shiela . . . yes, we are going for a walk. . . ."

"So that's Shiela!" exclaimed Frances, and she burst out laughing.

Alec looked at her in surprise. "Have you not seen Shiela?" he inquired. "Och, that is a queer thing . . . she is usually all over the place and there is no holding her at all. It is because of the puppies that you have not seen her. Shiela is a very good mother and she will not leave the puppies for long . . . but it is nice for her to have a walk now and then—so it is."

The walk through the fields was very pleasant and Alec was an interesting companion with plenty to say for himself. When he had pointed out the different farms—or crofts—and told her their names, and had introduced her to the snowy peaks in the distant range of mountains, Alec began to talk about the Home Guard and to wax enthusiastic upon the subject. "There's to be an

124

exercise on Saturday night," said Alec. "It is not the first we have had by any means but it will be a very special one, for the soldiers are going to take part in it—maybe you will have heard about it, Miss Field?"

Frances admitted that she had heard something about it from Captain Widgery.

"Is that so?" said Alec with interest. "He was talking about it, was he? He wouldn't have mentioned what the soldiers were going to do? He wouldn't have told you that?"

"No, he didn't," replied Frances.

"I was afraid he wouldn't," declared Alec with a sigh. "We'll just need to wait until Mr. MacDonald has seen the Colonel. Och, it will be a fine show. Some of the soldiers will pretend that they are the enemy—that is the idea—and we shall be hunting them over the hills. It is a pity you could not come out and see the fun." They had reached a gate by now and Alec opened it. "There is no need for me to come any farther," he said. "That is the farm over there—it is Mr. MacDonald's own farm—and when you have walked past the steading you will see the big gates with the MacDonald crest on them. It is only a quarter of a mile to the Castle, so you will be in good time for tea. It is a fine place. I am glad you are to see it."

Frances thanked him and said good-bye and walked on. Presently she turned and saw that Alec was still standing at the gate with Shiela beside him. She waved and Alec waved back.

Castle Cairn was somewhat surprising to anyone who expected to see a moated keep or an ivied tower, and Frances, as she turned a bend in the avenue and came upon it unawares, was greatly disappointed. It was a large house—not a castle at all —a large square, solid house with shining windows and well-kept paintwork. There was no reason why Frances should have expected anything different (except that she had been steeping herself in the Waverley Novels for the last ten days), and as a matter of fact until she saw the mansion she had not known what she expected to see . . . she knew now that she had expected to see Ellangowan Castle. It was so absurd that she laughed off her disappointment and, approaching over the neatly gravelled drive, she put out her hand and pressed the electric bell.

It was a cold day with a biting wind, but inside the house it was warm and comfortable. The carpets were thick and the curtains were draught-proof and there was central heating in the rooms besides large fires. Frances noted all this as she followed the old butler across the hall and into a large comfortably furnished morning-room; she noted the shine on the wood, the twinkle of the brasses. Having struggled with a large house herself, she was aware of the work entailed to keep everything in such perfect order, and she decided that Mr. MacDonald's housekeeper must be a capable person.

Mr. MacDonald was sitting in a large arm-chair by the fire. He rose and welcomed her warmly and declared that it was very good of her to waive ceremony and come to tea. "My cousin has been ill," he explained. "I meant her to call on you in the correct manner, but she has not been allowed out of the house and I wanted you to come. I was afraid that if I waited any longer you would have forgotten all about me."

Frances felt a little shy. She said somewhat awkwardly: "Oh no, of course not."

"My cousin keeps house for me," continued Mr. MacDonald. "She has done so since my wife died. It is good of her, because I am afraid she finds Castle Cairn very dull. Come and sit down, Miss Field."

Frances sat down. She said: "I thought it would be old."

"Old?" he repeated in surprise. "Oh, you mean the Castle! The old Castle was burnt down about a hundred years ago and my grandfather built this somewhat unimaginative but extremely comfortable residence in its place. You are not by any means the first person to be disappointed in Castle Cairn."

"It was just that I expected something different," declared Frances hastily.

"Cairn has suffered another invasion since I saw you last," said Mr. MacDonald, sitting down in the other chair and smiling at her. "A more pleasant invasion than that which took place in A.D. 700, and this time from the south."

"Yes," agreed Frances. "There are soldiers everywhere. I expect it seems odd to you to see them here."

"Very odd indeed," he replied. "It is strange to see them but even stranger to hear them talking. When one arrives at Euston one is prepared to hear Cockney spoken on every side, but to hear it in the wilds of Scotland is the strangest experience of all. . . . Oh, here is my cousin to tell us that tea is ready. May I introduce Miss Stalker, Miss Field."

They had tea in the big dining-room on the other side of the house. There were scones and sandwiches and home-made plum cake laid out upon the huge mahogany table.

"It's dreadful," declared Miss Stalker as they sat down, "it's simply dreadful not to be able to give people a decent tea."

"It's a lovely tea," said Frances.

126

"It wouldn't look so skimpy if you gave it to us on a smaller table," said Mr. MacDonald.

"We've always had it on the dining-room table," exclaimed Miss Stalker.

Mr. MacDonald smiled. "My cousin is conservative," he said.

"Of course I am," said Miss Stalker promptly. "My father was a conservative so I couldn't be anything else—not that I ever wanted to be anything else, of course." She sighed and added: "We used to have several kinds of cakes, and cream cookies and chocolate biscuits—I'm sure I don't know what Miss Field will think."

"Miss Field is no doubt aware of the fact that we are at war," said Mr. MacDonald gravely.

"Well, of course," said Miss Stalker in surprise. "Everyone knows that, but it seems so dreadful when people come to tea and you can't give them cakes or jam. I don't know what we're coming to, I'm sure. Half a pound of jam a month!"

Miss Stalker was a small woman with a large nose and thick black eyebrows—it was her nose and eyebrows that you saw first—the rest of Miss Stalker seemed to be attached to these striking features. After having apologised for the absence of proper food she busied herself pouring out the tea and said no more; perhaps this was just as well, for in a few words she had shown herself deficient in sense and humour. Mr. MacDonald enjoyed talking and Frances was a good listener, so before they were half-way through the meal she had learnt a great deal more about the history of Cairn.

Suddenly the door opened and Captain Tarlatan was announced. He looked surprised when he saw Frances sitting there, and she was equally surprised to see him. She was also a trifle embarrassed, for, since she had seen him last, she had thought of him so much and with such varying emotions. She felt a hot blush mounting in her cheeks, and the fact that she was annoyed with herself for this show of feeling did not help matters. Fortunately Captain Tarlatan was talking to his host, explaining that he had come on business and suggesting that he should wait until Mr. MacDonald was disengaged.

"Nonsense," said Mr. MacDonald firmly. "You will just sit down and have a cup of tea with us. It's a great pleasure to see you. The business can wait unless it is very important—there is nothing wrong, I hope."

"Oh no," replied Guy, sitting down and accepting a cup of tea from Miss Stalker. "There's nothing wrong. It's a splendid place for a camp; we're delighted with it. Colonel Thynne asked me to thank you very much indeed for all the trouble you have taken. He just wants to know if we may make another opening on to the road. It would be a great convenience to have another gate for the lorries, but I'm afraid it will mean cutting down a piece of the hedge."

"Of course," said Mr. MacDonald. "Of course—I'll send a man to do it to-morrow."

"We'll do it ourselves, sir," replied Guy. "There's no need for you to bother. We didn't want to do it without permission, that's all."

"And what about this exercise on Saturday?" asked Mr. MacDonald. "Have you thought out the details? I want it to be a good test for the Home Guard, not just a picnic."

"Oh, yes, that was another thing," said Guy. "I'm afraid we can't manage it this Saturday—we've just heard that we're being inspected—but Colonel Thynne said I was to ask if you could fix another day."

"Any Saturday will do," Mr. MacDonald replied. "It's exceedingly good of you to help us—just let me know when you can manage it."

"We'll let you know," said Guy. "We'll think up something pretty hot. I'm afraid it may disturb the game a bit—but—well, I'm afraid that can't be helped."

Mr. MacDonald sighed. He said: "I hate the birds to be disturbed, but, as you say, it can't be helped. Perhaps you could warn your men to be as careful as possible. The local people know to be careful."

"I'll warn them, sir," Guy promised.

Frances was trying to talk to Miss Stalker but it was uphill work, for Miss Stalker made no attempt to meet her half-way. She tried household subjects and inquired whether Miss Stalker was able to save sugar for jam-making, but even this failed to lure Miss Stalker out of her shell, so after a few minutes Frances abandoned her to her fate and lent an ear to the other conversation.

". . . but even before the war started we had been living on our capital for years," Mr. MacDonald was saying earnestly.

"I've heard it said before," admitted Guy. "But I'm no economist, I'm afraid."

"It is quite easy to understand," Mr. MacDonald replied. "You know what happens when a man starts to spend his capital, and the same thing is bound to happen when a government starts spending a nation's wealth. Death duties and suc-

128

cession duties are capital, but the Government has been spending the proceeds as if they were income. It would not be so bad if the Government raked in the money and invested it and spent the income—but that does not seem to have occurred to them. It does not require an economist to realise that a nation's wealth lies in the wealth of her citizens. Moneyed people are an asset to a nation, paupers are a liability. Take a man with an income of ten thousand a year, he is a valuable asset. The State can depend upon him for a definite yearly income. Then the man dies and the property—instead of passing to his son and continuing to yield the same yearly income to the State—has to be broken up and sold to pay death duties."

" I see," said Guy, nodding.

" You see," continued Mr. MacDonald, " every time a big estate is sold up it is a national investment sold out. No more yearly income will accrue from it to the State. It means that the Government has killed one of its geese, so *that* goose cannot lay any more golden eggs. In the last fifteen years or so the Government has killed off dozens of geese . . . soon there will be no more geese left, and therefore no more golden eggs."

" It seems very short-sighted," said Guy thoughtfully.

" It is short-sighted," replied Mr. MacDonald. " We have been suffering from short-sighted politicians for years. This dreadful war is due to myopia on the part of our politicians——"

" That's true ! " exclaimed Guy.

Mr. MacDonald smiled. " They wouldn't see and they wouldn't listen," he declared. " They never listen to people who try to tell them unpalatable truths. Lord Roberts warned them before the last war and they said he was in his dotage. Winston Churchill, Roger Keyes, Neville Henderson and half a dozen others warned them that Germany was on the warpath again, and all they did was to disarm faster and break up our battleships for scrap. . . . I don't know whether you have noticed," continued Mr. MacDonald, " it is rather an extraordinary thing; Churchill has never once said, ' I told you so,' or, ' If you had only listened to me,' He is a big man, there is no doubt of that,"

Chapter Nineteen

AFTER A little more conversation Mr. MacDonald rose and led the way to his study. It was a real "man's room" furnished with deep leather chairs and a large roll-top desk covered with books and papers. On the walls there were prints and maps and some good engravings.

Frances and Guy looked round the room with interest, and Guy pointed to the picture of a ship which seemed to be sailing across the land. "Is that a Viking ship?" he inquired.

"It is a fairly accurate drawing of a Norse galley," replied his host. "You can see the pointed prow and stern raised high above the deck, the single mast, the rigging of furled shrouds and stays——"

"But why is it sailing across the land?" asked Guy.

"Thereby hangs a tale—and rather a curious one," said Mr. MacDonald, smiling. "I can see that Miss Field is anxious to hear it."

"Of course I am!" cried Frances.

Mr. MacDonald began his story without more ado. "In the last years of the eleventh century there was a Scottish king called Malcolm Canmore. His wife was the saintly Margaret whose chapel can still be seen at Edinburgh Castle. Malcolm made a pact with Magnus Barefoot, a Norwegian king, and in this pact Magnus was given sovereignty over all the islands which lie off the west coast of Scotland. Some of our islands are scarcely separated from the mainland and others are separated from the mainland only at high tide, so to make the matter perfectly clear it was agreed that Magnus Barefoot was to have all land round which a helm-carrying ship could pass, and that he was to take possession by rowing round the islands. Magnus brought his ships round the south of Kintyre—or Satiri as it was called in those days—and as he rowed along he saw that the country was fertile and beautiful. Unfortunately for him, however, Kintyre is part of the mainland of Scotland—it is joined to the mainland by a narrow ridge of high ground between two arms of the sea—so Magnus could not sail his helm-carrying ship round Kintyre."

"I'm beginning to understand," declared Guy.

"Yes," agreed Mr. MacDonald. "You can see how his mind worked, can't you? Magnus wanted Kintyre and Magnus intended to have it, so he sat in his ship and had it drawn across the ridge of ground—just as you see in the picture. Wait a moment and I will read you the description." . . . Mr. MacDonald rummaged about amongst a heap of untidy papers and after some difficulty he found the passage to which he had referred. He cleared his throat and read: "'Magnus Barefoot had a small ship drawn across the ridge and the helm laid across in its proper form. The King sat in the poop and took hold of the helm-ball; and thus he got possession of all the country lying on the larboard side.' . . . It goes on to describe the scene in detail and says that Magnus wore a helmet of flashing gold and carried a red shield emblazoned with a golden lion; the hilt of his sword was of ivory inlaid with gold, and over his coat of mail he wore a short silken tunic of ruby."

"What an amazing spectacle it must have been!" exclaimed Guy.

"Yes," agreed Mr. MacDonald. "One can imagine the poor ignorant peasants standing by and watching the proceedings—wondering what on earth Magnus was doing."

"Sharp practice, wasn't it?" said Guy thoughtfully. "D'you think our friend Adolf is descended from Magnus Barefoot? He seems to have the same mentality——"

"Oh *no*!" cried Frances. "Hitler is worse. Of course it was a dreadful thing for Magnus to do but, after all, he took the trouble to keep to the letter of his pact. I've often thought that the worst thing about Hitler is that he has no sense of shame."

Mr. MacDonald nodded. "Yes, that is the very worst thing about him."

Guy was looking out of the window now. He pointed to a heap of ruins which showed between the trees. "Is that a chapel?" he inquired.

"Those are the ruins of the old Castle," Mr. MacDonald replied. "Many of the stones have been removed but I have put a stop to that."

"I suppose your family has lived here for hundreds of years."

"Yes, I am trying to write a short history of my branch of the family—just for my own satisfaction—but the fact is, I have got my notes into such a muddle that it has given me a distaste for the job. I wish I could find somebody with an orderly mind to help me with them, to docket them in chronological order——"

"Would I be any use?" asked Frances on a sudden impulse.

At first Mr. MacDonald refused to listen to the suggestion, but after some argument Frances managed to convince him that she would enjoy the work, and a day was fixed for her to come up to the Castle and go through the notes.

During this discussion Guy stood at the window with his hands clasped behind his back. His attitude was one of disapproval, but it was not until they had taken leave of their host and were walking home together that the reason for his disapproval became apparent.

"Why on earth did you offer to go and help him?" asked Guy.

"Why!" echoed Frances in surprise. "Because he wanted someone——"

"Let him find someone else."

"He can't," replied Frances in reasoning tones. "He can't find anyone to help him—besides, it would be rather interesting work."

"You had better be careful, Frances."

"Careful?"

"Yes, he likes you quite a lot."

"Likes me?"

"He's in love with you," said Guy bluntly.

Frances exclaimed in surprise. "Oh no," she cried. "Oh, what nonsense! He's quite old——"

They were walking back through the woods but now they stopped suddenly and by one accord. "What nonsense!" repeated Frances.

"Don't go," said Guy. "I don't want you to go, Frances."

Her heart was beating uncomfortably fast but she managed to laugh a trifle breathlessly. "I must go," she said. "I've promised——"

"I've warned you," declared Guy. "Perhaps you don't want to be warned. Perhaps you would enjoy being the chatelaine of Cairn Castle. He's got plenty of money, of course. You heard what he said about income-tax and death duties, so——"

"I think this is an extremely foolish conversation," said Frances firmly.

They walked on in silence, and Frances noted that her companion's brows were knit in a scowl of rage. She was not angry, but was amused and touched at his efforts to shield her . . . as if she could not look after herself! She was surprised, she was even rather pleased to find that she could annoy Guy so easily, that she could so easily produce that terrible frown; he was usually so much master of himself and of the situation.

By this time they had reached St. Kiaran's Chapel. It looked different to-day, for there was a cloud over the sun; it looked sad and deserted, but the spring still bubbled out of the hillside and trickled past the ruined door just as Frances remembered. As they were not on speaking terms at the moment, Frances forbore to acquaint her companion with the history of the place and led the way across the little clearing with a light step; but Guy, instead of following her, knelt down beside the spring and, cupping his hands, took a long drink of the sparkling water. Frances hesitated and came back. She watched him without speaking.

"What are you smiling at?" he inquired somewhat crossly.

"It's magic water," said Frances mischievously.

"What do you mean?" asked Guy.

"It's magic water," she repeated, trying not to laugh. "Mr. MacDonald told me all about it. This is St. Kiaran's Spring. Anyone who drinks this water will be married within a year."

Guy rose and wiped his mouth. "What nonsense!" he said.

"Yes, isn't it?" agreed Frances. "Absolute rubbish. Nobody believes in magic springs now—except the villagers, of course."

"Why don't you have a drink?"

"I'm not thirsty," she replied.

"I don't believe in magic water," declared Guy.

"No," agreed Frances. "No, of course not. We've agreed that it's nonsense, haven't we?"

Guy hesitated and then he said: "It's beautiful water. There's a queer sort of smoky taste about it. Why don't you try it?"

Frances laughed and shook her head; they walked on.

Suddenly Guy laughed. He said: "Don't let's quarrel, Frances."

"No, don't let's," she agreed, looking up at him and smiling with her eyes. "I should hate to quarrel with you—seriously, I mean."

"You aren't angry with me for saying that about old MacDonald?"

"It's nice of you to take an interest in me," she replied.

"Yes, isn't it?" he agreed.

She looked up at him again to see if he were joking, but his face was perfectly grave.

"I don't know whether you have noticed," continued Guy with a serious air. "I don't know whether you have realised what an extremely altruistic person I am. I have always been renowned for the way in which I sacrifice my own interests to the interests of my friends. For instance, when I was six years old I was very ill after eating a whole box of chocolates which belonged to my sister—I did it merely to save her from a similar fate."

"How absurd you are!" exclaimed Frances, laughing.

He heaved an extravagant sigh and replied: "But I hide a tender heart beneath my motley."

"A perfect example of double bluff," she retorted.

There was another silence and then Guy said in quite a different voice: "You are a most extraordinary girl——"

The woods were darker than ever to-day, not only because of the absence of sunlight but also because the deciduous trees were beginning to bud, to open pale-green leaves in the still air, but Frances did not notice the loneliness of the woods nor think of the people who had trodden this path so long ago on their way to see the saint; she had found before that it was impossible to talk to Guy Tarlatan without giving him the whole of her attention—even then it was difficult.

"Why am I extraordinary?" she asked, turning her head to speak to him, for the path was so steep and narrow that they were obliged to go single file. "You're always surprised when I say anything that isn't completely silly—you seem to have formed a low opinion of me."

"I haven't formed any opinion of you at all," he declared, "or perhaps it would be more truthful to say that I keep on changing my opinion every few moments. Just when I think I've got your measure you say something that doesn't fit—it's most unsettling. There's only one thing that I'm certain of . . . Frances, wait a moment. Let's sit down here on this fallen tree. I want to talk to you."

"You've been talking to me all the afternoon," replied Frances, hastening on.

"Frances——"

"Yes?"

"Why wouldn't you drink that water? It was awfully mean of you."

"Was it?"

"Yes; you let me drink it and then you wouldn't drink it yourself. I believe it's poisoned—why are you in such a hurry?"

"It's as pure as any water can be," replied Frances without turning round. "That's what Mr. MacDonald said."

"Oh, is it? I suppose you drank some—you and he together."

"No," said Frances.

They had reached the place where the burn poured itself into the sea, but the tide was out to-day, so instead of leaping straight into the sea with gay abandon it meandered across the beach and between the rocks. There were buds on the bushes now, and the larches, which had looked so dead, were veiled in a haze of green. There were a few primroses in the hollow beside the rock where Frances had frightened herself by picturing the tall figure of a Viking with golden hair and golden armlets.

134

"What a lovely place!" exclaimed Guy. "What a lovely, lovely place. Do you know what it's called, Frances?"

"St. Kiaran's Cove," she replied.

"St. Kiaran's Cove," repeated Guy; he hesitated and then added: "It's a natural harbour, isn't it?"

Frances saw what he meant. The spit of red rocks was like a jetty stretching out into the sea, sheltering the little bay. She thought again of the Viking ship, the ship full of golden-haired warriors, stealing in between the rocks with muffled oars. She imagined the tall figures stepping ashore and kneeling to drink at the burn. "Yes," said Frances; "I thought so when I was here before. I thought it would be a good place to land. In fact, I imagined that I saw——"

At this moment, before Frances had time to finish her sentence or Guy had time to ask her what she meant, they heard the sound of voices and the clatter of footsteps on the stones.

"Wait," said Guy, putting out his hand, but Frances did not want to wait. Frances was quite glad that her *tête-à-tête* with Guy had come to an end. She turned the corner of a big rock with Guy at her heels and found Major and Mrs. Crabbe on the beach; Major Crabbe, large and massive in his khaki uniform, and Elise, tall and willowy in a tweed coat and skirt. Frances was surprised to see them, for Elise was not the sort of person who enjoyed puddling about. Her shoes were unsuitable for walking in the sand, or for climbing amongst the rocks—Elise was essentially a townswoman—but here they were, and Frances reflected that their presence was probably due to the fact that Cairn offered very few distractions to its inhabitants. Major Crabbe was engaged in the ancient pastime of ducks and drakes (which, as everyone knows, consists of throwing flat stones in such a manner that they will hop upon the surface of the water), and Elise was aiding and abetting him by searching for suitable ammunition amongst the shingle. She looked up and saw Guy and Frances and waved her hand.

"Hallo!" she cried. "Where have you been? Come and play with Ned."

"Come on!" cried Major Crabbe. "Come on, Guy. I bet you can't beat my record—five hops—I'll take you on for half a crown."

"Damn!" said Guy below his breath, but he went down to meet them and Frances followed him.

Chapter Twenty

THE NEXT excitement at the Bordale Arms was the advent of Jennifer Crabbe. She arrived in a large car (with a good deal of luggage) and was carried into the hotel in the arms of her nurse. The hall was suddenly full of people who had heard the car drive up and wanted to see what was happening, but, far from being embarrassed at the crowd of strangers, Jennifer seemed delighted to see them and charmed with their attentions. She smiled at everyone and waved her hand in a queenly manner—there was something in the scene which reminded Frances of the arrival of Royalty.

"The wee lamb!" exclaimed Mrs. MacNair. "She has her mother's eyes."

She had her mother's elegance too—or so Frances thought. Frances had heard of Jennifer Crabbe from Winkie, but, even so, she was not prepared to see anyone so beautiful, so finished, so full of charm and personality.

Somehow or other the mere fact of Jennifer's presence in the hotel made a difference in the atmosphere of the place. The hotel felt more home-like, more friendly. Everyone in the house fell a victim to her charm and talked about her and boasted of her smiles. Frances made friends with Jennifer's nurse—a pleasant-faced elderly woman—and was therefore free to peep into the nursery when she felt inclined. She peeped in quite often and saw Jennifer having her supper, or Jennifer asleep in bed. She was invited to come into the bathroom and saw Jennifer having her bath.

It was amusing to see Elise with the baby. Elise tried so hard to be sensible and to disguise her pride in her daughter's beauty and charm. Major Crabbe made no attempt to disguise his feelings; his adoration of Jennifer was open and unashamed.

The day after Jennifer's arrival Winkie appeared and announced that he had come to see her, so Elise asked him to stay to tea. The nurse had gone out for a walk, and Frances and Elise and the two children had tea together in the dining-room. Jennifer ate her tea daintily. Occasionally she took part in the conversation.

"I'm going to marry her," said Winkie, looking at her with adoring eyes.

"Are you?" inquired Elise.

136

"You don't mind, do you, Mrs. Crabbe?" asked Winkie gravely.

"That depends," she replied with equal gravity. "It depends what sort of person you are when you grow up, and what you're going to be. I want Jennifer to marry a banker."

Frances was amused. She said: "Why a banker, Elise? Why not a peer of the realm?"

"Because I'm like Robinson Crusoe's father," replied Elise promptly. "I believe that the middle state of man—or woman— is the happiest and I want Jennifer to be happy. I don't want riches or high places for Jennifer, I just want happiness, that's all. A banker is settled and secure——"

"What is a banker?" asked Winkie. "How does a person begin to be a banker?"

Elise looked at her prospective son-in-law and smiled affectionately. "I thought you were going to be a soldier," she said.

"Well, I *did* think of it," admitted Winkie, "and then I thought of being a pilot in the Air Force, but now I've *quite* decided to be a banker. What does a banker do?"

"Winkie!" said Jennifer suddenly. She pointed at Winkie and smiled.

"Yes," said Winkie, nodding at her. "Yes, this is Winkie. You remember me quite well, don't you, Jennifer?"

"Nice Winkie," Jennifer said.

Winkie blushed to the tips of his ears. "You *see*," he mumbled, gazing at his plate. "You see . . . she likes me. Of course she's very young, but—but she likes me quite a lot already . . . and she's quite sensible . . . I mean, she knows things. She knows what she means, I mean. Dolly just says anything, but Jennifer is *quite* different."

Frances knew exactly what he meant, and she agreed that Jennifer was different. Nothing could have been more unlike than the two babies—the only thing they had in common was their extreme youth. She was thinking this over and wondering about it when Winkie changed the subject.

"I like people to be pretty," he observed, looking round at his three female companions with a satisfied air.

Elise laughed. She replied: "I'm glad you approve of us, Winkie."

"I like pretty people," Winkie said. "We had a terribly ugly nurse once. She had a crooked face and I didn't like looking at her. Of course you're different, Mrs. Crabbe. I mean, I would like you even if you were ugly."

137

"Are you sure?" asked Elise teasingly.

Winkie hesitated. "No, not absolutely honestly sure," he said at last. "You see, it's so difficult to *imagine* you being ugly."

Frances could not help laughing at this. She thought that Elise had had the tables turned on her very neatly.

Elise laughed too. "I think you ought to go into the Diplomatic Service," she declared.

Frances had not forgotten her "true promise" to take Winkie out in a boat, and now that the weather was settling down she arranged the matter with Alec. It was a beautiful afternoon and the sea was like glass—the expedition was a tremendous success in every way. Alec and Winkie liked each other at first sight, and before they had known each other for half an hour they were fast friends, chatting with each other gravely and seriously as if they were exactly the same age. Frances had noticed that these people had a genius for getting on with children—perhaps it was because they loved children, or perhaps because they were a little like children themselves. Alec offered to take Winkie out in the boat again whenever he liked, even if Miss Field were otherwise engaged, and Winkie accepted the offer with rapture.

"Would you really, Alec?" he said. "That would be *lovely*. I mean, of course, it's lovely to have Miss Field, isn't it? But you and I could go out together when it was too rough for ladies. I could help you, Alec."

"You could indeed," agreed Alec gravely.

"I'm small, of course," continued Winkie, "but I'm very strong for my size. You'd be surprised at how strong I am, really. I could help you to pull in the lines and to hoist the sail."

"I would be glad to have you and that's the truth," Alec said.

Alec was taking them out to his lines. There was just enough breeze to fill the big brown sail and to send them gliding over the water. The sun was warm and dazzling, the air was crystal clear. It was the most peaceful, beautiful scene that anyone could imagine.

"Alec," said Winkie suddenly. "Alec, what would you do if a German submarine suddenly rose out of the water just there, in front of the boat—what would you *do*, Alec?"

"That is a difficult question."

"Yes, but what *would* you do? It might, you know. It might suddenly rise up all gleaming wet and the water pouring down off the sides."

Alec looked somewhat alarmed and Frances was not surprised, for Winkie's vivid imagination had made the picture live. She could almost see the monstrous thing rising from the calm blue sea—just like a gigantic whale but a hundred times more dangerous. She wondered whether Winkie had ever seen a submarine break surface. If not, how did he know that the water poured down off the sides. Frances did not know this herself—she had never thought about it—but now that she thought of it she realised that it must be like that. As the submarine rose the water was bound to pour down its sides. . . .

Alec had evidently followed the same train of thought. " Have you seen one?" he asked.

" No, but I can imagine it," Winkie said. " I can see it happening if I want to. Would you ram it, Alec?"

" What would be the use?" inquired Alec gravely. " It would not do the submarine any harm to be rammed by a fishing-boat."

" Would you shoot it, then?"

" How would I do that?" asked Alec with the glimmering of a smile.

Winkie pointed under the seat. " That's your rifle, isn't it?"

" So you saw it!" exclaimed Alec, smiling broadly now. " Och, it's sharp eyes you have and no mistake. I thought I had hidden it under my coat. I did not want you to be seeing my rifle, Winkie."

" Why not?"

" Och, it is an ugly thing. I take it with me when I go out in the boat, for it gives me a safe kind of feeling, but it would not be much use against a submarine."

" What is it for?"

" It might be for a shark——" began Alec in a doubtful tone.

" It's in case you see an aeroplane," said Winkie eagerly. " That's what it's for. In case a Jerry suddenly swooped out of a cloud and attacked us."

" There are no clouds to-day," replied Alec, looking at the sky.

" That's what it's for—isn't it, Alec?"

" I would have a shot at it," admitted Alec.

" Of course you would. It would be splendid to bring it down."

" It is a long chance," Alec said. " It is not an easy thing to do, but my cousin was away at sea in a trawler and they were attacked by a dive-bomber and my cousin shot it down with his rifle, so there is no reason why I could not do the same thing. I would have a try at any rate. It would be a fine thing to do."

139

"Why aren't you fighting the Germans, Alec?" Winkie inquired.

Frances was somewhat embarrassed by her young friend's curiosity. She had often wondered why Alec had not been called up, but naturally she had not asked the reason for his exemption from military service. Winkie had no such scruples.

"It is because of my lung," replied Alec frankly. "I have a bad lung, you see. I went up to the office at Rithie, for I wanted to serve in the Royal Navy, but the doctor would not have me. It is a pity, because I am really very strong and I would have been useful, for I know about ships. I told the doctor all that, but he sent me away."

"You don't look ill," said Winkie, looking at Alec critically.

"I am not ill at all. My lung does not trouble me much now. I could have done the work quite well," said Alec. He smiled rather sadly and added: "Sometimes I wish that I looked ill. It is not a pleasant thing to be a young man and not in uniform."

Frances had a feeling that Alec had explained his disability for her benefit rather than Winkie's. He seemed glad to have been given the opportunity to explain. "You're doing very useful work," she pointed out.

"It is work that anybody could do," he said. "It does not satisfy me at all. I am thinking I might go to London for the fire-fighting—they would not bother about my lung there. Sometimes it is difficult to bear being left behind with the women and the old men—look, Winkie, there is a seal!"

The days were passing quickly, and Frances began to feel that this pleasant existence had been going on for months. It was such a peaceful, happy existence that she would have been quite pleased if it could have gone on indefinitely; but that was impossible, of course, for this was just a holiday, it was just an interlude between her old life and her new. Dr. Digby had written to her again, assuring her that she was quite capable of taking the post he had found for her and urging her to take it without delay, and she had received a letter from Mr. Fleming, the manager of the munition works, saying that he hoped she would decide to come and that the canteen would be ready in about three weeks. Three weeks seemed a long time in prospect, and Frances—secretly very glad of the delay—wrote to Mr. Fleming and said that she would come.

Now that she had made up her mind, and her holiday had a definite limit, Cairn seemed more beautiful and more lovable than ever. Spring had come, and to Frances, who had never before spent the spring months in the country, the beauty was amazing. The weather was a mixture of smiles and tears, of warm sunshine and silver showers. In the fields near the village and on the slopes of the hills there were lambs with black faces and tiny black legs, chasing each other and frolicking with gay abandon. Frances wanted to frolic too. There was magic in the air; magic in the sunshine, in the springing grass, in the flowers and the song of the birds, in the veil of tender green which was spreading rapidly over the earth. Frances saw the green buttons on the larches; she watched the chestnut tree outside her window, and every day there was a difference in it. The fat, brown sticky buds burst apart and the sheaths fell away, and the tiny fingers of tender green leaves spread themselves in the still air. It was a magic spring—or so Frances thought—she could not believe that spring had ever been so beautiful before. She said something of this to Elise, and Elise agreed with her.

"Perhaps it's because of the war that everything seems so beautiful," said Elise thoughtfully. "The war and all its horrors —and this peaceful, beautiful place . . . we appreciate it more. Perhaps it's because we know that our country is in danger, that all the things we value more than life itself are in danger. . . . I don't know. . . ."

The Crabbes were now the only people living in the hotel besides herself, and Major Crabbe could scarcely be described as living in the hotel. He came over when he could and was usually there at night, but there were evenings when Frances and Elise sat by themselves in the lounge with the windows wide open, reading or knitting and listening to the wireless. They had reached the stage of friendship when they could talk or not as they felt inclined—it was very pleasant. There were other evenings when people dropped in, the Listons or the Widgerys or some of the officers from the camp. Barry and Mark had discovered a grass tennis court behind the hotel and had spent a whole afternoon cutting and rolling it. The court was by no means level and it was very short, but it provided them with a good deal of amusement. The subalterns came over and played on it whenever they were free, and sometimes Tommy came and joined in the game. There was always more laughter than tennis when Tommy was there—she was a popular person. The tennis court provided the inhabitants of Cairn with free entertainment, and although the niceties of the game were lost upon them, they enjoyed seeing the white-clad figures leaping about and hitting the ball. The fence which surrounded the court was usually lined with people watching and commenting

141

upon the play. Sometimes there were soldiers in battle-dress amongst the onlookers—already the soldiers had found friends and sweethearts in Cairn.

One day when Frances was watching the tennis the Widgerys arrived with Angela, and a few minutes later Guy appeared. It was obvious that they had arranged a match and had met by appointment. Guy was clad like the others, in white flannel trousers and a tennis shirt open at the neck, and Frances, who had never seen Guy in anything but uniform, was surprised to see how different he looked . . . even his face looked different, younger and more carefree.

"Why aren't you playing?" he inquired, coming over to Frances and looking down at her. "Go and put on your tennis frock at once."

"I can't play," she replied frankly. "I never played tennis in my life, and I'm too old to start."

"Nonsense, you would soon learn," said Guy.

The others shouted to him to come, so there was no more opportunity for talk. He picked up his racket and went over to the net.

They started to play; Guy and Angela were partners against the Widgerys, and for some reason Frances wished that they had arranged it differently. She watched them for a little and then she gathered up her knitting and went indoors.

Chapter Twenty-One

FRANCES AWOKE with the feeling that something was going to happen to-day, something not particularly nice. She lay and wondered what it was, and after a few moments she remembered that this was the day she had promised to go up to the Castle and help Mr. MacDonald with his notes. . . . But I *want* to go, said Frances to herself. I'm very interested in the notes and I like Mr. MacDonald. Having assured herself of these facts, it was strange that her spirits remained low and that she had little appetite for breakfast.

The bus was just starting for Rithie when Frances came out of the hotel, so she asked the conductor whether he could take her as far as the Castle gates, and he replied, in the usual fashion of the Cairn inhabitants, that he saw no reason why he could not do so. Frances got in. She did not know why she had chosen to go to the Castle by a different route—it would have been just as easy to have walked along the cliff; but the cliff path was associated with Guy ... and Guy did not want her to go ... it was all rather silly, really.

The bus stopped at the big gates and she got out and began to walk up the avenue. It was a well-kept road, curving away over a moor like a grey ribbon. The moor was covered with brown heather and yellowish-green tufty grass; here and there were clumps of gorse bushes with a few yellow flowers on them. The day was silver—silent and cold—every now and then a few drops of cold rain fell; there was scarcely any wind but the clouds moved in from the sea slowly and steadily. Frances wondered where they all came from and where they were going, those heavy masses of pale-grey cloud. She remembered having read somewhere or other that all our bad weather comes from Iceland, that Iceland is the grave of worn-out cyclones; she remembered that before the war started (and weather bulletins on the wireless were discontinued) the B.B.C. announcer used to declare that " a V-shaped depression is approaching from Iceland." How cold and dreary it sounded—just like the day—cold and dreary and unfriendly. It was the sort of day that makes one feel small and defenceless ... undoubtedly Frances was experiencing a V-shaped depression of some magnitude.

Presently the avenue sloped down and entered a wood, a dank, dripping wood with moss growing upon the bark of the trees. . . . Frances shivered and walked faster. She had gone about fifty yards farther when the sound of shots broke the stillness—two shots in quick succession followed immediately by the most frightful screams. The screams died away in a sobbing sound and all was quiet again. Frances stopped dead in the middle of the road. She was petrified. Her heart thumped like a sledge-hammer in her breast. She stood there for a few moments listening ... and then Mr. MacDonald emerged from the wood and came towards her. He had a gun over his shoulder and a canvas bag on his back, and in his left hand he carried a rabbit swinging by its legs.

" Hallo, Miss Field!" he exclaimed. " I thought you would be coming the other way. It *is* good of you to remember your promise to come and help me——"

" It screamed," said Frances, pointing to the rabbit.

" Yes," agreed Mr. MacDonald. " Did it frighten you? I'm very sorry indeed. The poor little brute wasn't killed outright—it was inexcusable. I hate shooting rabbits, but the fact is we have nothing for lunch, and my cousin asked me to hunt for the pot. I have managed to bag half a dozen, so I think I have done

143

my duty." He opened the breach of his gun and emptied it. "There, the rabbits are safe now," he said, " so please don't look so sad."

Frances smiled. She realised that she had been rather foolish. The day and the stillness of the wood and her own peculiar state of mind had combined to frighten her. There was nothing to be afraid of, nothing at all, and Guy had been quite wrong.

They walked up the avenue together and soon came to the Castle; it was warm and pleasant inside the door, and there was a leaping fire of logs in Mr. MacDonald's study. Frances took off her hat and her oilskin coat and put them on a chair—she was determined to be very businesslike. "Let's get to work," she said.

Mr. MacDonald began to rummage in the drawers of his desk. "The notes are all here," he said. "They're in an awful mess. I'm afraid I've gone the wrong way about it from the very beginning. I should have dated the notes as I went along and kept them in proper order. They make me feel quite ill," he added ruefully.

Frances had no experience of dealing with this sort of thing, but she had come to help him with the notes, and she intended to do the thing properly. It was no use to sit and look at the untidy pile of papers . . . she began to sort them out into heaps and to clip them together in chronological order. The first set of notes related to a man named Sumarlid, or in other words " The Summer Soldier."

" He was the progenitor of our clan," explained Mr. Mac-Donald. " He lived about the year 1130. Then we come to Donald and Ewin and Ruari, his sons. Donald's son, Angus, was the first MacDonald—so called because he was the son of Donald—he lived in 1284. Ewin was the progenitor of the Mac-Dugals, and Ruari of the MacRuarys. There's a good deal about Angus MacDonald; he was small and dark, amiable and cheerful and witty—quite a nice sort of ancestor to have."

Frances was listening to Mr. MacDonald and trying to work at the same time. It would have been so much easier if Mr. Mac-Donald had not been such a talker, if he had stuck to the business in hand instead of trying to talk and work at the same time. It would take years to sort out the papers at this rate.

" Yes," she said. " He must have been nice. Here's something about Angus Oig—is that the same man?"

" He was the son of Angus. He helped Robert the Bruce, and was afterwards given the MacDugal Estates—the islands of Mull,

144

Jura, Coll and Tiree—which had belonged to the Lords of Lorn. Then his son, John, was dispossessed, but repossessed by David I."

" It says here that John was Lord of the Isles," said Frances, struggling to follow the story.

Mr. MacDonald nodded. " John became Lord of the Isles by marrying a sister of Reginald MacRuary. . . . He was the fifth generation from Sumarlid, and he had managed in different ways to collect all Sumarlid's estates. He had got the MacDugal Estates from the Bruce and the MacRuary Estates through his marriage. He also managed to collect Ross. The Lord of the Isles was a very important man."

" He was a king, really, wasn't he?"

" He was proud and powerful," agreed Mr. MacDonald, " and of course, like all proud and powerful men, he was envied and hated. His son succeeded him—there were four Lords of the Isles—and then in 1493 they lost everything. I've got some notes about that—yes—here they are. In 1493 the Lord of the Isles was accused of treachery; he was attainted and died in poverty. His son, Ian, came back to Kintyre and settled there, and it is from him that our family is descended. . . ."

They worked away for a little, sorting out the notes which related to the people mentioned. Frances clipped them together and numbered the pages.

When they had been working for some time, Mr. MacDonald looked up at her and smiled. " Order out of chaos," he said. " You have a neat mind, Miss Field. I couldn't see how I was going to start clearing up the muddle, but the muddle is clearing rapidly."

" Are you going to publish it?" Frances asked.

" Who would want to read it? No, I was just writing it all out for my own satisfaction, and for the sake of the family. I felt it should be done, and nobody else was interested enough to tackle it. The first part is a little dull, because I couldn't find out enough of the small details to make it interesting. . . , Now we are getting to the really interesting part."

" We'll call it Part II, shall we?"

He nodded. " That is an excellent idea. Part II will be the feuds between the clans—the internecine warfare. It lasted for several hundred years. I have bundles of notes about the raids and battles that took place on this very spot between the Mac-Donalds and the Campbells . . . the two clans were hereditary enemies——"

145

"Why were they?" Frances inquired.

The question was sufficient to start Mr. MacDonald off on his favourite subject; his eyes gleamed, he pushed the papers to one side—some of them fell on the floor—and proceeded to give Frances a long and detailed account of the two clans, of their rise to power, and of the factors which had made them enemies. Naturally he was prejudiced in favour of his own clan, so his account may not have been strictly impartial. He talked and talked—it was obvious that he preferred talking to writing; perhaps it was because he could find nobody to listen to him that he had started his history. Frances made one or two attempts to stem the tide and to get back to business, but they were somewhat feeble attempts, because she was aware, before she made them, that they had little chance of success. . . . She was forced to abandon the papers and to give all her attention to the speaker. She learned that both clans had prospered by their allegiance to Robert the Bruce, but the Campbells continued to prosper and increase with tremendous rapidity. They increased in numbers more rapidly than the MacDonalds, and became more powerful and required more land. Scotland was torn by factions, and the Campbells were always on the winning side—they had a habit of taking fortune at the flood. After Flodden the internecine warfare was intensified, and the Campbells spread southward into Kintyre and gradually ousted the MacDonalds from their territory. Frances heard of the last struggle of the MacDonalds for their patrimony in 1614, and she heard of the Battle of Dunaverty. It was a sad story. The whole struggle from the very beginning seemed unnecessary and unreasonable—or so Frances thought. A little understanding, a little give and take between the clans, would have saved so much misery and bloodshed. She thought, as she listened, that all history was like that; it was all a muddle and a struggle. Men had always fought for power and for land; they were still engaged on the same miserable business. Would it ever end, or would men continue to fight and kill each other for ever and ever? Would the human race ever learn to live and let live in peace and friendship?

The booming of the gong for lunch stopped Mr. MacDonald in the middle of a sentence—he gave an exclamation of annoyance and looked at his watch. "I had no idea it was lunch-time," he said. "I'm afraid I have talked too much, but I wanted to give you an idea—an outline of the story."

"It's been most interesting," Frances said. She spoke sincerely, for it had been very interesting indeed.

Mr. MacDonald rose and showed Frances into a bedroom where she could tidy herself. There were silver brushes on the table and clean towels hanging on a rail beside the fixed basin.

"Don't hurry," he said. "My cousin always has the gong rung ten minutes before lunch is ready. It is the only way to prevent me from being ten minutes late."

He left her and went away, and Frances tidied her hair and washed her hands. She was drying her hands on the towel when the door opened and Miss Stalker appeared.

Miss Stalker stood and looked at Frances without speaking (without making any reply to her guest's conventional greeting), and Frances felt a sudden twinge of dislike for the woman, of something that was almost akin to fear.

"We've done quite a lot this morning," Frances said, trying to speak cheerfully.

"Are you coming back?" asked Miss Stalker.

It was a strange question, and Frances did not know how to answer it. The docketing of the notes was not finished, it was only half done, but somehow or other she was not particularly anxious to come back. She had a feeling that it was a waste of time trying to help Mr. MacDonald; he had lost interest in his history. She had a feeling that even if the notes were put in order the history would never be written. . . . "We haven't finished the job," said Frances at last.

"What were you doing all the morning?" asked Miss Stalker, coming nearer to Frances and gazing into her face. "You weren't working all the time. He was talking—I heard him when I passed the door. You can't work and talk at the same time."

Frances had finished drying her hands; she turned and hung the towel on the rail. She discovered that she was really frightened of Miss Stalker now—her hands were trembling as she hung up the towel—there was something horrible about the woman; it was a relief to turn her back on that nose and those aggressive eyebrows.

"Why didn't he ask me to help him?" continued Miss Stalker in the same somewhat breathless voice (it was as if she had been running upstairs). "I've been here for six years and he's never asked me to help him with his notes."

"Perhaps he thought you were too busy."

Miss Stalker hesitated and then she nodded. "I'm very busy," she said. "It takes a lot of time to run a house like this. . . . Lunch is ready, so we had better go down. It's only rabbits, of course."

" I like rabbits," said Frances.

" Stewed rabbits," said Miss Stalker. " We can't get meat every day."

" No, of course not," said Frances.

They went downstairs together and, as they went, Miss Stalker continued to complain about the rationing and to bemoan the fact that her guest would have to eat rabbits for lunch, and Frances, who was somewhat trembly about the knees, continued to assure her that it didn't matter.

Mr. MacDonald was waiting for them in the hall, and they went in to lunch. He was in very good spirits, assuring Frances that she had been of the greatest assistance to him and that he was beginning to see daylight through the muddle of his notes. As they sat down he took up the story of the clans at the exact point where he had been interrupted, and continued to talk without ceasing while they ate their soup. Frances was glad of the monologue, for she was upset by her extraordinary interview with Miss Stalker, and would have found it difficult to take part in a conversation—as it was, she said " yes " and " no " at the proper places and did her best to eat the food which was offered to her.

" I'm afraid you don't like rabbits," said Miss Stalker, interrupting Mr. MacDonald in an account of a particularly daring foray by the MacDonald clan. " I did my best to get veal, or mutton cutlets, but the butcher wouldn't give me any meat. He said we had had our week's ration already. He's *very annoying* sometimes. I really think we ought to try another butcher."

" It isn't his fault," Mr. MacDonald said.

Miss Stalker shook her head. " I don't know about that," she replied. " There seemed to be plenty of meat in the shop, so why couldn't he stretch a point and let me have a few cutlets?"

" It would have been against the law."

" We've always been very good customers—big bills every month."

" Everyone must share alike," replied Mr. MacDonald testily. " That's why meat coupons have been introduced. I've explained the whole thing to you before—not once but several times."

Frances had recovered a little; she had recovered sufficiently to be amused at the by-play. Mr. MacDonald did not like being interrupted and brought to a standstill when he was astride his hobby-horse.

" You might have caught a salmon," said Miss Stalker, returning to the subject of lunch.

" The river was too low," replied Mr. MacDonald shortly.

" You might have tried."

148

"*The river was too low,*" he repeated, accentuating every word. "No salmon in its senses would come up a river unless there was sufficient water——"

"Perhaps Miss Field doesn't like salmon either," said Miss Stalker in sorrowful tones. "Quite a lot of people don't like salmon—cutlets would have been best, because everyone likes cutlets."

"The discussion seems very unprofitable," declared Mr. MacDonald with a frown. "The fact remains that you couldn't get cutlets and I couldn't get salmon, so Miss Field is forced to eat rabbits. One imagines that she might enjoy her lunch better if she were allowed to eat it in peace."

"I hope she likes peaches," said Miss Stalker, who seemed impervious to snubs. "They're tinned, of course. If I could have got cream we might have had pêche melba. . . , We always used to have cream."

"I like rabbits and I like peaches," began Frances; she had been trying to find an opening ever since the discussion began. "I like anything, really. I'm not at all particular about food."

"We used to have such nice food," said Miss Stalker reminiscently. She was a person who liked to have the last word.

Frances could not help wondering what Mr. MacDonald and his cousin talked about when they were alone—they were an ill-assorted couple and seemed to have nothing in common—perhaps they did not converse with each other at all, but just dwelt beneath the same roof and went their own ways. She wondered what Mrs. MacDonald had been like, and decided to ask Alec (he was her stand-by for any information about the people and the district). Had Mrs. MacDonald been interested in internecine warfare? Had she been interested enough in the subject not to be bored at having it served to her at every meal? Frances had been very interested in it—and still was—but she had begun to think that one could have too much history . . . she was approaching the moment when she would have had too much Mr. MacDonald. She realised this quite clearly.

"When will you come back?" asked Mr. MacDonald as he saw her off at the door. "What morning would suit you best—or would you rather come in the afternoon?"

"I'll let you know—may I?" Frances replied. "Perhaps one day next week. You aren't in any hurry, are you?"

"No," he said. "No, of course not." But his face fell and Frances felt a brute.

"You could go on with it yourself now," she pointed out. "We finished the first part, didn't we?"

" Yes," he said. " Yes, it has been very good of you to help. . . .
I had hoped . . . but of course you have other things to do."

Frances shook hands with him and came away. She saw, now,
that Guy had been right and that she ought not to have gone at
all.

Chapter Twenty-two

GUY HAD said that Ned Crabbe was one of the best fellows you
could meet in a day's march, and now that Frances saw him more
frequently she realised that it was true. He did not talk much but
what he said was always worth listening to. There was something
staunch and dependable about him, he was absolutely sincere.
Frances began to see why Elise was so devoted to her husband
—it had always been easy to see why he was devoted to Elise.
One evening when Major Crabbe came over he found Frances
and Elise listening to the nine o'clock news. He signalled to
them not to speak and sat down beside Elise on the sofa.
The news was bad. Our forces were being evacuated from the
Greek ports, they were being bombed from the air and there were
not enough British planes to protect the transports. There was
trouble brewing in Iraq. The Germans were saying that we
intended to invade Spain. Tobruk's outer defences had been
penetrated by an enemy force of tanks and infantry.

Everything seemed to be going wrong at once, and when the
news was over Frances looked at Major Crabbe and asked him
what he thought about it.

" We're going through a bad patch," he said. " It was unfortunate that we couldn't send more help to Greece—very
unfortunate—but we must hang on to Egypt. We daren't risk
losing Egypt and the Suez Canal. It must have been damned
hard for Wavell to decide how many troops he could spare."

" It seems terrible to have to leave them to their fate—the
Greeks, I mean."

" It is terrible," agreed Major Crabbe, " but we've got to beat
the Bosche. When we've beaten him the Greeks will be all right
and they know that. The Greek business is a bad show but it's
only a side-show, really. It may have lengthened the war, but it
won't make any difference in the end. Hitler knows that better
than anyone. The only way Hitler can win is by a direct attack
upon the British Isles—or by preventing American help from

reaching us. America has realised this and will take care that it doesn't happen."

"Then you aren't—you aren't worrying?" Frances said.

He smiled. "I left off worrying about the ultimate conclusion of the war when Roosevelt signed the Lease and Lend Bill," replied Major Crabbe. "The actual help that's coming to us from America is tremendously important, but there's something more important still. Roosevelt knows we're going to win. . . . Look at it like this," said Major Crabbe, leaning forward and speaking very earnestly. "Roosevelt is an onlooker. He sees the whole situation from afar—sees it in perspective. His policy is the result of the careful weighing up of all the factors in the case—that's why I hang my hat on what Roosevelt thinks. Of course America has always hoped that we would win, but last year after the French collapse she was very much afraid that we were going to be beaten. Now she sees we *can* win and she's going to help us up to the limit of her resources. She's making us magnificent tools—I was talking to an R.A.F. fellow and he was tremendously enthusiastic about those 'Havocs' they're sending over: 'perfectly marvellous' were the words he used—and if I know anything about the Americans, they'll make sure we get those tools safely. What would be the sense of spending millions of dollars on munitions and letting them go to the bottom of the sea?"

"Not much, really."

"Not much," agreed Major Crabbe. "The Americans are too—too practical to do the thing by halves. If they're going to do a thing at all, they'll take care to do it thoroughly."

There was silence for a few moments and then Major Crabbe continued: "I came across rather an interesting idea the other day. It was a suggestion by an American—I can't remember who it was—that America and ourselves should make a pact—the same sort of agreement we offered to the French. I'm no politician, so I'm a bit hazy about the details, but it seems to me that it would be a stupendous advantage to the two great democracies if they could link up with each other and pool their interests. They would be partners—not only for the war but for the peace —partners for all time. They would be partners in building up that new world we hear so much about."

Frances had never heard Major Crabbe speak so much before —he had a quiet, deliberate way of speaking which gave weight to his words.

"The whole English-speaking world," said Elise thoughtfully. "All of us pulling together. It sounds marvellous—would it be possible, Ned?"

151

"Why not?" he asked. "Our interests are identical. We believe in the same things; we *want* the same things—peace and decent behaviour and a fair chance for everyone. There couldn't be another war—ever—if the thing could be made to work. Churchill and Roosevelt between them could keep the whole world in order." He rose and knocked out his pipe. "That's what I think, anyhow," he said. "I don't pretend to be a politician or an economist . . . but . . . that's what I think."

"Are you going back to the camp?" asked Elise in surprise.

He nodded. "I've got to go back," he said. "I just want to have a peep at Jennifer."

"Don't waken her," said Elise, looking up and smiling.

Frances went up to bed in a thoughtful mood. She felt cheered by what Major Crabbe had said; she felt as if she could see a break in the dark clouds of war. She remembered everything that he had said, but one thing especially stuck in her mind and she knew that she could never forget it. "We want . . . decent behaviour," Major Crabbe had said. Frances thought that the phrase epitomised all that we were fighting for.

One of the pleasant features of Cairn was the fact that it was a good place for sleep. There was no need to woo sleep in Cairn: one dropped off peacefully the moment one's head touched the pillow and slept solidly until the morning. One night, however (it was shortly after Major Crabbe's statement of faith), Frances experienced a very peculiar dream. She was in a railway station—a small station situated on a main line—and she was waiting for a train to London. The train was approaching rapidly and she was aware that this was the train she must catch; she waved her hand to make it stop (waved her hand to the engine-driver as if the train were a bus), but the train did not slacken speed. It approached and thundered through the station at express rate, and the noise was so loud that it woke her. She woke suddenly with a start but the noise of the train still filled her ears, roaring away into the distance, and after a few moments she came to the conclusion that the noise was real and that it must have been an aeroplane flying over the house. She sat up in bed and rubbed her eyes and looked at her watch—it was half-past one.

Just then there was a knock on the door and Elise looked in.

"Frances," she said in a whisper. "Frances, are you awake? Did you hear it?"

"Yes," replied Frances. "It seemed pretty near."

Elise came in; she was in her dressing-gown and her hair was in a net. " I think I shall take Jennifer down to the cellar," she said. " Do you think I should? Perhaps it's silly to disturb her——"

" I don't know," Frances said.

" Perhaps I should just let her sleep," said Elise doubtfully. " I suppose the chance of another bomb dropping in Cairn is very slight—what do you think?"

It was unlike Elise to be undecided, to ask for advice. Frances considered the matter carefully: she thought the risk was slight, but it was there—somebody in Cairn might have been careless and left a crack of light showing—she did not feel that she could take the responsibility of advising Elise to leave Jennifer where she was. " I think you should take her down," said Frances at last. " It's better to be on the safe side. I'll put on some clothes and come too—there's another one."

The second plane roared overhead and sped away, and Frances leapt out of bed and dressed as quickly as she could. When she went into the nursery she found Elise and the nurse making their final preparations. They rolled Jennifer in blankets and as they did so she opened her eyes and smiled at them. " Good-mornin', Mummy," she said in a sleepy voice.

" Good-morning, darling," said Elise tenderly, " . . . but it isn't time to get up yet." She gathered the bundle into her arms and led the way downstairs. The nurse seized the mattress and Frances took the pillow and the rest of the blankets and followed quickly.

The little procession went through the hall and into the kitchen premises and down a steep stone stair. Frances saw that there was a light in the cellar—Mrs. MacNair and Annie were there before them.

" There you are!" exclaimed Mrs. MacNair. " I heard you getting up and I knew you would be bringing the wee lamb downstairs. We can lay the mattress on the floor; there is no draught and it is a fine dry cellar, so she will take no harm. . . . Och, the wee creature, she's smiling at me!"

Elise put her baby on the mattress and tucked her in firmly with the blankets. " It's all right, Jennifer," she said. " Go to sleep, darling. Mummy will pat you." She knelt down and patted Jennifer soothingly. . . . In a few moments Jennifer's eyes were shut and she was breathing quietly and easily.

" The wee pet!" said Mrs. MacNair. " Och, she is a good bairn. It was just as well to bring her down—she will be quite safe here. Mr. MacNair says there is several feet of stone in the roof of the cellar—it is very safe."

The cellar was a long-shaped vault with arches and alcoves. It was warm and dry and the walls and the roof were of solid stone and tremendously thick. At the other end of the cellar there were wine bins—some of them full of bottles—but there was no wine in the outer part where they intended to sit. Mrs. MacNair had brought down some chairs during the last raid and had left them there, and some wooden boxes as well. She began to arrange them conveniently.

"If somebody had told me when I married Mr. MacNair that I would be spending some of my nights sitting in this cellar I would have thought they were mad," declared Mrs. MacNair forcefully, "but now it seems a natural thing to do. We will have a cup of tea. I put the kettle on as I came through the kitchen."

"I'll infuse the tea," Annie said.

"Are you frightened to go up?" asked Mrs. MacNair. "I can do it myself, if you are frightened."

"Och, I'm not frightened," declared Annie. She went up the stairs and disappeared.

"She is a good girl," Mrs. MacNair said. "A wee bit scatter-brained, maybe, but her heart is in the right place. I am hoping she will not lose it to one of the soldiers," added Mrs. MacNair with a smile, "There will be a lot of hearts lost in Cairn before the war is finished—so there will."

"There's another plane," said Jennifer's nurse suddenly.

They listened. The plane approached rapidly. The noise of its engines grew louder and louder, reverberating through the vaulted cellar till it sounded like the noise of half a dozen express trains.

"I think there are several of them," said Frances, raising her voice so as to be heard through the din.

"Mercy!" exclaimed Mrs. MacNair. "Mercy me, it sounds as if it were coming in at the door——"

Fortunately, however, the plane—or planes—did not attempt this somewhat difficult feat but passed overhead and roared away into the distance, and a few moments later Annie came down the stairs with a tray of tea-things.

"That was a near one," she said cheerfully. "The whole place shook with it—you wouldn't hear it down here."

"We heard it," said Mrs. MacNair dryly.

Frances was surprised at Annie's sang-froid, for she remembered that Annie had been horror-stricken at the idea of living in London and at the thought of bombs ("I'd be scared all the

154

time," Annie had said), but now the test had come and Annie was not scared at all; she was sitting on an old wooden box with a cup of tea in one hand and a biscuit in the other and was chatting in a friendly manner with Jennifer's nurse. . . . "It's quite an easy pattern," Annie was saying; "you slip one and knit one and pass the slipped stitch over. I'll give you the pattern to-morrow if you would like it——"

Some people were like Annie, thought Frances; some people thought they would be frightened but were not frightened at all, and there were other people—like Aunt Zoë—who were exceedingly brave in anticipation but who failed to maintain their courage when the testing time arrived. Frances wished that she knew enough about psychology to understand the reason of these different reactions to danger. It would be interesting. Her own reaction—now that she thought of it—was of a third type. She was a little frightened in anticipation and a little frightened when the test came, but fortunately she was able to control her fear. She pushed it into a corner of her mind and barricaded it in. This left her mind perfectly clear and free to function properly. Of course, one had to keep an eye on the barricade, thought Frances, smiling to herself at the absurd simile; one had to see that it was holding firm and keeping the fear-beast from bursting out and making a nuisance of itself. . . .

Mrs. MacNair was talking to Elise. "I wakened everybody," she was saying. "Mr. MacNair gets the yellow warning, of course, because he is in the Home Guard, but when the red came through I went round and wakened everybody, and small thanks I got for my trouble. Mary—that's the cook—turned over in her bed and grunted when I told her that the Jerries were here—she is a wee bit deaf, of course—and the others were not for moving either, but I felt I had done the right thing, for I could not take the responsibility of letting them sleep. If anything happened I would never forgive myself."

"I think you were right," nodded Elise. "I wouldn't have come down if it hadn't been for Jennifer. You can take risks for yourself but you can't take them for other people."

Two more planes had passed while they were having tea, passed over and gone, but now there was a different sort of noise. They stopped talking and listened.

"There are several planes wheeling about——" began Frances.

". . . and that's machine-gun fire," added Elise.

"They'll be fighting!" exclaimed Annie with shining eyes. "It will be one of our own. . . . Och, that's fine! I've been sitting here listening to them going over and wishing I could get at them with my own hands." She rose as she spoke and made for the stairs.

"Where are you away to?" cried Mrs. MacNair.

"To see——" replied Annie, disappearing with a swirl of her skirts.

"I think I'll go too," said Frances, rising. "We shan't see anything, of course, but still——"

"In the name of fortune!" exclaimed Mrs. MacNair.

There was quite a crowd of villagers on the terrace above the harbour and Frances joined them, for the terrace made an excellent grandstand. Everyone was gazing out to sea. The noise was terrific now—the noise of engines zooming and the clatter of machine-guns. In the bright moonlight and against the curtain of dark-blue sky there was a spirited dog-fight taking place: two planes—no, three—whirling, diving, climbing, and jinking round each other, mingling trails of white vapour and tracer bullets. . . . They overshot each other and banked steeply . . . and climbed and dived again. It seemed incredible that they could manœuvre like that without colliding with each other in mid-air. . . .

Someone—a woman—seized Frances by the arm and said: "Can ye see them? Which is oors?"

"Oors is the fighter—the wee yin," said a man's voice close by.

Suddenly something fell. It was a small object—or so it seemed—it dropped down into the sea and sent up a fountain of spray . . . and almost immediately one of the planes began to lose height . . . it was falling quite slowly . . . turning over and over as it fell . . . it looked like a dry leaf fluttering through the air.

"It's one o' the Jerries," said the man who had spoken before, and Frances, glancing at him, saw that he had a small telescope glued to his eye.

"Are ye sure, Ben?" demanded the woman. "Ye're not just saying it——"

"It's a Jerry," repeated the man. "It's a dommed Jerry—but I'll need to get out the boat all the same. . . ."

"Will I come and help ye?" asked a fisherman with a snow-white beard.

"I'll be quicker mysel'," declared the first man. He shut his telescope with a snap and ran down the steps.

"Take care the other Jerry doesn't machine-gun ye, Ben!" cried the woman in anxious tones.

"He wouldn't, would he?" Frances exclaimed.

156

" Aye—wouldn't he? It wouldn't be the first time——"

The pilot of the other bomber had his hands too full to pay any attention to the fate of his comrade, or his would-be rescuers; he circled round pursued by the fighter; he banked and dived, firing short bursts . . . suddenly he broke away and came zooming towards Cairn harbour with the fighter on his tail. The two planes screamed overhead . . . they were so low that they almost seemed to touch the chimneys of the hotel, so low that the little group on the terrace flung themselves on the ground . . . and now they were past . . . now they were merely two specks disappearing over the hills, and the roar of their engines and the staccato clatter of machine-guns died away in the distance.

It was over so suddenly. One moment the noise and the tense excitement of battle, and the next moment silence and the calm night.

The bomber which had fallen into the sea had almost disappeared by this time. One wing, sticking up above the water, was all that remained of it. The boat had already left the harbour and was pulling out towards the wreck, but Frances did not think it would be in time. " They have collapsible boats, haven't they?" she asked.

" Aye, but they don't seem to be using it," replied the old fisherman.

They waited—it was the last scene in the drama, a silent, melancholy aftermath of battle. The little boat from Cairn reached the spot where the plane had sunk. It circled several times; it paused there, rocking gently on the swell . . . then it turned and made for the shore.

" They're drooned, I doot," said the woman who had spoken before. She sighed and added: " Maybe they've mothers waiting for them at hame."

" That's war," declared the fisherman with the snowy-white beard. " Their deaths lie at Hitler's door, like the deaths of millions of other folks more innocent than them——"

Chapter Twenty-three

SATURDAY WAS the day fixed for the Home Guard manœuvre. It was a day of brilliant sunshine and soft showers of rain. Tommy came over about seven o'clock, and she and Frances had dinner together at the little table in the window.

" It's a great night for Cairn," declared Annie as she brought in their fish and put it before them on the table. " They're all on the hop—the whole lot of them. It's a great thing for the Home Guard to be going manœuvring with real soldiers. Donald Fraser's almost beside himself. He was in the bar a wee while ago, but he wasn't there for a drink. He's wanting to keep a clear head for the night's work."

" What did he come for?" asked Frances, smiling at Annie's excitement.

" It was for advice," replied Annie seriously. " Mr. MacNair is his Section Leader, and Donald was wanting to know whether he would take his old gun or his new one. They've given him a grand new gun from America and Donald's as proud as punch, but he likes the feel of his old gun better—it's more friendly, so he said. Mr. MacNair said he could take which he liked but he wasn't to fire at all. He was to remember it was just a game, Mr. MacNair said.

" Goodness, I hope they won't shoot each other!" exclaimed Tommy in some alarm.

" They've been told not to," Annie pointed out.

The object of the exercise was to give the Home Guard a test of efficiency and to see whether a force could land anywhere in the vicinity and make its way to Cairn Castle without being observed and intercepted. As it was impossible to land from the air, it had been agreed that the soldiers from the camp (who were taking the part of the enemy) should be allowed several hours free from observation to get to their positions. At zero hour the exercise would begin and the Home Guard would sally forth to find them. Alec had explained all this to Frances and had then asked, somewhat ingenuously, if she knew where the soldiers intended to " land." Fortunately Frances was able to reply with perfect truth that she had not the slightest idea.

" Do you know where they're going to 'land,' Tommy?" inquired Frances when Annie had gone away.

" No, Midge wouldn't tell me," she replied. " Midge was very secretive about the whole affair—he seemed pleased and excited about it."

"Excited!"

"I know it seems absurd, but I know Midge so well. . . . I suppose it will be rather fun . . . hide-and-seek *is* rather fun, don't you think so?"

Frances had never played hide-and-seek in her life, for it is impossible to play it alone, so she was not in a position to judge whether or not the game would be fun played on a large scale. She did not reply to Tommy's question because she was thinking of Captain Widgery and trying to imagine him enjoying a game of hide-and-seek with the Home Guard, trying to imagine him becoming excited over the prospect. She found this quite impossible to imagine—it was out of character. Barry and Mark might enjoy the exercise—and even Guy—but not Captain Widgery. . . .

"What are you dreaming about?" Tommy inquired.

"Nothing," said Frances hastily.

It was such a lovely evening that they decided to go for a walk along the cliffs. Frances was anxious to show her friend St. Kiaran's Chapel, and there would be plenty of time to go there and back before dark. The sun was declining westwards, making a golden path across the sea, and the shadows of the two girls were long and thin, spread out upon the grass.

"I'm worried about Guy," said Tommy suddenly. "He used to pop in and see me quite often, but I haven't seen him for days."

"Perhaps he's busy."

"Perhaps," agreed Tommy doubtfully. "But he isn't too busy to go up to the Thynnes' or to take Angela to the pictures at Rithie."

Frances was silent for a few moments—she remembered the tennis match.

After a little Tommy continued: "I used to like Angela. She was rather a dear until she got spoilt by too much attention. Her mother is a fool—hasn't the slightest control over her and encourages her to be silly. I used to think she would be the very person for Guy, but I don't think so now."

"No," said Frances; "but I shouldn't have thought that Guy——"

"You wouldn't, would you?" Tommy agreed. "Guy isn't easy to please, but men are funny creatures. Sometimes the very nicest men fall for the most impossible women."

"Yes," said Frances. She didn't believe for a moment that Guy and Angela——

"I've got to go away for a day or two," said Tommy when they had walked on for a little in silence. "I shall have to go and see my mother; she hasn't been very well. As a matter of fact it fits in quite nicely, because Midge is going to London for a few days to see someone at the War Office. I said I would go with him, but Midge isn't keen on my going to London. He will be busy, of course."

"Yes," said Frances. "You won't be away for long, will you?"

"I don't want to go at all," said Tommy in a thoughtful voice. "I hate the idea, really. It seems absurd, doesn't it?"

"Absurd?"

"Yes. I mean, it seems absurd to be so—so upset at the idea of going away for a few days."

"It will be nice to see your mother."

"She's a darling," Tommy declared. "She's a perfect pet . . . and that's why I can't understand myself at all. I keep on telling myself how lovely it will be to see her . . . but there's a sort of cloud. . . . I can't explain it, but somehow or other I feel as if—as if I were coming to the end of something."

"But, Tommy, if it's only for a few days——"

"I know," said Tommy. "It's quite ridiculous."

They were talking so earnestly that they scarcely noticed where they were going. Frances saw the world through a haze, but she knew the way so well by this time that there was no need to think about it. She turned right at the fork and led Tommy up the steep path through the woods.

"We've been talking about me all the time," said Tommy suddenly. "You're rather a mysterious person, Frances."

"I don't mean to be," replied Frances, smiling.

"Perhaps not, but I was thinking about you this morning and I suddenly discovered how little I knew about you—nothing at all, really. You listen to all I have to say but you never mention your own affairs."

"They're so dull."

"All the same, I think you're beginning to live," declared Tommy.

Frances laughed. "Perhaps I am," she said. "At any rate, I'm beginning to understand what you meant when you said I hadn't begun to live."

By this time they had reached the clearing where the little chapel was situated and, as Tommy was tired after the climb, they found a sheltered spot and sat down with their backs against a wall. Frances endeavoured to interest her companion in the history of the place, but, although Tommy listened patiently to all that she was told, she did not seem very enthusiastic about it. It was a trifle disappointing, of course, for Frances expected others to share her enthusiasms, but presently she realised that it takes all sorts of people to make a world. Tommy was more interested in her fellow-creatures than in things ; she lived and moved and had her being in the present . . . so it was quite natural that she should not experience the thrill of being in contact with the past. Having made this discovery, Frances stopped bothering and a little silence fell. The light was fading now and it was getting very late, but it was still warm and comfortable where they were sitting.

"It's peaceful here," said Tommy at last. "I'm getting rather sleepy. I haven't been sleeping very well lately."

"Perhaps we should go back."

"Why?" inquired Tommy. "There's nothing to drag us back. It's nice here."

"Would you like to come and see the chapel and the spring?"

"Not specially," replied Tommy frankly. "I know it's a great *want* in me, but I never was very interested in history. You go and poke round by yourself—I know you're longing to."

Frances rose. "All right," she said. "I won't be very long." She left Tommy sitting there and went into the little chapel ; there was not enough light to see the carving on the slabs, but she did not mind that. It was not the slabs she had come to see— not really—she had another purpose in mind. She clambered over the fallen masonry and made her way down to the spring, and as she went she looked about her in a somewhat guilty manner. There was nobody about, of course ; it wasn't likely that anyone would be here at this hour of night, and Tommy was probably asleep by this time.

Frances had brought a little horn cup in her pocket. She took it out and filled it with the sparkling water . . . then she hesitated and looked round again. It was very quiet in the clearing, nothing moved. The sun had gone down but the sky was still clear with reflected light. The sky was lovely : it was pale mauve and amber. There were no shadows now : it was the twilight hour, the magic hour when everything looks different from normal, when white flowers shine like stars in the gloom. . . .

I don't believe in it, of course, thought Frances, looking at the brimming cup. I don't believe there's anything in it—it's just nonsense. . . .

She drank. It was lovely water, very, very cold and very clear.

She recognised the smoky taste of which Guy had spoken—it was a queer taste, but pleasant. Frances filled the cup again and drank some more. No good to do it by halves, thought Frances, smiling at her own foolishness.

The deed was done and Frances was drying the little cup with her handkerchief when she heard a slight sound and, looking up, she saw two people, a man and a woman, at the other side of the clearing. They had just come out of the woods from the direction of the Castle and were standing at the edge of the trees talking to each other earnestly. Frances, feeling slightly ashamed of her magic potations, withdrew behind a piece of ruined wall and waited for them to pass. She could see them—though not very clearly—but they could not see her. They were too much interested in each other to be observant of their surroundings. The man was in uniform; he was tall and broad-shouldered. The woman was small; she had a light-coloured scarf over her head. It was so still that Frances could hear the murmur of their voices mingling with the murmur of the spring. They were discussing something. The man was urging his companion to come forward and she was hanging back.

Suddenly he seemed to lose patience with her. He walked forward and looked to the left and right. " Don't be a fool," he said loudly. " We can't go back . . . the rag-tag and bobtail of Cairn . . . it's the woods for us, my girl." He took her hand and they disappeared into the thickest part of the woods.

Frances knew now who the man was—it was Widgery. She tried to think ; she tried to be sensible and calm and matter-of-fact. She tried to make up her mind what she should do. . . . Ought she to tell Tommy what she had seen? I can't tell her, thought Frances. I don't know whether I ought to tell her or not, but I *can't*. She thought about it again and began to wonder whether she could possibly have made a mistake. Perhaps it was not Widgery after all. She had not seen him clearly because the light was so dim ; she had recognised him by his voice and by his words. . . . She was certain in her own mind that the man was Widgery but she could not have sworn to the fact. She decided that she must hold her tongue ; she must wait and ask Guy—he would know what to do.

Frances straightened herself. Her muscles were so cramped by the intensity of her feelings that she felt quite stiff. She knew that she must go back to Tommy now. It was almost dark and Tommy would wonder what on earth she had been doing. She must go back to Tommy and talk to her as if nothing had happend, as if everything were perfectly all right.

Poor Tommy, thought Frances. It's dreadful. It's simply horrible. I always knew he was a horrible man. I always wondered how she could possibly love him. . . . That was the worst part of it, of course—Tommy loved him.

Tommy was sitting in exactly the same position; her eyes were shut but she opened them when Frances approached. "Hallo!" she said. "I wasn't asleep—not really—I was just drowsing and dreaming. Funnily enough, I thought I heard Midge's voice."

"You couldn't have heard him," said Frances quickly.

"No, of course not," agreed Tommy.

Frances was aware that, although they were agreed upon the point, they meant something quite different—it was just as well that Tommy had not understood.

"Poor Midge!" continued Tommy, stifling a yawn. "Poor darling Midge. I wonder if he's enjoying himself as much as he expected."

"You'll get cold sitting here," said Frances.

"It's lovely—not cold a bit."

"We've got to get back, and it will be dark going through the woods. Do you know it's nearly midnight?"

"It isn't really. I know your watch says twelve o'clock, but really and truly it's only ten——"

Frances laughed. "I'm not going to argue with you," she said. "The clocks in the hotel will all be saying twelve—not at the same moment, of course, but within about twenty minutes of each other—and if we don't hurry back we shall be locked out for the night."

"It wouldn't matter," declared Tommy, but she rose and followed Frances down the path. It was very dark beneath the trees, and after they had stumbled on for a few minutes they decided to link arms and hold each other up.

"Frances," said Tommy in a low voice. "It's rather fun doing this together."

"I shouldn't like it if I were alone," Frances declared.

The path seemed longer and steeper in the dark, but presently they saw the sea glimmering between the trunks of the trees and knew that they were nearing St. Kiaran's Cove . . . a few steps farther on and they were out of the trees and looking down on to the shore. Suddenly they stopped by one accord, frozen stiff with astonishment. The moonlight gleamed on the water and lit up the scene with a ghostly radiance, and there, in the little bay, were two large rowing-boats full of soldiers. One of the boats had drawn in beside the spit of rock and the men were disembarking. The other boat was waiting its turn, bobbing up and down on the slow swell. For a moment Frances was terrified . . . and then she heard Tommy's chuckle and realised how foolish she had been.

"It's the manœuvres," whispered Tommy. "What a lark! Let's hide and watch them pass."

At one side of the path there was a rock screened by some bushes—it seemed an admirable place to hide. The two girls climbed on to the rock and arranged themselves as comfortably as they could. They could see the path and they could see straight down into the little bay.

The disembarkation took place in silence: the men got out of the boats and crouched on the rocks, waiting until their comrades were ready. Then an officer made a signal and they all rose and followed him. They came straight across the rocks to the path. It was obvious that their leader knew exactly where he was going, and this was not very surprising for their leader was Guy. After Guy came one, two, three . . . twenty men in single file. They passed the rock where the girls were hidden, passed like dark shadows, climbing easily and following carefully in each other's footsteps. They passed so near that Frances could almost have touched them with her hand. It was thrilling. Even though she knew that it was "only a game," Frances was thrilled to the core. Her heart thumped so madly that it seemed as though they must hear it. They passed and filed away—it was like a long dark-green snake winding up the path. Mark was the last man to pass, he raised his head when he came to the rock where the girls were hidden, and they saw his face, shining white in the moonlight. For a moment Frances thought that he had seen them, and then she realised that he was looking up at the moon. They passed and filed away, and the sound of their stealthy footsteps died away in the distance.

Tommy chuckled again. "Fun," she said. "Hide-and-seek. I wonder if they'll get through to the Castle. I wonder how Guy knew about this path."

Frances knew exactly how Guy knew about the path but she kept the information to herself.

"It was a detachment from B Company," continued Tommy. "That's Guy's company, of course, and Mark is his company officer. I counted twenty of them."

They scrambled down off the rock and went on, but they had only gone a few steps when a tall figure in uniform loomed out of the darkness and barred their passage.

"Hallo!" said Tommy. "Is that Sergeant Findlater?"

There were five khaki-clad figures standing round them now, and Frances found the fact a trifle alarming, but Tommy appeared unperturbed.

"Oh, it's Corporal Brown!" exclaimed Tommy in a friendly voice. "I didn't recognise you at first. It's a lovely evening, isn't it? I'm Mrs. Widgery, in case you can't see me in the dark."

"Yes, but where have you come from?" asked the man in some bewilderment.

"Oh, we were sitting on a rock," replied Tommy. "We saw the others pass. We're just on our way back to the hotel."

"I'm afraid you can't go," he said.

"What!" asked Tommy in surprise.

"It's orders," he explained.

"Your orders don't affect us."

"They affect us," he said firmly. "Orders is that nobody's to pass this way."

Tommy laughed. "But we aren't playing," she said.

"My orders is that nobody's to pass," repeated Corporal Brown in stubborn accents. "I'm sorry about it, but there it is. Nobody *is* to pass, so nobody *can* pass."

"You know me——" began Tommy.

"Yes, ma'am," agreed the Corporal. "I know you all right—it would be a funny thing if I didn't—but orders is orders. There wasn't anything about me using my discretion about who was to pass, so if you were the Queen herself it would be just the same. We've to wait here for thirty-five minutes and if they haven't come back by then we've to row back to camp. Nobody's to pass, that was what the Captain said. You heard the orders, Melton."

"Yes, that's roight," agreed one of the other men in a deep bass voice.

Tommy saw that it was no use to press the point. "Oh, well, I suppose we shall have to wait here until you go."

"That's all," agreed the Corporal in a relieved tone, "and it's only twenty-six and a half minutes to wait now."

One of the men spread his coat on the bank and the girls sat down. It was quite dark but there was a half-moon floating in the sky. The sea gleamed like pewter. Tommy lighted a cigarette. She offered some to the soldiers, but Corporal Brown refused and they all followed suit.

"We're on duty," he explained.

"We're at war," declared one of the other men with a chuckle.

"We're Germans landing in Britain," said a third.

165

"Have you killed us?" asked Tommy cheerfully.

"No," replied Corporal Brown. "We've taken you prisoner, that's all. We aren't out to kill women."

"What's happening, exactly?" Tommy inquired.

Corporal Brown hesitated and then he said: "I don't suppose it matters, telling you now. There's four column's converging on Cairn Castle. There's thirty men from each company taking part in the exercise."

"Four columns?" repeated Tommy. "I suppose you've got a fifth column inside the Castle."

The Corporal did not understand the allusion—neither did Frances for that matter—so Tommy explained what she meant. "It was when General Franco was marching on Madrid," said Tommy. "Somebody asked him how many troops he had, and he replied that he had four columns with him and a fifth column in Madrid itself. *Now,* of course, the term 'fifth column' has passed into everyday use and is taken to mean—well, to mean traitors, really, but that wasn't General Franco's meaning."

"I never knew that," declared the Corporal. "I've used the term myself but I'm—er—blowed if I knew what it meant."

"Which company is Captain Widgery with to-night?" asked Tommy suddenly.

"He isn't taking part in the exercise," replied Corporal Brown.

"He's the Adjutant, you see, ma'am," added one of the other men.

"I know he's the Adjutant," declared Tommy, laughing. "I know that to my cost, but he's taking part in the game, I can tell you that for certain."

There was a little silence. Tommy had spoken so confidently that nobody liked to contradict her.

"Perhaps he's with A Company," said Tommy. "Major Liston is away just now, so——"

"There's someone else coming," said Melton suddenly.

They all cocked their ears and listened. Frances heard the sound of a stone rolling down the path, but that was all she heard.

"It's them coming back," said Corporal Brown below his breath.

"No," said Melton.

They listened again.

"It may have been a rabbit," suggested one of the other men.

"No," said Melton. "It was someone—two people, I think.
166

They've gone back now—must have heard us talking or smelt Mrs. Widgery's cigarette—anyhow, they've gone back."

"How can you possibly tell?" asked Tommy with interest.

"I'm a country man," he replied.

"He's a poacher," explained Corporal Brown. "That's what he is in private life."

They all laughed and Melton joined in the laughter.

"I've always heard that poachers were very useful people to have in a regiment on active service," Tommy said.

They chatted quietly after that. Tommy was always friendly, sincerely friendly, with every soul she met, and every soul she met was friendly in return. Frances had sometimes wondered how she had learnt to adapt herself so that all kinds and conditions of people were perfectly comfortable with her. To-night Frances made the discovery that Tommy did not adapt herself consciously—Tommy loved her neighbour and that was why her neighbour loved her.

"It's thirty-three," said Corporal Brown at last. "Thirty-three minutes. They must have got through."

Tommy got up and stretched herself. She said: "Well, it will be your fault if the hotel's shut and we have to spend the night on the beach. Good-night, Corporal Brown."

"We'll row you back," he said. "It'll be easier for you than walking back in the dark—it's on our way. We'll drop you off at Cairn Harbour . . . wait a moment, though. We must give them the full time."

The two prisoners were escorted over the rocks to the spit of rock where the boats were waiting, and Frances noticed that there were five men guarding the boats. (The exercise was being conducted in an exceedingly war-like manner—but of course it would be no use to have the exercise at all unless it was properly carried out.) Melton—the poacher—had made himself responsible for Frances and was holding her firmly by the elbow, and she was glad of his help for it was difficult to see where she was going.

"It's slippy, isn't it?" Melton said. "It's dark too—not much of a moon to-night. You aren't cold, are you, miss?"

"No, not a bit, thank you," replied Frances.

"You didn't mind being kept back, did you?" asked Melton anxiously. "The corporal couldn't do nothing else. It was orders —Captain Tarlatan's orders."

"We didn't mind at all," declared Frances with perfect truth.

"I'm glad B Company got through," said Melton. "B Com-

167

pany's the best in the regiment, and Captain Tarlatan—well, he's the best officer. There's no one like Captain Tarlatan, that's what I say."

Frances had thought from the first that Melton was a very intelligent man—she was sure of it now.

Chapter Twenty-four

SUNDAY WAS a quiet day at Cairn. Frances had hoped that Guy would come over from the camp, for she wanted to speak to him about the Widgerys, but Guy did not appear. He had been out all night, of course, so perhaps he was resting. On Monday morning Frances walked over to Sea View (she was worried about Tommy and could not keep away). She found Tommy very busy putting her house in order.

"I'm leaving this afternoon," said Tommy. "I'm going to Aberdeen. I told you about it, didn't I? You can have the house if I don't come back—if I'm killed on the road or anything —you can have the house and everything in it, everything except Midge."

"Tommy, what *is* the matter?" inquired Frances in dismay.

"Nothing," said Tommy. "Nothing at all. That's the ridiculous part of it. Everything has fitted in splendidly. I've managed to save enough petrol to get to Aberdeen and I've got my petrol coupons for this month to come back with. I'm starting immediately after lunch and spending the night in Glasgow with a friend. Midge is leaving for London to-morrow morning and we're both coming back on Saturday. Everything has fitted in perfectly—just like a jigsaw puzzle."

"Well, then, why——"

"It's fitted *too* well," Tommy declared. "There's bound to be a snag somewhere. I've got a feeling that it's a horribly big snag. I don't *want* to go."

Frances comforted Tommy as best she could, and they kissed each other when they parted.

"That's the first time we've kissed each other," said Tommy, smiling a trifle sadly. "Wouldn't it be—wouldn't it be strange if it was the last time, Frances?"

"Nonsense," said Frances, trying to laugh but not succeeding at all well. "Absolute nonsense, Tommy. We're friends——"

"Yes, of course we are," Tommy said.

It was raining hard in the afternoon, but **Frances felt so restless**, so worried and upset, that she put on her oilskins and went for a walk. She returned late for tea and found Guy Tarlatan in the lounge. He was drinking a cocktail and smoking and turning over the pages of an old and extremely tattered *Punch*.

"Hallo, Frances," he said. "Where have you been? I thought you would be in because it's such a foul day. Do you like walking in the rain?"

"Sometimes," said Frances. She hesitated and then added: "I wanted to see you, Guy. I wanted to tell you something."

"Go ahead," he replied, smiling at her.

Frances sat down beside him. She had taken off her sou'-wester, and her hair was in a mess, but she was not thinking about her hair. "It's Tommy," she said. "I'm terribly worried about Tommy . . . there's something wrong."

"Something wrong?" he said. "There's always been something wrong. Widgery is selfish."

"Selfish!" she exclaimed, almost laughing at the absurdity of the description.

"Selfish to the bone," nodded Guy. "He thinks and cares for nobody and nothing except himself. He admires nothing but himself. He's the vainest man on earth. I'm just about through with Captain Middleton Widgery if you want to know the truth."

"Yes," said Frances, "but the fact is——"

"Tommy hasn't the slightest idea how to manage him," continued Guy, "and that's odd, you know, because—well—because she's rather clever at managing people—no, that isn't what I mean. I mean, she has an instinct for getting on with people."

"Oh, yes," agreed Frances.

"So it's very unfortunate indeed that her instinct should fail her where he's concerned."

"Yes," said Frances again.

"It's because," said Guy gravely—"it's because she loves him too much. Never love anyone too much, Frances. It's the very devil. It puts you so hopelessly in their power. It makes you such a coward. You're afraid to—to say anything when you're with them, and then, when you aren't with them, you find all sorts of things you might have said. You make up your mind that you'll say all the things next time—and then you don't."

Frances had a feeling that he had forgotten about the Widgerys and she brought him back firmly to the subject. "I wanted to tell you," she said. "It's about Captain Widgery. I saw him in the woods. I'm practically certain it was he——" She hesitated. She had known it would be difficult to tell Guy, but it was

169

even more difficult than she had expected. She felt herself blushing furiously—that absurd blush always made her angry.

"He was with a woman, I suppose," said Guy.

"How did you know?"

"It wasn't very difficult to guess. Who was the woman, Frances?"

"I don't know. It was dark—at least it was half dark. I recognised him by his voice and by something he said."

"Was it a woman from the village?"

"It might have been. She had a light scarf—or perhaps it was a shawl—tied over her head. I didn't know *what* to do," said Frances earnestly. "I couldn't make up my mind what I ought to do—so I thought I'd tell you."

"What can I do?" he asked.

"I thought you'd know what was the right thing," said Frances.

He smiled at her. He had a very charming smile. "We must do nothing," he said. "Do nothing and say nothing . . . now that you've spilt the beans we can enjoy ourselves. Have a drink, Frances? Well, have a cigarette? I've been so busy over that blinking exercise that I haven't seen you for days."

"I saw you on Saturday," said Frances.

"Where?"

"Where do you think?" she asked, smiling at him. "I was so near you that I could almost have touched you—you and your invaders!"

"You weren't in the woods?"

Frances told him about their adventure, she told him everything that had happened . . . there was only one omission in her story: she did not tell him about her drink at the magic spring. . . .

When she had finished and Guy had stopped laughing he took up the tale himself and gave Frances a short account of the night's operations. "It was a good show," he said. "It really was a most useful night's work—not only for the Home Guard but for ourselves as well. The other columns approached the castle from the land—they were supposed to be parachutists—but I knew about that path so I said I would approach from the sea. You saw us arrive and disembark; they did it well, didn't they? When we got to the chapel we lay doggo for a bit while Mark took a couple of fellows and did a bit of scouting. I was rather amused when one of the fellows discovered the spring—they all had a drink, every man jack of them. I didn't tell them the awful fate they were bringing upon themselves." He paused and smiled, and Frances smiled back. "I had another drink myself," declared Guy. "I thought I might as well do the thing thoroughly while I was about it."

"Yes," agreed Frances. "If you are going to be married it *is* better to be thoroughly married——"

"Mark scouted round for a bit and then he came back and said there was a detachment of the Home Guard farther up the path, so we divided the men into two lots. Mark's detachment was to show itself and draw off the defenders while we nipped past . . . the plan worked splendidly. We made a detour and came up near the ruins of the old castle; we hid there for a bit and then slipped in at the dining-room window, and there we were. When old MacDonald got back he was a bit chagrined, but he was very decent about it. We were the only people who managed to get through without being spotted; the others were all mopped up before they'd gone half a mile. It was pretty good work on the part of the Home Guard."

"You got through," Frances said.

"I know, but it wasn't really very fair. We wouldn't have got through if I hadn't known the lie of the land. A real invader wouldn't have the local knowledge unless he managed to get hold of a Quisling." Guy rose and looked out of the window—the rain was coming down in sheets.

"This is an awful place when it's wet," said Guy a trifle fretfully. "Why don't they have a billiard-room?"

"We could play some other game," suggested Frances.

"What sort of game?" he asked. "Can you play shove halfpenny, Frances?"

She saw there was a twinkle in his eye, so she replied gravely: "No, I'm afraid not, but perhaps I could learn."

"It's a very difficult game," declared Guy. "If there had been a billiard-table——"

"There's a backgammon board," Frances said.

He laughed. "Well, why not? I haven't played since I was a child, but we'll have a shot at it if you would like to."

Frances fetched the backgammon board (she had seen it lying on the shelf below the Waverley Novels). They put it on the table and set out the pieces. At first Guy was not very skilful—nor very interested—but after two games, which Frances won quite easily, he drew in his chair and settled down to it in earnest. Frances had always been able to beat Uncle Henry two games out of three, but she discovered that Guy was quite a different antagonist. He was cautious—as all backgammon players should be—but his caution was leavened with dashes of recklessness which took her by surprise. In the third game Frances was very nearly gammoned; she only avoided the disaster by throwing double sixes twice running.

He grinned at her and said: "Frances, you prayed."

"What?" asked Frances in surprise.

"You prayed," he repeated. "It isn't fair to pray. When we were small Elise and I used to play golf together, and it was considered exceedingly bad form to pray for your putt to go down—it was *almost* cheating. You must have prayed for double sixes, I'm afraid."

"No, honestly," said Frances, smiling.

They arranged the pieces for another battle. "It's a good game," he said. "I'd forgotten what an awfully good game it is. Come on, Frances, I'm going to gammon you this time."

They were still playing when Elise came into the lounge. She crossed over to the table and watched them. "Look," said Elise, leaning on Guy's shoulder and pointing to the board. "Look, Guy, you silly ass, you could have made a point in your inner table."

"Go away," said Guy. "Go and play with your baby. We're busy."

She laughed and sat down near the fire and took up her sewing. She was making a frock for Jennifer and embroidering it with daisies.

"Where is your baby?" asked Guy. "Where is my beautiful niece?"

"In bed, of course," replied her mother.

"Is Ned coming over?"

"No."

"I'll dine with you if you like."

"I *would* like," replied Elise, smiling at him fondly, "but the fact is I promised to dine with Tillie. Jack is away and she's feeling dull, so I promised I would go. It's a frightful nuisance——"

"Oh, damn," said Guy. "I can't talk and play backgammon at the same time. You've taken me again—I didn't notice that blot—and your inner table is full. How unkind you are, Frances!"

"Perhaps you would like to dine with me," said Frances rather shyly.

"Yes," said Guy. "Yes, let's dine together and go for a walk afterwards—it has stopped raining now."

It had stopped raining and the clouds had vanished as if some-one had taken a broom and swept the sky clean. Frances had seen this happen before at Cairn—it was one of the beauties of the place. One never knew from hour to hour what the weather would be; clouds blew up suddenly and filled the sky, and then, just as suddenly they were gone.

"We might walk along the shore," Guy continued. "It would be rather nice, wouldn't it? The tide is going out."

"Are you sure?" asked Frances in significant tones.

"Perfectly certain," he replied. "As a matter of fact I make it my business, now, to know what the sea is doing."

"Why?" asked Elise, looking up from her work.

"Because," said Guy. "Because—oh, just because it's a good thing to know. Time spent on reconnaissance is seldom wasted."

"So you reconnoitre the sea?"

"Daily," nodded Guy.

Chapter Twenty-five

FRANCES AND Guy dined together at the little table in the window, and as there was nobody else in the dining-room they were able to talk freely. Guy seemed different to-night; he was quiet and graver than usual—it was almost as if he were thinking of something, as if he had something on his mind—but in spite of this their conversation was more intimate and friendly, and Frances felt more at ease with him than she had ever felt before. He began to tell her about his boyhood and his school days and about the miseries of never having a settled home. Frances had heard something of this from Elise, and now she was hearing the same story from Guy's point of view.

"It was like a dark cloud on one's horizon," said Guy. "The other fellows at school looked forward to the holidays—they counted the days—but I didn't. They went home to their parents, they had ponies and dogs, they looked forward to seeing their familiar haunts. I never knew where I was going—sometimes to one set of relations and sometimes to another. Very often there was a muddle over it. I used to worry and worry. I lay awake at night for hours when all the other fellows were snoring away like foghorns. It was the same for Elise, of course—she was at a school at Bournemouth—but somehow or other I don't think she worried quite so much as I did."

"It must have been very bad for you," said Frances.

"It made me a freak," he replied, smiling at her. "It made

173

me different from the other fellows—boys don't like freaks, they like people who are the same as themselves. I suppose it was because I had a different background. At any rate it took me a long time to learn to behave like other people . . . and I'm still different inside," added Guy, laughing.

" Don't you think everyone feels like that—different inside?"

" Not everyone, but I believe you do."

" Of course I do," cried Frances, " and I haven't learned to behave like other people. I'm still a freak."

He looked at her rather strangely, so strangely that Frances dashed into hasty speech. " Didn't your parents understand?" she asked. " Didn't they write and arrange about your holidays?"

" Of course they wrote," said Guy; " but letters from India take weeks to come, and sometimes Elise and I had no idea where we were going to spend our holidays until the very last minute. That was bad enough, but what was worse was the feeling that our relations didn't want us, that they were just having us because there was nowhere else for us to go. Sometimes we spent the holidays with an aunt at Beckenham; she had three girls, lumpy, uninteresting girls. There was one occasion when a dreadful thing happened—at least it seemed dreadful at the time. It was arranged that we were to go to this aunt and then one of the girls developed whooping-cough. Elise had just had whooping-cough at school, so it didn't matter for her, but I hadn't had the foul complaint. At the very last minute everything was upset, and I was packed off to another aunt at Margate—I shall never forget what I felt like. You see, Elise was all I had and I was all she had; we scarcely knew our parents. It seemed the end of the world to be going to Margate and not to be seeing Elise. The cousins at Margate were much older than I was and made no secret of the fact that I was a confounded nuisance—I've no doubt I was. At any rate I was miserable and I got miserable letters from Elise. Suddenly I felt that I could bear it no longer; I felt I *had* to see Elise, so I just walked out of the house and went. I got a bus part of the way and I walked and got lifts. I arrived in the middle of the night and threw stones at Elise's window and she came down at once. She wasn't a bit surprised to see me, in fact she was expecting me. The Margate people had telephoned to say I had vanished, and Elise was quite certain I was on my way to see her. Of course there was a tremendous row between the two aunts—they didn't like each other much at the best of times—but fortunately the Beckenham aunt took our part and said I was to stay there for the rest of the holidays
174

and risk the whooping-cough and, as I was there already and possession is nine points of the law, the other aunt couldn't do anything about it. The fact was the Beckenham aunt was rather pleased because I had walked out on the other aunt," declared Guy, laughing.

"I don't wonder you're devoted to Elise," said Frances.

"She's a splendid person, isn't she?"

"And so beautiful."

"I'm glad you and Elise like each other," said Guy in a thoughtful voice.

They had finished dinner now, so they strolled out into the street. Some officers had just arrived from the camp and were standing outside the door talking and smoking, and Guy introduced them to Frances.

"I've heard of Miss Field," declared Captain Rackham, "and I've seen her several times, but I haven't had the pleasure of speaking to her before."

"Fox is a foxy beast," said one of the others.

They all laughed, and Guy joined in the laughter quite cheerfully.

"Have you got a sister, Miss Field?" asked Captain Rackham.

"No," said Frances in some surprise.

"That's a pity," he said, shaking his head. "That's a great pity. I was going to suggest that she might like to come to the Bordale Arms for a holiday."

"Half a dozen sisters wouldn't be too many," declared one of the other officers.

"We're going for a walk," said Guy.

"You wouldn't like me to come with you, I suppose?" asked Captain Rackham.

"Your supposition is correct," replied Guy, smiling at him in a friendly manner.

"Two's company, Racky," one of his friends reminded him.

Guy extricated himself and Frances from the little group, and they walked down to the shore. It was a lovely evening. The trees had been washed by the rain and every leaf was sparkling in the sunshine, the air was fresh and there was a delicious earthy smell.

"Which way shall we go?" asked Guy, pausing at the harbour. "Shall we go north along cliffs or south across the bay?"

Frances did not mind which way they went, she was happy to be with Guy. "It doesn't matter which way we go," she replied, and Guy agreed that it didn't. As a matter of fact they were both wrong, for a good deal depended upon their choice.

They went down from the rocks on to the sand, and the big bay stretched before them, gleaming in the sunshine. The tide was out and the wet sands were dazzling to the eyes.

"We'll walk along to the point, shall we?" suggested Guy. "We could come back through the woods. You're sure you wouldn't rather go by the cliffs, Frances?"

"I don't mind a bit," she said.

Frances had decided to tell Guy about her life at the Wheelers' —to tell him all about herself. He had asked her before what she was, and she had refused to tell him, for she had felt that the slight mystery was a sort of shield, but now he had told her so much about himself that he deserved something in return. . . . Frances was no longer frightened of Guy, she did not need her shield. They walked along in silence for a few moments. Frances was trying to find words to begin her story, so she had no time to wonder at Guy's silence or to guess its meaning. As is so often the way after a short silence, they both began to speak at the same moment.

"Frances, I have been trying to ask you——" began Guy.

"Guy, I wanted to tell you——" began Frances.

They looked at each other and laughed. "Ladies first," said Guy.

"It was just that I wanted to tell you what I used to do," said Frances. "You asked me once. It isn't very interesting, really. I used to live with an uncle and aunt in London and keep house for them."

"The story of your life in one short sentence."

"Yes, I told you it wasn't interesting. You see, my father and mother died when I was a child——" She stopped. Somehow or other she had become aware that Guy was not listening. She looked up at him in surprise and saw that he was gazing along the sands, shading his eyes from the glare with his hand to his forehead.

"Look," he said. "Look—there's Angela. It *is* Angela, isn't it?"

Frances shaded her eyes too. The sands were deserted except for one small figure at the other end of the bay. She could not be sure whether or not it was Angela, but it might be.

"Perhaps she's going to see Tommy," said Frances. "Perhaps she doesn't know that Tommy has gone——"

Guy had taken out his glasses and was focusing them. "By Jove it *is*—it's Angela! I think I'll—yes, I must speak to her— you understand, don't you?"

He was off like an arrow before Frances could answer; he was running with long strides, covering the ground easily and without effort; he ran so well that his feet scarcely seemed to touch the ground.

Frances stood still. She was a humble-minded person, but even humble-minded people have their pride. . . . She was surprised and hurt and angry and humiliated all at the same moment. It was rude . . . it was more than rude, it was unkind. Frances had been feeling so friendly towards Guy, she had been feeling more than friendly. She had begun to tell him about herself and he had not wanted to hear. It was Angela, and not Frances, that Guy was interested in . . . it was Angela. . . .

Frances had never experienced such a storm of feeling before. Her knees felt so weak that she was forced to sit down on the sand. She took up handfuls of sand and squeezed them so that the grains trickled between her fingers. Tears of mortification stung her eyes . . . she had made herself too cheap. She had been too friendly with him. She had asked him to dine with her . . . he couldn't very well have refused.

The storm was passing now, and Frances was beginning to feel cold and a trifle sick; she was beginning to think about the whole thing more calmly and reasonably. (Am I making a mountain out of a molehill? she asked herself. Was it quite a natural thing to do, to ask me to come out for a walk and then leave me to rush off after Angela?) But however calmly and reasonably she thought about it, she could not see that it was anything but rude . . . outrageously rude . . . unkind. She reminded herself that these new friends of hers had a different standard of behaviour from that to which she was accustomed— they took things for granted and their manners were easy-going —but in spite of their easy-going manners, Frances had never found them lacking in consideration, she had never found them unkind, quite the contrary. Frances was forced to realise that it must have been a very strong motive which had induced her late companion to desert her like that . . . a very strong motive indeed. She looked back. "Guy has taken a great deal of interest in Angela lately," Tommy had said, and Tommy had returned to the subject of Guy and Angela more than once. Guy had said himself that Angela sparkled in an amusing manner. . . . Frances was aware that *she* did not sparkle at all. Angela was attractive, she was younger than Frances; she was the Colonel's daughter and was therefore one of the regiment, inside the fence. Frances had realised long ago that the regiment was clannish, that it was a little society complete in itself; she had realised that it was not snobbery, they did not fence themselves in deliberately, they had

177

never tried to shut her out—in fact, they often went out of their way to draw her inside the fence—but their own society was congenial, and their community of ideas and interests resulted in a common attitude towards life, and this made a bond between them which overcame the differences in their natures. No two people could have been more different than Tillie and Elise, but they were friends, they were both inside the fence . . . so it was natural that Guy and Angela . . .

Frances looked back further and remembered that very first night when they all met at the Bordale Arms. Guy and Captain Widgery had both offered to walk home with Angela, but Guy had been so insistent that he had won the day and carried her off in triumph.

Frances waited for a little. She had a faint hope at the back of her mind that Guy might return to her and explain everything. (She imagined him running back to her across the sands and saying: " Awfully sorry to leave you like that, but I had to give Angela a message.") But Guy did not come back—he and Angela had both disappeared; there was not a soul to be seen. She got up at last and went back to the hotel. The little group of officers was still standing at the door and a burst of laughter met her ears as she approached.

" Hallo, Miss Field!" exclaimed Captain Rackham. " What have you done with Fox?"

Someone else replied for her. " Oh, she got bored with him and pushed him into the sea. Now's your chance, Racky."

They all laughed, for they were in the mood when any joke, however feeble, seems the soul of wit. Frances's mood was very different. It was an effort to smile; it was an effort to pass them, to cross the hall and run upstairs. She shut her bedroom door and turned the key, and stood with her back against it looking round the room.

PART III

GUY

Chapter Twenty-six

GUY HAD won the mile at Sandhurst and, as he had been running a good deal in the last few months (running being a part of the new training system), he made pretty good time across the long stretch of sands; but Angela had had a long start and had reached Sea View some minutes before him. Guy paused at the door to recover his breath (he had no wish to put himself at a disadvantage by entering upon a delicate interview incapable of speech), but he was in such excellent training that his heart soon ceased to pound uncomfortably and his lungs resumed their normal functioning. Guy opened the door and walked straight in, and he found—exactly what he had expected to find—Widgery and Angela locked in each other's arms. In spite of his preparedness the scene disgusted Guy a good deal more than he had anticipated, for it is one thing to expect and another to see.

" Are you practising for a film, or what?" he inquired, trying to speak lightly.

They sprang apart and faced him. " What the devil d'you mean by forcing your way in here!" cried Widgery in furious tones.

" I've come to take Angela home," replied Guy.

" What the hell has it got to do with you? Can't you see when you aren't wanted? Angela hasn't any use for you——"

" I haven't much use for Angela——"

" Then why the hell can't you leave her alone?"

" I'll explain all that presently," replied Guy, trying to speak quite calmly. " Meanwhile Angela had better go home. She can go home by herself—yes, that would be better, there are several things I should like to say to you——"

" Guy," began Angela in a breathless voice. " Guy, you don't understand."

" No," agreed Guy. " No, and I don't want to. You can explain the whole thing to your father. Perhaps he'll understand——"

" You wouldn't!" she cried. " Oh, you beast, Guy! There's nothing—nothing wrong——"

179

"Your ideas of right and wrong are different from mine," declared Guy.

"Keep your ideas to yourself," Widgery exclaimed. "Get out of here before I break your neck——"

"Come and try," said Guy evenly. He had been spoiling for a fight with Widgery for weeks; a hundred small incidents had fanned the flame, and now it seemed as if zero hour had arrived. Guy was glad. He was pretty certain that he could thrash Widgery, for, although Widgery was bigger, he was not in such good trim . . . and Widgery was angry. Guy was angry too, but he had himself well in control—his was a cold rage.

"Come and try," said Guy again.

Widgery hesitated. He said: "Don't be such a fool. It's nothing to do with you——"

"Of course if you're afraid," said Guy with a short laugh. "It's easy to scheme and lie and carry on with women behind your wife's back—but there's a soft streak in you, Widgery . . ."

Widgery came at Guy, but Guy stepped aside nimbly and dealt him a stinging blow on the ear as he blundered past. Then Widgery turned and hit Guy in the stomach. It didn't hurt much, but it annoyed him a good deal; he lunged forward to Widgery's face with a right that had a good deal of weight behind it. Widgery moved his head and the blow met air . . . before Guy could recover Widgery grasped his arm and kicked him savagely on the shin. It was painful, but Guy was quite pleased about it, for it absolved him from any rules . . . this was not to be a gentleman's fight. Guy seized Widgery round the waist and tried to throw him, but he couldn't manage it. They swayed to and fro, Widgery battering at Guy's face when the opportunity occurred. . . . All this time Angela was screaming; she seized Guy's coat and tried to pull him away. This hampered him considerably, for he had no wish to hurt Angela . . . he tried to push her to one side, and, as he did so, Widgery wriggled and slipped from his grasp.

Guy stepped in and hit Widgery as hard as he could. He had aimed at Widgery's chin, but again Widgery had moved his head and the blow took him on the shoulder . . . he staggered but recovered himself and came at Guy again. Guy eluded him and hit him as he passed, harder than before. It was a satisfactory blow, for it landed fair and square on Widgery's face. Guy was feeling grand now, for he knew he could lick Widgery—he had him taped.

"Stand up and fight like a man," said Guy.

Widgery stood up; he hit out with his left, but Guy warded
180

the blow with his right arm and followed it up with a punch with his left. Widgery feinted with his left and landed a right on Guy's cheek, but he had overreached himself and Guy was able to get in another punch with his right before Widgery was ready. Widgery seized Guy's arm and twisted it, and Guy with his other hand forced back Widgery's head. They struggled for a moment, and then Widgery turned sideways; he stumbled against the table, and the table fell with a crash. . . . Angela screamed again.

"Go home," said Guy a trifle breathlessly. "I told you to go home, Angela."

Widgery had picked himself up and was coming for Guy; he had lost his temper completely and his arms were flailing like the sails of a windmill. Guy waited for him, intending to step aside and punish him as he passed, but Widgery leapt at Guy's throat and forced his head back, kicking him again. It was an unpleasant moment, but Widgery was breathing heavily, and his grasp was not so strong. . . . Guy managed to twist himself free.

Guy stepped back to get room for the straight left which was going to finish the fight . . . he stepped back, but there was something behind him . . . a footstool . . . he felt himself falling backwards . . . he fell with a crash.

When Guy opened his eyes it was dark, but there was a yellow pinpoint of light moving about the room. He had not the faintest idea of where he was or what had happened.

"Is it an air-raid—" he asked.

The light came nearer and now he could see that it emanated from an electric torch the battery of which was at its last gasp. He could see the torch and part of a hand.

"Who is it?" asked Guy.

"It's Tommy," said Tommy's voice. "I'm trying to find some matches."

Guy's head ached horribly, but his brain was clearing. He was beginning to remember what had happened . . . Widgery . . . he had fought Widgery . . . had Widgery knocked him out? No, by Jove he had almost finished the fellow . . . and then . . . then he had fallen over that blasted stool. What had happened after that, and what on earth was Tommy doing here?

"What's happened?" asked Guy rather faintly.

"Heaven knows," replied Tommy. "If you don't know what's happened, how should I? If only I could find a match——"

"Here's a match," said Guy.

181

The torch had flickered out completely by this time, but Tommy groped about and took the box from his hand. He heard her drawing the curtains across the windows and then the scrape of a match, and in another moment the room was filled with golden lamplight.

"Good lord!" exclaimed Tommy.

Guy was not surprised to hear this exclamation, for he was aware that the room must look somewhat disordered. It is impossible for two large men to fight a mill in a sitting-room without causing a certain amount of damage.

"Good lord," said Tommy again. "What on earth has been happening?"

"I fell," said Guy. "I fell over that blinking stool and hit my head." He sat up as he spoke and felt his head. There was a lump on it and his hair was sticky. His fingers were covered with blood when he looked at them—it must have been the castor of the chair. Apart from the bump on his head the only injuries he had received were a swollen cheek and a severe bruise on the shin.

"Guy, you look as if you had been fighting!" declared Tommy, gazing at him in surprise.

"Do I?"

"And the room looks like it too," she added.

"My head feels awfully queer," said Guy a trifle fretfully. "I must have hit it on something as I fell." He had hoped to distract her attention from the condition of the room, and his ruse was successful, for Tommy was a sympathetic creature.

She knelt down beside him and examined his wound. "It's bleeding," she said in dismay. "Oh, Guy, no wonder your head feels queer. I shall have to cut some of your hair and put a wet dressing on it——"

"Shove on iodine," said Guy. "Iodine's the stuff."

Tommy found some iodine and dabbed it on with cotton-wool. She fetched a pot of ointment and applied it to his cheek, then she sat back and demanded an explanation.

"I told you," said Guy. "I fell over the stool. What are you doing here? I thought you were on your way to Aberdeen."

"You thought I was on my way to Aberdeen, so you came here to see me—or was it Midge you came to see?"

"Midgey, of course—but why did you change your mind?"

"I had a puncture," she replied. "And the spare tyre was flat. It took ages and I knew I should be frightfully late getting to Glasgow . . . and so—so I just changed my mind and came home. I had a feeling that something was wrong. What happened, Guy?"

"I fell and bumped my head," said Guy again. "I must have knocked over the table as I fell."

She looked round the room. "I don't believe it," she said. "What were you *doing*? Where's Midge?"

"I wish Elise were here," declared Guy. He felt quite unable to deal with the situation himself. Ought he to tell Tommy the truth? His head still felt muzzy and his brains had turned into cotton-wool.

"Where's Midge?" repeated Tommy.

"I don't know," replied Guy. He would have given quite a lot to know where Widgery had gone and whether he had taken Angela with him.

"Was Midge here when you came over?" asked Tommy.

"I don't remember," mumbled Guy. "Yes, I believe he was, really . . ."

"Guy," said Tommy earnestly, "Guy, you're frightening me. I must know what happened. I simply must. If you don't tell me I shall begin to imagine all sorts of horrible things."

He looked at Tommy doubtfully. He was very fond of her. He had tried his best to help her and to shield her. If Tommy began to imagine things . . . but she could not imagine anything more horrible than the truth. How could he possibly tell her? Now that Guy had begun to think it over in cold blood he was a trifle ashamed of the part he had played. He realised that if he had not been so furiously angry he might have handled the situation better. Why hadn't he knocked on the door and warned them of his presence? He might have pretended that he had blown in to see how Widgery was getting on; he might have pretended that he saw nothing strange in Angela's presence; he might have offered to walk home with her and got her away without a scene—he had got her away from Widgery before. Would it have been better to have used diplomacy rather than force, or would it have just put off the evil day? Guy did not know; he only knew that he had hoped to give Widgery a thrashing and had failed—he had made a complete fool of himself.

Guy rose, somewhat gingerly, and sat down in a chair. His head spun round, but he managed to steady it.

"How do you feel now?" asked Tommy anxiously.

"Not too good," he replied.

Tommy glanced at him and then went and fetched a bottle of whisky. She poured some into a glass. "Will you have it neat?" she asked.

"No, half and half," replied Guy. "I've got to get back to camp."

"You can't," she said. "I'll make up the bed in the little room."

"No," said Guy. "No, I must get back."

"But, Guy——"

"No, honestly," he said. "It wouldn't be a good thing—I mean, I must go back." He realised that things were already in such a frightful tangle that the sooner he got out of here the better. It would add to the confusion if he spent the night at Sea View. "I'm better," he said, smiling at Tommy. "I'm feeling fairly all right now, and the fresh air will do me good."

"But you aren't fit——"

"Yes, I'm quite all right."

"Why not lie down for a little——"

"No, really," said Guy.

Tommy followed him to the door. "Guy, please," she said, laying her hand on his arm. "Please, Guy, tell me what happened. You know I'm quite a sensible person, don't you?"

"Yes, of course, Tommy, but I've told you——"

"Was Midge here when you fell?"

"Yes," said Guy.

"He was here!" exclaimed Tommy. "He was here when you fell and went away and left you lying on the floor?"

"No—of course not. He couldn't have been here, could he? He must have gone before that."

"Where did he go? He intended to sleep here to-night."

"He changed his mind," said Guy. "He didn't tell me where he was going."

Tommy hesitated. She said: "Well—perhaps he went to Rithie for the night so that he wouldn't have such an early start in the morning. He's going to London, you know."

"Yes," agreed Guy with relief. "Yes, I expect that's what he did."

"He's taken all his things, his shaving tackle and everything, so he must have done that, mustn't he?"

"Yes, that's what he's done," declared Guy in a cheerful tone. "That's the explanation of it. I must go now," he added, patting her hand. "You aren't afraid of being left here alone, are you?"

"No," said Tommy doubtfully.

He took no notice of the doubtful tone in her voice. "That's good," he said. "That's splendid. You'll be quite all right. I can't stay with you because—because I must get back to camp.

184

I'll come over and see you in the morning—or send someone—yes, I'll send Mark over first thing. Good-night, Tommy."

" Good-night," she returned.

"Lock the door, won't you?"

"Yes, of course."

He walked down the path to the gate. It was very dark and cloudy. It was so dark that Guy felt as if he were inside a box. He could see nothing at all. He stood still for a few minutes and shut his eyes . . . when he opened them, he found he could see a bit better. Fortunately he knew the path well; he knew every little hump and hummock on the way . . . he walked on, and as he walked he turned everything over in his mind. He hated leaving Tommy there alone, but what else could he do? It would not be long until the dawn, already there was a faint greyness in the eastern sky. He hurried on when he noticed that greyness, for he wanted to get back to his quarters unseen. He did not want anyone to know that he had spent most of the night at Sea View. Everything was in such a muddle that it made his head ache to think of it, and it would add to the tangle if his absence from his quarters was discovered.

There were sentries round the camp, but Guy knew where they were and he knew the lie of the ground like the palm of his hand. He turned to the left when he got near the camp and approached it through a thick belt of undergrowth. Curiously enough, Guy had suggested to Colonel Thynne that this belt of undergrowth should be removed—it was not sound to have cover of this nature so near the camp—but although Colonel Thynne had agreed with the principle, he had taken no action in the matter. Guy smiled to himself—it was rather funny, really. He crept up through the undergrowth and saw the sentry standing near the hedge. The sentry stood there for several minutes—perhaps he had heard something—then he moved on. Guy waited for him to pass and then crawled through a gap in the hedge and made his way along the ditch. The sentry was walking up and down. When his back was turned, Guy made a dash for it. He ran about fifty yards and then threw himself face downwards on the ground. Another sentry was coming. The second sentry passed quite close to Guy, but it was still very dark so he did not see him. The two sentries met and exchanged a few words and then parted again. Guy waited until both their backs were turned and then made another dash. He reached the nearest hut and turned the corner. (As he stood there, listening, he decided that he must speak to the Colonel again about that belt of undergrowth—it was very unsound indeed.)

Dodging in and out of the huts and avoiding the guard-room, Guy came at last to his own quarters and went in. It was a comfortable hut and he was lucky enough to have it to himself. Everything was in perfect order. His servant had put out his pyjamas and turned down the blanket on his camp bed. It was pleasant and reassuring to find everything just as usual and to see all his own belongings—Elise's photograph, his desk with a half-finished letter on it, his dressing-gown hanging behind the door; so much had happened since he had left this room that it was difficult to believe he had not been away for days. . . .

Guy undressed, folded his clothes neatly, and turned in.

Chapter Twenty-seven

IT WAS half-past eight and Guy was just finishing his breakfast in the mess when Barry appeared at his side and said: "Telephone for you, sir. It's Mrs. Crabbe. Shall I take a message?"

"No, I'll come," replied Guy, swallowing a mouthful of sausage and wiping his mouth—"and, Barry, tell Mark I want him, will you?" Guy went into the ante-room and seized the receiver. "Hallo, Elise!" he said. "Hallo, is everything all right?"

"I'm all right, if that's what you mean," replied Elise. "I just rang up to tell you that Frances has gone."

"Gone!" cried Guy in amazement. "Gone where?"

"So you *are* interested!" said Elise's voice in his ear.

"You know I am," said Guy. "I mean—look here——"

"You had better come over and see me."

"Yes, I will. I'll come as soon as I can, but look here——" He stopped, for the wire had suddenly gone dead . . . "Hallo!" he cried, waggling the bar up and down. "Hallo, Elise—I say——" There was no reply at all. He was talking to vacancy. For a moment he wondered whether he should ring her up and then he decided that it wouldn't be much use. He couldn't tell Elise anything over the telephone; it would be better to hurry through his work and go over and see her.

Guy had various things to do before he could get away. His company was training this morning, so he went out and had a look at the men, and had a talk with Sergeant-Major Bliss. While he was there Mark appeared, and he told Mark to go over to Sea View, explaining that Tommy had had a puncture and had come back and was there alone. "Don't stay long," said Guy.

186

"Just nip over and see how she is. I'll be in the Company office. I'm going there now."

B Company office was at the other side of the camp. Guy walked over and found a good many things to settle; it was always the way when you were in a hurry to get through. There were three cases of discipline—two of the men had returned late off pass and the third had used obscene language to Corporal Brown. As a rule Guy was apt to err on the side of leniency (he preferred to reason with his men and used punishments such as C.B. as a last resort), but this morning he did not feel like being lenient, so the three men got what was coming to them, and were marched away feeling somewhat dazed. (". . . and a good thing, too," declared Sergeant Findlater in the privacy of the sergeants' mess. "There's been too much of this sort of thing 'appening in the Company. It's 'igh time someone was made an example of.")

Having polished off his defaulters, Guy read some letters that had come in and dictated one or two replies, and by this time Mark had returned from Sea View with the news that Mrs. Widgery said she was O.K., but looked a bit under the weather. "D'you know what's the matter with her, sir?" inquired Mark somewhat anxiously.

"I expect she's feeling lonely," said Guy shortly. "I want to speak to the C.O. I'll have to go. You can finish up here."

It was twenty minutes to ten, and Orderly Room was at ten o'clock, but the Colonel was often early and Guy wanted to speak to him before the other officers arrived. Guy had decided that he must tell Colonel Thynne about Angela and Widgery—perhaps he ought to have done so before. He was walking across the field when he saw the Colonel's car arrive, so he shouted and waved madly and ran after it, and the Colonel drew up.

"I wanted to speak to you, sir," said Guy breathlessly.

"After Orderly Room——" began Colonel Thynne, looking at his subordinate officer in some surprise.

"No, now," said Guy. "It's very important, sir."

"What's happened?" asked the Colonel.

"It's private," said Guy. "I really think we should—should go into your room, sir."

Colonel Thynne parked his car and led the way to his room. He sat down and waved Guy to a chair. "Now, what is it?" he inquired. "I haven't very long, because I want to go over one or two files before Orderly Room. . . . You look a bit bedraggled this morning, Guy."

"Yes, sir," Guy agreed. He felt bedraggled. He also felt slightly sick. This was going to be a frightful interview. It was all the more frightful because Guy was fond of Colonel Thynne; he was rather an old woman in some ways and apt to be somewhat obstructive, but there was something very likeable about him. He looked fresh and bright and cheerful—a little like a robin—and he was smiling kindly at Guy. Guy felt like a murderer.

"Go ahead, Guy," said Colonel Thynne. "Out with it—I can't sit here all day."

"It's so difficult——" said Guy. "The fact is I don't know how to tell you . . . but I'm sure I ought to tell you. . . ."

Colonel Thynne's face had changed completely. He said gravely: "Well, Guy, if you are sure you ought to tell me you must tell me, that's all. Is it something to do with the battalion?"

"No," said Guy.

"Nothing to do with the battalion?"

"No, sir."

Colonel Thynne looked at him in bewilderment. "Is it something to do with one of my officers?"

"No," said Guy, "at least I mean yes, it is really."

"Guy!"

Guy had realised that this was not the right way to tell his story—to allow it to be dragged out of him bit by bit—he dived straight into it without hesitating any longer. "I was walking on the sands yesterday evening and I saw Angela. I saw her go up to the Widgerys' cottage. I knew Tommy was away—she left yesterday afternoon to go to Aberdeen—so I went after Angela and I found her there. She was there with Widgery."

"With Widgery? You mean——"

"Yes," said Guy. He did not look at the Colonel. He looked round the little office and out of the window. There was a curtain on the lower half of the window, but he could see the sky through the top half—it was very blue.

"Angela!" said Colonel Thynne in bewilderment. "Angela and Widgery . . . but I thought you . . . I thought Angela and you——"

"No, sir," said Guy. "We're friends, of course, but—that's all." He got up as he spoke.

"Don't go," said Colonel Thynne. "I can't understand—I can't believe—there must be some mistake. Angela went off yesterday in the car. She's gone to spend a few days with her grandmother. Are you sure she didn't just drop in to see the Widgerys and say good-bye?"

"Quite sure."

"But, Guy——"

"I wouldn't have mentioned it to you unless I had been quite sure."

"No—no, of course not; but—but I can't understand it. Angela and Widgery—it's incredible."

"I told Angela I was going to tell you," added Guy.

"You told her——"

"Yes, it's been going on for some time. I told her it had to stop or else I would tell you about it—but it hasn't stopped."

"So it was that!" muttered the Colonel, staring at Guy in a blank sort of way. "So that's what it was! Angela has been—different lately, but I thought——"

Guy leaned forward. "I thought I ought to tell you," he said urgently. "I felt I must tell you so that you could take steps. There's no time to be lost."

"Yes—yes, of course. Something must be done. It's a terrible blow . . . I don't know what to do."

"I think you should go after them, sir," said Guy.

"Go after them!" cried Colonel Thynne in quite a different voice. "Good heavens, you don't mean she's gone with Widgery! You can't mean it—the thing's outrageous. . . ."

It was odd—or at least it seemed odd to Guy—that Colonel Thynne should have been so blind where Angela was concerned and yet so easy to convince. It was almost as if he had half known about it before, or at least had suspected that something was wrong. Half-way through the conversation Guy had been afraid that Colonel Thynne was going to let the whole thing slide; he had been afraid that Colonel Thynne was incapable of dealing with the matter in the way it should be dealt with . . . and then, all of a sudden, Colonel Thynne had come to life and grasped the situation in both hands. He was certainly alive now. A steady stream of unprintable language was issuing from his lips (and Guy was able to deduce that if and when Colonel Thynne managed to get hold of Captain Widgery, the latter would have an unpleasant time), but this did not interfere with the arrangements which Colonel Thynne had begun to make for his departure. He was pulling out drawers and turning over files of papers as he spoke; he was jotting down notes on a pad. He opened the safe and took out a bag of keys and emptied them on to the table.

"You're going, sir," said Guy.

"Going! Of course I'm going. I'll catch the swine at the War Office. He's got an appointment with Featherington at eleven-thirty to-morrow—I'll go south by the Night Scot—find me a train from Rithie to Glasgow. Here's a time-table , , , you're doing Adjutant in Widgery's absence, aren't you?"

" Yes, sir."

" You can go on doing it, then. Rackham can take over B Company. I'll see Major Crabbe after Orderly Room . . . and Guy, we don't want this wretched business to get about."

" No, sir, of course not."

" We can't hush it up altogether because Widgery will have to go—there's nothing else for it. I shall tell Ned Crabbe, of course. He may be able to advise me—sound fellow, Ned Crabbe —but we don't want a lot of talk."

" No, of course not."

" We've got to think of Tommy . . . devilish hard on her."

" Yes, sir."

The Colonel hesitated. He put a bunch of keys down on the table and looked at Guy. " Guy," he said, " I don't know what I shall do when I see the fellow. I suppose Tommy will divorce him. I suppose he'll want to—to marry Angela——"

" Don't let him," said Guy.

" No, that's what I feel ; he's——"

" He's rotten all through," said Guy earnestly.

Colonel Thynne sighed. He said : " Well, we had better go over to Orderly Room—it's after ten."

" Need you take Orderly Room, sir ? " asked Guy. " Couldn't Major Crabbe take it ? "

" I'll take it," said the Colonel shortly.

Guy had never liked or admired the Colonel so much as he did at Orderly Room that morning. He was a trifle paler than usual, but he was perfectly controlled. It seemed to Guy that the business which they had to conduct was more trivial than usual, that the R.S.M. was slow and stupid, that the suggestions about various matters which emanated from the other company commanders were trifling and absurd. Several minutes were spent in a discussion as to whether or not the " Black Bull " at Rithie should be placed out of bounds for the troops. The R.S.M. was of the opinion that this should be done at once—there were two barmaids—he didn't like the look of them. Dicky Sale, who commanded D Company, declared that the barmaids were quite respectable girls. Guy knew nothing about it one way or the other and cared less.

At last it was over and they came out. Dicky Sale stopped outside the door to light a cigarette. He said : " The old boy's a bit white about the gills this morning—looks as if he's been on the tiles."

Guy hesitated. He felt like hitting Dicky—it took all his
190

strength to beat down his anger and to keep his mouth shut. . . .
After a few moments, he laughed.

"What's the joke, Fox," Dicky inquired.

"Nothing much," replied Guy. He had suddenly thought
how surprised Dicky would have been if he had received a hefty
punch on the jaw.

Guy was longing to get away. He was full of impatience to see
Elise and find out why Frances had gone and where she had
gone to, but everything conspired to delay him. He was to be
Adjutant, now, in Widgery's place and this would entail a great
deal of extra work—different work from what he had been
doing. It was a compliment to be chosen for the post, and the
extra five bob a day would be a welcome addition to his pay, but
he was sorry to give up B Company. Guy had dealt faithfully
with B Company and had got it into very good trim—it really
was rather a wrench to give it up. Racky would do it quite well,
of course ; he was glad Racky was getting it. He found Racky
and told him that he would hand over in the afternoon, and then
he had to find Mark and tell him the news and listen to Mark's
mingled congratulations and lamentations . . . and then he was
waylaid by Sergeant-Major Bliss, who had heard about it—heaven
alone knew how—and he was obliged to listen patiently to more
congratulations and lamentations.

"All through France," said Sergeant-Major Bliss, "and never
no trouble . . . and there isn't many officers you can say the same
for—I mean, that you can see eye to eye with about everything
—but, of course, I knew we wouldn't 'ave you long, sir. I mean—
well—an officer like yourself, sir, is pretty well bound to get on—
and I wouldn't wish anything else, sir, I'm sure. As regards being
Adjutant, there isn't anyone else would do it 'arf as well, if you
don't mind me saying so, sir ; but I 'ope Captain Rackham will
see eye to eye about the training—B Company being the best
company in the battalion, as you and I know, sir, I shouldn't like
to see anything different—not but what Captain Rackham isn't
a very nice officer—it's only just about the training—will 'e see
eye to eye?"

"Of course he will," said Guy. "You'll get on like a house on
fire with Captain Rackham. Everything will be just the same.
It's very nice of you, Sergeant-Major—I mean, it's good of you
to say you'll miss me. We've pulled together a long time now."

"Yes, sir, through thick and thin as you might say."

"Yes," agreed Guy. "Yes, by Jove we have . . . I'm damned
sorry to give up B Company, I can tell you, but I shall always be

interested to—to see how it goes on and all that—and—and I want to thank you for all you've done. B Company wouldn't be what it is if you hadn't been so keen——"

"It won't be the same without you, sir."

"Yes, it will," declared Guy. "It will be just the same if not better. I shall be down on you like a hundredweight of bricks if it isn't!"

They laughed—though perhaps not very heartily—and they shook hands very heartily indeed.

After this somewhat painful interview, Guy rushed about the camp seeing people and making necessary arrangements. It was a quarter-past twelve before he ran his car out of the garage and set out for Cairn, and even then he had several things on his mind —things which he knew he ought to have done. I can't help it, thought Guy, as he trod on the accelerator and streaked out of the gate. I can do all that in the afternoon. I can't put my mind to anything until I've seen Elise and found out about Frances.

Chapter Twenty-eight

ELISE WAS waiting for Guy in the lounge. She was sitting at the window sewing. She looked up as he came in and said: "Guy, what have you been doing to Frances?"

"What have I been——"

"Yes," said Elise. "Don't look so surprised. You must know what you've been doing."

"I haven't done anything," declared Guy. "I don't know what you mean. Where has she gone?"

"Why do you want to know? I won't have you playing fast and loose with Frances; she doesn't understand it—she isn't that sort of person."

"Fast and loose!" cried Guy.

"I've got very fond of Frances lately," added Elise.

"So have I!" said Guy frankly.

Elise looked up again from her work. "How fond?" she asked.

Guy hesitated, and then he said: "Well, if you *must* know, I want to marry her."

"You might do a lot worse," said Elise.

They were silent for a few minutes, and then it was Elise who spoke first. "Did you ask her?" she inquired.

"No," replied Guy. "No, I didn't. I tried several times but

192

something always happened—and she was so elusive, somehow. It was awfully difficult to get hold of her, if you know what I mean. I liked her from the very first moment but I couldn't understand her—I don't understand her *now* as a matter of fact. Sometimes she seems one sort of person and sometimes another . . . but I want to marry them all," added Guy with a grin.

Elise laughed. "That's a good thing anyhow," she said.

"Yes, isn't it? One afternoon I pursued her out on to the rocks. We got cut off by the tide—I never told anyone because it sounded so damned silly—and Frances behaved like a brick. She was splendid really—never turned a hair nor said what a mug I was——"

Elise burst out laughing.

"Oh, you can laugh if you like," said Guy, "and as much as you like, but the fact remains. I knew then that she was the woman for me. We talked for hours, and I flattered myself that I had got to know her pretty well and that she—well, that she wasn't exactly indifferent to my charms, but the next time I saw her she seemed to have drifted away again, and I had to start at the beginning. Since then I've been trying to—to get hold of her. I've had several opportunities, but I wasn't sure of her—I mean, I didn't want to rush in too soon or anything. It was frightfully *difficult*," declared Guy, sitting down and running his fingers through his hair. "It was *frightfully* difficult . . . there was Mr. MacDonald, too——"

"What on earth has he to do with it?"

"I don't know really," replied Guy. "I thought he liked her and that she was rather interested in him. We met at the Castle one day, and she offered to help him with his notes. It was odd, I thought. I mean, she's usually so shy and retiring, and she seemed so matey with the old boy. It gave me a bit of a shake . . . so it went on until last night." He hesitated, and then continued in a lower tone: "Last night was *different*, somehow. We seemed to hit it off better than ever. We seemed to be absolutely in tune. I thought it was perfectly all right, and I was just going to take the plunge when——when I saw Angela. I thought Frances understood, but, of course, she can't have understood. She must have thought—oh, lord!" exclaimed Guy, breaking off as the inference became clear. "Oh, lord, what a mess I've made of it!"

"I don't know what you're talking about," said Elise.

"It was a misunderstanding," explained Guy. "It was about —about Angela, really."

"About Angela?"

" Yes, you see——"

" I see you've mismanaged the whole thing."

" I've been a—fool," said Guy bitterly.

He had always told Elise everything—or nearly everything—so it was not difficult to tell her the whole story, and somehow, as he told it, things became clearer in his own mind.

When he had finished Elise said nothing for a few moments, and then she said: " You were right to go straight to Colonel Thynne."

" Yes," agreed Guy. " That was the only 'right' thing I did. Everything else that I did—or tried to do—was a complete failure. You always say it's no use meddling with other people's affairs. Why don't you say 'I told you so'?"

Elise smiled. " And then *you* would say 'How like a woman!' —but as a matter of fact you had to try and help them. You couldn't have stood aside and let them rip."

" I wish I had."

" No," said Elise, shaking her head. " No, you couldn't, Guy. You might have succeeded if you'd had a little luck."

Guy saw that this was true, and it comforted him a little. " I've seen it coming for some time," he said. " That's why I tried to amuse Angela, that's why I took her about a bit. I took her over to Rithie one afternoon—to the pictures—and I spoke to her seriously about it. She said there was nothing in it at all, that it was just fun, that Widgery amused her. I pointed out that it wasn't much fun for Tommy, and she was quite reasonable. She said she would be more careful. I felt much happier about it after that. Then Frances told me she had seen Widgery in the woods near St. Kiaran's Spring—with a woman. Somehow or other I had a feeling that it was Angela; anyhow, it roused my suspicions again. That was why I dashed after Angela last night. I wish I had left them to stew in their own juice," added Guy bitterly.

" You had to try," said Elise again. " You might have succeeded. Angela is very fond of you."

" Nonsense!"

" It isn't nonsense. She would have married you if you had asked her——"

" Absolute nonsense," declared Guy. " Why does everyone think that? Angela is quite amusing but she isn't my idea of a wife—never was—and this business with Widgery is proof positive that Angela never had any use for me."

" It isn't, really," replied Elise. " I think that was how the affair with Widgery started. Angela wanted to show you——"

" No——"

" Yes, honestly . . . and then she got swept off her feet. Widgery is very attractive, you know."

" Attractive!" exclaimed Guy.

" He's so vital," said Elise thoughtfully.

Guy uttered a few partially muffled statements anent Widgery and his progenitors.

" Oh, yes," said Elise, smiling. " I agree with you, of course. He isn't the type that appeals to me at all, but he *does* attract some women. . . ." She hesitated and then added in a different tone: " . . . Tommy adores him."

" I know," said Guy, nodding. " It's amazing . . . as a matter of fact it was really for Tommy's sake that I mixed myself up in the affair. Poor Tommy. You had better go over and see her."

" Yes," said Elise with a sigh. " Yes, I must. I'll go this afternoon."

" Good! That's settled. Now what about Frances? Where has she gone?"

" She has gone back to her aunt," replied Elise, " and if you take my advice you'll try to wangle a few days' leave and go after her. It will be much easier to explain everything if you see her."

" Much easier . . . besides, I want to see her. Where does the aunt live?"

" But, Guy, don't you know?"

" Would I be asking you if I knew?" inquired Guy impatiently.

" I don't know either," said Elise.

They looked at each other, and Elise felt inclined to smile at the consternation on his face. " But you said you knew where she had gone!" he cried.

" I knew she had gone back to her aunt. Do you mean to say you don't know where the aunt lives?"

" Funny, isn't it?" said Guy grimly. " Awfully funny, isn't it?"

" But Guy——"

" It was a sort of joke," he continued. " I wanted to know about her, but she refused to tell me, so I said I would guess. I couldn't, of course. There was something very mysterious about Frances. We kept up the joke all the time—until last night—and she had just begun to tell me——"

Elise had opened her bag and was holding out a half sheet of paper. " That's all I know," she said. " Annie brought it to me this morning after Frances had gone. She left by the early bus."

The letter read as follows:

Dear Elise,

I have been offered a post at a canteen and have decided to take it because it is time I was doing something useful. I feel I ought to see my aunt before I start work, so I am going to spend a few days with her first. I hate saying " good-bye " and I know you feel the same (we discussed it one day, didn't we?), so I know you will understand why I am writing " good-bye " instead of saying it. Good-bye, Elise, and thank you very much for being so kind to me. I have enjoyed our talks more than I can say. I have had a very happy holiday at Cairn, and have learnt a great deal. When I am settled in my new job I will write and tell you how I get on. I hope I shall see you again some day. Please give my love to Tommy. I do hope she is all right, and that she will feel happier soon—and please give my love to Jennifer and Winkie.

Much love from
Frances

The letter was very short—it was little more than a hasty scrawl—but Guy took some time to read it. He read it over several times before he looked up. " I must find her," he said at last.

Elise nodded. " Yes, you must find her. She probably left her address with the MacNairs."

He jumped up and made for the door. He still had the letter in his hand and Elise did not ask him to return it.

After Guy had gone Elise sat and thought about all he had told her. It was a tangle, but it could be unravelled, and nobody would be any the worse except Angela. It was a great pity about Angela—she was so young to have wrecked her life—Elise was sorry for her and very sorry for her parents. Freda Thynne ought to have kept some control of Angela—but, unfortunately, Freda was foolish. Elise was sorry for Tommy as well, but she decided that, in the long run, after Tommy had recovered from the shock, she would be much happier. She had never been really happy with Widgery; her life had been one of constant strain. There would be a chance of happiness for Tommy now. Tommy would go to Aberdeen, to her mother; that was the best thing for her to do. Having settled all this in her own mind, Elise's thoughts were free to turn into a much more pleasant channel— she thought of Frances Field. It did not matter who Frances was nor what her history had been, it was *what* she was that mattered. Frances was a dear. She was good and sweet and comfortable; there was something very attractive and refreshing about

Frances. Elise thought she would suit Guy admirably . . . and she would be a very nice sister-in-law, very nice indeed. Elise had often worried about Guy, and wondered whom he would marry. She was so devoted to Guy that nobody seemed good enough—only the best was good enough for Guy. She wanted Guy to marry someone really nice, firstly for his own sake, of course, but secondly for purely selfish motives ; she and Guy had always been such tremendous friends that it would be a disaster if Guy were to marry someone Elise did not like—or someone who did not like her. Then, latterly, Elise had begun to be afraid that Guy would never marry at all, and would become a confirmed bachelor, lonely and cynical—there was a trace of cynicism in Guy which might easily develop and warp his character—she had worried about that ; she had decided some months ago that it was high time Guy found a wife. Guy was so particular, so fastidious ; he hated lipstick and scent and coloured nails, he loathed affectation. Several girls had fallen rather heavily for Guy—nice girls too—but he had not even noticed the fact ; he had remained heart-whole. Now, at last, Guy had found someone he could love. He had said nothing about " love," of course, but Elise knew Guy so well—she did not need her t's crossed nor her i's dotted where Guy was concerned.

Elise smiled to herself. It was unfortunate that when at last he had found someone to suit him he should lose her like this—careless of Guy—but in a way it was not a bad thing. It would have been a pity if Frances had been too easy, and Frances *might* have been too easy, for she was without wiles and had been deeply in love with Guy for some time. (Elise had realised this, of course, and had gone out of her way to warn Frances of what she must expect if she married a soldier. She had warned Frances, not because she wanted to brown her off, but because it was only fair that Frances should understand what she was in for. Unless she loved Guy enough to marry him with her eyes open she wouldn't be much use as a soldier's wife. Frances had not understood why she was being warned, but that didn't matter.) It would have been a pity if Frances had been too easy to win, for men were such odd creatures . . . men liked to pursue . . . men appreciated their game so much more if it were difficult to approach . . . and Guy was no exception to the rule. It would do Guy no harm to pursue Frances, no harm at all. In fact, if Frances had not been Frances—so absolutely straightforward and honest, so childlike and innocent of wile—one might almost have suspected that she had disappeared like this on purpose to . . . but not Frances, no, definitely not. It was odd that Guy could

197

not understand Frances (thought Elise). She was crystal clear. You could see right down to the bottom . . . but perhaps that was the very reason he could not understand her . . . he could not believe that there was nothing hidden, nothing kept back. Frances might be mysterious about the past—about where she had lived and what she had done—but Frances, herself, was the least mysterious woman that Elise had ever known.

Chapter Twenty-nine

ELISE WAS not used to walking—she considered walking a much overrated form of amusement—and when she did happen to go for a walk she liked a flat surface underfoot, so she was tired and hot and not quite so trim and elegant as usual when she arrived at Sea View. She had not been there before, and she had heard a great deal about the house—both for and against—so she looked at it with interest. The site was magnificent, of course, nobody could deny that, but site was not everything. Elise shared Captain Widgery's partiality for modern plumbing, and she was aware of Sea View's deficiencies in this respect. She liked comfort when she could get it, but, when she could not get it, she did without it uncomplainingly ; there were more important things in life than comfort . . . there was love, for instance, and kindness and consideration . . . you could do without electric light. . . .

Elise would have taken even more interest in the little house if her mind had not been full of what she was going to say to Tommy. She had been considering what she would say all the way through the woods, and she was still considering the matter . . . she would try to make Tommy see that it was not the end of everything. She would try to make Tommy take a long view. Tommy must put all this miserable business behind her and go forward ; she must be made to think of the future.

The door opened as Elise went up the path, and there was Tommy standing in the doorway, her face very white and strained and her eyes larger and greener than usual.

" I was just coming to see you," Tommy said.

" I wish I'd known," declared Elise, sinking into a chair. " It would have saved me a good deal of trouble." Now that she was here, face to face with Tommy, all her carefully prepared sentences vanished from her mind. She did not know how to begin to tell Tommy what she had to tell her. She could not meet Tommy's eyes.

"Go on," said Tommy. "Tell me. You've come to tell me something horrible, haven't you?"

"Yes," said Elise. "Yes, I'm afraid so, Tommy."

"Go on," said Tommy again.

"Angela," said Elise in a breathless sort of voice. "Angela and—and Midge."

There was a little silence and then Tommy said: "Yes . . . I —I think I knew all the time . . . but I pretended to myself that I didn't."

"Oh, Tommy——" said Elise, holding out her hand.

Tommy did not take the hand—perhaps she did not see it—her own two hands were clasped tightly together. She said in a hard voice: "Tell me everything, please."

"I don't know very much——"

"Guy knows."

"Not very much, really."

"They fought—Guy and Midge," said Tommy slowly. "Yes, that's what happened. They fought over Angela—she would like that."

"They didn't really," said Elise quickly. "Not in the way you mean. Guy hasn't any use for Angela."

Tommy laughed—it wasn't a very pleasant sound. She said: "That's another thing I tried to make myself believe . . . that Guy and Angela . . . and I almost succeeded. It's funny how you can deceive yourself. Have you ever tried to deceive yourself, Elise?"

Elise did not answer. She hesitated for a moment, and then she said: "It's awfully hard to bear. I know it must be. In a way it's harder for you than if he had been killed."

"No," said Tommy quickly. "Oh, no, you don't understand. He's still here—in this world, I mean. There's still hope. I just feel as if he were very ill—as if it were a sort of illness——"

"But Tommy——"

"An illness," said Tommy again. "Of course it may be a long illness, but some day he will recover. I'm sure of that."

"You can't mean——"

"I suppose you think I haven't any pride. I haven't really—not where Midge is concerned. I mean, I love Midge so much—I want him——"

"Tommy, dear——"

"He's different from other people," continued Tommy in a strained sort of voice. "He—you can't judge him by the same
199

standards. He's very like his mother. You haven't seen his mother, have you? She's a Creole . . . she's very beautiful . . . I understood Midge better after I had seen her. I know Midge so well—other people don't understand him. You have to—to make allowances. . . ." Her voice broke off suddenly, and she hid her face. "I can't go on living without him," she whispered.

"Oh, Tommy—poor darling!" cried Elise. She rose and put her arm round Tommy's shoulders.

"I knew," Tommy whispered. "I knew all along . . . ever since that first night at the hotel . . . but I wouldn't let myself see. I hid my head like an ostrich and pretended everything was all right . . . I'm such a fool over Midge . . . I love him so . . . I can't be sensible with Midge."

Elise patted her shoulder and said nothing. It was better to say nothing than to say the wrong thing. Elise did not understand. (How could you go on loving a man when he treated you like that? How could you go on wanting him when he did not want you?) Elise *could* not understand, so she kept her mouth shut.

"What am I to do?" said Tommy at last.

"You must go home to your mother," said Elise. "That's the best thing—it's the only thing to do."

"But Midge—what will happen to him? He has to be back on Saturday. . . . Oh, I suppose he can't come back, can he?"

Elise did not try to answer this. She was aware that Colonel Thynne was on his way to London. What would he do? What arrangements would he make? "We'll just have to wait and see what happens," said Elise vaguely. "Meantime you must go to Aberdeen."

"No," said Tommy. "No, I can't go and stay with Mother."

"Of course you can. Ned will take you over to Rithie and see you into the train. It's much the best plan."

"I can't go to Mother," declared Tommy. "I just simply *can't*. Mother wouldn't understand. She would be angry and upset ; she would say—dreadful things about him, I know she would."

Elise thought this not unlikely, for she herself was longing to say dreadful things about him. "All the same, I think you should go," she said.

"I couldn't bear it," said Tommy, shaking her head. "It would mean a row—it would mean constant rows. Mother is a darling pet, but she's too like me—I mean, we both say things without thinking—and Mother has never been fair to Midge."

"You must think of the future——" began Elise.

"Yes, I know," agreed Tommy. "That's what I'm doing. Some day Midge will come back; Angela will bore him after a bit."

"But you aren't going to sit down and wait for that to happen?" Tommy did not answer.

"Oh, Tommy, I can't understand it at all!" cried Elise.

"Of course you can't," replied Tommy with a wan ghost of a smile. "I couldn't understand myself either unless I happened to be me. It's awfully good of you to—to come over and see me, but you must just let me go my own way. You mustn't worry about me. I shall be all right."

"Of course I'm worrying about you. Tommy, my dear lamb, you can't go on living here by yourself—if that's what you're thinking——"

"Why not?"

"Because everyone will know about it. Everyone in the regiment is bound to know—or at least to suspect. People will wonder why Midge has gone."

"I hadn't thought of that," said Tommy slowly. She hesitated, and then added: "No, I couldn't stay on here, could I? I couldn't face Mark or Barry or—or any of the other babes. They would be—be sorry for me. I couldn't bear that . . . and the Thynnes . . . no, I shall have to go."

"Ned will take you to Rithie," said Elise, patting her hand. "He'll take you over to-morrow morning. Your mother will be awfully pleased to have you."

Elise was very tired indeed when she got back to the hotel; she was tired and miserable and utterly bewildered. The only ray of hope in the darkness was that Mrs. Fraser would be able to persuade Tommy to see sense, and the ray was not a very bright one. Elise decided to write to Mrs. Fraser and explain matters and warn her to treat Tommy with care. It would be a difficult letter to write, for it would have to be very tactfully worded, but it was worth trying. Anything was worth trying, anything to prevent Tommy wasting her life, wearing herself out, making herself miserable over that worthless man. If only Tommy could be made to see sense, if she could be persuaded to divorce him there might be a chance of happiness for her. Then Widgery—would he marry Angela? Would the Thynnes want that? Elise decided that if she were the Thynnes she would not want Angela to marry him. There was no hope of happiness in that sort of marriage.

Elise was having tea by herself in the lounge when Guy came in. "Nobody knows," he said, flinging himself into a chair.

"She left no address. I rang up the Listons—Tillie knows nothing. I asked the MacNairs, and I spoke to the man who drives the bus. I pursued an old woman who went to Rithie this morning in the same bus as Frances, and she volunteered the information that the luggage was labelled Euston . . . *Euston*," repeated Guy. "That's a tremendous help, isn't it?"

Elise hesitated with the teapot in her hand—for the first time the possibility that Frances had really vanished into thin air flashed across her mind. She was appalled. "But someone must know!" she exclaimed.

"Who?" inquired Guy angrily. "Who would know? I've spent hours pursuing people and questioning them, and they all think I'm half-witted. I'm beginning to think so myself. I'm up to the eyes in work and my brain is like dough. I can't think of what I'm doing. I've got the most appalling headache."

"Doesn't Alec——"

"No, he doesn't. He looked at me in amazement and said that he thought Miss Field was a great friend of mine. He suggested I should ask you."

"But it's absurd," said Elise. "People don't vanish like that and leave no address——"

"That's nice to know," said Guy.

There was a little silence. Guy rang the bell with unnecessary force and ordered a whisky and soda—a double one—and his temper was not improved when Annie informed him that he could not have it until six o'clock.

"Bring it for me," said Elise hastily. "I can have it because I'm staying in the hotel—that's right, isn't it, Annie?"

"Of all the idiotic laws!" exclaimed Guy, when Annie had gone to fetch it. "Of all the damned silly, fussy, old-womanish laws! I don't know what we're coming to. We're supposed to be fighting for freedom, aren't we? If this is a free country, why can't you turn round without being throttled by red tape? Why can't you get a drink when you need one?"

"She'll write to me," said Elise soothingly. "She said in her letter that she'd write and tell me how she gets on."

"Oh, yes, I dare say," agreed Guy with a mirthless laugh. "She'll write to you in a month or two—if she hasn't forgotten us all by that time."

"Do you think Frances will forget us?" asked Elise in a quiet voice.

Guy hesitated. "I'm a beast," he said. "I feel—I feel all wrong—all twisted into knots. I want to *do* something at once, not just sit down and wait."

Elise knew the feeling, she wished she knew how to help him.

"Oh, well," he said, after a little silence. "Oh, well, there's nothing to be done. I shall just have to sit down and do my lessons like a good boy . . . they've made me Adjutant," he added.

"Oh, Guy, I'm so glad—and Ned will be delighted. He has always said you would make a splendid Adjutant. Aren't you pleased?"

"I suppose I am," mumbled Guy. "I mean, I would have been pleased if I'd heard about it yesterday."

Chapter Thirty

DURING THE next few days Guy's friends had rather a difficult time. They could not understand why Fox, who was usually a pleasant, cheerful comrade, had suddenly become a bear, and a very bad-tempered bear at that. Nobody could please Fox, nobody could get a smile out of the fellow. His servant could do nothing right, the mess waiter could do nothing right, the clerks in the orderly room were in hot water up to their necks. It was thought by some that Fox was taking his new job too seriously and that it had got on his nerves, and by others that he was suffering from a liver chill. Captain Rackham was of the opinion that Fox was in love.

"You mark my words, there's a blitz coming," declared Sergeant Findlater in the privacy of the sergeants' mess. "That's why 'e's making things 'um. 'E wouldn't make things 'um for nothing—not Captain Tarlatan. Mark my words, there's a blitz coming."

"There's a blitz going on now," growled Sergeant Stokes, the orderly-room sergeant, who was the chief sufferer from the new broom. "You'd know if you were me. I wasn't too keen on Captain Widgery as an Adjutant—he did as little as he could—but I'd rather have him than Captain Tarlatan, who does a sight too much."

"You got slack, that's what," retorted Sergeant Findlater.

Sergeant Stokes snorted and went away. He was aware that there was more than a grain of truth in the accusation, but still . . .

Guy was glad of the extra work. He was glad to find that the orderly-room staff needed gingering up; it did Guy good to ginger them. He was in a very unenviable state of mind. for he was desperately in love, miserably unhappy and furiously angry. He was angry with Elise and all the other people who surely ought to know something about the woman they called their friend; he was angry with himself for being such a fool; he was even angry with Frances.

Why didn't Frances understand? asked Guy of himself, raising his head from a file of papers he was trying to put in order. I thought Frances understood. I thought it was perfectly clear. I thought she realised I was only trying to head-off Angela because of Tommy—Oh, hell, I shall never get this file in order!

Ned Crabbe was commanding the battalion in the Colonel's absence, so he and Guy were thrown into very close contact (the Adjutant works in the C.O's. office and is his right-hand man). Ned had been aware for some time that Widgery was a bit slack; he had spoken to Colonel Thynne about it, and had suggested in a tactful manner that someone else might do the job better and show a little more keenness for the work, but the Colonel had hummed and hawed and replied that Widgery was not doing badly and that he disliked changes—it wasn't a good thing to keep changing round. Nothing more could be said, of course, though quite a lot might be thought—it was Ned's opinion that, if things were not entirely satisfactory, changes were indicated and should be made. This being so, Ned was not sorry to see the orderly-room staff being gingered up and made to toe the line, and he left Guy to get on with the job. Ned knew the inner reason for Guy's restlessness, and was glad that he could work off steam in a useful way. Ned was very sorry for Guy, and was ready to make allowances for him, but none were needed as regards his own contacts with Guy—Guy was the perfect Adjutant. They had always been tremendous friends, Ned and Guy; in the first instance because they both adored Elise, but afterwards because they liked each other. They were intimate and "jokey" in private, but on duty their conduct was circumspect. Guy was particularly careful not to presume upon his relationship with Ned, particularly careful to maintain his position as a subordinate officer. It was rather pleasant to work together, and they found much to admire in each other. Guy thought— *By Jove, old Ned will make a clinking C.O.*, and was quite unaware that at the very same moment "old Ned" was thinking— *Guy's got brains. He'll go far unless I'm very much mistaken.*

One day, when the morning's work was over, Major Crabbe got into his car. "I'll be back at three," he said. "I'm going out to see that patrol exercise at three-fifteen. I want you to come too."

"Yes, sir," said Guy. "I'll have the letters ready for you to sign."

"There isn't anything important, is there?"

"Only the one to S.D.3," replied Guy. "That ought to go—the others can easily wait."

Major Crabbe hesitated. "Come over and have lunch, Guy," he said. "Elise was saying she hadn't seen you for a day or two."

"But what about the letter?"

"It isn't as urgent as all that."

Guy was pleased at the suggestion. He nipped round to the other side of the car and got in, and, now that they were off duty, his manner changed, for he was no longer the Adjutant, he was dear old Ned's brother-in-law.

"Has Elise heard from Tommy?" he inquired as he settled himself in the seat.

"No, we haven't heard a thing since I took her over to Rithie and saw her off to Aberdeen. Elise rather hoped she would send a wire—there was a raid in Glasgow that night."

"We'd have heard soon enough if she hadn't arrived," replied Guy.

"That's what I told Elise."

They shot out of the gate, acknowledging the salutes of the sentries, and turned left towards Cairn. Guy noticed as they went that a small fatigue party was busily engaged in clearing the undergrowth at the far end of the camp. He smiled to himself and commented upon it to his companion.

"Yes," agreed Ned Crabbe. "It ought to have been done before. It was you who suggested it, I think."

"It's a pity the old boy's coming back," declared Guy, following out a logical train of thought.

Ned laughed. "He isn't a bad old stiff. You have to keep prodding him, that's all. By the way, I had a letter from him this morning. You had better read it." He felt in his pocket as he spoke and held out a letter to Guy. Guy read it with interest.

Baddely's Hotel,
Kensington

Dear Crabbe,

I hope to be back on Monday. I saw Widgery at the War Office. We had a stormy interview, and I was obliged to threaten him with legal action. I had seen a lawyer and he told me the line to take. Finally, I went back with Widgery to the hotel and saw Angela. I had some difficulty in persuading her to leave him, but not as much as I had expected. I fancy she had discovered that he was not all she thought. Angela is here with me. She realises now that she has been extremely foolish, to say the least of it. When I go north she will go to her grandmother for a long visit. Widgery is leaving the regiment. He will be seconded in the meantime and will take up an appointment in one of the new Hush Hush units. I see no reason why anyone should know what has happened except ourselves. Tarlatan can be relied on to be discreet. The only reason for disclosure will be if Tommy wants to divorce Widgery. She would be more than justified in doing so. Perhaps you will be good enough to find out her intentions so that I can consult my lawyer. Naturally I should prefer for Angela's sake that the affair should be allowed to drop, but Tommy must be our first consideration. Angela must stand the racket if necessary. The whole affair has been a bitter pill for me—but I need not enlarge upon it. You will understand what I feel. I thought it a good opportunity to see Featherington while I was in town. I succeeded in getting some useful information from him about training, etc. He has promised to keep us in mind and to arrange some tactical exercises in collaboration with aircraft. (I shall explain fully when I return.) You will be pleased to hear about this.

Kindest regards to yourself and Elise.

Yours,
A. T. Thynne

" It's awfully like the old man," said Guy, handing the letter back.

" Yes," agreed Ned. " I'll have to answer it. Elise says Tommy won't want to divorce him—but we don't know for certain. A thing like that can't be arranged all in a minute! It requires thought."

Ned Crabbe sometimes said that his wife was a pillar of the post office, and that the enormous sums which the Government derived from post-office revenues were largely due to his wife's passion for correspondence. Elise was one of those useful people who carry on an information bureau for the benefit of their friends. She received letters from all over the world. People wrote to her from India, from China, from Malta and Mauritius, from Bermuda and Egypt and Ceylon. She had letters from the North-West Frontier, from Singapore and the Gold Coast, in fact, from practically every spot where the British Army is known, and she had letters from places such as Buenos Aires and Lisbon, where military attachés and their wives and families are still to be found. People wrote to Elise giving all their news, saying that Bill had left school and gone into the R.A.F., and that George was somewhere in the Middle East—nobody knew where—that Jean had had twins and Dorothy's children were in the throes of whooping-cough, and Pamela was engaged to a Lieutenant-Commander in the Navy—a charming man—and they always finished up by asking what had happened to Frank, and where Lilian was now, and whether Alison's eldest boy was old enough to take an active part in the war; whereupon Elise immediately seized her pen and wrote a long letter in reply, giving all her own news and all the news she had gathered in from her other correspondents. The posts at Cairn were irregular in the extreme. Sometimes letters arrived early in the morning and sometimes not until the afternoon, but, somehow or other, once you had got used to this peculiarity, it was quite pleasant to have a surprise, and to receive a bunch of exciting letters when you had ceased to expect them. On this particular morning the post was late in reaching Cairn, and Elise received several interesting letters just before lunch. She was expecting Ned to lunch, so she put them aside until afterwards, noting that one was from Betty, who was living on the fat of the land at Srinagar, and another was from Evelyn, who was having a pretty thin time at Bristol. The third letter bore an Aberdeen postmark, but it was not from Tommy; Tommy's bold and dashing calligraphy was too well known for there to be any doubt about that. As Ned had not yet arrived, Elise decided to open the letter, so she opened it and, like all sensible people, she looked at the end first, to see who it was from. The signature was Tamara Fraser, so the letter was from Tommy's mother.

Hailes Park,
Aberdeen

My dear Mrs. Crabbe,

Thank you very much for writing to me. I was horrified to hear about Middleton, but not really surprised, for nothing he could do would *surprise* me. I entirely agree with everything you say, and especially I agree that the best thing that could happen would be for my poor Tommy to free herself from Middleton. I would have advised her to do so—very tactfully as you suggest—but unfortunately I have had no opportunity. Tommy has not come to me after all. She sent me a wire from Glasgow saying that she had decided to go south and would write later and let me know her address. Since then I have heard nothing at all and I am really quite *frantic* with anxiety. I wired to my cousins in Hampshire, thinking that she might have gone there, but they wired back that they had not seen her. I would go south myself if there was any chance of finding her, but it is not much use when I have no idea where she is, and of course she may write to me. I hope for a letter by every post. I had hoped that Tommy might come here and help me; there would be plenty for her to do. This house has been taken over by the military authorities as a convalescent home, and I am doing the catering, which keeps me very busy. Of course I *could* get away if I knew where Tommy was—I should just *have* to go to her—but it would not be very easy. Do you think Tommy has gone to London to find Middleton? I *hope* not. I try to comfort myself by thinking that she may have decided to take up some form of war work. If only Tommy could see Middleton in his true colours and could escape from the extraordinary influence which he seems to exercise over her—it is such an *evil* influence! Oh, how happy I should be if Tommy could free herself from him! You will think I am quite mad to write all this to you, but your letter was so kind and understanding and I have nobody here to talk to about it. Can you suggest anything that I could do?

With kindest regards, and again many thanks for writing to me.

Yours very sincerely,
Tamara Fraser

Elise had no time to digest this letter before Ned and Guy arrived; in fact, they found her with it in her hand. She greeted them a trifle vaguely and handed the letter to Ned (for she and Ned shared all their correspondence), and in return Ned fished out Colonel Thynne's epistle and handed it to Elise. They went in to lunch still talking about the two letters and trying to decide whether anything could be done. Guy could not help thinking how odd it was that both Frances and Tommy should suddenly disappear into thin air.

Chapter Thirty-one

SOMETIMES GUY worked amongst the orderly-room files with a mad frenzy, and sometimes he found himself unable to work at all, and one afternoon when he was in the latter condition he pushed aside a batch of correspondence anent weapon training, and rising from the table he seized his cap and walked down to the shore. He had decided to walk across the bay and have tea with Elise—he could talk to Elise about Frances. The tide was out and the rocks were bare, and Guy suddenly perceived a small figure in a red jersey and grey shorts standing upon a pinnacle of rock and waving a spade to him—it was Winkie Liston. Guy was not in a sociable mood; he had already avoided Mark with some difficulty, but Winkie was different since Winkie was innocent of crime. Winkie could not be expected to know anything about Frances Field, so Guy was not angry with him. Guy waved back and went down to join Winkie on the rocks.

Winkie looked a great deal better than the last time Guy had seen him; there was a pink flush on his cheeks and he had put on a little weight; in addition to these signs of health, Guy was delighted to notice that his hands and knees were dirty and there was a large rent in the sleeve of his jersey.

" Hallo, what are you doing?" inquired Guy.

" Come here!" yelled Winkie. " Come *here*, Jennifer's uncle! I'm playing house-agents. I'll show you how to. I'll teach you if you like."

Guy sat down and gazed into the small pool indicated by Winkie's outstretched finger. " What's the idea?" he asked.

" They're hermit crabs," Winkie explained. " *Those* are hermit crabs and *those* are empty houses. . . . Look, look, there's one changing!"

Guy looked and was amazed to see one of the crabs come out of its own shell and insert itself into another which Winkie had placed conveniently near.

" Hurrah!" cried Winkie, leaping up and down like a lunatic. " Hurrah, hurrah, I've let a house! I'm an awfully good house-agent."

" Do they often take your houses?" asked Guy with interest.

" Not terribly often," replied Winkie, " but just often enough for it to be exciting when they do. Sometimes they look at a house—feel it all over with their claws—and then make up their

209

minds not to move—just like real people do. As a matter of fact that's what you did."

"I did?" asked Guy in bewilderment.

"Yes, as a matter of fact you did. We found a very big hermit, you see, and it was you, and we found a very, *very* big house for you to move into, but you decided not to."

"Did I really?" asked Guy, smiling with amusement. "Perhaps it hadn't electric light——"

"It had everything," declared Winkie. "It even had a fridge so you could have had ice in your whisky if you wanted it. The house-agent lady and I chose a specially nice house for you. Will she come back?"

"What?" asked Guy.

"Will the house-agent lady come back here?"

"Do you mean Mrs. Widgery?"

"No," said Winkie. "Mrs. Widgery doesn't know any games or stories. She's just like other grown-up people."

"Oh, I see," said Guy in a disinterested tone.

Winkie was somewhat displeased. He was disappointed in Jennifer's uncle. He sighed so gustily that Guy was forced to take notice.

"What on earth's the matter with you," asked Guy.

"It isn't me, it's you," replied Winkie sadly. "You're not so interesting as usual, that's all."

Guy could not help laughing. "No, I'm poor company for anyone at the moment," he agreed.

"Have you got a pain?" asked Winkie with rather more sympathy.

"No," said Guy. "No, it isn't that."

"Perhaps you've got toothache," suggested Winkie. "Toothache is horrible, but the best thing to do is to have it pulled out. That's what I did."

"No, I haven't got toothache either. I'm just—just a bit worried."

"I'll tell you a story," said Winkie kindly. "It'll take your mind off. I know an awfully interesting story—not a silly one about fairies—but an *awfully* interesting one. The house-agent lady told it to me, and——"

"Not just now," said Guy. "I'm going up to the hotel to see Jennifer's mother." He rose and smiled at Winkie and wandered off.

Winkie was even more disappointed in Jennifer's uncle, he shook his head sadly and returned to his game, and the incident was closed.

Elise was giving Tillie Liston tea in the lounge when Guy strolled in; she waved the teapot to him in a hospitable manner, so he crossed over to where they were sitting and endeavoured to make himself agreeable.

"Hallo!" he said. "Yes, it is a lovely day. I've just been talking to Winkie on the shore. He's looking ever so much fitter."

"Yes," said his mother, but she said it doubtfully, and somehow or other Guy became aware that he had interrupted a conversation about the young man.

"Tillie is worried," said Elise.

Guy was not surprised to receive this information, for he had known Tillie for years and had never seen her in any other condition; but he made solicitous noises and forbore to look at Elise in case he should smile.

"Yes," said Elise. "Tillie is very worried about Miss Cole."

"Miss Cole!" exclaimed Guy, accepting a cup of tea and selecting a scone from a plate on the table. "What's the matter with little Miss Cole?"

"Nothing," said Tillie hastily. "I mean, she's quite well. It's just that she doesn't seem to be able to manage Winkie any more. He's got so independent lately, and Jack said I was to let him have more freedom to roam about—but it's very difficult."

Guy was surprised. He liked Miss Cole and he liked Winkie, and it always seems strange when two people one likes fail to like each other.

"Tillie will have to get rid of Miss Cole," said Elise firmly.

"Oh, dear!" moaned Tillie. "I don't know what to do. She's so good with Dolly. I'm afraid Winkie is getting to a very unmanageable age. He's *very* naughty sometimes."

Guy thought of the small dirty figure on the sands; he seemed to see the trustful eyes gazing into his. "Nonsense," said Guy. "Anyone who had a grain of understanding could manage Winkie with one hand. What's Miss Cole been thinking of?"

Elise smiled to herself, for she had hoped that Guy would interest himself in this business. Guy needed something to think about and Tillie would listen to what Guy said—Tillie was the sort of woman who is more ready to listen to advice from a man.

"Do you really think so?" Tillie was inquiring. "Miss Cole says he's *very* difficult. She has a theory that Miss Field upset Winkie and undermined her authority."

"Miss Field—what has she to do with it?"

Tillie nodded. "Doesn't it seem absurd? I told Miss Cole it was absurd, but she sticks to it that Winkie's naughtiness dates

211

from the day they met Miss Field in the bus—the day they went to Rithie for Winkie to have his tooth out——"

"I didn't know Winkie *knew* Miss Field," said Guy.

"Oh, yes, they were friends. She took him out in a boat and another day she played with him on the sands. Winkie is always asking when she is coming back."

Guy did not reply at once, for he was thinking—perhaps Frances was the house-agent lady——

"I wish Jack were here," said Tillie in anxious tones.

"He'll be back soon," replied Elise soothingly. "He's been away for ten days, hasn't he, so he'll be back about the end of next week——"

"The end of next week!" echoed Tillie in despairing accents.

There was a short silence, and Guy glanced at Elise. He knew Elise so well, they were so much in tune with each other's minds, that he was certain she was "up to something." She wanted him to *do* something—probably something unpleasant.

"You must just get rid of Miss Cole," said Elise at last. "It's bad for any child to be pulling against authority, and especially bad for Winkie, because he's such a highly-strung, sensitive creature. Guy's right. If you take Winkie the proper way you can do anything with him. You say yourself that you can't go on as you're doing, so you must make up your mind to part with Miss Cole or else to send Winkie to school."

"To school! But we couldn't—he's far too young—and he's so delicate—so difficult with his food—besides, we couldn't afford it——"

"Of course you can't," agreed Guy. "Elise only meant to show you that there was no alternative."

The door of the lounge opened and Winkie appeared. He stood there for a moment smiling like the sun on a May morning. His face was streaked with mud, his clothes were covered with sand, his grey shorts were in tatters round his bare legs. There was an angry-looking scratch on one of his shins and the blood from it was dripping on to the carpet. . . . His mother gazed at him; she seemed to be stricken dumb with consternation at his appearance.

"Hallo, Winkie, what have you got in your pail?" asked Guy.

"A fish," replied Winkie, coming towards them, still with that beaming—almost blinding—smile upon his dirty face. "A real live fish. I caught it myself in a pool. I had an awful job to catch it."

"Good man! Let's see it," said Guy.

Tillie was recovering a little. "Winkie, your clothes——" she began in horror-stricken tones; but Elise interrupted her, leaning forward, and putting a hand upon her knee and saying in a low voice: "Look at his face."

"My clothes!" said Winkie, looking down at his ragged shorts in surprise.

"It's all right," said Guy, putting an arm round his shoulders and drawing him near. "Your mother understands that boys are bound to get dirty when they're catching fish. She doesn't mind a bit . . . where's the fish, Winkie?"

The fish was extremely small, but it was a real fish with fins and a tail; Guy did not know whether it was an infant haddock or whether it was a small species of fish—perhaps it was a minnow. They discussed it seriously, their two heads close together as they peered into the pail.

Tillie looked at them and then she smiled at Elise. "You're quite right," she said in an undertone. "It's just that he has always been so delicate . . . but what about his leg?"

"My leg!" said Winkie, looking up. "Oh, it's nothing. It was a rock, that's all. I'm sorry about my shorts, but the rock had scratchy sort of shells on it."

"We'll put a bandage on your leg," said Elise, rising and holding out her hand. She was quite glad of the excuse to remove Winkie from the scene, for she hoped that Guy would talk to Tillie seriously.

"Look here, Tillie," said Guy. "You've got to realise that Winkie is a boy. It's good for him to get dirty and tear his clothes—just think of what he was like when he came to Cairn—this place is going to make a man of Winkie."

"Yes," said Tillie. "You're quite right, of course. Oh dear, it's so difficult! Miss Cole will be furious about his clothes."

"It will give you a good excuse for sacking her," replied Guy, somewhat brutally.

"Oh, Guy, I don't think I can!" cried Tillie, looking at him with frightened eyes. "It seems so awful to tell her to go . . . after all she has done for the children. It isn't that I'm frightened of her, Guy, it's just . . . it seems so ungrateful."

"She'll get another job quite easily," declared Guy.

"You don't understand," said Tillie—and, of course, this was perfectly true. How could Guy understand? Only Tillie herself knew of all the anxieties which she and Miss Cole had shared. Only Tillie knew of the times when they had taken it in turns to walk the floor for hours on end with Dolly when she was teething, and how she and Miss Cole together had agonised over

213

Winkie when he was feverish and miserable and the doctor had been almost certain—but not quite—that it was appendicitis. Miss Cole had been splendid then; she was always a tower of strength when anything went wrong—when the children were ill—she was always calm and cool and capable. Miss Cole had been with Tillie for years; she was as much a part of Tillie's life as the children themselves, and it was only lately that she had begun to be—to be not quite so satisfactory. Just lately Tillie had begun to feel that Miss Cole was becoming too—well, just a trifle too possessive. She was taking everything into her own hands. She was beginning to run the whole house. She was not content to share the children's affections, but was actually trying to oust Tillie altogether and usurp her place with Dolly and Winkie. She had succeeded with Dolly—Tillie realised this—but Winkie was different. Winkie resented Miss Cole's authority.

"Oh, Guy, you're right!" said Tillie at last. "You and Elise are quite right. She must go—but I don't know how on earth I'm going to break it to her."

"You can tell her quite nicely," said Guy in a comforting manner. "You can say you've noticed that Winkie is getting too much for her or something like that, and you can offer to find her a good post."

"Yes," agreed Tillie. It sounded easy enough but she had no illusions on the subject; she was aware that she was in for a most unpleasant time.

"I'll tell you what we'll do," said Guy suddenly. "I'll come up with you if you like. I won't come in, of course, but I'll wait in the garden while you do the deed. You'll know I'm there, you see. . . ."

Chapter Thirty-two

AFTER A good deal of discussion, it was arranged as Guy had suggested, and he and Tillie and Winkie set off together for the bungalow on the hill. During the walk the conversation was concerned with the fish, and was conducted entirely by Winkie and Guy. Tillie walked along with a white, set face, and her lips moved slightly all the time. It was not difficult to guess that she was engaged in framing sentences which would convey her intentions to Miss Cole as tactfully as possible.

"Will it live?" asked Winkie for the third time. "Will it grow into a big fish—big enough for mummy to have for break-

214

fast? Will it be a herring when it grows up? Do you think it's quite happy in my pail? What do you think I ought to give it to eat? I should like to give it something to make it grow very quickly. What do you think would make it grow very quickly, Jennifer's uncle?"

Guy answered all these questions as best he could—which was not very satisfactorily.

"You don't know much about it, do you?" said Winkie at last with his usual frankness.

When they reached the bungalow Tillie pressed Guy's hand and hurried up the steps—she was muttering to herself now and was obviously keyed up to concert pitch—and Guy led Winkie to the summer-house.

"But it's my bed-time," Winkie said. "It *must* be nearly my bed-time, and Miss Cole will be angry if I don't go in—she'll be angry anyhow when she sees my shorts——"

"You're staying up a bit later to-night," said Guy.

"Am I?" inquired Winkie in surprise. "Why am I staying up later? I haven't been specially good."

"Because—because you caught the fish, of course," said Guy in desperation.

They went into the summer-house and sat down. It was warm and sunny and sheltered from the wind, and it had a lovely view over the sea. The tide was half-way up the bay—it was coming in fast—and far away on the point you could see the little house where the Widgerys had lived. Guy searched about in his mind for something to amuse Winkie and to ward off any more awkward questions. "What about that story?" he inquired. "You said you knew a very interesting story . . . by the way, I suppose the house-agent lady is Miss Field?"

"Yes, of course," replied Winkie. "She taught me the game, you see, and she told me the story." He wasted no more time on explanations, for he loved telling stories and it was so seldom that anyone wanted to listen, and he realised that if he did not start off at once Jennifer's uncle might change his mind and decide that he did not want to hear it after all. Winkie perched himself on the edge of the table and began his tale, and as he had an exceedingly good memory, he told it in almost the same words as it had been told to him.

"Once upon a time there was a princess, and she lived in a lovely palace in the middle of London; but the princess was very lonely and had a dull time because she was invisible. It was a spell, you see. She had all sorts of nice things to eat—ice-cream and strawberries and things—but she had nobody to play with.

People couldn't play with her, or talk to her even, because she was invisible; they didn't know she was there."

"That was hard luck," said Guy.

"Yes, wasn't it? Well, one day when the poor princess was feeling specially sad—because she had nobody to play with—a kind old magician came along. It wasn't Merlin, it was another magician called Digby. Some people thought he was just an ordinary doctor, but he wasn't; he was a very powerful magician. He was sorry about her being lonely, so he broke the spell with his magic and the princess escaped—and where do you think she went? She went to Cairn."

Guy looked at Winkie. "She came here?" he said slowly.

"Yes," said Winkie. "She came here to Cairn—wasn't it fun? It makes the story sound—sort of *true*, doesn't it?"

Guy had been thinking the same thing. "What was the princess's name?" he asked.

Winkie was delighted to find he had awakened the interest of his audience. "I don't know what her name was," he replied, "but we could think of a name for her, couldn't we?"

"No," said Guy. "No, Winkie, I'd much rather hear the story exactly as Miss Field told it. Go on, there's a good lad."

"Well, she came to Cairn," continued Winkie, "and, of course, she had lots of people to talk to. At first it was difficult to talk, because she wasn't used to it, but after a bit she got quite good at talking—she found her tongue—it was funny to have lost her tongue, wasn't it?"

"Go on, tell me more."

"It's a good story, isn't it?"

"The best story I've heard for years," declared Guy.

"There isn't really very much more after that. I *rather* wanted her to live happy ever after; but, you see, after the spell was broken she was just an ordinary person, like you and me, and it's only fairy princesses who live happy ever after."

"Yes, I see."

"Well, that's all," said Winkie, "and I think I had better go in now because they seem to have forgotten all about me."

"They'll fetch you when they want you," declared Guy. "It's quite all right, Winkie. Tell me what the girl did at Cairn."

"I don't know what she did," said Winkie sadly. "I wish I knew. I rather wanted to see Miss Field and ask her whether the girl went on living at Cairn or whether she ever went back to the palace in London."

"Yes," agreed Guy. "I should like to know that too."

"I don't think she would go back to the palace, because she was so lonely when she was there."

"You don't happen to know where the palace was—what part of London, I mean?"

"No," said Winkie, shaking his head. "The palace was called Wintringham Square, but——"

"What?" exclaimed Guy.

"Wintringham Square," repeated Winkie. "It's an awfully silly name for a palace. It was called that because it was a square sort of palace—at least that's what I thought."

"No," cried Guy. "By Jove—it was called that because—because that was its name! Winkie, you're the most sensible person in the whole of Cairn. In fact, you're the only person in Cairn who has any sense at all. Would half a crown be any good to you?"

"Half a crown?" asked Winkie, looking at Jennifer's uncle to see if he had suddenly gone mad.

"No, five bob," said that worthy, fishing in his pocket and producing four separate shillings and two sixpences and tucking them into Winkie's grubby little hand.

"But what's it for——?"

"It's a prize," declared Guy. "It's a prize for remembering the story so well—and especially for remembering the name of the palace—that's what it's for."

"Golly!" exclaimed Winkie in amazement.

Guy got up. He was so excited that he could not sit still a moment longer. He would wangle leave somehow—they must give him leave—and he would go to London and find her. Wintringham Square . . . that was where she had lived, of course, so if he went to Wintringham Square he was bound to find her. She might be there now—at this very minute—she had said that she was going to stay with her aunt. There were several things he must do before he left. It would be difficult to get away, but Ned would understand. Ned would let him go. . . .

Winkie was counting his money, gloating over it like a small miser. "Need I put it into my savings bank, Jennifer's uncle?" he inquired.

"No," replied Guy. "It's to spend. You're to buy anything you want with it."

"Golly!" exclaimed Winkie again.

At this moment the front door of the bungalow burst open and Miss Cole appeared; she looked neither to the right nor to the left, but rushed down the steps and through the gate and

217

disappeared from view. There was such an air of madness about her departure that Guy took to his heels and pursued her at top speed. He saw her in front of him when he reached the road, and he overtook her quite easily just before she got to the beach.

"I say, what's the matter?" he inquired.

Miss Cole stopped at once. Her face was extremely red and her breath was coming in gasps. "Oh!" she cried. "Oh, it's you! Oh, Captain Tarlatan, I'm so miserable I don't know what to do. Mrs. Liston says—says I'm to go away. I *can't* believe it. I've done—you've no idea what I've done for them—and now—and all because of Winkie—oh, dear!"

Guy did not know what to say. He felt like a villain.

"You're so sympathetic," continued Miss Cole. "You *understand*, don't you? I've done all I could—nobody could have done more—I've loved them all and given my best. Dolly is so sweet—dear little Dolly! How can I leave her and go away! She's so devoted to me, she's so sweet and funny—her funny little ways—how can I bear it! Oh dear!"

She sat down on the sand, and Guy sat down beside her. He felt that the least he could do for Miss Cole was to listen to her.

"I've done my best," she continued in a calmer tone. "I've tried to lay the foundations of their characters. I've tried to teach them from the very beginning, to bring them up really well —and now it's all lost—all my work. Oh dear, we were all so happy together . . . until just lately. Just lately everything seems to have gone wrong. Winkie—it's all Winkie, of course—Winkie has been so disobedient, so different from what he was before. He used to be such a dear little boy—but now——"

Guy said nothing. He was aware that nothing need be said.

"Mrs. Liston spoils him," complained Miss Cole. "Everyone spoils him. Of course he has been ill, but you can't go on making allowances for ever. People don't understand how difficult Winkie is, how terribly difficult to manage. They think he's such a dear little boy because he talks in that old-fashioned way. Really and truly he's very stubborn indeed—underneath—very stubborn." Miss Cole hesitated, and then she continued in quite a different tone of voice. "It began—it all began when he got to know that Miss Field. It was she who put Winkie against me —he was always a thousand times wilder and more independent when he had been with her. She made him cheeky too."

"How could she?" asked Guy.

"You may well ask," replied Miss Cole, taking Guy's words in a different sense from the perfectly plain and straightforward
218

sense in which Guy had intended them. " How *could* she have been so—so unkind—as to put Winkie against me? It wasn't *right* of her to do it."

" But she didn't," said Guy. " I mean, she couldn't change Winkie's attitude to you? It isn't possible. Besides, she wouldn't do a thing like that."

" Oh, wouldn't she? You don't know what she's like. I knew she would do me a bad turn if she could—I knew it from the first."

" I don't think there is any need to discuss Miss Field," said Guy.

" No," replied Miss Cole. " People like that always come to grief in the end. I'm a great believer in poetic justice—aren't you, Captain Tarlatan?"

Guy did not know what she meant, and he wondered whether she herself knew what she meant by poetic justice. He was beginning to feel that he had listened to Miss Cole long enough, but he did not know how he was going to get away from her.

" Poetic justice," repeated Miss Cole. " That's what comes to people who interfere and poke their noses into other people's affairs."

Guy was rather amused at this. He wondered whether his misfortunes could be classified as poetic justice—he thought this over while Miss Cole elaborated her theme. It was true that he had poked his nose into other people's affairs and had got severely punished for his trouble . . . but he would find Frances now and all would be well—thanks to Winkie and also thanks to Miss Cole. It was curious how the thing had worked (thought Guy), for, if Miss Cole had not fallen out with Winkie so seriously that Tillie had been obliged to sack her, Guy would never have listened to the story and would never have heard of Wintringham Square. If Miss Cole were to be believed, it went right back to Frances herself, for Miss Cole blamed Frances for Winkie's rebellion. Was that poetic justice or was it the long arm of coincidence? wondered Guy, smiling to himself at the trite phrases.

Miss Cole rose and dusted the sand from her skirt. It had done her good to talk—Captain Tarlatan had been so kind and sympathetic—already she was feeling a good deal better, already she was beginning to get used to the idea of leaving the Listons. After all, Cairn was exceedingly dull. There was no picture house and no shops worthy of the name . . . and they would have a fine time with Dolly when she had gone . . . that would show Mrs. Liston. . . .

Chapter Thirty-three

ONCE GUY was actually in the train on his way to London he felt
a different creature, for he was doing something active—he was
on a trail. He travelled by night and should have arrived early
in the morning, but the train was delayed by a serious air-raid,
and it was ten o'clock before it reached Euston. He bathed and
breakfasted at the Station Hotel, for he felt grubby and unkempt
after his night in the train, and then, leaving his luggage at the
hotel, he strode out into the sunshine to look for a taxi. He
found one standing on a rank, and calling the driver asked him
if he knew Wintringham Square.

"South-west," replied the driver tersely. "It'll mean a bit
of a day-tour, but I'll get ye there O.K."

"Carry on, then," said Guy, getting in.

Guy had not been in London for months, and he was anxious
to see for himself what damage it had sustained from the recent
raids. Some parts looked just the same as usual, but other parts
showed the scars of battle. Here and there Guy saw crumbling
masonry; he saw houses which looked as if they had been sliced
in half with a gigantic knife. One house, which must have been
damaged quite recently, reminded Guy of Elise's doll's house.
The whole front was gone, and one could see straight into the
rooms—there were beds and chairs and tables standing in their
accustomed places; there was flowered wallpaper on the walls—
somebody's home had been shattered past repair. In other places
workmen were busy demolishing smoke-blackened masonry, or
shoring up tottering walls with timber struts . . . then for some
time Guy was carried through streets which looked perfectly
normal, streets which apparently had not suffered at all from
enemy action. The taxi driver went by back streets, narrow and
twisting and sometimes blocked by drays. Guy had lived in
London at one time and he prided himself upon his knowledge of
the city, but to-day he was being taken through districts he had
never even heard of.

"You're taking me by a very roundabout route," said Guy at
last, pulling back the window which shut him off from the
driver.

"It's quicker in the long run," replied the man. "I told ye
it would mean a bit of a day-tour. Fact is we're supposed to
220

keep clear of the main streets when we can—saves blocks. Don't want blocks with Jerries coming over."

"They don't come much in the day-time, do they?"

"Not much—scared of our lads—still, ye never know. Sometimes we gets a stray Jerry."

They came at last to a district of large squares—one leading out of another—and here the driver slowed down and looked about him. "Ought to be 'ere somewhere," he said. "It's some time since I was in this part. Ah, there it is—Wintringham Square—wot number did ye say, Guv'nor?"

"I didn't say any," Guy replied. "Just drop me out here."

The taxi drew up at the kerb, and Guy got out and paid the driver. Then he straightened his back and looked round . . . this was Wintringham Square.

When Guy had heard at Cairn that Frances had mentioned Wintringham Square he had thought, *that's easy, I'll go there and find her*, but now that he was actually on the spot it seemed a good deal more difficult. It was a large square with gardens in the middle, and there were houses on all four sides . . . he counted the houses and found that there were sixty. Frances might be living in one of these houses with her uncle and aunt or she might not; she might have lived here once, years ago, and gone away; she might never have lived here at all. Guy's heart sank. He realised what an optimistic fool he had been . . . all the same, it *was* a clue and the only clue he had. He could go round the whole square and ask at every house. It might take days. . . .

He looked round the square again. How deserted it was, how quiet and peaceful! It was a sort of backwater, and the hum of London was like the distant sound of the sea. There were no children or nurses to be seen as there would have been in peacetime. There was nobody about, nobody except an errand boy on a bicycle.

Guy crossed the road and spoke to him. "Do you know anyone here called Field?" he asked.

"Field!" repeated the boy. "In this 'ere square d'yer mean? No, I don't know nobody called that." He got on to his bicycle and pedalled off.

Guy walked round the square looking at each house (he had started at number 60, so the numbers went backwards). They were all exactly the same, these Victorian houses, and yet they were all different, for the people who lived in them had impressed them with a different personality. Some of the houses were well cared for, with good paintwork and shining door-knobs; others

221

looked as if they had come down in the world . . . most of the houses were residential, but one or two had brass plates with dentists' names on them, and there was one large nursing home. So far Guy had seen no doctors' plates, and that seemed odd for Wintringham Square was a sort of place in which doctors like to live. It was not one of the very expensive squares, but it was quiet and pleasant and eminently respectable.

Guy had now walked round three sides of the square and had come to the fourth. Ah, there was a doctor's plate. He stopped and read it.

J. DIGBY, M.B., Ch.B.

Guy gazed at it with dawning comprehension. What was it Winkie had said? " He was called Digby. Some people thought he was just an ordinary doctor, but he was a very powerful magician."

" I've found her!" cried Guy . . . his heart nearly choked him . . . he bounded up the steps and pealed the bell. . . .

Just at that moment a car glided up to the kerb and stopped, and a man got out—an old man with white hair and rather a bushy white moustache.

" You're Dr. Digby!" exclaimed Guy breathlessly.

" Yes, is it an accident?" asked the doctor, pausing with one foot on the steps.

" No, it's—it's Providence," declared Guy, seizing the doctor's hand and shaking it.

Dr. Digby laughed. " I hope Providence hasn't decreed that I've got to go out before I've had my lunch."

" No, of course not," said Guy earnestly. " I'll wait. I don't want you to go anywhere—I just want to ask you something, that's all."

" You'll have had your lunch, I suppose."

" Yes," said Guy. " I mean no—but it doesn't matter. I had breakfast late. The train was late in arriving."

" Where did the train arrive from?"

" From Glasgow," replied Guy.

" But you're not a Scot——"

" No, I've been stationed in Scotland. I came south to see you —at least I think so—I mean, I didn't know that you were here, but I'm sure you're the very man I want to see——"

Dr. Digby was hungry; he had not breakfasted late, so he cut short these incoherencies by inviting the excited young officer to have lunch with him. Guy replied that he would wait.

He did his level best to avoid sharing the doctor's meal, for he was aware that catering was difficult, but the doctor would take no denial, and in a very few minutes they were sitting opposite to each other at a large mahogany table eating an excellent piece of boiled cod and drinking beer out of two large tankards.

"I've an appointment at two-thirty," said Dr. Digby, "so there's not much time. You can talk to me while we eat and tell me why you've come all the way from Glasgow to see me."

"It's just this," said Guy. "Do you happen to know Frances Field?" He paused and waited for the doctor's reply in a fever of impatience.

"Yes, I know her well. This is her uncle's house," replied Dr. Digby.

Guy looked round the room.

"Yes, she used to live here," said the doctor. "I rented the house from Mr. Wheeler when my own house was blown to bits. It's a bit on the large side, but——"

"Where is she?" Guy inquired.

"She's not here," Dr. Digby replied, smiling at Guy's impatience. "I've just told you I've rented the house. The Wheelers are in Devonshire."

"Is Frances with them?" asked Guy.

The doctor hesitated and then he said: "Why do you want to know?"

"I must find her."

"But why?"

"Because——" said Guy. "Well, because I want to ask her to marry me."

Dr. Digby grinned. He said: "You've put all your cards on the table. I suppose you think I should do the same?"

"That was the idea," admitted Guy.

"But supposing Frances Field would rather I didn't tell you where she was?"

"Oh, but——"

"This is how I see it—if Frances had wanted you to have her address she could have sent it you herself . . . and, as she's done nothing of the sort, I'm forced to the conclusion that she's not particularly anxious for you to have it."

"But I must see her!"

"Will she want to see you?"

Guy hesitated. "I think she will," he said.

"But you're not sure?"

"It's like this, you see. I'm almost sure that she—er—likes me, but we had a sort of—well, a sort of misunderstanding. I thought that she understood . . . but she thought that I . . . well, it was a misunderstanding . . . and then, before I could get hold of her to explain the whole thing, she had vanished and I've been trying to find her ever since."

"Ah, that was the way of it!" said Dr. Digby, and, although his face was as grave as a judge, his eyes were twinkling.

Guy nodded. "It sounds idiotic, doesn't it?"

"I hear quite a number of things that sound idiotic," Dr. Digby replied. "Sometimes the things are not so idiotic as they sound. . . . If you'd been here last Friday you'd have seen Frances," he added.

"I thought you said she was in Devonshire?"

"I said the Wheelers were . . . help yourself to another piece of cod."

Guy did not want more cod. He said: "You will tell me, won't you, sir?"

"I think so," said Dr. Digby. "Yes, I think I will . . . but I should like to know a little more first. Did you meet Frances at Cairn?"

Thus encouraged, Guy plunged into the story; he told Dr. Digby everything—all about Winkie and how he had heard the name Wintringham Square—and Dr. Digby listened and nodded and chuckled. He did not give Guy the information he wanted until nearly the end.

"Well, I think you deserve a reward for your trouble," he said at last. "Frances is at Manburgh in Hertfordshire. She's at the Belton Works. She went there on Friday and she's to manage the canteen. I can't give you her address in Manburgh, but if you go to the Belton Works and ask for Mr. Fleming he will be able to put you in touch with her. You can mention my name to Fleming—I'll give you my card—he's a friend of mine. He'll not be best pleased if she throws up her job," added Dr. Digby thoughtfully.

Guy realised that this was true. He said quickly: "It doesn't matter. I mean, if she wants to go on doing the job I can wait for her. I can wait if I know that everything is all right."

"Mind you, there's to be no nonsense," said Dr. Digby as he saw Guy off at the door. "I've given you her address and you can go and see her and explain the misunderstanding, but I'll not have you pestering Frances. There's to be none of that."

"If you don't trust me——"

"But I do," declared Dr. Digby with a chuckle. "If I hadn't trusted you, I'd never have given you the child's address . . . and what's more I hope you'll be successful. Frances is a lonely sort of creature—always has been—but she's a grand girl, and I'm old-fashioned enough to think marriage is a woman's best career. You'll let me know what happens."

"Of course I will. Thank you, sir. Thank you very much indeed. I'll be—Frances will be all right with me. I mean——"

"I know fine what you mean," said the old doctor, patting him on the back. "Away and find Frances. She'll be pleased to see you if I know anything about it."

The town of Manburgh was in some confusion when Guy arrived, for it had been badly bombed the night before. In fact it was the Manburgh blitz which had delayed the Night Scot and had made Guy late in arriving in London.

"They'll be back to-night, I shouldn't wonder," said the porter as he carried Guy's bag to a taxi and heaved it in. "Two nights running—that's the rule."

It was quite true, of course. The Luftwaffe usually bombed the same town two nights in succession—and we did the same thing with German towns—it was good strategy, for the A.R.P. Services were bound to be a trifle less efficient the second night, and the fire-fighters would naturally be tired.

"Was there much damage?" Guy asked. "Were the Belton Works hit?"

"The bombs were mostly in the town," replied the man. "A lot of 'ouses were wrecked. The Belton Works are outside the town and Jerry didn't get them."

"'E would 'ave liked to," declared the taxi driver, joining in the conversation. "The Belton Works is wot Jerry wanted—so they're saying."

Guy went straight out to the Belton Works. It was nine o'clock by this time, and he realised that it was too late to find Frances to-night, but he decided to go to the works and get her address so that he could look her up early in the morning. He was still impatient, but he felt that if he knew where she was he coudl rest; she might be living in a hotel—probably was—and if so he could go and stay the night under the same roof.

"There's the Belton Works," said the driver, pointing to half a dozen enormous factory buildings situated in a large park. "They're new. They've jus' bin built, but they're going full swing night an' day. They won't let you in unless you got a pass —nobody can't get in."

"I'll try, anyhow," Guy replied.

There was a little delay at the gate, but Guy was in uniform and his manner was assured. He produced Dr. Digby's card and asked for Mr. Fleming, and after a little discussion and some telephoning he was informed that Mr. Fleming would see him.

Mr. Fleming was a Scot; he was younger than Dr. Digby, but was rather like the doctor in many ways. He had the same type of face—somewhat dour, but changing to genuine kindliness when lighted by a smile—and the same keen grey eyes. " Well, Captain—er—Tarlatan," he said, " and what can we do for you?"

" It isn't business," said Guy. " I'm very sorry to disturb you, but Dr. Digby said you wouldn't mind. Could you give me Miss Field's address?"

" Miss Field? Oh yes, the canteen manager."

" It's dreadful to disturb you at this hour, but it's rather important——" began Guy.

Mr. Fleming smiled. " This hour!" he said. " All hours are the same to me. We're working night and day. I'm afraid I can't tell you where Miss Field is living, but if you go over to the canteen you'll find her there. She's getting everything into order. It's opening to-morrow." He came with Guy to the door of his office. " What do you think of it?" he asked, waving his hand. " Eighteen months ago the place was a park—not a bad effort, is it?"

Guy could hardly believe it. The great buildings which were dotted about the grounds were filled with the hum of machinery; there were men in overalls, and women in white coats. Huge trucks, laden with strangely-shaped pieces of metal, were running from one building to another on small-gauge rails. The whole place was a hive of well-organised activity.

" It's marvellous," said Guy.

" Aeroplane parts," said Mr. Fleming. " Don't spread it abroad. I'll take you round the whole place to-morrow if you like."

" I'd like it immensely," Guy replied. He realised that it was Dr. Digby's recommendation which had gained him an entrance to the Belton Works—that and his uniform, of course.

" It's one of the biggest factories in England for aeroplane parts," continued Mr. Fleming with justifiable pride. " We got started in January and we're working eight-hour shifts—you'd be pretty surprised if I could give you our production figures. It's production that's going to win this war. Production is the key to victory."

" Yes," said Guy, smiling, " but production wouldn't be much use without the men to use the machines. You've got to admit that."

Mr. Fleming admitted it generously. "Oh yes, *you're* all right," he said. "It's for you we're working—and you're fighting for us. It's a partnership. Neither of us would be any use without the other . . . your men and my factories . . . between them they'll do for Hitler and his gang. Curious about Hess, wasn't it?"

Guy had not come here to talk about Hess, so he agreed that it was very curious indeed, and before Mr. Fleming could say any more on the subject he asked which building was the canteen.

"None of them," replied Mr. Fleming. "We're using Lord Belton's mansion house as a club for the operatives—Miss Field is going to live there and look after the place when we've got it all in order. It's a beautiful house—several hundreds of years old—with a magnificent staircase and drawing-rooms with parquet floors. We've turned the old banqueting hall into a canteen—I suppose you think that's vandalism."

"We're fighting for something more important than banqueting halls," said Guy.

"That's true, but still . . . I don't mind telling you I had a few qualms when we started to turn the place inside out. It seemed wrong, somehow. Well, I won't keep you. There's the house . . . over there amongst those trees. You're sure to find Miss Field, she's an indefatigable worker. Sorry I can't come with you. . . ."

Chapter Thirty-four

GUY WALKED across the park in the direction indicated by Mr. Fleming and, once he had turned his back upon the bustle and hum of the works, he felt as if he were in another world—an older and more peaceful civilisation. The light was fading fast, but there was a moon floating clear and cold above the treetops, and, between the two lights—the fading light of day and the growing brilliance of the moon—Guy saw the old mansion house take shape before his eyes. It was a stately house, large and imposing and beautifully proportioned; it was built of yellowish stone weathered to a dull chrome colour. Somehow or other it gave Guy a feeling of satisfaction. It was beautiful and old and permanent. It looked as if it had grown out of the soil of England; it was part of England's heritage. Guy knew now what Mr. Fleming had meant when he had spoken of vandalism.

The front door was standing open, so Guy walked in and

found himself in a large hall with statues standing in the corners. Lord Belton had evidently left the statues behind when he moved out of his ancestral home—probably because he had no other place to put them. The staircase was very fine; it was a double staircase going up from each side of the hall and meeting in the middle . . . the banisters were of wrought iron. Guy opened several doors and looked into the rooms. They were furnished with chairs and tables—these were the rest-rooms. The large drawing-room was full of ping-pong tables and there was a battered piano at one end of it. After some trouble Guy found the banqueting hall, which had been turned into a canteen. It was so large that it reminded him of a chapel, and this resemblance was further accentuated by an enormously high vaulted roof that went right up to the top of the building. There were small tables about the room; some of the tables had vases of flowers on them. and some were laid—as if for a meal—with knives and forks and spoons. Against the wall near the door where Guy had entered, there was an enormous refectory table of fumed oak. This was the only piece of furniture which really suited the room, and Guy decided that this—like the statues—must belong to Lord Belton. He wondered what Lord Belton thought of it all, whether he minded . . . but it was not much use minding, and Lord Belton was a sensible sort of fellow (Guy knew him slightly), so probably he made the best of it.

Guy was standing there wondering what to do next, when a very pretty dark-haired girl came out of a side-door with a tray of cutlery in her hands.

" Is Miss Field here?" asked Guy.

" Not at the moment," replied the girl, looking at Guy with interest. " She's gone over to see Mr. Bridge—he's the assistant manager—but she won't be long."

" May I wait here for her?"

" Yes, of course. Perhaps you'd like a cup of coffee or something?"

" That would be very nice," said Guy gratefully. He sat down at one of the little tables and, as he did so, he discovered that he was very tired. It was not surprising, really, for he had been on the go all day, and last night in the train he had been too keyed up to get much sleep. He had been keyed up ever since he left Cairn, keyed up and straining forward. He had found Frances now—actually found her—and in a few minutes they would be face to face. What should he say to her? How should he begin? He turned it all over in his mind and decided that he must not frighten her; he must not take it for granted that she

228

would be pleased to see him. First of all, he must tell her how distressed he had been to find she had left Cairn, and then he must explain about the Widgerys and about Angela . . . after that he could go on and tell her of his struggles to find her, and all about Dr. Digby. The misunderstanding must be thoroughly cleared up and everything must be put right. Then, when Frances really understood, and everything was clear between them, he would say . . . he would ask her whether . . . he would tell her that he had loved her all along from the very first moment that he saw her. He would remind her of that day when they got marooned on the cliffs and she had been so splendid. He would tell her that he had known then that she was the only girl in the world for him and that unless she would marry him—no, that wouldn't do. He would say, " Frances——"

" Here's your coffee and this is Pamela Durward bringing it to you," said the dark-haired girl's voice at his elbow.

Guy looked up and smiled at her. " Thank you very much, Miss Durward. This is Guy Tarlatan thanking you."

" You aren't her brother, then?"

" No, just a friend," replied Guy.

Miss Durward lingered; she seemed in the mood for conversation. " How do you like this room?" she inquired. " We've been working at it like slaves, and now it's finished and we're opening properly to-morrow. We're expecting a good old crush at eleven—that's when the morning shift gets a break. Of course the house has been open—the rest-rooms and all that—but the canteen was just in a hut; it wasn't much of a place."

" Have you other people to help you?"

" Oh, rather—but most of them are voluntary. Frances and I and another girl are the only whole-time workers. We earn our crew, I can tell you. . . . I hope we get some sleep to-night," she added, stifling a yawn.

" You didn't get much last night."

" No . . . we don't *bother* much about the raids unless we get stuff dropping fairly near, but the noise keeps you awake—that's the worst of it."

" Haven't you got a shelter?"

" Yes, but we just carry on. The operatives have to carry on or production would be slowed down." She laughed and added: Production is conversation topic number one in this place—we think of nothing else. The figures are given out every week, and if they've gone up everyone is as pleased as a dog with two tails—myself included."

" And if they go down?" inquired Guy.

229

"They don't," replied Miss Durward promptly. "They g
up and up and up. This canteen is going to send them soaring t
the skies."

"How?" asked Guy.

"Oh, I was just ragging," she replied. "The canteen can
make very much difference except that when people are well fe
in a pleasant place it increases their efficiency; but you must le
us keep the illusion that we're helping production. . . . Hallo
d'you hear that?"

Guy listened, and far away in the distance he heard a siren, th
eerie wailing sound of the alert. He also heard a faint poppin
noise which he knew to be distant gunfire. "Jerry seems to be in
the neighbourhood," said Guy.

She nodded. "That's Truckford siren, and those are th
Truckford batteries. You'll hear our own siren in a fe
moments. I think I'll make for home."

"Hadn't you better wait?"

She shook her head. "I want to get home. I must have som
sleep before to-morrow. Cheerio. Frances won't be long now—
she always locks up the place herself."

Guy sat on. The room was in darkness except for one electri
lamp on the table where he was sitting and one light above th
door which led into the hall. It was such an enormous room tha
the other end of it was in darkness . . . what a huge shadow
cavern of a room! To-morrow it would spring to life; it woul
be full of men and women snatching hasty meals between thei
periods of work.

The Manburgh siren was wailing now—Guy hated the sound
He wondered why it was necessary to have such a dismayin
noise as a warning that the enemy was approaching. Wouldn
it be better (for psychological reasons) to have an enlivening ca
to arms, the note of a bugle or a drum, instead of that distress
ful yowling that froze the marrow in one's bones? The gunfir
had come nearer . . . that barking was obviously the Manburg
A.A. guns . . . and that was a stick of bombs—three explosion
one after another, not very loud but loud enough to make th
windows rattle—and now, quite distinctly, he could hear th
sound of planes.

Guy wondered where Frances was. He wished she woul
come. There must be a lot of stuff falling round about, shel
splinters from our own guns if nothing else. The noise wa
increasing every moment, the bark of guns and the roar of th
planes. Guy rose to his feet with the subconscious urge to g
and look for Frances and just at that moment the door into th

230

all opened and Frances was there. She stood in the doorway
with the light shining on her hair and turning it to gold.

"Guy!" said Frances in amazement.

Guy was stricken dumb. He could not begin his carefully prepared explanations; he could not even say her name. He gazed
at her in absolute silence.

It was then, at that moment, while he was still staring at
Frances, that Guy heard the bomb coming. He had heard bombs
coming before—that curious, quite unmistakable squealing
sound with a background like the rending of coarse calico—he
had heard it in France at a village where he was billeted, he had
heard it in Belgium and again at Dunkirk, and he was aware that
when you heard that sound there was only one thing to do and
you hadn't much time . . . Guy leapt at Frances, seized her in his
arms, flung her on the floor, rolled her under the big, solid
refectory table and spread himself on the top of her . . . the
bomb burst.

For a moment or two Guy was absolutely stunned by the crash
of the explosion . . . it was an appalling crash . . . it was the
loudest and most devastating noise he had ever experienced . . .
the whole place rocked upon its foundations like an earthquake.
After the explosion came the crash and clatter of falling
masonry, the rending, tearing sound of tortured timbers . . . the
air was filled with the stench of cordite. . . .

There was silence for a moment, and then another avalanche
of masonry, stones and rubble poured down from the walls and
the roof; they clattered down and stopped, and then clattered
down again . . . every now and then there was a louder crash as
the beams and stones were loosened from their places and a
larger chunk of wall tottered and fell.

After a few minutes, the avalanche of stones ceased to fall,
and Guy opened his eyes and sat up. His ears were singing, but
he was unhurt, and as Frances had been underneath him, he had
very reason to believe that she had escaped injury. He saw that
he had fainted—perhaps that was just as well. He looked round
the room upon the most extraordinary scene he had ever beheld.
The bomb had fallen on the outer wall, shearing away the wall
and part of the room . . . through the large gap bright moonlight
was pouring in, flooding the scene with silvery light. The floor
was a mass of huge, jagged stones and beams and rubble. Clouds
of dust and plaster filled the air . . . eddying, floating, falling
and settling inches deep upon everything. Beams, torn and
lacerated, jagged and splintered, stuck out from the walls—they
looked to Guy as if they had been clawed out of the walls by a

giant with a pickaxe. While Guy looked, another piece of wall began to sway and totter . . . the next moment it fell with another crash and the stones bounded on the other stones which were heaped on the floor and were flung in all directions.

His first idea had been to get Frances out of the place as quickly as he could, but now he changed his mind, for he noticed that the outer wall, where the gap was, had been cracked from top to bottom and a huge piece of masonry which had been torn from its moorings was balanced on one end of a beam in a most precarious fashion . . . Frances was safer where she was. The table was solid and the wall behind the table was solid too—it was the inner wall of the house and seemed more or less secure. To get Frances out he would have to carry her across the room to the gap, he would have to scramble over the heaps of fallen stones. It would be better to wait until a rescue party arrived—people who knew what to do. He had heard no more bombs, so perhaps the raiders had been driven off . . . it was to be hoped that the factory had escaped destruction. . . .

"Guy," said Frances, faintly.

He looked at her and saw that her eyes were open. "Are you all right?" he asked anxiously.

"I thought I was dead. The noise . . ."

"Yes, it was some noise. You aren't hurt, are you?"

"No," she replied. She sat up and shook back her hair—it was full of dust and plaster—her eyes widened with horror and amazement as she looked round. "Oh, the poor house!" she said. "Oh, the poor, poor house—it was so beautiful, Guy."

Guy did not reply. He was looking round with an anxious expression on his face . . . he smelt fire . . . where was it? Was it just a waft of burning wood from some other bomb—an incendiary—near by, or was it *here*? A tongue of flame shot out from the door at the other end of the room, a red and yellow flag of danger. . . .

"We'll have to move," said Guy, rising to his feet.

Frances had seen it too. She crawled out from under the table and stood up beside him.

"Frances," said Guy quickly. "We're going to get out of here safely—of course we are—but just in case—Frances, it's all right, isn't it?"

"Yes, it's all right, Guy."

"You'll marry me, Frances?"

"Yes, of course," she said.

He looked at her and saw she was looking up at him—and smiling. "Aren't you ever frightened of anything?" he asked.

"Only of mice," she replied.

Guy knew it wasn't true. She was frightened (of course she was frightened), but that didn't matter. It was the gesture that mattered—the brave gesture—he loved her for it. He held out his hand and she put hers into it . . . together they began to climb over the huddle of stones and rubble to the gap in the wall.

The stones crumbled beneath their feet; there was glass everywhere; there were jagged beams with nails in them; there were huge chunks of stone which had fallen from the vaulted roof. The fire was spreading with incredible rapidity—little tongues of flame were advancing towards them, licking up the wood, dry as tinder, which lay among the debris on the floor. The place was filled with a red glow and with acrid smoke which made them cough. They struggled on and all the time Guy kept looking at the wall . . . the cracked wall. It was tottering and the beam that supported it was swaying . . . they reached the gap now, and Guy climbed out. He turned and held out his arms and Frances flung herself into them . . . at that moment the wall fell with a crash. It fell inwards, but a small avalanche of rubble and dust poured down from the roof, knocking them over and half burying them.

Guy rose. He was dazed and bruised but apparently sound. He picked Frances up in his arms and went down to meet the rescue party which was coming up the drive.

Chapter Thirty-five

"THANK GOD you're safe!" exclaimed Mr. Fleming. "Is there anybody else in the place? Miss Durward? No . . . that's good. Put her down here. The grass is dry as a bone. Where's the doctor?"

Guy laid Frances on the grass, and an elderly man came forward and knelt down beside her. Guy watched him anxiously as he ran his hands over her in a competent manner. They were alone now—the three of them—for Mr. Fleming and the rest of the party had gone on to the house with the fire-fighters.

"Is she—badly hurt?" asked Guy, moistening his dry lips with his tongue.

"No," replied the doctor. "I can't find anything except a simple fracture of the arm——"

"But why is she unconscious," asked Guy, bending over and gazing at her white face and closed eyes.

233

" Shock probably," replied the doctor, " or perhaps slight concussion. We'll get her off to the hospital. What about yourself?"

" I'm perfectly fit. Are you sure she's all right? No internal injuries or—or anything?"

" I can't be sure, of course," replied the doctor, looking up at Guy; " but I don't think there's much wrong. Are you related to her?"

" We're engaged to be married," said Guy.

" I see. Well, I don't think you need worry unduly. Do you want to go with her to the hospital?"

Guy hesitated. He looked at Frances and then he looked at the house. Flames were leaping up and shooting through the windows. The fire-fighters were running out their hoses; Mr. Fleming was standing on the terrace waving his arms and calling out directions to the men.

" I think I ought to help them," said Guy at last.

" It would be good of you," nodded the doctor. " Fleming is rather worried in case the fire spreads to the factory. The wind is in that direction."

" You'll look after Miss Field?"

" Yes, I'll get her off to the hospital at once."

Guy looked at Frances again. Her dead white face and hurried breathing terrified him, but apparently the doctor was not anxious about her . . . and he, himself, was powerless to help her. He felt that his duty lay in the other direction . . . he could do something useful there. He delayed no longer, but strode off towards the house to join in the battle of the flames.

It was the most amazing night that Guy had ever spent. It was a night of terror and excitement and gruelling work. The roar of the flames, the crash of falling stones, the hiss and splutter of the hoses filled his ears. He worked with the men, dark figures so blackened with smoke that it was impossible to know them apart. Mr. Fleming was the only one amongst them that was recognisable; he was in the forefront; he seemed to be everywhere at once, giving help where help was most needed, and shouting encouragement in a hoarse, cracked voice. After they had been working for some time Guy began to feel as if the fire were possessed of devilish intelligence and malignity. No sooner had they managed to get it under control at one place than it burst out with renewed fury at another place. Guy was singed, he was soaked to the skin and then singed again. His clothes were blackened and charred, he was choked by smoke, and his hands were scorched and lacerated. The fire was in the rafters now and the dry beams, which had supported the roof for hundreds of years, were blazing furiously . . . and then the roof fell in and the flames shot upwards until they seemed to touch the sky.

"It's a fine beacon for Jerry," said a man who was working beside Guy.

"But Jerry's gone home with his tail between his legs," said another man . . . they both laughed.

"Trust our lads to chase them off," said the first man with pride and satisfaction in his voice.

"What about the works?" asked Guy.

The second man glanced in his direction, and replied: "They're safe. This was the only bomb in the place."

"There's a Jerry down at Truckford," said another. "Tom says——"

"Here, mister! Look out!" cried the first man, leaping at Guy and pushing him backwards with such force that Guy lost his footing and fell. Guy was about to expostulate when there was a terrific crash and a blazing beam descended upon the exact spot where he had been standing . . . he realised that the man had saved his life. He looked about him to see where the man was, to thank him, but they had separated now and Guy did not see him again. To tell the truth, Guy was doubtful whether or not he would have recognised the man, for they were all like sweeps, their teeth shining whitely in their blackened faces. This was just one of the many incidents which occurred during that amazing night. There was another incident of a somewhat different nature in which Guy was the principal actor. After the roof fell, there was still one corner of the building which remained standing, blazing like a furnace and sending out sparks in all directions. The sparks were flying towards the nearest factory building, and this was what they were trying to prevent. . . . Guy seized a ladder and reared it against a crumbling wall and started to mount with his hose. He had placed his foot on the first rung when he felt a hand on his arm and, turning his head, found himself face to face with Mr. Fleming.

"The wall's crumbling," said Mr. Fleming in a croaky voice. "It's not safe."

"It's all right," replied Guy. "And it's the only way to get a hose near enough——" and with that he threw off Mr. Fleming's detaining grasp and mounted.

Fortunately the wall was solidly built and remained firm, and Guy was able to direct the jet of water into the heart of the blaze.

Soon after that the walls began to fall. They tottered and fell one after another, scattering showers of sparks and burning wood, which set fire to dry grass and palings and to a stack of fuel which was piled up in a yard; but these fires were not serious and were quickly stamped out. Daylight came and by now the flames were dying down. The hoses were still playing upon the glowing heap of stones, but the chief danger was past, the fire was under control.

Guy saw that he was not needed now, and as he was very weary and his hands were somewhat painful, he withdrew from the battle and climbed a bank and sat down. He looked at the place—it was incredible that a few hours ago a splendid mansion had stood there. It was incredibly sad. He felt that something had died, something beautiful and fine, something that could never be replaced . . . the stones, the timber, the magnificent workmanship which had gone to the making of Belton Park were irreplaceable. Guy tried to " see " the house as he had seen it before. He tried to erect it in his imagination out of the blackened heap of ruins which was all that remained of it . . . suddenly he found Mr. Fleming standing beside him.

" What a night! " Mr. Fleming said.

" I wish we could have saved it," said Guy.

" The house was doomed from the first," declared Mr. Fleming in his hoarse croak. " The timbers were old and dry. We've saved the works."

Guy nodded.

" Wonderful," continued Mr. Fleming. " Grand work. I was sorely afraid at one time that the fire would spread, but we kept the flames in check. I don't know how to thank you for your help."

" I didn't do more than you or the other men."

" You did as much as any two of us put together," said Mr. Fleming firmly. " My heart was in my mouth when you went up that ladder——"

" It was nothing. The wall was perfectly sound."

" I saw you rush in just as the roof was falling and drag one of my men to safety."

" They'd have done the same," replied Guy.

Mr. Fleming hesitated and looked round. " We can do no more here," he said. " You'll be wanting to go over to the hospital. I'll take you."

Chapter Thirty-six

ELISE WAS sitting in the lounge at the Bordale Arms Hotel having
tea. She was feeling somewhat blue. For one thing the weather
had broken and the rain was coming down in sheets—soft warm
rain falling with such persistency that it gave one the impression
that it would go on falling for months—and for another thing
Ned had told her that he would be over at tea-time, and he had
not turned up. Elise ought to have been used to disappointments
of this nature caused by the exigencies of the Service, but she was
not and never would be—it was quite useless to try not to expect
Ned; there was something inside her which strained and yearned
for Ned without ceasing. He would come, of course; he might
be here any minute, for he had not phoned to say that he could
not get away. Something had happened to delay him at the last
minute—he would come when he could. Colonel Thynne had
now returned from London and resumed command of the
battalion, but Guy was still away and his absence entailed extra
work for Ned. Nothing had been heard from Guy since his departure, but he was expected back on Monday, so perhaps he had
thought it not worth while to write. (Elise wondered whether his
quest for Frances had been successful; in her heart of hearts she
was of the opinion that it was a wild-goose chase.) Once Guy
was back and had settled down properly, perhaps Ned would be
able to get a few days' leave. His leave was long overdue. Elise
sighed and poured out a cup of tea, and at that moment Annie
came in with a sheaf of letters.

" They're late again," said Annie apologetically. " It was
the van this time. It broke down between here and Rithie, and
Mr. Walker's saying they'll need to get a new van. It's an
awful ramshackle affair and that's the truth." She put the letters
on the table and added: " They're not such important letters
to-day, so you'll not mind them being late so much."

Elise could not help smiling. She knew that Annie took a tremendous interest in her correspondence. " How do you know
they aren't important?" she inquired.

" They're not from abroad," replied Annie promptly. " They're
just ordinary stamps on them."

This was one way of judging the importance of a letter, but it
was by no means infallible, for Elise noticed that one of the

237

letters was from Tommy and another from Guy . . . no letter
from " abroad " could be more important than these.

Guy's letter was much the longer. It covered five closely
written sheets in a somewhat crabbed hand, so she put it aside for
a moment and read Tommy's letter first.

Ivy Lodge
Winklesham, Surrey

Darling Elise,

I meant to write to you before but I knew it wouldn't be
easy, so I kept on putting it off. I expect you're pretty fed up
with me for not going to Aberdeen, but I never said I would
did I? I just felt I couldn't face mother—I came here instead
to Midge's mother. It was dreadful of me, but I told you I
hadn't any pride, besides, I knew she would understand and she
did. She loves Midge too, you see. I expect you know that
Colonel Thynne came to London and took Angela away, and
you probably knew that Midge had got a new appointment. I
can't say much about that because it's supposed to be hush
hush. The only thing you don't know is the most difficult to
tell you, but I expect you can guess. You're rather good at
guessing things. Midge loves me, you know. He does really
It isn't any use saying that things will be different in future
because, of course, they won't. I mean, Midge wouldn't be
Midge if he were different. Well, that's all except that I'm very
happy, so don't worry about me, Elise—but don't forget me
will you? I should hate you to forget me. I miss you all very
much—even poor old Tillie—it's rather grim leaving the regiment and starting afresh in a strange place. I feel as if I had
too few clothes on or something. It's a draughty sort of feeling. I haven't written to Frances because I don't know whether
she knows anything, poor babe, so please give her my love—
my dear love—and my very dear love to your beautiful self

Yours ever,

Tommy

Elise read the letter twice and then she put it down and thought
about it. The letter brought Tommy so clearly before her eyes
that she might almost be sitting opposite in that empty chair. If
only she were sitting there, thought Elise. If only I could get
hold of Tommy and talk to her . . . but what would be the
use. Tommy had made up her mind and nothing that anyone
could say or do would persuade her to change it. . . . I shall miss
Tommy horribly, thought Elise.

She sighed and picked up Guy's letter, hoping that it contained more welcome news.

Bardonald House,
Manburgh.

My Dear Elise,

I've found her and everything is all right. I proposed to her in the middle of a perfectly hellish blitz with pieces of masonry falling all round us. After that we were both very nearly killed but not quite. As a matter of fact, I got off with a few bruises and Frances got off with a broken arm and slight concussion. It was a marvellous escape. I'll tell you all about it when I see you. The doctor says Frances must take it easy for a bit, so we think the best thing is for her to come to Cairn with me. You'll look after her, won't you? We shall travel north next Friday—yes, I know I'm supposed to be back on Monday, but Ned will have to get my leave extended because Frances won't be fit to travel till Friday and I can't leave her behind. She might disappear again or there might be another blitz, and I shouldn't be here to look after her, so you must just tell Ned that if I am to be court-martialled I must just be court-martialled, that's all. As a matter of fact, the doctor says he will give me a certificate if necessary, so perhaps I shan't be court-martialled after all. Now, don't worry about me, Elise, because there is absolutely no need to worry. I got my hands burnt in the fire, and at the moment they are swathed in bandages, which accounts for this peculiar scrawl. They are a bit painful but will be all right in a day or two, I can hear you saying " What fire?" and " Why Manburgh?" and cursing me for telling you everything back to front, but you must make allowances for me because I'm nearly off my head. (I daresay you can remember what you were like when you and Ned were first engaged. If you can't, I can. You were both quite potty.) The whole story of how I managed to find Frances is far too long to write, so you will have to wait for details until we come north. I ran her to earth at Manburgh, where she was working in a canteen in Lord Belton's old house. Then the blitz came—see beginning of this letter—and then the fire started and raged like an inferno. I never saw anything the least like that fire, it was a terrific blaze, and the house was burnt to a cinder in spite of all our efforts. It was such a beautiful old house too. However, we managed to prevent the fire spreading to the works. They are very important works, and it would have been pretty serious if they had been damaged. I am

staying with Mr. Fleming at the moment—see above address—
and shall remain here until Friday, so you can ring me up if
you want to speak to me. Mr. Fleming is the manager of the
aforesaid works; they are the apple of his eye, and if anything had happened to them I don't know what he would have
done. He has got a bee in his bonnet about my fire-fighting
activities and wants to put in my name for the George Medal
—perfect rot, of course. The old boy deserves one himself if
anyone does. Now for the really important part of my letter.
There are one or two little things you might do for me—for
Frances and me. We want to be married soon. Life is short
and there is no just cause or impediment! I suppose the conventional thing would be to go to Devonshire, where her uncle
and aunt are living, and be married there, but neither of us
sees much object in trailing from one end of Britain to the
other when we could get married just as easily at Cairn.
Besides, I have had all the leave I am likely to get for some
time, and the long, double journey would be the worst thing for
Frances. If the uncle and aunt want to see Frances married
they can come to Cairn; but Frances does not think they will.
Old Dr. Digby might come—but you don't know anything
about him, of course, and I can't start explaining about him
now. I thought, perhaps, you might make inquiries and see
whether we could be married in the little church at Cairn . . .
thank you very much. Then there is another thing—what
about Sea View? Did I hear you say "What about it?" or
have you caught on? Honestly, I think it would suit us, for,
with all its disadvantages, it is a dear little house and conveniently near the camp. It was Frances's idea and I think it is
a good one. You might get hold of Alec and ask him about it.
Frances says he is Ellen MacNair's brother-in-law. I don't suppose Tommy will be coming back (have you heard from her?),
so unless the furniture has already been removed we could just
take the house over as it stands. The only thing I refuse to
have in the house is that blue-pencil footstool. I shall have
great pleasure in taking it out on to the rocks and chucking it
into the sea—Frances says I may if I like! Frances understands everything now. She says—like you—that I might have
succeeded in my efforts if I had had a little luck. I go and sit
with her in the hospital whenever they will let me in and we
discuss all sorts of things. Frances thinks it is "awful" of me
to ask you to do all these little jobs, but I have explained that
sisters are created on purpose to be useful. She has not got one
of her own yet, of course. There are so many things that I

want to say to you, Elise—serious things, I mean—that it would take me all night to do the job properly. Fortunately, you will understand most of them without being told. You will realise from this crazy letter that I am as mad as a hatter with happiness. Frances is the most marvellous person in the world, the sweetest, bravest—but if I once begin to write about Frances I shall never stop. I really must try to be sensible. One of the most pleasing features of the affair is that you and Frances are so fond of each other—the two dearest people in the world—it makes everything quite perfect. You and I have always been pals, haven't we, Elise? Ned made no difference; he just came inside the fence and there were three of us—and now there will be four. That's all, really. Here's the doctor arriving to take off my bandages—I know it's going to hurt like hell.

Yours ever,

Guy

Chapter Thirty-seven

THE Bordale Arms Hotel woke to activity at an unusually early hour. Annie was the first person in the house to get out of bed. She rose and opened her window (she always slept with it hermetically sealed) and gazed out at the most beautiful June morning she had ever seen. It was just the right sort of day for a wedding—so Annie decided—and especially suitable for the marriage of two people like Captain Tarlatan and Miss Field. He was so tall and strong and tanned—a fine figure of a man if ever there was one—and she was so sweet and pretty with her fair hair and her blue eyes. Annie sighed and her thoughts strayed to Corporal Brown. He was a fine figure of a man too . . . last night they had walked up to St. Kiaran's Spring and had partaken together of the magic water . . . but dreaming here wouldn't get the work done, and there was more to do than usual with the wedding luncheon and all, so Annie turned from the window and leapt into her clothes and clattered downstairs to get about her business.

Elise opened her eyes and saw the sun shining. Her heart rose with happiness and satisfaction at the sight. Guy and Frances deserved a lovely day for their wedding . . . besides, it was much more pleasant for everyone when the sun shone ; everyone would feel more cheerful. Elise had made all the arrangements, so she was particularly anxious that things should go with a swing. She lay and thought and wondered whether she had remembered all the small details which were so important. The wedding was to take place at twelve o'clock in the village church, and after that they would all return to the Bordale Arms for the reception . . . then the luncheon, of course. Elise frowned, for the luncheon had been the most difficult part of the affair. Guy and Frances had insisted that all the officers of the Green Buzzards should be bidden to the feast, and, although some of them had been obliged to refuse (the camp could not be denuded of officers even for a wedding luncheon), a great many of them had obtained special leave. Some of the wives were coming too. They had found accomodation at Rithie, and a bus had been chartered to bring them over for the day. In addition to the regimental guests, there was old Dr. Digby, who had arrived the night before, coming all the way from London on purpose to be present at the ceremony. Elise was glad he had come; he seemed a dear and he was the only representative of the bride's relations. Mr. MacDonald and his cousin were coming . . . and the minister, of course . . . it was a big party to feed in war-time. However, Elise and Mrs. MacNair had put their heads together and had solved the food problem as best they could with the means at their disposal. The drink problem was easier; it had been left to Mr. MacNair, who had spent a good many hours in the dim recesses of his cellar. . . .

After the luncheon there would be speeches, of course, and then Guy and Frances would walk across the bay to the little house which was ready and waiting for them. Elise had conquered her aversion to pedestrian exercise and had made several visits to Sea View—they were much more pleasant and fruitful visits than her first—she had interviewed Ellen and had seen that everything was in apple-pie order; she had filled every vase she could find with roses and sweet peas to welcome the couple to their new home.

Elise thought of her own wedding. She had been married in Calcutta and, as her father was the C.O. of the battalion at the time, the wedding had been celebrated with pomp and circumstance. She thought of the presents, the bridesmaids, the pretty frocks, the huge wedding cake which she had cut with Ned's sword. She remembered the fuss and excitement—too much noise—one had lost sight of the real meaning of the ceremony, it had been covered up with confetti and coloured paper streamers. This way was natural and simple. It was a good way; two people who loved each other making their promises in a little village church and walking home together—starting life as they meant to go on.

Frances opened her eyes and the first thing she saw was the chestnut tree outside her window. The white candles were faded now, but the sun was shining on the bright green leaves so that they glowed with emerald light. She lay for a little between sleeping and waking, wrapped in rosy dreams . . . how happy she was —far happier than she deserved—happier than anyone had a right to be in a world so full of misery. She had been happy ever since her return to Cairn, for everything was perfect. Guy was perfect, of course, and Cairn in June was paradise. Who could want more than " the time and the place and the loved one all together "?

243

Cairn in June . . . bright sunshine, cool breezes, blue sea: long days fading softly into the half dark which is Scotland's summer night: trees bright in their summer green, rising tall and stately above a brilliant blue carpet of wild hyacinths: gorse blazing, golden, on the hillside: pale-green bracken, waist-high, and full of yellow pollen: hawthorn, sweet as honey: rhododendrons at their gorgeous best, shining like white and red and purple lamps amongst their dark-green foliage: bell-heather in sheltered nooks: cowparsley in the meadows: sphagnum moss, pale pink and green, in the moist places near the burn. Spring had been lovely, thought Frances; there had been magic in the sweet spring air, but summer was breath-taking in its beauty, in its colour and fragrance.

Frances did not get up to breakfast, for Elise had insisted that she should remain in bed until it was time to dress. She had no idea of the reason for this decree (perhaps the reason was that Elise had breakfasted in bed on her wedding morning), but Frances was so fond of her sister-in-law-to-be and, to tell the truth, so completely under her beneficent thumb, that, although it seemed a waste of time to stay in bed when she was perfectly well and the sun was shining and the birds were singing like mad and all Cairn was inviting her to come out, she stayed there obediently and demolished a boiled egg with enjoyment. By half-past ten, however, it had become impossible to remain dormant another moment, so Frances rose and began to dress. Her arm was so much better that she was able to use it, so she was not dependent upon outside help. She was brushing her hair when Elise opened the door very cautiously and peeped in.

" Oh, you're up!" exclaimed Elise in surprise.

" I couldn't stay in bed any longer."

" Guy rang up," said Elise. " He has just heard that he is being awarded the George Medal for his gallantry at Belton Park——"

" Elise! How marvellous!"

" Yes, it's splendid," said Elise, smiling happily. " I'm so glad about it."

" Oh, so am I," declared Frances. " And Mr. Fleming will be delighted. He kept on saying that Guy ought to get the George Medal—but Guy just laughed. Is Guy pleased about it?"

" Of course he's pleased. It's a splendid distinction. He pretends that he did nothing to deserve it, but that's just Guy's way."

Frances nodded. She knew Guy's way by this time.

" Nobody knows about it," continued Elise. " Guy doesn't want anyone to know until the award is made public."

Frances was silent. Her feelings were somewhat mixed. She was proud and glad, of course, but at the back of her mind there was the uncomfortable knowledge that Guy must have been in terrible danger. Frances had suspected this at the time, but Guy had comforted and reassured her by making light of the whole affair . . . he had been in no danger worth speaking of: he had taken jolly good care of himself: he had just given them a hand with the pumps . . . but Frances was aware that the George Medal is not awarded to people who take good care of themselves. It is certainly not won by yeoman-service at the pumps.

"Elise," began Frances, searching for words to explain her feelings on the subject. "Elise, I'm very proud of Guy, of course, but——"

"I know," said Elise, nodding. "I know exactly how you feel, but it's over now and he's perfectly safe, so the best thing is not to think about it any more. I'll do your hair for you, shall I?"

Frances surrendered the comb at once, for there was nobody to beat Elise in the ticklish business of coaxing hair into deep, smooth waves and entrancing curls. "What else did Guy say?" asked Frances.

"He said a good deal," replied Elise, smiling reminiscently. "I couldn't get away from the phone and I knew Mrs. MacNair was champing about the hall waiting to get on to the butcher. First of all Guy wanted to know if you were still here and——"

"Still here!" echoed Frances in amazement.

Elise laughed—that light, soft laugh that Frances had grown to love. "Guy's quite mad," she declared. "I've never known Guy so absolutely crazy before. He says he is going to make a speech at the luncheon, and heaven knows what he will say. He's in the mood to say anything mad—anything that comes into his head."

Frances looked up a trifle anxiously.

"It doesn't matter," Elise assured her. "Everyone knows Guy —they won't mind what he says."

"Did he send me any messages?" Frances inquired.

"Hundreds," replied Elise. "I told him I couldn't possibly remember them all, so then he said I must remember to tell you that immediately after his speech you and he are to make a bolt for it and disappear—you are both to fly for your lives."

"Why?" asked Frances in bewilderment.

"Oh, because he doesn't want to waste the whole afternoon sitting in a stuffy room listening to fatuous asses making speeches. He wants to go home with you. I don't blame him, really."

"We could bathe," said Frances, looking at the sea with yearning eyes.

Elise shivered. "So you could," she agreed.

"What else did he say?" asked Frances.

"He said it was a lovely day; the sun was almost as bright as your hair, but the sea wasn't nearly as blue as your eyes," replied Elise gravely. "Then he asked if I were quite sure you were still here and if you were still willing to marry him."

Frances laughed.

They talked about various matters after that until at last Elise glanced at the clock and said it was time for the final preparations. Elise herself was already attired for the wedding and, as usual, she looked cool and elegant. She was wearing a silk frock of navy-blue and white with little buttons from neck to hem, and her hat was a navy-blue straw, very crisp and shiny, trimmed with a bunch of small white flowers.

"You look lovely, Elise," said Frances. "You *always* look lovely, of course. I believe you would contrive to look elegant and stylish if you were dressed in sackcloth."

"That would be rather difficult," laughed Elise.

Frances's frock was lying on the bed ready to put on—it was made of heavy silk in a soft shade of blue—she lifted it carefully and slipped it over her head and Elise arranged it for her.

"You should always wear blue," declared Elise as she stood back and looked at Frances with pride and affection. "It suits you better than anything. It's a darling frock, Frances."

"You don't think it's too——"

"It isn't too anything," said Elise firmly. "It's quite perfect. I like the way the bodice fits into your figure, and the pleated skirt gives it style . . . now for your hat."

The hat was a skull-cap of the same soft blue silk with a little wreath of forget-me-nots round the edge. Frances pulled it snugly on to her head and Elise arranged the golden curls round it.

They were still engaged upon the important task when the door suddenly burst open and Annie appeared with a large bouquet of pink and white roses.

"Och, I forgot to knock!" exclaimed Annie.

"It doesn't matter a bit," replied Frances, smiling at her.

"I'm that excited I don't know if I'm on my head or my heels," continued Annie. "Mary's running round in circles like a scalded cat——"

"Is that for Miss Field?" asked Elise, pointing to the bouquet

246

"I'll be forgetting my head next," said Annie. "Yes, it's for her. It was a soldier brought it. He's waiting to see if there's any message."

"No, there isn't any message, thank you," replied Elise, taking the bouquet and handing it to Frances.

It was from Guy, of course. Frances had known that he was going to send her a bouquet but she had never imagined anything so magnificent as this . . . it was the largest, the most beautiful bouquet of roses she had ever seen. She stood quite still for a moment, holding the flowers and drinking in their fragrance; the tears were pricking behind her eyes.

"It's a very nice bouquet," said Elise in a matter-of-fact tone. "It gives you the finishing touch, doesn't it?"

"She's just beautiful," declared Annie, gazing at the bride with eyes like saucers.

Dr. Digby and Ned Crabbe were waiting in the lounge. The former was walking about impatiently and consulting his watch at frequent intervals. "These clocks are all wrong," he declared. "The right time is one minute *to*. We shall be late, Major."

"It's a woman's privilege," replied Ned, smiling, "and Frances is worth waiting for. Elise will see that she doesn't keep him waiting longer than is good for him."

"Fine woman, your wife," observed Dr. Digby.

"Yes," said Ned simply.

He had hardly spoken when Elise and Frances came down the stairs and declared themselves ready to start, but now Dr. Digby's hat had disappeared into thin air, and this circumstance delayed them further.

"I had it a moment ago," declared Dr. Digby. I laid it down on the hall table—I take my oath on that. Somebody must have moved it."

After a hurried search the hat was discovered beneath a chair in the lounge, where its owner had put it " for safety "; he seized it and crammed it on to his head, and the little party sallied forth into the sunlit street. As the church was less than two hundred yards away, Elise had decided that it would be simpler to walk the distance than to bother with a car, but she had not realised what an interest Cairn was taking in the proceedings or she would have decided differently. The whole village seemed to have taken a holiday and to have turned out to see them pass. The street was lined with old men and women and children and young women with babies in their arms. Elise was amazed at the crowd; she had not known that there were so many people in the place.

Fortunately, the people of Cairn knew how to behave themselves
they were perfectly quiet, so that except for the uncomfortable
feeling that hundreds of eyes were focused upon herself and he
companions, Elise would not have known that they were there
. . . she glanced at Frances to see how she was feeling, but France
was walking in a sort of dream. There was a strange other
worldly beauty about Frances to-day; she seemed full of radi
ance, as if a light were shining within her, illuminating her face

More people had clustered round the church door and the
church itself was packed. It was not dim and cool as Episcopa
churches are, but was full of bright sunshine streaming in
through the plain glass windows, stretching right across the
building like a *cheveaux de frise* of shining golden swords. The
organ began to play the " Wedding March," and Frances put he
hand on Dr. Digby's arm and began to walk up the aisle. She
was glad of that firm, kind arm, for her dream was suddenly
broken and she realised that everyone was staring at her . . . and
then she saw Guy waiting for her at the communion table and
everything else was forgotten.

Chapter Thirty-eight

CAIRN HIGH STREET was still full of people waiting to see the
wedding party go back to the hotel. The bride and bridegroom
went first and the guests followed in pairs or in little groups
talking and laughing cheerfully. It was such a lovely day tha
nobody could help feeling cheerful, the sun was so warm and
golden and the sea so blue. Mrs. MacNair had arranged the
lounge for the reception; she had ransacked her own garden and
those of her friends and the whole room was a mass of flowers—
there were banks of flowers in every corner, hollyhocks an
lupins, roses and sweet peas, the air was heavy with their scen
The bride and bridegroom stood near the window and the guest
filed past, congratulating them and shaking hands. The Liston
were amongst the first to arrive. Tillie was looking much mor
cheerful than usual; she was quite smart in a two-piece suit o
beige and brown and a beige hat trimmed with brown ribbon.

Winkie had a new grey flannel suit, of which he was ver
proud. " It was a lovely wedding," he said gravely as he held u
his face for Frances to kiss. " I hope you'll come to my weddin
too."

"Of course she will," said Guy. "She's Jennifer's aunt, now."

The room was filling fast and the noise of talk and laughter was growing louder every moment. Frances saw Dr. Digby making jokes with the minister, she saw Mr. MacDonald talking to Elise. Mark and Barry and Captain Rackham were grouped about a tall, fair girl whom Frances had not seen before. . . . All her friends were here, all except one, and somehow or other Tommy was so clear in Frances's imagination that she found herself looking round the room for the slim figure, the heart-shaped face, the sparkling green eyes. Angela was not here either, of course, but Colonel and Mrs. Thynne had come. Mrs. Thynne was looking a little out of tune with her surroundings, but the Colonel was laughing and talking and obviously making an effort to join in the fun.

Presently, at a given signal, the whole party streamed into the dining-room, and were shown to their places at the long table which stretched from end to end of the room. There were far more men than women, of course, and the seating of guests had caused Elise a good deal of thought, but she managed her difficult job so tactfully that everyone seemed pleased with the arrangement. Frances had Guy on one side of her and Colonel Thynne on the other; Dr. Digby was sitting next Elise—an arrangement which suited him down to the ground. Mr. MacDonald had a very pretty woman on his right, but was talking earnestly to his left-hand neighbour, who happened to be Major Crabbe, and Frances felt pretty sure that Ned would know a good deal about internecine warfare before the repast was over. Miss Stalker had been placed beside Major Liston, for he was a kind-hearted creature and could be depended upon to entertain her to the best of his ability.

The luncheon was excellent. They started with salmon and went on to chicken and ducks, accompanied by large bowls of fresh green salad and new potatoes. The pudding course had been the chief difficulty, for the strawberries were not yet ripe, but Mrs. MacNair had made gooseberry tarts which looked and tasted delicious. Mr. MacNair had found a bin of champagne in the recesses of his cellar, and although it was a trifle past its prime and had lost a little of its sparkle, it added greatly to the party spirit.

After lunch the minister proposed the health of the bride and bridegroom, and this was drunk with great acclamation; Dr. Digby replied for the bride in a neat and very amusing speech; then Colonel Thynne arose and welcomed " the new recruit " in

a few well-chosen words. When he sat down there were cries of
" The bridegroom!" and " Come on, Fox!"

Guy rose to his feet at once. His face was grave, but there was
a fleeting twinkle in his eye, and Frances, who knew that little
twinkle well, had a momentary pang of anxiety . . . and then
she saw Elise smiling at her from the other end of the table, and
remembered what Elise had said. " Everyone knows Guy—they
won't mind——"

" Ladies and gentlemen," said Guy gravely, " on behalf of my
wife and myself——"

(Here he was interrupted by cries of " Good old Fox!" and
" Well said!" and other evidences of approval.)

" . . . on behalf of my wife and myself," said Guy firmly, " I
wish to thank you for your good wishes and for all the kind
things you have said about us. Far be it from me to say that
these eulogies are undeserved—I have too much confidence in
your judgment—but it is gratifying to find that we are appreciated
at our true worth. Frances—as you and I are agreed—is indeed
' the top of admiration,' and you have said that I am one of the
best fellows going—a statement with which I heartily con-
cur. . . ."

(Guy was violently interrupted at this point by shouts of
" Modest Violet!" and, " Oh, that's what you think!" and other
interjections of a ribald nature).

" Yes," said Guy, nodding his head gravely. " Yes, my wife
and I make an admirable couple. There is no doubt of that. It
would be difficult to find a couple to match us in good looks and
sterling worth . . . but it would be immodest to stress this circumstance," declared Guy with tremendous gravity, " and modesty is
a virtue which I have always respected in others and cultivated
in myself." He paused until the laughter had subsided and then
continued:

" I have been told that the correct thing for me to do is to
thank you all for coming here to-day and seeing us married, but I
have decided that this is quite unnecessary, since you were all very
anxious to come and are thoroughly enjoying yourselves. The
marriage feast was super excellent, thanks to the excellent work
of the commissariat under the good generalship of Mrs. Crabbe
and Mrs. MacNair, and the bubbly—though a shade less bubbly
than it should be—is nevertheless a pleasant and exhilarating
beverage."

(Cries of " Hear, hear!" and " Mrs. Crabbe!" and " The
commissariat department!")

" It may interest you to know," continued Guy, " that during the last fortnight I have received a great deal of advice from my friends. In fact it was hurled at my head both in and out of season. Some of the advice which I received was good advice—which means that it coincided exactly with my own ideas, of course—and some of it was bad—which means that it did not. I was the recipient of congratulations and commis erations——"

(Cries of " Shame! ")

" Yes, *commiserations*," repeated Guy, shaking his head. " It was the bachelors of my acquaintance who had the temerity to commiserate with me on my approaching nuptials. I feel bound to stress the point so that my married friends may be exonerated from blame by their wives. One might think that bachelors would know very little about matrimony, but that did not prevent them from offering advice on the subject. The advice which I received was conflicting and confusing. Some people assured me that marriage was an excellent institution and that it would be the making of me, while others declared that it would ruin my career, and quoted the aphorism, ' He travels fastest who travels alone.' Speaking as a married man——"

(Here Guy was interrupted by jeers and cries of " Two hours married, old boy! " and " Vast experience, haven't you! ")

" Speaking as a married man," continued Guy in firm accents, " and nobody here can question my undoubted right to speak as a married man, I strongly advise all my bachelor friends to remain single, because——"

(Roars of laughter greeted this statement and Racky was heard to murmur, " Regretting it already, poor devil! ")

" To remain single," repeated Guy, raising his voice above the din, " for the simple reason that the only woman in the world who is my idea of a perfect wife is already safely and soundly married to me."

Guy waited for the second burst of laughter to subside and then he continued: " Some of you seem to be of the opinion that my wife and I have not known each other very long and that we have taken the plunge into matrimony with undue celerity, but time is relative—as Professor Einstein would tell you if any of you had the patience to listen to him or the brains to understand him—and when two people have been through fire and water together, or, to be chronological, water and fire, they get to know each other pretty quickly. Before we go further," said Guy, dropping his voice and speaking in a more confidential tone; " before we go any further I should just like to say that my wife is the most courageous woman the world has ever seen. She laughs at tempests and smiles at bursting bombs. Man-eating lions, rogue-elephants and charging buffaloes leave her cool and un-ruffled. There is only one thing on earth which has the power to strike terror in her breast, and what that one thing is I am bound not to divulge. Thus you will see, ladies and gentlemen, that Mrs. Tarlatan is a fit mate for a man like myself, whose courage is renowned through the length and breadth——"

(Here Guy was interrupted for some moments by wild cries of dissent and comments of a derogatory nature.)

" Did someone say, 'Draw it mild?'" inquired Guy, looking round upon the assembled company with a ferocious scowl. " Let me tell you, ladies and gentlemen—and brother-officers—that I have no intention whatever of drawing it mild. If a man can't draw it strong on his wedding-day I should like to know when he can."

(Shouts of " Not once he's married, that's certain!")

" I have often listened to other fellows making speeches on their wedding-days," continued Guy with a thoughtful air. " Invari-ably the poor fish have made a hash of it. They have either lost their heads completely or put their foot in it up to the knee; they have stammered and stuttered themselves into nervous wrecks or produced speeches of such bathos that I felt I wanted to crawl under the table." Guy paused and looked round and his flashing eye rested for a moment upon several of his brother-officers whose nuptials had taken place within recent years. Some of them had the grace to blush. " Poor fish!" said Guy sadly. " What a golden opportunity wasted! The bridegroom's speech is the opportunity of a lifetime, for it is the one occasion when a man is sure of getting a hearing. His friends have got to listen to him whether they want to or not. . . ."

(Cries of " Worse luck!" and " You seem to be making the most of it!" and other exclamations of a similar nature were heard on all sides.)

" Yes, I am making the most of it," declared Guy. " This is the first speech I have ever made, and for all I know it may be the last. Where had I got to? Ah, yes, the bridegroom. I am aware that the bridegroom is supposed to be of small acount on his wedding-day. Some people have the impertinence to think that he is not the best man, but if there happens to be anyone present who thinks he is a better man than I am, he has only got to say so and I am willing to take him on."

(Shouts of delight from the younger members of the party and cries of " Any time you like!")

Guy smiled and continued: " The bridegroom is the most im-portant person present—much more important than the bride—

or he is the prime mover in the whole affair (the case of Queen Victoria and Prince Albert is merely the exception which proves the rule); it is the *man* who woos and pursues. Sometimes he has to pursue his quarry from one end of the country to the other before he runs it to ground. Is the hunter to be considered of less account than the quarry?" demanded Guy triumphantly. He paused and looked round, but for once there were no dissentient voices to be heard. Perhaps his audience was too dazed by the strangeness of Guy's smile to find anything to say.

Guy had now come to his peroration; he drew a long breath. "My wife and I——" declared Guy in ringing tones. "My wife and I, having braved the perils of the deep and the perils of the air, having encountered tempest and blitz and won through by our—by the combined forces of our personal courage and endurance, are now preparing to set out upon the path of matrimony with high hearts and—er—er——"

"Low heels," suggested Racky.

"Thank you, Racky," said Guy. "With high hearts and low heels. The path is a bit stony at times—so my much-married brother-officers have informed me—and, therefore, it is obvious that low heels are the correct wear . . . and now, if you will excuse us, we shall withdraw in a graceful fashion and leave you to eat, drink, and make merry to your hearts content. . . ."

Hand in hand Guy and Frances rose and made a dash for the door.

There were loud cries of " Here, I say!" and "Where are you going?" and "Look out, they're escaping!" Some of the more temerarious rose to their feet with the intention of following the happy pair and dragging them back to provide the company with further amusement, but they were foiled in their attempt by Ned Crabbe.

Ned had managed to reach the door in time to open it for the bride and bridegroom, and now he had shut it firmly behind them and had placed his back against it. Ned was smiling . . . and across the breadth of the dining-room his eyes sought the eyes of his wife. . . .

She nodded. Ned had done it beautifully.

THE END

SMOULDERING FIRE

D. E. Stevenson

In the romantic setting of loch, mountain and ruined castle this popular woman's author weaves a delightful story around the startling happenings at Ardfalloch Glen.

WINTER AND ROUGH WEATHER

D. E. Stevenson

James and Rhoda Johnstone return from their honeymoon to the hill-farm on the Scottish Borders—and to the dramas of their many neighbours ... "Miss Stevenson knows just how to draw a full measure of amusement from every situation." *Scotsman*

BRIEF SUMMER

Mavis Heath-Miller

The charming story of what befalls Jo and her fiancé one brief summer when a famous actress and her brother come to stay in the village ...

RETREAT FROM LOVE

Maysie Grieg

Ann had to become a model in order to get to the bottom of her family's unhappiness—and becomes deeply involved in the world of fashion and its strange personalities ...

THE MAN FROM OUTBACK
Lucy Walker

Mari was whisked off to Australia to mend a broken heart, but
Station that no white woman had visited in 20 years was hardly a
ideal place.

THE DISTANT HILLS
Lucy Walker

A marriage of convenience between two people who misunderstan
each other's motives.

OVERTURE TO DEATH
Ngaio Marsh

The lady had one hand on the black keys of the piano, one hand c
the white, and suddenly the keys between were red. "Admirab
mysterious" *Daily Mail*. "Very real characters . . . sureness
touch" *The Times*. "A model detective story" *Times Lit. Supp.*

SURFEIT OF LAMPREYS
Ngaio Marsh

"Ghoulish enough to set the blood tingling, the scalp itching wi
apprehension" *Evening News*.